MAJESTIC

MAJESTIC

Whitley Strieber

G. P. PUTNAM'S SONS NEW YORK

G. P. Putnam's Sons
Publishers Since 1838
200 Madison Avenue
New York, NY 10016

The lines from the Eighth Elegy of the *Duino Elegies* by Rainer Maria Rilke,
translated by David Young, are reprinted by permission of W. W. Norton &
Company, Inc. Copyright © 1978 by W. W. Norton & Company, Inc.

Library of Congress Cataloging-in-Publication Data

Strieber, Whitley.
Majestic / by Whitley Strieber. — 1st American ed.
p.   cm.
I. Title.
PS3569.T6955M35   1989   89-8495 CIP
813'.54—dc20
ISBN 0-399-13469-7

Printed in the United States of America
1   2   3   4   5   6   7   8   9   10

ACKNOWLEDGMENTS

I would like to acknowledge the kind assistance of Stanton Friedman, William L. Moore, Jaime Shandera, Walter Haut, Dr. Jesse Marcel, Jr., and Anne M. Strieber for their advice in the preparation of this novel.

It is a work of fiction that is based on fact. I have used the names of historical figures, and invented all others. Newspaper stories quoted are entirely authentic except for the use of this convention. Insofar as it reflects the truth, this book is the outcome of the patience of those who have helped me. Any errors are my own.

This book is dedicated to the memory of
Colonel Jesse Marcel,
an unknown hero.

Through official secrecy and ridicule, many citizens are led to believe that unidentified flying objects are nonsense. To hide the facts the Air Force has silenced its personnel.

—ADMIRAL ROSCOE H. HILLENKOETTER,
First Director of the Central Intelligence Agency
From the *New York Times*, February 28, 1960

Introduction

It was my misfortune to have some really good luck.

If I'd had the good sense to go along with it, I would have left this story alone. It's the scoop of the century, but it has almost certainly ruined my career. And I was about to escape my job with a dreary suburban weekly and go to work for a semiofficial urban daily. Now I'll never report for the *Washington Post.* I'll never enter the fabled halls of the *New York Times,* unless it is with somebody else's sandwiches in my hands.

So what is this thing that has ruined me?

I won't hide the fact that I was researching an April Fool's piece for my paper—or rather, my former paper—the Bethesda *Express.* We were going to get a good laugh out of an obvious absurdity that is believed by at least half the population.

I wasn't fired because I failed to turn in this story. That wasn't exactly it. What got me canned was that I found out it was all true. What I wrote struck my editor as being a joke on him.

He did not think this was funny.

Like the whole community of journalists, he was convinced that the subject is nonsense.

I have met the man who did this to us. Insofar as it is about any one person, this book is about that man.

His name is Wilfred Stone and he lives here in Bethesda, along with a few thousand other Washington retirees. For most of the past year he's been sitting in his backyard quietly dying of lung cancer. During the last six months he and I have been collaborators. As much as I can stand to be his friend, I am that.

At first Will was almost ashamed to tell his story. Secrets like

11

his are their own very ugly pornography, and it was terribly painful to him to reveal them.

But he got used to it, finally became passionate about it. What started as sparse muttering ended in a torrent of searing human anguish, a howl for forgiveness from the edge of the grave.

I have viewed my role in our collaboration as that of facilitator. This book is Will Stone's confession. My job has been to support his effort, to fill in backgrounds, to do what legwork was necessary, and to provide my vision of this desperately troubled man.

I met Will because he sent the *Express* a response to a nasty review I'd published. I trashed a book written by what I assumed to be an obvious charlatan.

This is not a big town, and his letter was the only response in support of the professional liar.

In my own defense I can only repeat that I was also one of Will's victims.

When it came time to do the April Fool's story and I needed a sucker, he looked like a strong contender.

Will acted like he'd been waiting for a call from someone like me—which I suppose he had. Everything he does is structured in terms of bait and hook.

He is a subtle man, too subtle to just walk into my office with an armload of the most extraordinary and terrible secrets that the United States of America possesses.

Considering just how much he has wanted to tell his story, and how little time he has, waiting for me to take the bait must have been very hard.

He lives in a dark old house on a street that was fashionable thirty years ago. I went there to connect with my victim.

And became his.

He sounded like an old freight train as he huffed slowly down the hall to answer my knock at his door. After he opened it he leaned against the jamb to catch his breath. Then he straightened up and a huge, complex smile came into his face. I say complex because it was not a smile like yours or mine.

It was the saddest expression I have ever seen.

He took me into his grim living room with its grim furniture and thick, silent carpet. The curtains alone added cheer. They

12

were odd—white oilcloth or parchment with yellow flowers pressed between the layers.

We sat down. I didn't know what to expect, even what sort of questions to ask.

He pushed his big, wobbly face into mine and said without preamble, "The damn thing is real and I can prove it." I thought, oh boy, paydirt.

"What damn thing?"

"The whole damn thing." He pulled himself to his feet and rolled out of the room. A moment later he was back with a cardboard box full of documents, photographs and cans of movie film.

At first I thought it would be the usual sort of junk, fake pictures, news clippings, nutty tracts.

The first thing I saw was a clear color photograph of what appeared to be a dead alien. It was attached to the autopsy reports that appear later in this book.

The authenticity of the photo was so obvious that it affected me like a blow on the head. The blood drained from my face; I literally reeled.

Every tiny detail seemed true, the pale skin, the injuries, the oozing fluid, the black, sunken eyes.

The documents went on for pages and pages. I have reproduced the most critical ones in this book. But there were thousands of others, and God knows how many more are hidden even from Wilfred Stone.

I sat there in that dim room reading, looking at picture after picture, all of it stamped with things like CLASSIFIED—ULTRA and TOP SECRET—MAJIC.

It became clear to me that nobody could have faked this, not all of this, not with the detail and perfection of it.

For me the world crumbled. Everything I believed was called into question. All my expectations, my understanding of the way things were, all of it was shattered.

When he heard a droplet of sweat snap against the memo I was reading he put his hand on my shoulder. "I want to get the story out before I die."

I just looked at him. I could only think that I'd been living in a false world with a false history.

Everything important was secret. I looked down at the documents spread around me on the floor. They were terrifying, both for their contents and for their ominous-looking secrecy stamps. I was seeing levels of classification I hadn't known existed.

His possession of these documents was clearly illegal. If I assisted him in any way I was headed for jail.

This was when good sense and good luck came into conflict. This story had things like joblessness and jail and disgrace written all over it.

"People have a right to know. They had a right to know forty years ago."

He sat there, the slightest of smiles on his face. Was he trying to look pleasant, to win me over? Will does not smile well. This time words like "snake" came to mind.

But, dammit, I couldn't take my eyes off the stuff he was showing me! The most incredible story in history. And it was literally lying in my lap.

The truth was in the hands of a sick, helpless old man.

And he was putting himself in mine.

Overnight I thought about what was obviously an offer.

To publish this story would be mad.

And yet . . . . At about four in the morning I decided the hell with it and finally went to sleep.

When I got up I grabbed the phone and called an old friend of mine, Jeb Strode. We'd roomed together two years at American University. He went on to law. I bought a cheap Sony tape recorder and became a reporter.

Now he pulled down a couple of hundred thousand a year keeping lobbyists out of jail. I figured he could afford the ten minutes it would take to answer my question.

"I'm crazy," I said. "I slept on this and decided to forget all about it."

"So you called a lawyer while he was still under a pile of housecats with his eyes closed."

"How could I reveal highly classified information and stay out of Danbury?"

"Danbury is the nice federal jail. That isn't where they would put you. I see lots of steel doors and guards with Gila monster eyes."

"What's a Gila monster?"

"Something unpleasant. Don't even think about it, Nicky."

"I have to."

"We never had this conversation. But if you *really* want to do this, your only hope is to publish your book as fiction. They'll figure if they hit you, it'll tell the world it's all true. You might make it."

So this is fiction. Everything in it—all the documents, the briefing papers, the interviews—is fiction. The story is fiction. Will is fiction and so am I.

Only the newspaper stories and Admiral Hillenkoetter's statement are real. You can easily check them, so what's the point?

Even if I don't go to jail, I have become a martyr to my issue. My career is dead.

But it's worth it, because the issue is enormous: what is at stake is the whole future of mankind. The coming of the visitors is as pivotal an event as the original spawning of the human race.

It is incredible that this event has been kept secret.

As director of the Majestic Agency for nearly forty years, Wilfred Stone is the man most responsible for that secrecy.

Let him try to explain himself. I cannot. And I thank God that I don't have to face his conscience in the night, or when he goes to his dying.

—NICHOLAS A. DUKE
March 15, 1989

Foreword by Wilfred Stone

I was among the architects of one of the worst mistakes that has ever been made, and this is my final throw, my magic bullet, my effort to make it right.

In the end it is going to be up to you; my generation has already cast itself upon the rocks. We who fought World War Two and the Communist menace have only one legacy beyond the armed and furious world we have given you.

In 1947 somebody from outside this world attempted to form a relationship with mankind. First contact fell to the United States government. Fresh from victory and full of pride, our generation failed the test. We made a horrible mess of it. We did not understand the subtle and terrifying—the magnificent— thing that they were. We made the simplistic assumption that they were something like us—but from another planet. We failed to see the truth. Failed utterly.

If I may, let me begin with an explanation.

Do you know the word *empath?* It is the invention of a writer, but it is a true word, a fine word. An empath is somebody who so completely identifies with the nature of another that they assume that nature. If you met a perfect empath, or a whole city or nation of perfect empaths, and you introduced them to a vicious psychopath, the empaths would become monsters.

Because they lack experience, children are empaths. They are blank and clean. At my age it is clear that the whole of adulthood is an attempt to recover that innocence. History is also such a journey, an attempt to return to the forest.

These others—who appeared to us as aliens—are empaths,

but not because they lack experience. They have returned to the forest; they are not men, they are beyond that. Like very young children, they are empty of knowledge: they have become conscious animals. And that is a beautiful thing. In the sight of God they are almost angels.

They came here to help us find our own version of this wise innocence. We who faced them did not even begin to understand. We did not understand the awesome portent of Walt Whitman's lines:

> There was a child went forth everyday,
> And the first object he looked upon,
> that object he became . . .

And so when we called them terrible, that is what they became. "Be as little children." What did He mean? Why did He say it? We have become lost on our long journey back to the woods. When we detonated atomic bombs over Hiroshima and Nagasaki we distorted history, setting ourselves on a path that leads not to the forest but to extinction.

We achieved absolute terror, a darkness so deep it could not be penetrated, not even by light so bright that it vaporized the eyes. Wise innocents that they are, the others saw our predicament and came to rescue us.

"Regard the lilies of the field," He said. Why, we who are naked in the rain? If we surrender to the wind and the rain they will be our saviors; the flowers will be our deliverance. We do not need economies, nations, churches. We need only one another—and the ability to give and bear true love.

This is the message of the others. They thus represent absolute and total change, the collapse of economic civilization and the end of days. They are freedom; the soul in the open sky. Because they stand for such radical change we in the government saw them as a threat to the United States.

Instead of proclaiming their arrival up and down the land as we should have, I participated with a group of men who hid it behind a curtain of denial and ridicule. We posted guardians at the gates and spread a net of rumors and lies to protect our secret knowledge.

We have with our lies created the impression that an excursion of the pure is an invasion by monsters from the depths of our own psyche.

In the Bible when a man looks upon the face of an angel he will often cry out, "Woe is me," or, "I have sinned," or other such words. This is because he sees in those dark angelic eyes a clear reflection of what he truly is.

In the eyes of the others we who met them saw ourselves.

And there were demons there.

Part One
THE FIELD OF BONES

We can only know
what is out there
from an animal's features

for we make even infants
turn and look back
at the way things are shaped

not toward the open
that lies so deep
in an animal's face.

—RAINER MARIA RILKE
Eighth Elegy, *Duino Elegies*

Chapter One

Will enthralled and horrified me. While his complete authenticity was obvious, I nevertheless felt that I had to do some basic research.

He claimed that the story had begun in Roswell, New Mexico, in July of 1947. He named names, dates, places, showed me news clippings and memoranda.

Fine, I would see for myself. I took a week off (I was still being fed by the *Express*) and got a super-saver to Albuquerque, rented a Vega and drove the hundred-odd miles south to Roswell.

It took me about ten minutes to fall in love with the town. Roswell is American perfect, a middle-sized city at peace with itself. It's an agricultural community with a smattering of light industry. The streets mix fifties modern with older architecture. Everywhere I went—the motel, the radio and television stations, the local newspaper—I was struck by the fact that this place was populated by decent people. Honest people.

At the Roswell *Daily Record* they were frank about the story. Everybody in town knew about it. The fact that something real had happened in July of 1947 and been covered up turned out to be an open secret across most of southern New Mexico.

Will tells me that I won't feel so much anger when I get older, but I felt anger now, interviewing people, walking the site of the crash near Maricopa, viewing the ruins of the old ranch on which the disk fell.

I was choked with bitterness. I'd dismissed the whole UFO question with a laugh and I'd been a *dupe!*

My ego was involved and I thought I'd never get over hating Will.

One of the most annoying things about him is how wise he is. He knew that I wouldn't always despise him.

I wish I could comfort that old man somehow, but he is beyond words, beyond touch, beyond everything.

South of Roswell stand the empty remains of the Roswell Army Air Field, now being transformed into an industrial park.

I walked that crooked tarmac on a warm spring day, and let the ghosts of the past rise up around me. There was no feeling of elegy or remembrance. I was angry, and the ghosts were angry, too.

At least two of those ghosts, and possibly a third, were not human. I wondered if they looked back also, and if they did not remember the night that they arrived, and died.

Through the ten o'clock dark they came, silent and slow, watching the streets of Roswell unfold below them. More carefully they were watching the flight line, counting the planes, counting the bombs.

At that moment the 509th Strategic Bomber Wing stationed at Roswell was the only atomic bomber force in the world.

Perhaps they came to warn us, or perhaps theirs was a more subtle mission. But Roswell could not have been chosen by accident. Will explained to me that they have a definite tendency to appear right in the middle of our most sensitive, most dangerous, most heavily guarded military installations.

This was one of the things that caused the hostilities. "Be as little children," Will says. Indeed, innocence does not know secrets and it does not know fear. But mankind is not the only earthly creation that fears death. Everything fears it. And when there is resurrection every living thing will be delivered, from the crawlers in the mud to the high bishops, and fear will be swept from the earth forever.

When *they* came, everything was afraid.

Birds awoke as they passed over, and fluttered nervously. Coons and bobcats screamed, opossums hissed. Babies shrieked in the night.

When they came it was midnight in Washington. Will Stone was a young man then, struggling to create a postwar career for himself in the Central Intelligence Group, soon to become the C.I.A. He knew nothing of what was happening in distant New Mexico.

His memory of what he was doing that night is nevertheless vivid. This shouldn't be surprising; we tend to recall exactly where we were at moments of great crisis.

A familiar wartime question: "What were you doing when you heard about Pearl Harbor?" Will Stone remembered: he was standing in a department store looking at some ties. "Where were you when the Japs surrendered?" He was drunk in Algiers.

What was he doing on the night of July 2, 1947?

He was lying in bed in his apartment worrying about the fact that he was having political problems at the office. Instead of working on the Russian desk he was off in a backwater, helping the Algerians put an end to French colonialism.

Betty and Sam White were sitting on their porch in Roswell sipping lemonade and watching the sky. It was a beautiful night, with storms off to the west and stars overhead.

I know just what they said, just how they acted. I've read their files—and all the other files that Will has—many times over.

I've tried and tried to see where Will and the others went wrong, to understand if there is anything in God's world that might help us now.

"What's that," Sam asked his wife back on that lost night.

"I'm not real sure," she replied in her twangy voice.

"I'm gonna call the sheriff." He got up from his chair with a creak of porch boards and a grunt.

The object was round and brightly lit—glowing, in fact. It made no sound as it swept northwestward across Roswell.

Beneath its thin blue light people went about their business. Except for the Whites, nobody noticed a thing.

At the Army Air Field the radar operators did not glance up from their glowing screens. The lookout on the tower was facing the other way, and never broke the imaginary monologue he was delivering to Dorothy Lamour.

Bob Ungar, on his ranch seventy miles northwest of Roswell, watched the storms with a critical and uneasy eye. He was totally unaware of what was approaching from the direction of town.

Bob's concern was the damned clouds.

They could drop hail as big as a sheep's eye. Hail like that could knot a man's skull or batter his animals until they were crazy. He'd also found his share of sheep braised by lightning, lying stiff in the scrub.

The worst part was the way they'd bunch up on the fences during a bad storm, frightened by the thunder and trying to shelter from the rain. You'd find them in heaps, and the ones at the bottom would be smothered.

Bob pitied the poor, dumb things. I know he did, because I know exactly what kind of a man he was. I admire him unabashedly.

He died in the sixties, old and dried to straw by the desert.

Walking the path of Will Stone I spoke to Bob's wife, Ellie, now a very old woman. She lives in an adobe cottage—really little more than a hut. Of course she's been wracked by time, but there is within her a light such as you don't often see. I spoke to her of her husband, and their old house that is in ruins now, and a long time ago.

I can imagine Bob standing on his back porch on that night, squinting into the dark west.

A long, cool gust swirled out of the dark. The air grew eerie. The last five nights he'd saddled up his horse, Sadie, and gone out to help the sheep. It hadn't made a lick of difference. They'd gotten themselves killed anyway.

You'd think sheep had been going through thunderstorms for a long time. But this bunch, they got all worked up over a little sheet lightning, forget the thunder and wind and the hail.

He heard the sheep faintly, far off now, moaning and bleating.

Meanwhile the glowing object left the outskirts of Roswell and the Whites lost it in the darkness.

Cats that had leaped into bookshelves looked out. Dogs that had run under houses scrambled back to their master's sides. Babies that had been screaming began to sniffle and coo. Children sighed in their beds, their half-formed nightmares subsiding.

Lightning flared across the west, and the Ungars' radio crackled. ". . . tornado five miles south of Caprock . . ." Then the static returned.

"Oh, Lord," Bob said.

"That's way away from here." Ellie reached toward him, then withdrew her hand.

"A hundred miles isn't nothin,' not s'far as these storms are concerned."

"We'll get through," she said.

"I moved the sheep up that draw. They got a little shelter in there."

"I worry about the water comin' down there."

"Don't you worry now."

Some dance music came out of the radio. Fox-trot music.

"Where is your gingham dress?"

"In the cedar chest."

"Will you put it on for me?"

She smiled the strong, accepting smile that he loved, and went into their bedroom. When she returned she was wearing the dress. She swayed to the music. He took his work-thin wife in his arms, and danced with her as the lightning flashes flickered.

"Oh, Lordy," she said, "do you remember the night we decided to get married? The conga line?"

How they had danced! "Old Joe really got that conga goin'."

"Bobby, I think that was the happiest dance of my life."

He closed his eyes and bent his head to her woman-smelling hair, and saw the black window float past.

At that moment there was a crack of thunder and the rising roar of wind. The radio was drowned out. He turned it off; no use in wasting the battery.

The wind came sweeping around the house, shaking the boards, screaming in the eaves, bringing with it the perfume of the range, sweet flowers, sage, dust. He imagined his animals out there in the storm. They'd be milling, nervous, ready to stampede all the way to the wire if lightning struck nearby.

He wondered how it could help but strike them. Looking at it, he realized that he'd never seen another storm quite like it, not in all of his years on this New Mexico land.

He doused the lamp. "Ellie, come look."

They went out onto the porch together. The storm was a huge, glowing wall of clouds. It seemed to ride on a forest of lightning bolts. "I've never seen so much lightning," Ellie said.

25

"If it comes over the house—"

"Look at the way they strike."

"Yeah. 'Lightning never strikes twice in the same place.' So much for that idea." He turned away. "God help the small rancher," he said bitterly.

They went to their bedroom. He took off his clothes and sat on the bed rolling a last cigarette. They lay back together, sharing drags. After a while she put her hand on his chest.

And then they slept.

His father came to him, his face lit as if by the light of a lantern. Astonished, he stared. He was aware that this was a dream, but amazed at how real it was. There was Dad, his lean, hard features, his dark eyes, his grim-set mouth. "Dad," Bob said. "Dad!" His father didn't say anything, but Bob felt like some kind of a warning had been given. He woke up feeling very afraid. A lot of time had passed; he'd been asleep for hours. Ellie beside him was snoring.

Long thoughts started whispering through his mind. He wondered why he lived like this. His poor ranch couldn't last. But then what the hell would happen to him? He worked this place. "I'm a sheepman." He could say those honorable and proud words.

He noticed, through his dark reverie, that there was an awful lot of light in the room. He opened his eyes, thinking for an instant that he'd overslept and it was daylight.

The room was full of soft, blue light. He sat up. A fire? There was nothing to burn. They had a wood cookstove but it was just embers now. And the lanterns were out. His nostrils dilated, but he smelled no smoke.

Not the barn! He vaulted out of bed, burst through the house and into the restless night.

The barn was fine, but there was some kind of lightning in the sky the likes of which he had never seen before. It looked like a huge star floating around below the clouds. It was so big and so close that he stifled a shout of surprise and jerked back against the screen door.

He stared up. The thing was sliding and floating in the air, and it was hissing. A sort of shock went through him. He was all covered with tingling. His heart started thundering.

It must be a burning plane. Oh, Lord, coming down on the house! It got closer and closer, practically blinding him with its light.

"Ellie, God, *Ellie!*"

There was an answering murmur from the house.

"Ellie!"

The thing was hissing and buzzing, and there was a buzzing in the middle of his head. He grabbed his temples.

High-pitched children's screams mixed with the buzzing, and then Ellie came urging the kids along, her own voice all shaky.

He went toward her, turning his back on the thing, which was now almost on top of him. As he ran toward them the buzzing got so loud that he almost couldn't bear it. The world seemed to go round and round and he felt himself falling. For a second it seemed as if he was floating upward, but then he hit the ground with a thud.

Ellie and the children were already out the backdoor. The thing went buzzing and skipping and jerking through the air above them. Then it was skimming the hill, then it was a glow behind the hill.

He heard the most god-awful sound he had ever heard in his life: an explosion to beat all. It was a huge clap of a sound, it winded him, it shook the back windows right out of their frames, it made Sadie scream in the barn and the chickens start squawking in the coop. Ellie and the kids were screaming, and Bob heard his own voice too, rising against the echoes of the blast.

And then, quite suddenly, there was silence. And the night returned.

And that's how it began, pretty much. In the secrecy of that late hour, thus did our innocence perish.

From the Roswell *Daily Record,* July 8, 1947:

ROSWELL HARDWARE MAN AND WIFE
REPORT DISK SEEN

Mr. and Mrs. Sam White apparently were the only persons in Roswell who have seen what they thought was a flying disk.

They were sitting on their porch at 105 North Foster last Wednesday night at about ten minutes before ten o'clock when a large glowing object zoomed out of the sky from the southeast, going in a northwesterly direction at a high rate of speed.

White called Mrs. White's attention to it and both ran down into the yard to watch. It was in sight less than a minute, perhaps forty or fifty seconds, White estimated.

White said that it appeared to him to be about 1,500 feet high and going fast. He estimated between 400 and 500 miles per hour.

In appearance it looked oval in shape like two inverted saucers faced mouth to mouth, or two old-type washbowls placed together in the same fashion. The entire body glowed as though light were showing through from inside, though not like it would be if a light were merely underneath.

From where he stood White said that the object looked to be about 15 feet in size and making allowance for the distance it was from town he figured that it must have been 15 or 20 feet in diameter, though this was just a guess.

The object came into view from the southeast and disappeared over the treetops in the general vicinity of Six-Mile Hill.

White, who is one of the most respected and reliable citizens in town, kept the story to himself hoping that someone else would come out and tell about having seen one, but finally today decided that he would go ahead and tell about seeing it.

Chapter Two

Even after all these years I could see the terror in Ellie's face as she told me her story. I sat across from her in her home, and listened to her remarkable tale.

Hers was a humble place, with a cigarette-marked Formica table in the kitchen, a couple of chairs and an enormous television dominating the tiny living room. As we talked and sipped coffee from big mugs, "Jeopardy" rollicked along in the background.

"I remember that noise was real loud, Mr. Duke."

It took some little time for their ears to adjust to smaller sounds. When they could hear again, they realized that the sheep were actually shrieking. Ellie thought the plane had hit right on top of them.

"One of them big bomber planes crashed," she said to Bob.

"Lord, woman, I know it."

"Go out there! Saddle up Sadie and go out there!"

He pulled on jeans and boots and threw his slicker over his T-shirt. Grabbing a hat, he dashed out to the barn to get the horse.

She was skittish, rolling her eyes back at him as he worked. " 'S all right, baby doll," he murmured, " 's all right, babe." He got the saddle thrown and cinched and led her out of the barn. She snorted when the sheets of rain hit her, and she looked at him like she thought he was absolutely crazy.

The night was filthy black and he hadn't brought a lantern. He made it up the hill behind the house by using lightning flashes. Sadie couldn't help him, she had no way to know where she was going.

I can see him now, his hard, stoic form in the lightning flashes, a shadow on a horse beneath the streaming brim of an old hat.

Being with his widow, surrounded by the shabby objects of their lives, looking at the stern, deeply humorous photograph she has of him, I chose him unreservedly as the man I would want to represent me to a higher world.

Human society and government being what they are, Bob Ungar never saw more of our visitors than a little wreckage. Instead their first encounters were with the likes of Will Stone.

If Bob Ungar had met them living and vital on that night, everything would surely have been different.

Once he reached the top of the hill the screaming of the sheep was louder, reaching his ears clearly through the peals of thunder and the soughing of the wind.

Then he heard another noise, something completely new. It was a terrible, ragged wailing. Sadie flared her nostrils and tossed her head and stomped.

What was that? It was the strangest, most savage noise he'd ever heard. Nothing made a sound like that, not a fox, not a coyote, not a bobcat being soaked by a storm.

I suspect that at least one of the unknown beings was on the ground at that time, probably blown out of the craft by what was later found to have been an explosion that hadn't destroyed the whole thing.

Wilfred and his associates later found three bodies, but they were miles from the Ungar ranch. I don't think anybody ever found the fourth one, who fell on the ranch.

And who probably lived a little while.

If so, then we came very close to having Bob Ungar be the first person to meet the visitors in full consciousness and in the flesh.

But for a horse . . .

With no warning Sadie bucked. It was the last thing he was expecting out of his docile old lady horse and he found himself rising into the air before he really knew what had happened.

He came down sideways in the saddle and she bucked again. This time he ended up in the mud. He hit so heavily his jaw snapped and he saw stars. Before he could get up Sadie was heading back to the barn at full gallop. Her hooves rattled off into the dark.

The screaming of the sheep mixed with that savage noise. "God," Bob said, "oh, God."

He turned and went back down the hill hobbling and slipping along after his horse.

Half an hour later he slammed through the screen door into the kitchen and pulled his 12-gauge out of the gun cabinet. He tucked a couple of lead solid shots into the chambers. Ellie grabbed his shoulder. "Bob!"

"Somethin's out there, honey!"

"What? A coyote?"

"It scared that old horse so bad she bucked me off!"

"Bucked *you* off?"

"Come on, Ellie, wake up! Somethin's out there!"

"A cougar?"

"No cougar ever sounded like that."

Then there was a lull in the storm and they both heard it. Ellie grabbed Bob as the children came rushing out of their room bawling. The family huddled together in the kitchen. When lightning flickered the shotgun shone blue and mean, and gave them all comfort.

The sound was full of agony and incredible sorrow.

"Is it a man?" Ellie whispered.

"I don't rightly know." He held her tighter.

"They found us," Billy said. His voice was so solemn and quiet and firm that both of his parents looked at him with surprise in their faces. But he said no more.

When Billy grew up he joined the Navy and told all who cared to listen just exactly what had happened on the Ungar ranch.

About a year after he had finished his tour his car was found abandoned on a road in northern California, and that was the end of him.

I asked Will Stone whether or not he had been responsible for the death of this talkative young man. His reply had an eerie resonance. "People go with them," he said. He would say no more.

The gaps that Ellie had left in her interview with me were filled in by Will, working from the yellowing transcripts of old interviews with the family.

"I hope it's not some poor flier burned in the crash," she remembered telling Bob. She did not ask him to go back out and he didn't move. He felt guilty. He thought, "I am probably letting some poor soul die."

Over the next hour the storm raged and the cries slowly died away. The more he heard them the more Bob became convinced that they weren't human noises. No human being could make a sound like that, not even a man burned and in agony.

It had to be an animal, he thought. Some poor, hurt animal.

He was surprised by dawn. It didn't seem like he'd been asleep, and here it was pushing six. He stirred himself, sat up from the couch and stretched his neck. He still had his boots on and his legs were stiff. When he straightened them his knees cracked and he felt better. Ellie and the kids slept huddled together, their faces as soft as dew. Compared to them he was like a big old mesquite tree, all bark and thorns. He went into the kitchen and opened the breadbox, cut off a slab of bread and spread it with grape jelly. He pumped up some water and drank it in deep, grateful draughts. He would have liked coffee, but he was in a hurry to see what had happened last night.

He felt guilty. A plane had crashed and he hadn't gone out to help the poor bastards. A howling animal had scared him away. By the thin light of morning he was just plain ashamed of himself.

I know this because he admitted it to Joe Rose, the man who interrogated him while he was being held in the brig at Roswell Army Air Force Base.

He was even more ashamed when he went into the barn and found Sadie standing there still in her saddle and bridle. She gave him a sad, accusing look. How could any man who worked with animals ever leave a horse saddled half the night?

He would have unsaddled her immediately, but he couldn't do that. He had to use her right now.

As he mounted her he mumbled that he was sorry. Then he headed up to the pastures to see what he could see. She trotted right along; she was a faithful animal.

He went first to his sheep. In spite of himself he pressed Sadie to a canter. It was his expectation that he was going to find that a plane had crashed into his flock.

The morning was as quiet as the night had been noisy, and he didn't like that. Were they all dead? Was it that bad?

Sadie cantered smartly. Her ears were cocked forward as if she, also, was listening for the sheep.

Then he saw them bunched up in the shallow draw. There was no crashed plane, in fact no sign of damage at all. He couldn't see any carcasses. The sheep were grazing, some of them milling.

He made a little sound of relief in his throat. They were all right, and putting them here had been a good idea. They'd stayed away from the fences.

Sadie suddenly reared up. She whinnied then came down hard, stomping at what Bob thought was a sizable snake. He knew better than to interfere with a horse killing a rattlesnake, and let her have her way until he realized that the thing she was trampling into the muddy ground was no reptile.

He backed her off and peered down. Her chest was heaving, and she was extremely skittish.

What he saw down in the mud appeared to him like a thick belt of black webbing. He didn't know what to make of it.

After looking a moment longer to be certain that it wasn't a rattler, he dismounted his horse.

She pawed and snorted. He held the reins tightly; it was a long walk back to the house.

He bent down and with his free hand drew the black strap out of the mud.

Where were you when the hand of man first touched a thing of angels? I know where I was: unborn in 1947. I was produced later, in the last, disillusioned years of the baby boom. I wasn't exactly an unwanted child, but I suspect that my dad, at least, would have preferred a new Pontiac.

It looked like burned plastic, but it was floppy. Sadie's eyes rolled and she stomped. She tossed her head, nearly pulling the reins out of his grasp. Holding her tightly, he remounted with the stuff in his free hand.

She began craning her head around. What the hell was the horse so fired up about? It was obviously some burned scrap from the plane.

One thing about the webbing that fascinated Bob was its weightlessness. He squeezed it. You'd think you could just tear something this flimsy to pieces. He pulled at it. The stuff was tough.

Finally he tied it on behind him—and nearly got dehorsed for the second time in as many days. The instant it touched her skin Sadie reacted as if he'd hit her with a hot branding iron. She screamed and bolted forward, straight into the outer edges of the flock.

Her fear infected the sheep at once, and they started running. He'd have a damned stampede on his hands if he didn't watch out. He reined Sadie back hard and clicked his tongue at her. But it was to no avail. The horse was in a first-class panic.

What the hell. He pulled the piece of junk off her back and threw it as far as he could.

She calmed down then. But now the sheep were desperately rearranging themselves to avoid the thing. He sat open-mouthed watching this display of animal craziness.

Rather than get himself into trouble with Sadie, he resolved to wait until the ground dried a little and bring out his old Jeep to get the damned thing.

After inspecting his animals he rode up to the head of the little draw and looked around. There was nothing in the immediate area, but in a distant pasture there seemed to be an awful lot of rubble. Little bits of stuff shining in the morning sun, thousands upon thousands of them.

It was a good thirty-minute ride over there, which meant he wouldn't make it back for breakfast until nine. He wanted some decent food in his belly before he approached that mess. He could have used some whiskey, too, but he didn't hold with drink during the morning. Coffee, though. Ellie's coffee.

At the meal he said nothing about the wreck. He ate a couple of eggs and some Spam, and drank two big mugs of coffee. The kids drank milk and ate Post Toasties. As usual Ellie had coffee and a cigarette. She sang while she was cooking, "It was a long time ago, long time ago. . . . " He didn't know the song.

"You see the plane, Dad," Billy asked.

"A lot of little pieces."

"Can we go?"

Ellie turned from the stove. "No."

"Well," Bob said.

"Bob, there might be—"

He thought of that sound. "Your ma says no," Bob said.

"Momma, please." Mary's voice was intense. "We all oughta go. Not just Dad."

"If there's a man hurt he might need help." Billy was, as always, a matter-of-fact kid.

Bob looked into his coffee. He should have gone out there last night. Somebody might have died because of him.

"Go on, kids," Ellie said. "But you stay away from dead men. You don't want nightmares."

Bob drove to the sheep, his kids sitting silently beside him. Ellie stayed behind.

The sheep still wouldn't come within fifty feet of the black plastic. Bob got out and went to it, the mud sucking at his boots as he walked through the mire created a while ago by all the stomping hoofs. He picked up the plastic. You closed your eyes, you could feel its texture, but it definitely had very little weight.

No weight. And yet when he tossed it into the back of the Jeep, it fell normally. It ought to float in air, like a feather or like smoke.

"What is it, Dad?" Mary touched it gingerly.

"I'm not real sure. A piece of the plane."

They got in the truck and he drove carefully out of the draw.

They bounced and rattled along the sandy borders of a wash, then turned and headed up toward the pasture he'd seen from horseback. Soon he could see the wreckage again, still lying scattered along a low rise, glittering in the sun.

He drove up to the edge of it, then stopped the engine. They all climbed out. It looked just like somebody had taken the tinfoil from a thousand cigarette packs, torn it up and scattered it over tens of acres. The rubble was spread in a long sort of fan, as if whatever had created it had come sliding into the ground out of the southeast. He picked up a piece of the foil. It was strange stuff. Tough. You couldn't even think about tearing it. And it was light, too. Like the webbed belt it had no weight at all.

"This isn't pieces of a plane," Billy said. He held some of the stuff in his cupped hands. When he let it go, it fell like a handful of dry leaves.

"Look," Mary said. She bunched up a piece of the foil until it was no bigger than a pill. Then she let it go. Instantly it bounced back into its former shape.

"Damn," Bob said. He did it. The same thing happened. Again he tried tearing it. Nothing.

Billy put some of it on a stone and beat it with another stone. It didn't even scratch.

How anything as tough as this stuff could ever have gotten torn up like this just beat all, as far as Bob was concerned. Must have been a whale of an explosion. The stuff was stronger than metal and yet thinner than cellophane. And blown all to hell.

Then he saw a gleam of violet coming from under a largish sheet of the foil. He lifted the sheet, tossing the two-foot square over his shoulder. The way it fluttered in the air reminded him of the flickering wing of a butterfly.

What he saw on the ground confused him even further than he was already confused. There lay a T-shaped object a couple of inches long, made of what looked for all the world like balsa wood, with violet glyphs covering it. He looked at it for a long time. He did not touch it. Others were I-shaped.

There were also pieces of what appeared to be waxed paper, and on these had been painted rows of little figures that Bob surmised were numbers.

Mary picked up a piece that hadn't been written on and held it up to the sun. "Look, Daddy."

Bob saw the faint outlines of yellow flowers. He took the sheet in his own hand. It was as if there was a subtle design, or maybe even real flowers pressed between the layers. They were beautiful, like yellow primroses. Evening Primroses.

You couldn't do anything to the paper, either. It didn't burn or tear. It was as tough as the foil.

Bob surveyed the field of rubble. The sun shone down, but no birds sang. A creepy sensation overcame him, and he wished he hadn't brought his kids.

The only sound was their own rustling breath. His big, familiar pasture seemed strange and dangerous and full of mystery. He did not like this, did not like it at all.

Where were the birds? There had always been plenty of birds around here.

What devilment had gone on last night?

"Were there bobcats crying out in the storm?" Billy asked.

Bob did not answer. He could imagine the devil screaming like that. Then, with a toss of his head, he dismissed the thought.

"Somebody gotta clean this place up," he said. "Who's gonna do it?"

"It'd take ten loads in the Jeep."

"I'd say more like a hundred, son. We'd be at it for a month."

He surveyed the mess, and felt hopeless. There was so darned much of that tinfoil and other junk he could hardly believe his eyes.

Who the hell would do it? He couldn't haul all this crap out in his Jeep, not in a month of work. And what about the gasoline? A man had to think about the cost. At a dime a gallon, ten dollars' worth of gas at least.

He walked around, turning over pieces of the rubble with his toe, trying to see if he could find some insignia, something more than the little violet squiggles. But there was nothing, not a number, not a name.

"Hell." This wasn't what he wanted to see. He couldn't expect the AAF to deal with this mess unless it was theirs. But this didn't look like any sort of military stuff he'd ever heard of.

Maybe it was secret. Secret stuff. Them and their damned secrets, they'd really made a mess of one man's pasture.

He reached down and picked up one of the pieces with the violet writing on it. The thing was balsa wood, but it was so hard he couldn't dent it with his fingernail. It looked like balsa, he could see the grain. It was at least as light as balsa. But how could it be so damn hard?

The letters were inlaid into the gray surface. What did they say? He couldn't make out a bit of it. Was it Jap? Maybe that was it: the Air Force was testing some kind of Jap secret weapon they'd captured from old Tojo.

"Banzai," he muttered. Then he tossed the little piece of wood aside.

He strode forward, moving steadily up a long rise. Now he could see signs of fire. Some of the pieces of foil were melted, others showed signs of scorching.

He listened to the silence. It made him want even more

urgently to get his kids out of here. What kind of thing was it that terrified dumb sheep and horses and made birds fly away? Whatever bothered the animals about this stuff probably ought to bother him, too.

Then he realized that there weren't even any insects buzzing around here.

The place was totally silent, and he knew that even the little things, the insignificant things, had been frightened away.

He whirled around, sure that somebody was coming up behind him. But there was only the kids standing in the sun, their skin golden, their faces solemn.

"Come on, y'all. Lets get some of this stuff picked up and put in the back."

Each of them dumped an armload of the wreckage into the Jeep. Then they got in. Bob pulled the choke, then hit the starter. She ground and gasped and finally chugged to life. He put her in gear and she went lurching off, tires spinning and whining in the wet, sandy dirt.

"Move," he growled, whipping the wheel around and gunning the motor to get out of an especially bad area.

Then he was on dry stone and doing twenty. She rattled like a can of marbles, but she got them home three times as fast as horses, and for that he was grateful.

Ellie had heard them come rattling down the hill, and was waiting at the kitchen door. He stopped the truck and turned it off, then got out.

His wife looked small and fragile, just pretending all that strength of hers.

He gathered her in his arms.

"Is it bad?" she asked.

"There's somethin' funny."

"Are all the men dead?"

"There weren't any men, Mom," Billy said.

"There was wax paper, like, with yellow flowers pressed in it."

"It's all about like this." Bob showed her the back of the Jeep.

She was a practical woman, and because it didn't make sense she didn't comment. She gave them all beans and potatoes for lunch. Bob ate in silence. Afterward he said, "Don't you kids go back up there without me."

"Should you tell the sheriff?"

"As soon as I get to town I'll do it."

She was silent after that, going about her work. How slim she was, this woman who had been swayed by his love. He listened to her movements, the shuffle of her slippered feet, the occasional sigh.

That afternoon he got a frozen-up windmill gear and had to spend a couple of hours working on it. Before he knew it the sun was heading toward the horizon and it was time to knock off. He thought no more about the field of rubble and the sheriff. Maybe it was some kind of test glider. That would explain the seeming lack of victims. After he finished work he sat at the table drinking coffee and smoking.

In the back of his mind he'd been thinking that the Army Air Force might show up on its own, but as evening fell he had to conclude that they were not coming today.

Late that night he was awakened by light outside brighter than the moon. He pulled on his boots and went out. A blue searchlight was darting down from a huge, dark object that hung soundlessly in the sky, blackening out the stars.

The searchlight went on and off in the dark, darting down now and again. It moved toward the pasture where the wreckage lay.

Perhaps the fourth being was rescued on that night.

I think not, though, because it was heard again.

Bob expected the Air Force to show up the next morning, but they didn't. He waited a few days. Still nothing. Finally, on July 7, he got in his Jeep and went rattling off toward Maricopa. He told the sheriff's deputy to tell the Air Force to get out to his place and claim its own.

When the sheriff called the Army Air Field in Roswell, they had no idea what he was talking about, but they went out anyway, to see what had so upset one of the region's stolid ranching men.

Chapter Three

The Chronicle of Wilfred Stone

It would soon be the responsibility of my friend Joe Rose to get Ungar under control. He would do it with the same ferocious subtlety that appeared when we were fishing for trout, and that he had used on former Gestapo agents when he interrogated them.

Now I dislike fishing, but in those days I was young and full of murder, and loved the game of it and the kill. I inherited the sport of fly-fishing from my father, and many of the other gentlemen in CIG had done the same.

Back in July of 1947 I was—God, let me see—I was thirty-four years old. I'd just had my birthday. I was born on Friday, June 13, 1913. I walk under ladders and seek out black cats.

Thirty-four. I was healthy from my years in the Office of Special Services. Now I am bent and flabby and cancerous from my years in MAJIC. The wages of sin.

But what delicious secrets I know. I am so terribly afraid . . . and that, too, is delicious.

Don't let me pretend to be a hero. I am no hero. Spies are not glamorous. We gather and protect secrets, which are power. We control your lives and you don't know it.

When the history of this era is written, it must certainly be called the Age of Secrets. I will state the matter simply: Everything important is classified.

Everything.

Public knowledge has degenerated to a form of entertainment. I should know. The control of the public mind has been my lifelong profession and horrible fascination.

Official secrets are the snare of modern life. If you don't know them, you're helpless. If you do, you're trapped.

July 6, 1947: The previous week I had been roped into a peculiar sort of a project. The Board of National Estimates had asked the Central Intelligence Group what it would mean if the rash of "flying disks" being reported nationwide resulted in contact with spacemen. We did not yet know of what had happened in Roswell, but there had been so many other sightings reported in the last few months that our interest was piqued—at least officially.

Because I'd made no secret of the fact that I was unhappy on the French desk, I was given this bit of silliness to amuse myself.

I was in the process of completing the intelligence summary that would answer the BNE request. What, if anything, did we know about these spacemen, if they even existed? Why were they here? Were they hostile? Communistic? I worked diligently away in my dingy office at 2430 E Street, the headquarters of the CIG.

My official employer was still the OSS. The military was battling the President over the establishment of the CIA, and the National Security Act was at that time under debate in Congress.

The best friend of the Central Intelligence idea in those days was General Hoyt Vandenberg, soon to become commanding general of the United States Air Force. But he wanted the CIA on his own terms, as a military toy, not as an independent civilian agency.

An old Socialist and gentleman named Norman Thomas once said, "Where the secrets start, the republic stops." We were ignorant and proud men and we did not believe that. Had he known what he was helping to create, Vandenberg would never have done it. He was a great man, and I love him still.

The Central Intelligence Group was populated from three or four different directions. OSS people. FBI people. Military intelligence people. A prescription for chaos, but it worked fairly well. We were united in our desire to turn back communism. Well, perhaps a few of us were a little more cynical—but for the most part, we were united.

Flying disks were the merest diversion, and my intelligence

estimate was expected to be the work of an afternoon. The disks had started appearing in numbers only in June, and nobody viewed the matter very seriously.

During the war a little work on the question had been done by the Army Air Force. So we already had a dossier of unsolved mysteries and unusual phenomena, collected on an ad hoc basis when Army Air Force Intelligence was assessing the "foo-fighter" phenomenon toward the end of the war. We had concluded in 1946 that the "foo-fighters" were some sort of unknown phenomenon "possibly under intelligent control."

They represented a form of chaos, the intrusion of a powerful and provocative unknown into human affairs. I will not lie about it: The AAF was telling us that there was something going on, but they had no idea what to make of it.

I had worked through the July Fourth holiday, which I viewed as a minor sort of a tragedy.

I would have enjoyed spending my Fourth banging around the Snake Pit at the Mayflower Hotel looking for unescorted chorines, or crawling the Statler-Carlton circuit in search of a party.

Since the war I'd been uncomfortable with anything but the most casual relationships. I had nightmares about a French operative named Sophie, and about the North African I also lost, Jamshid, who was little more than a child. Often I would wake up in tears, but be unable to remember which of them had broken my sleep.

I disliked myself pretty thoroughly, because I thought I had been a less than brilliant spymaster, and I had wasted their lives.

I assumed that Admiral Hillenkoetter, who had just replaced Vandenberg as CIG director, realized these things about me. He knew that I felt useless on the French desk even though French politics was what I knew best.

As I worked on my intelligence estimate I found a peculiar pattern hidden in the old reports, and I did not like that pattern at all. If I was right about it, then the disks were far more dangerous than we had ever imagined.

So much for a few days' lark: the facts began to bother me.

What the hell was going on? Were they Russian, or some sort of Nazi or Jap secret weapon hidden until now?

They certainly appeared to be damned dangerous.

As the nights wore on, my olive-drab gooseneck lamp would attract more than its share of june bugs, moths and mosquitoes, until I would be sitting there at midnight in a cloud of darting insects and billowing cigarette smoke.

It was immediately clear that there would be no purpose served in repeating the assessment that the Army Air Force's intelligence unit had already provided about the "foo-fighters."

We needed to go deeper than to simply say that they might be under intelligent control.

If my suspicions were even directionally correct, we had to find out what was going on and find out fast, because we were at war. We were being invaded.

My method of gathering information was much less simple and straightforward than what the AAF had done, which was to view gun-camera photography of "foo-fighters" and interview pilots who had seen them.

I was looking for possible earlier instances of *contact* that might tell us more about the motives and intentions of our strangers.

1947: We were the victors. We had telephones and radar and DC-4's, with DC-6's just beginning to appear. We had Good Humor bars and weather balloons. We had captured German V-2 rockets. We had Albert Einstein and J. Robert Oppenheimer. We had the atomic bomb, and there were bigger bombs on the way.

We were lost in the dark and didn't know it.

The world went on, swathed in that beauty you can never quite touch, the beauty of a radio's voice drifting through the evening, of a woman waiting in a bed, the smell of bourbon at three A.M., of swimming in a dark pool, of watching children sleep. . . .

But there was also something else. There was that field near the tiny hamlet of Maricopa, New Mexico, and what was in that field.

It was there that the others waited. And not for some abstraction like mankind or the nation. They waited for each one of us individually—for me, for you, and for each trembling child.

In time each of us, every one, will face them.

In due time.

July 8, 1947

National Board of Estimate
INTELLIGENCE ESTIMATE ON FLYING DISK MOTIVES

Prepared by Office of Research and Analysis,
Central Intelligence Group
Copy 1 of 2

Purpose

The purpose of this estimate is to assess the motives of possible nonhuman beings piloting so-called "flying disks."

Background

From June 1947 there has been a dramatic increase in the sighting of "flying disks" in the United States, primarily in the Western states. On 24 June Mr. Kenneth Arnold, a fire-appliance salesman, took off from Chehalis Airport in Washington State to assist in the search for a Marine Air Transport C-46 that had disappeared in the Cascade Mountains. Mr. Arnold observed nine disk-shaped objects "skipping" through the air at a relatively high velocity. Over subsequent weeks there have been a large number of similar sightings, the best documented of which took place on July 4. A United Airlines DC-3 passenger-type aircraft was passed by nine disks while flying over Idaho on a flight to Seattle, Washington. Both pilots and nineteen passengers observed the disks, which were described as being larger than the aircraft.

These and other sightings may possibly be related to the sightings that have been reported consistently since 1946 by B-29 crew on transarctic missions. Photographs have been made, usually with gun cameras or ground reconnaissance cameras that suggest an intention on the part of the pilots of the devices to allow observation and/or photography to take place. Other objects are weather balloons distorted by a combination of wind and pressure effects at high altitude, flocks of birds reflecting the sun from their wings while flying in close formation, and clouds smoothed by wind.

Because of the substantial number of confirmed sightings and photographs, this estimate of the possible intentions of the craft occupants has been prepared.

Summary

It is possible that there is a relationship between a number of unsolved cases of disappearance and possible flying-disk activity, and that the flying disks could represent an extremely provocative and quite unusual phenomenon involving the permanent abduction of citizens into unknown conditions in a subterranean, undersea or outer space context. Should the occupants of the disks increase their level of activity, as it now seems apparent that they will, it is probable that the population will be terrorized, should large-scale disappearances occur and become known. The revelation that the government is helpless to act would then lead to public panic and a permanent loss of governmental credibility.

Detailed Analysis

This analysis will cover a number of cases of an unusual nature that appear to be related to the

presence of strange nocturnal lights and/or flying-disk activity.

At 3:15 on the morning of 4 October 1871, an un-
dertaker named William Robert Loosley awoke and
took a walk in his garden in the town of High Wy-
combe, Buckinghamshire, England. Mr. Loosley
recorded subsequent events in a manuscript that
was locked away until 1941. The ms. has been au-
thenticated by British antiquarians. It probably represents an example of a "probe" from some
sort of nonhuman intelligence.

When he went outside, Mr. Loosley observed a
light like a star move across the sky. He then
heard a clap of thunder, which, in view of the fact
that the sky was clear, struck him as strange. The
lighted object flew lower, stopped, then dropped
in a "falling leaf" pattern into some nearby
woods. This pattern of motion is also characteristic of modern flying disks.

The next morning Mr. Loosley went into those
woods and observed something metallic in a pile
of leaves. He soon uncovered a strange metal container approximately 18 inches long and covered
with knobs.

The thing moved and, making a sound like a lock
clicking, opened what appeared to be an eye behind a glass lens. Then another eye opened and
emitted a beam of purple light. A third eye extended a thin rod.

At this point Loosley decided to vacate the
area, and began to move away—running, no doubt.
To his considerable consternation the machine
followed, leaving a trail of three small ruts. He
observed that similar ruts crisscrossed a nearby
clearing.

The metal box shot a claw out into the brush and

grabbed a rat, which it killed with a flash of purple light. It then deposited the carcass in a panel that opened in the side of the machine.

The device then rushed after Mr. Loosley, who ran off in a panic, only to find himself being herded toward a larger machine, which appeared from a nearby clearing. He observed a "moon-like" device in the sky which seemed to be signaling with lights. He managed to escape from the machines and return home. The next night he observed a light come down from the sky, then rise up again and disappear into the clouds.

The fact that this account was written in 1871 greatly diminishes the likelihood of hoax. Robots of the sort described are only just now being speculated about in circles considering methods we might employ to explore planets such as Mars and Venus. It may be that Mr. Loosley observed a robot on a reconnaissance mission, and that it has now been followed by a larger expedition. If so, we can anticipate that it will be exploratory in nature as well, and that it will almost certainly center on analysis of the human species, which would have been the most interesting discovery made by the earlier reconnaissance.

It may be that human beings have since been successfully taken by strange machines.

The first seemingly related case of disappearance in U.S. history took place on 23 September 1880 near the town of Gallatin, Tennessee. At approximately three-thirty on that sunny afternoon, Mr. David Lang, a farmer, dematerialized in front of five witnesses, including his wife, his two children, his brother-in-law and a local judge.

The brother-in-law and the judge had just

pulled up in a carriage. Mr. Lang moved toward them across a field, followed by his family. Without warning, he simply ceased to exist. There was no cry, no sign of distress. Mrs. Lang, distraught, rushed up and pounded the ground where he had been walking. All that afternoon and into the night the field was searched. Subsequently the county surveyor determined that there were no hidden caves or sinkholes in the area of the disappearance.

The subsequent April, seven months later, the children heard their father crying distantly underneath the field. He seemed desperate and tortured, and was begging for help. His voice gradually died away and was not heard again. Where he had last been seen, there was a circle of withered yellow grass twenty feet in diameter.

The family moved away from the farm.

It can be surmised that Mr. Lang was not removed aboveground, but rather was taken into the earth and kept alive there for some months, judging from the cries that were heard the next April. What the poor man suffered during that time, and what finally put him out of his misery, can scarcely be imagined. It may be possible that another robot machine was sent, which waylaid this man from underneath the earth, in view of the fact that the device sent in 1871 had failed to capture a human being by more straightforward means.

In 1909 a child of eleven, Oliver Thomas, disappeared upon walking out of a Christmas Eve party at his home in Wales. Other partygoers heard a scream that seemed to come from the air above the house. No trace of the child was ever found. Was this an example of ambush from above?

In 1924 two British pilots crashed in the desert not far from Baghdad. Their craft was located shortly thereafter, and footsteps were discovered leading away from it. The footsteps stopped in the sand. There were no signs of a skirmish. No trace of the pilots was ever located. In view of the fact that there were bandits in the area where this disappearance took place, it is possible that the pilots met with foul play. However, British colonial authorities investigated the case thoroughly over a period of months, and found absolutely no trace of the men. None of their equipment or personal effects ever appeared for sale in the souks. British authorities have not yet closed the case.

In the winter of 1930 a profoundly disturbing incident took place in Canada. Trapper Arnaud Laurent and his son observed a strange light crossing the northern sky. It appeared to be headed for the Lake Anjikuni area. The two trappers describe it as being alternately bullet-shaped and cylinder-shaped. It can be assumed from this that it was an object of irregular configuration that was tumbling as it moved.

Another trapper named Joe Labelle had snowshoed into the village of the Lake Anjikuni people, and been chilled to discover that the normally bustling community was silent, and not a soul was moving in the streets. Even the sled dogs, which would normally have bayed welcome, were silent.

The shanties were choked with snow, and not a chimney showed smoke.

The trapper found the village's kayaks tied up on the shore of the lake. Inside the shanties the trapper found a further surprise: there were meals left hanging over fires, long grown old and moldy, apparently abandoned as they were being cooked. The men's rifles were still standing by the doors. This really frightened the trapper, because he knew that these people would never leave their precious weapons behind.

He reported his discovery to the Royal Canadian Mounted Police, who investigated further. They discovered that the town's dogs had died of hunger, chained beneath a tree and covered by a snowdrift. More disturbingly, the town graveyard had been emptied. The graves were now yawning pits. Despite the frozen ground, the graves had been opened and the dead removed.

The RCMP continues the case opened to this day. A check with their records department indicated that the matter remains unsolved, and despite a search of the whole of Canada and inquiries throughout the world, not a trace of the missing twelve hundred men, women and children has ever been found.

There are many other cases of disappearance in the air and at sea, but this small group appears to be the most unusual and the most likely to be related to an otherworldly presence.

Unfortunately we know nothing of the fate of most of these people. Only in the case of Mr. Lang can we even speculate. He was apparently left to languish in some sort of subterranean prison, presumably dying when his food and water ran out.

Were the hardy Eskimos moved to some other world, to plant the human seed among the stars? Was Mr. Lang examined, tested and then abandoned to his fate? And what of the little boy, and the two pilots? Did they end up in machines similar to the one that menaced Mr. Loosley?

It is possible that we are observing the outcome of a scientific study of the human species that uses stealth to accomplish its end of obtaining human specimens.

The fact that human specimens are gathered at all indicates that the beings doing the study consider us animals. That they are not returned reveals that our lives are of limited value to the nonhuman beings, if that is what they are. That the whole process takes place only in secret indicates that the beings realize that we would resist if we knew the truth. In other words, they are doing this despite the fact that they know we are sentient creatures.

It is likely that the public will initially greet the appearance of aliens with welcome and delight. Should arbitrary abductions take place, however, the cheering will shortly become a collective scream of horror.

People will then demand protection, looking to the government—and specifically the Army Air Force—to provide it. Given our present lack of knowledge, the Air Force will in all probability fail to do so. This will result in a loss of faith on the part of the American public at least as great as that experienced by the Third Reich in the last quarter of 1944, when even the most propagandized population groups finally understood that Germany would lose the war.

Thus we will be faced with a dispirited and hostile public on the one hand, and cruel and all-powerful aliens on the other.

Conclusion

If these cases of disappearance are indeed related to the flying disks, the conclusion can be drawn that the strangers are interested in us but do not have any regard for us. This is obviously a dangerous and highly undesirable state of affairs, and steps should be taken to correct it at once.

Recommendations

1. The public should be insulated from any certain knowledge that the disks are real until such time as we have a clear understanding of the nature and motives of their occupants, and can effectively maintain control over our own land and airspace, offering the public the protection that it mandates.
2. Every effort should be made to obtain samples of a flying disk as soon as possible, barring only hostile military action. This should be viewed by the AAF as its number one worldwide priority.
3. Because of the extremely disturbing nature of the phenomenon—and our helplessness—the whole affair should be given the highest classification rating that we possess, and should also be the subject of a rigorous propaganda campaign centered on denial. This campaign should be socially pervasive, so that it will continue to be effective even if a considerable number of disappearances take place.
4. Under no circumstances whatsoever must the public be allowed to become aware of the probable seriousness of this situation, and of our impotence to act. The only way to be certain that they will remain ignorant is to impose the highest level of security ever achieved. If we are to maintain the impression that the gov-

52

ernment can provide essential security, this must be done at any and all cost.

5. Should a disk land, or any debris be left behind, extreme efforts must be made to obscure the real meaning of the event. The fact that the strangers are real must not be revealed to the public until we understand their motives, and have gained effective control of their activities within the sovereign territory of the United States of America.

Chapter Four

In 1947 the most dangerous thing in the world consisted of twenty-four B-36 bombers polished to a high degree of shine. I have photographs of them standing along the flight line, back when Roswell Army Air Field had some meat on its bones.

Will Stone gave me the pictures, of course. He handled them with the excessive caution of the very old. When he looked at them there was hunger in his eyes. "The times were dangerous," he said. And he smiled that shattering smile of his.

Our tradition of stalemate has made the use of atomic weapons seem improbable. But in July of 1947 it had been just twenty-four months since the U.S. had used such weapons against Japan, and the prospect of those good machines taking wing for Moscow was an immediate and fascinating possibility.

What the hell were those bombers doing in New Mexico, the chiefs of staff asked. Move them to Europe, give them a straight shot at the Kremlin.

One thing was certain, and that was that the 509th was ready. Every pilot had thousands of bomber hours. Every one was a combat veteran, many from both the European and Pacific theaters. Everybody had clearances, even the cooks and janitors. The intelligence group was superb, the best air intelligence officers in the Army Air Force. Arguably theirs was the most sensitive command of its kind in the Army, and maybe in the world.

When I met some of those pilots I did not particularly like them. I doubt if there are twenty of them left; the ones I met ferried the debris found on the Ungar ranch to Eighth Air Force HQ in Fort Worth.

which came alive with a pale, fluorescent flutter. Hesseltine raised the large shade. It revealed a wall map of New Mexico. There were various colored pins in this map, representing the presence of radar installations and air bases. A large section marked off by black dotted lines was labeled, "Proving Grounds." This area, which would become the White Sands Missile Range, was where the captured German V-2 rockets were being tested.

Hesseltine pulled down a parallel ruler that was attached to the map and maneuvered it until one side was in the middle of the dot that represented Roswell.

"A hundred and twenty miles north-northwest? That isn't anywhere. No installations nearby."

"What about a stray from the proving ground?" There was always a possibility that a rocket had gone off course.

"No problems since last month. And that baby got found two weeks ago."

Gray now walked over to the map. "Private aircraft?"

"It's a restricted flyover area. There would have been an intrusion alert."

Gray stared at the map. "That's flat, miserable country. What does the man run?"

Hesseltine, from a suburb of Philadelphia, hadn't the least idea what ranchers raised in godforsaken deserts. "Dunno," he said, "maybe lizards."

"There wouldn't be any money in that."

"Why, sure there would," Hesseltine said eagerly, realizing that Gray had taken his absurd remark at face value. "Plenty of money. Lizardskin wallets."

"It's not very likely, Hesseltine."

"A stray private flier was forced down in a storm. It's a matter for the civilian authorities," Hesseltine said. He covered the map. "Raise the blinds, Winters."

"Yes, sir."

"Not yet, Mr. Winters," Gray said. He put his finger on the map. "The flier was well within restricted airspace when he was forced down. We're required to examine the wreckage." He picked up a telephone and called the sheriff's office in Maricopa. "This is Major Gray at Roswell."

"Yeah?"

"I just read your report on the plane that went down on the Ungar place."

"He came in this morning. Says it's a big mess. A bunch of tinfoil that you can't tear. I guess you guys know all about it."

"We'd like to take a look at the wreckage. Can you give us driving instructions?"

"Bob can do that himself. He's down in Roswell. You'll find him at Wooten's on North Main."

"I know the place."

"You get your directions from Bob. We haven't been out there. No call for us to go, not if you guys are going. It's way the hell out in the middle of nothin', where that plane went down."

Gray hung up the phone. "Looks like this could be an all-nighter. We gotta go find the rancher. He's apparently buying ranching paraphernalia at Wooten's."

Only Major Gray would use a word like that in ordinary conversation. Paraphernalia.

"You mean reins and scabbards and whatnot?"

"I guess. We'd better get going if we expect to get out there before dark."

Hesseltine glanced at his watch. It was past three. When Gray got rolling, he was perfectly capable of continuing all night if the matter seemed important enough to him. "Why not first thing in the morning," Hesseltine asked briskly.

As he had feared, Gray had other ideas. "I think that we should go out there immediately, Lieutenant. And take Walters of CIC."

There was no point in arguing. Hesseltine called Counterintelligence. Walters wisely decided to come in his own Jeep.

Hesseltine would have liked to take a Jeep, too, but he knew that Gray preferred his staff car. Hesseltine kind of enjoyed getting in Jeeps and putting on his dark glasses and sitting with his foot up on the dash like a pilot being ferried out to the flight line. He had washed out of pilot training due to his tendency to become sick during maneuvers such as taking off, landing, and flying through smooth, clear air.

Hesseltine was convinced that he was second-rate. As far as he was concerned every officer in the Army Air Force who was not a flight officer had failed.

That Gray did not share his feelings was incomprehensible to Hesseltine. The best men flew fighters, as Gray himself had during the war. Second-best were on bombers and other aircraft. The rest were nowhere.

He was so humiliated by his failure that he would obsessively deadhead on bombers, taking the tail-gunner position. Nobody ever knew that his flight bag contained dozens of neatly folded canvas airsickness containers . . . nobody but Will Stone, who must at some time have ferreted it out of him.

It is obvious from reading his meticulous notes and diaries that Will was obsessed with details like that, almost as if they might somehow provide the tiny, critical bit of information that would explain why things went so wrong.

Gray had once caused Hesseltine to run to the can with his cheeks puffed out by simply saying the word "tailspin" and whirling him around a couple of times in his chair.

Gray was one of those men who viewed such miseries as the will of God. "The Almighty made you quick to get an upset stomach," he had said earnestly as Hesseltine came staggering back from the men's room.

Gray was also the man who had floored a viciously drunk captain from another bomber wing with a single, appalling left uppercut that had lifted this two-hundred-pound monster off the floor of the Lackland Army Air Force Base Officer's Club in Texas.

It was one of many reasons that Hesseltine resented Gray, and found it interesting to needle him. Now that there was no war to fight, the fact that the mild and methodical Gray could sometimes be enraged was about the most fascinating thing left in Hesseltine's life.

As I write, I try to imagine those two men as they were then. Strength. Promise. A little arrogance, perhaps. Now they are both dead, Gray after a long and distinguished career.

Six months after the Roswell incident Pete Hesseltine began to hit the bottle so hard that he became pretty much of a professional at it. He died alone in a walkup in Sacramento, California, in September of 1955. He was not yet forty years old.

But on this day they were both young and at least somewhat

happy, two victorious soldiers looking forward to glowing careers in the finest military organization in the world.

They went down the long, plywood corridor that led from their office to the front of the building and out into the blazing parking lot. As they crossed it soft tar stuck to the bottoms of their shoes. Gray seemed almost to prance as he moved along. He was a spit-and-polish dresser.

"Gonna have to stay up half the night polishing the bottoms of our goddamn shoes," Hesseltine said.

"Why polish the bottoms of our shoes?"

"You can't eat off floors that have tar on them."

"Is that an example of your wit?"

"Maybe it's wit. Or maybe I'm just crazy."

"I think the former." Gray stepped into an especially soft spot and lifted his right foot out with a loud smack.

The concrete apron of the runway started just the other side of a chain-link fence. On it were six jeeps lined up in a neat row, waiting to ferry crew to the planes, which stood in the distance shimmering with heat. There were no flights planned for this afternoon, and the line was quiet.

Hesseltine fitted his aviation glasses to his face and looked longingly toward the rows of planes. Slowly he walked toward the car. In his mind he was, no doubt, running down a checklist, starting motors.

The car was hot to touch, hotter to sit in. With a long sigh he started it and nosed it out of the lot.

Walters's Jeep pulled in behind them, driven by a grim-faced PFC Winters, who had been dragooned into the job.

Once they were on the two-lane blacktop that led over to Roswell, Hesseltine lit a cigarette and tuned in a radio station. A show called *Sundown Roundup* was on, and they listened in silence. He knew that Gray didn't particularly like country music, and also that he was too polite to twist the dial if Hesseltine appeared to be enjoying himself. Hesseltine snapped his fingers in time to the thin caterwauling of a lonesome cowboy. He hated the goddamn West. He would gladly have given an entire paycheck for a hoagie.

They drove through the town, past the restaurants, the bars, the general stores, the offices of the *Daily Record*. Hesseltine glanced back with longing as they left the last of the bars behind. He was a man for a tall, cool one. He had a possibility of a date tonight, and he was damned if he was going to waste time out on some godforsaken ranch with Gray and Walters when he could be dancing with a WAAF at the Nixon Bar. He nosed the Chevy wagon to the sidewalk in front of Wooten's. The Jeep came in beside them. Gray got out of the wagon and trotted into the store.

Hesseltine sat staring after him. Soon Walters came up to the car and leaned his head in. "Whaddaya think?"

"Wild goose chase. Some private plane went down in a storm."

"Funny place for a private plane to be. Middle of nowhere."

"Flying Albuquerque-Roswell. Blown off course a few miles. Makes perfect sense."

Walters regarded him, nodding slowly. Compared to Walters, Gray was a real card. "Could be Russian," he said in dark tones. "Up from Mexico, or even from the coast. A recce plane launched from a sub. After a look at the 509th."

"Didn't make it."

"How do we know? Maybe it had a *good* look and radioed everything back to the sub."

It struck Hesseltine as damned unlikely and he said so.

"Well, Lieutenant, you may be right. But look at the stakes. Stalin wants, more than anything else in the world, to know exactly where the 509th is located, and its immediate orders."

"But he can't *get* here. Surely not, Mr. Walters."

"That isn't a CIC problem. You S-2s are supposed to be savvy in that department."

Major Gray came out of the store. "That's a good man, that Bob Ungar. I like men like him. Honest as the day is long. Friendly as hell." He held up a hand-drawn map. "He can't lead us out, he's got too much to do here in town. But he gave me very explicit instructions to his house. His wife and kids are there."

The tiny convoy started up again. A thought crossed Hesseltine's mind. "What kind of kids?"

"Daughter, he mentioned. Son he has with him."

"Daughter?"

"A *kid*, Lieutenant. Twelve years old."

Hesseltine got quiet.

Beyond the clutch of Mexican shacks that ended the town Hesseltine picked up speed. Unable to stand any more of the whining music he spun the dial. A bad dance band pounded away at "Begin the Beguine." Father Coughlin screamed over waves of static. A woman explained that certain cactuses were edible. Somebody talked about how the DuBarry Success Course could bring more dates, more fun. You followed at home the same methods used at the Richard Hudnut Salon in New York.

Hesseltine spoke longingly about a girl in a pale gray suit tapping along in heels. He wanted that sweet and anonymous image with an ache that made him fall silent.

"They take the money of innocent kids," Gray intoned. "Nobody around here is ever going to look like she got within fifty miles of Richard Hudnut."

"Give me one of those Fifth Avenue dames. I'd take her up to the Rainbow Room and dance her until she dropped. These New Mexico girls have sand between their teeth."

"I wouldn't know. Jennine—"

" 'Jennine, I dream of Lilac Time—' "

"Please, Lieutenant."

"I thought it was your song. You and Jennine."

"The way you sing it, it's nobody's song."

They swept off the blacktop onto a dirt road. The Jeep dropped way back to avoid their dust cloud.

They drove at a steady forty-five miles an hour, for three hot and dismal hours. When they stopped the shadows were long and the katydids were already singing.

They were in Maricopa, a town that consisted of ten houses strung along the roadside, a store, a bar and a gas station.

Everybody got down from the vehicles. Walters stretched his back, took off his sunglasses and began cleaning them with his handkerchief. His PFC driver whapped at his own uniform, bringing up clouds of dust.

"I'll bet that bar is full of cold beer," Hesseltine said. Nobody acknowledged him, but I have no doubt that PFC Winter's eyes rolled.

"I'll go in and confirm these instructions," Gray announced. Walters went with him.

"You want a beer, Private?"

"Yes, sir."

"Our commanding officer will fail to realize this."

"Yes, sir."

"End of story, Private."

"Yes, sir."

Gray and Walters came hurrying back like men about to miss a train. "The road is about half a mile back toward Roswell," Gray said. "Then another thirty miles to the man's house. It's just a track."

It was far worse than that. Hesseltine waited for the Chevy to break an axle.

Amazingly, it didn't happen. This may have been because of the number of gates they had to open and close was so great that they never managed to get past twenty before they had to slow down again.

"The cattleguard hasn't been invented yet in New Mexico."

"Apparently not, Lieutenant."

"This is gate number sixteen."

"I haven't been counting."

Soon they arrived at a miserable hovel that was distinguished only by a tiny flower garden in the front yard. The garden had sunflowers in it, and a few fat little cactuses with yellow flowers on them. Two kids, shy and afraid, cowered by the side of the house.

"Look out," Hesseltine muttered to Gray. "They might be commie dwarfs disguised as scared kids."

To Hesseltine's surprise, Gray stomped his foot against the floorboard of the car. He glared a moment at his junior officer.

"Close your window, Lieutenant," he snapped as he wound up his own. "Breaches of security are always a serious business, especially in a sensitive area like Roswell. For all we know, those kids *are* Commies and ready to report our least move to their cell leader. The fact that we're here on this ranch could be common knowledge in Moscow inside of an hour!"

Hesseltine was so taken aback by this outburst that he guf-

63

fawed before he could stop himself. Gray glared at him. "You've got to take this seriously, Hesseltine."

"I'm sorry, sir. It's just that I've blown a date, and—"

"I understand perfectly. But we have to do this. And do it right."

"I agree, sir."

The porch had an old couch on it that was covered with a piece of canvas. The couch was sprung and there were places where animals had torn at the stuffing.

Gray was not a large man, but he felt huge in this little adobe-brick house. He knocked, the sound echoing flatly in the dark room beyond the rusty screen door.

Soon a shadow appeared moving forward from the back of the house, a woman gliding swiftly and crookedly along. She appeared behind the door, hesitant, her face clouding at the sight of the uniforms. She had a cigarette between her lips, which she took into her fingers. "Can I help you?" she asked, her voice soft.

Gray felt pity for her until he saw the flashing strength in her eyes. As he had many times before, he thought now that he did not understand these tough New Mexico people. "I'm Major Gray of the Roswell Army Air Force. This is Lieutenant Hesseltine and Mr. Walters." He did not introduce PFC Winters. The soldier, in any case, was lingering out by the Jeep.

"Come on in," Ellie replied, opening the door. The two children, who had been standing on the steps, now crowded past to be with their mother. "Go back outside, now," she said, "you let these men be. They're important Army men and they don't need kids to bother them." She herded them toward the back of the house. "They've never seen Army men so close," she added. As she spoke she smiled, and Gray was surprised without understanding why at how her smile made him feel.

For all his self-assurance Gray was an uneasy and open-hearted child of America. Her poverty spoke to him of his childhood seeing Okies on the road and hoboes in the back alley behind the white bungalow where he ate meals of collard and steak and cornbread. He had bounced along in the backseat of a clean little Essex, and heard his father say things like, "God has blessed us among the cursed millions, and we must never forget to thank Him."

One afternoon his father sat beneath the blooming wisteria in the backyard with tears streaming down his face. After that things had slowly gotten harder and harder. The Essex went, the refrigerator became an ice box again, the radio broke and was not repaired, and the leaves of autumn rolled down the street.

But there were also pennants won and comic books read and Baby Ruths eaten, and the sonorous majesty of Latin Club declamation contests. "In partem gloriae venio," and all the rest of it, Virgil and Cicero and the compressed fury of Seneca's plays.

The Grays had been a raft of neat, diminished pride in the shabby Midwestern ocean. These people were even worse off, and that scared him and made him hate them a little, and also feel tender toward them. Two generations ago most of the New Mexico settlers had set off westward from the ruins of Virginia, leaving their silk collars and magnolia evenings forever behind. They had slipped from grace and tumbled down into poverty's labyrinth of musty, rugless rooms and chipped white bowls on the dinner table.

"My husband's out back. I'll get him to come up." She left the living room, and in a moment her voice came again, low and hard and shockingly loud, "The Air Force is here!"

Hesseltine fidgeted with a bit of frayed cloth on the arm of the easy chair in which he was sitting. Gray stood nervously contemplating the large picture of Christ on the cross that hung over the mantel of the ancient, blackened fireplace. On the mantel there was also a picture of a lean, young man and a girl beside him.

"Would you like coffee," the woman said in her murmuring, prayerful way. Gray imagined the family before its picture of Jesus, praying against their frayed lives and the dry, hot desert where they made their living. He could not have been more wrong, of course. The Jesus was there for the colors, which Ellie thought matched the chair. And it was good for the kids.

Although all three men had declined coffee, the woman was making it anyway when her husband came banging into the house. He loomed through to the living room like a great caricature of Abraham Lincoln, stooping under the door and crossing directly to Gray. Walters and Hesseltine jumped to their feet.

"How in the world did you beat us," Gray asked.

"There's a road in that passes north of Arabela. Cuts off fifty miles."

"Oh."

"I thought I told you about it."

"We'd better get out to the crash."

"We can't."

"Can't?"

"It'll be dark before we get there. No use goin' until mornin'."

Gray could see by the looks on Hesseltine's and Walters's faces that they were just as appalled as he was.

"We got you each a plate of beans," the rancher said affably. "And coffee."

Gray managed to smile. Walters was impassive. Hesseltine looked like he was thinking about going AWOL. Winters had come to the door and stood there hesitantly. "Bring in that half of bourbon," Walters growled. The PFC produced a well-sucked half-pint of Old Granddad, which Walters handed to each man in turn.

Gray drank a swallow to be sociable. Hesseltine, he noticed, knocked back a couple of long pulls.

"That hit the spot," the lieutenant said. "Pardon me for drowning my sorrows. As of fifteen minutes from now I'm standing up the best-looking WAAF captain in Roswell."

"You better hope she doesn't put you on report."

"I like your sense of humor, Major Gray."

"Thank you, Lieutenant."

The rancher's wife called them into the kitchen, where they hulked around the table. When Gray saw how sparse the meals were, he knew that the woman had stretched four helpings of beans to eight. Even so, each plate had a little scrap of fat back on it along with the beans, and the coffee smelled rich and good.

They sat down to the crowded table. "This is some of that stuff," the rancher said. He put a couple of small pieces of tinfoil on the table.

Gray felt a flush of anger: he recognized it as foil from a burst weather balloon. He picked up the scrap of material. "Did you see the plane?"

"Lights. Heard the explosion. Then the next night y'all's blimp came over with the searchlights, but it missed the wreckage."

Gray frowned. "Blimp?"

"Sure. That big gray blimp."

Walters looked at Gray, took the foil from him. He held the stuff in his hand, staring down at it. Abruptly he crushed the foil to a tiny ball, then put it on the table.

To Gray's amazement, it sprang back to its original shape.

"You can't burn it or tear it," the rancher said as he spooned up the last of his beans. "I don't wonder, you couldn't put a bullet through it, either."

Gray met Walters's eyes. The CIC man's face was literally drained of color. "Let's go out to the Jeep," he said evenly. "Get those maps."

Outside, it was immediately obvious that Walters wasn't looking for any maps. "What the hell is going on here," he asked.

"I don't know."

"What is that stuff?"

"Frank, I've never seen anything like it before in my life."

"And a blimp!"

"Experimental aircraft, maybe."

"Something you wouldn't know about?"

Gray didn't like to think that experimental aircraft would be tested in the squadron area without his knowledge, but it was possible. "Could be," he answered.

"I don't like it. There isn't a hangar in New Mexico that can hold a blimp."

"Texas, then. Blimps can fly long range."

"Real long range. Like from Russia. If you ask me, this could be some kind of new goldbeater's skin. Incredibly tough. Suitable for a long-range spy blimp, or even a bomber."

Both men knew what a bomber could do to the 509th if it struck while there were atomic devices on the flight line.

"Hiroshima'd look like a picnic," Gray said. He tried to imagine the scope of the disaster, but his mind rejected it.

"Two blimps. One of them blows up in a thunderstorm. The other one comes searching for the remains."

"They have a hell of a big radar signature."

"They can also fly low and slow, Don."

"Low and slow all the way from Russia. Damn, that's scary."

They went back inside to find that the rancher and his family were already going to bed.

As he passed the couple's bedroom door, Gray glimpsed an old iron bed with yellow sheets and a dresser with a half-empty bottle of Trushay hand cream on top. He felt a pang of loneliness; Jennine used Trushay. He wished that he'd called her before he came out here. Suddenly he was facing Russians in the night, and he was uneasy.

"I think we'd better hang watches," he said when the four soldiers were alone together in the living room.

"I agree," Walters said.

"What're we worried about, coyotes?" Hesseltine sounded disgusted.

Gray explained to him. "Russians. This stuff is most probably some kind of goldbeater's skin, used to cover a blimp. The rancher saw another blimp last night. Long-range Russian blimps after the 509th."

That stopped even Hesseltine. The PFC's eyes were wide.

"I'm armed," Walters said. He produced a police special from under his jacket. "The man on watch carries it in his belt."

"Is it a regulation weapon?" Gray asked. "I didn't think civilians could carry weapons on base."

"Consider me a cop. That's what counterintelligence is, kid. Police work."

Gray didn't know Walters all that well, but he'd always had a lot of respect for the man. His background as a police detective combined with his toughness and brains made him one of the best counterintelligence men that Gray had ever met. With communist fifth columnists, fellow travelers and spies said to be everywhere, good men were needed to protect the 509th.

He lay on his back with a couch cushion for a pillow. First PFC Winters went on watch, then Hesseltine. Gray had decided that the postmidnight hours were the most dangerous, and assigned them to himself and Walters. There would be four two-hour watches from nine P.M., then reveille along with the rancher, who ordinarily got up at five.

He must have slept a little, because Hesseltine's place was empty and the PFC was snoring peacefully when he opened his eyes again. Walters had been sawing Z's from the second they'd snuffed the oil lamp. Gray lit a cigarette.

He could easily imagine Russians sneaking around out here. He thought of the goldbeater's skin. How the hell had they done it? He'd never seen anything even remotely like it. Incredibly tough. Incredibly light.

Suddenly Hesseltine was whispering in his ear. "Your turn, boss."

Gray looked at his radium-dial watch. "You've got it, Mr. Hesseltine." He stubbed out his cigarette in the ashtray he'd brought down to the floor. "Any sign of anything?"

"It's been quiet, except for the porcupines, badgers, ferrets, owls, coons and coyotes. Not to mention the things that scream."

There was nothing screaming now. As a matter of fact it was absolutely quiet, absolutely dark and about as lonely a place as Gray had ever been in. The Milky Way came right down to both horizons. Even a tiny constellation like Lyra stood out clearly. The only way you could tell where the land started was that there were no stars there.

Gray wished he had another cigarette, but you didn't carry lights on watch. He stood in front of the house beside the bulk of his staff car. It would have been nice to see if he could pick up some dance music, but he supposed that all the radio stations would be shut down by now.

One-fifteen. As his eyes slowly adjusted to the dark he took a walk around the house. He moved up toward the barn, which was small and ramshackle. There was a horse snorting inside, and he could hear sheep bleating somewhere off in the distance. There were rustles and shuffling sounds and occasional low growls in the brush.

Once he was startled to see what he thought might have been a glow on the horizon, but it disappeared and he didn't see it again.

An hour passed.

Then he heard a noise unlike any he had heard before. It cut through him like a white-hot blade.

Walters and the rancher and Hesseltine came pouring out the kitchen door. PFC Winters stood behind them.

69

"What the hell was it," Walters breathed.

"Damned if I know," Gray said. The scream was still echoing in his head. "What about it, Mr. Ungar?"

The rancher was standing very still, staring into the black night. "I heard it right after the crash. I lived here all my life, and I never heard anything like it before."

Gray's fingers closed around the piece of foil in his pocket. In his mind there had formed a question, but he did not yet know how to put it into words.

"Goddamn," Hesseltine said softly.

The rancher backed up against his screen door.

From inside the house a child keened, and Mrs. Ungar offered comfort in a shaking voice.

Ungar whispered, "The other night when I heard it, I thought nothing could sound like that but the devil."

"It's real," Walters said. "We all heard it."

They were silent, then, and so was the night.

Chapter Five

In part I have written this in an attempt to understand why Will Stone and the others did what they did. Why did they choose to decide that these others were dangerous?

One of the things that I originally understood the least was the mind of Will Stone and by extension all the other Will Stones that choke the bureaucracies of the world.

I can read his diaries, listen to him talk, read assessments of him, sit across from him and watch him slowly choking on his cancer, and never actually see him. The moment I leave him, it is as if he has never existed. The curse of living with too many secrets is that a man's own meaning also becomes a secret. He loses himself in the machinery of his knowledge.

I keep thinking that, if only I understood exactly what was so strangely *unformed* about the man I would also know why he failed so dismally to grasp the sublime aim of the others. Somehow he translated their offer of help into a deadly challenge.

I suppose it was an offer of help. Surely it must have been. What would happen to us, I wonder, if we were attacked by an army whose weapons were so subtle that we could not understand even that we were at war?

I am fascinated by the contrast between Stone and Bob Ungar. The one is alive and yet more indistinct than a shadow. The other—long dead—is vivid with meaning and sense and even grace.

I can imagine the morning that he took the military party to the crash site. Major Gray's report reveals nothing of the emo-

71

tions, of the sinew and color of the experience. But I can imagine.

Dawn at the Ungar ranch would be marked by quiet kitchen bustle and the smell of strong coffee. Judging from the uneasiness he reports feeling, Don Gray would have been sleeping fitfully.

Perhaps the clink of dishes made him open his eyes. It was still pitch dark, but the entire Ungar family was already at breakfast. Walters was with them, slopping down coffee and chewing on a big piece of bread.

Gray woke up the others, tucked in his shirt and went to the table. The meal consisted of coffee and bread spread with a thin coating of grape jelly. He thought of steak and eggs at the officer's club. Roswell AAF was a good life. Challenging to be an intelligence officer in a place where it really mattered. A good outfit. Excellent facilities.

Coffee and bread. Not even a glass of water to wash it down, let alone milk or juice. They couldn't have drunk the water even if it had been offered. These people used cisterns. The Air Force warned you to drink only from approved water supplies as soon as you set foot on base. And stay away from animals that might have fleas: New Mexico had fifty to a hundred cases of bubonic plague a year. Not to mention astronomical polio statistics and a substantial amount of TB in the Mexican population.

Don was just as glad that the coffee was well boiled.

Ungar wiped his mouth against the back of his hand. "Let's get on out there. I've got a lotta other stuff to do today."

He pulled his ancient Jeep up to the house. His daughter and son got in with him. The four soldiers rode in Walters's much newer Jeep. Gray and Hesseltine sat in the back, deciding that it was best to leave the staff car behind.

They bounced over the desolate land for about half an hour. Gray could see a mountain ahead, but it never seemed to get any closer. The land undulated in great, shallow waves. Spanish daggers and chorro cactus dragged along the sides of the Jeep. Tough clumps of dry grass waved in the morning breeze. Out where the land was flat tumbleweeds bounded along.

They came to the top of a rise and he saw the crash site. His practiced eye told him at once that something had blown up as it was traveling in a westerly direction. Debris had fanned out from a point about a hundred yards below the base of a hill. The wreckage covered an area about a quarter of a mile long.

They stopped the Jeeps. "No large debris," Hesseltine said immediately.

"What was it?" Walters asked.

Gray spoke. "The lack of large debris does suggest a balloon or some such thing."

The rancher walked into the mess. "I want y'all to take a look at something." He pointed at the ground. "Those things."

Gray saw some small balsa beams, some shaped like the letter I and others like a T. He picked one up. It was marked by violet hieroglyphics.

"Cyrillic?" Hesseltine asked.

"No," Walters said as he examined it.

"Jap?"

Gray looked at the writing. It was vaguely reminiscent of Egyptian, but there were no familiar animal shapes. "I've never seen anything like it before."

The little girl held up a piece of what seemed to Gray to be parchment. There were rows of little squiggles on it. They were pink and purple, and Gray couldn't make anything out of them at all.

"Maybe they're numbers," Hesseltine said. "The way they're in columns like that."

The little girl held another piece of the parchment up to the sun, the disk of which had just cleared the horizon. "You can see yellow flowers inside. Its real pretty."

The torn pieces of parchment were abundant, and all four soldiers picked them up and held them to the sun. "Cornflowers," Gray said.

Walters grunted. "Primroses. Cornflowers are blue."

"You can't burn it, bend it, tear it or nothin'," the rancher said. "Just like the tinfoil."

PFC Winters spoke. "What I think you all have here," he said in his drawl, "is the pieces of one of them flying disks like folks've been seeing."

Nobody replied. Suddenly Walters grabbed a large piece of

73

foil and began struggling furiously with it. He pulled it, ripped at it, stood on it and tried to stretch it. Nothing.

Finally he took out his pistol. "Okay, folks, we'll see just how strong this stuff really is." He laid the three-foot-square piece of material out on the ground and fired into it.

There was a blast from the gun, and the foil swarmed into the ground behind the bullet. "That tore it," the PFC said. He and Walters pulled it out of the ground.

The flattened bullet was lying in the middle of the foil, which was completely unmarred.

"You sure that's not Cyrillic on that paper," Walters asked again.

The bullet just lay there, flattened. The foil shone in the sun. Gray took out his Old Golds and with shaking hands pulled the foil from around the few cigarettes that remained in the pack. He took a piece of the strange metal in one hand and the cigarette wrapping in the other.

The metal was thinner by a considerable margin. He was a methodical man, and not quick to make decisions. He carefully returned the cigarette wrapping to the pack and put his cigarettes in his pocket. He then picked up a piece of the parchment and attempted to burn it with his lighter. It would not burn.

"Nothin' burns," the rancher said. "And the wood doesn't break."

Walters grabbed a piece of the wood. It bent like rubber. No matter how he twisted it around he could not make it snap. Finally he threw it to the ground. "What the hell is it?"

Gray looked at the PFC. "I think you're absolutely right, soldier. I think what we have here is the remains of an exploded flying disk."

"Oh, Lord," Walters said. "What are they doing here? What are they up to?"

"Maybe just looking around," Hesseltine replied.

"By dark of night? In secret? I hardly think that's all they're doing." Walters looked grim. He had taken his pistol from his shoulder holster and stuck it in his belt.

"We don't know what they're doing," Gray said. There was annoyance in his voice. He didn't like loose speculation. They weren't equipped even to think about things like intent. "What we need to do is gather up as much of this stuff as we can, and get it back to the field pronto."

"We ought to recce the whole site," Hesseltine said.

The four of them walked it, making rough measurements and kicking under the sheets of foil, the wooden beams, the parchment, looking for any large objects.

It took them about an hour to examine the area and fill the jeeps with as much debris as they could conveniently carry.

When they returned to the house they transferred some of the material to the rear of Gray's wagon. Then they headed back to the field. The rest of the stuff remained with Walters.

Don Gray was now excited, even elated. He had forgotten the cries in the night, and was now thinking only of the incredible thing they had found. It was one of the most momentous discoveries in history, and he had made it. Just absolutely incredible.

"We are going to have a hell of a lot of work to do on this," he said to Hesseltine.

"What work? This is gonna be Eighth Air Force business. Pentagon business. We've done our work. You'll see. The brass is gonna be all over this thing."

"Maybe and maybe not."

I believe that this was the moment that Donald Gray became a hero. To his own considerable surprise, he found that he had formed a powerful conviction about this. It was not going to be a military secret.

"What about the threat to the 509th? I mean, why are they out here in this godforsaken place, anyway? Could be because it's close to the squadron." Hesseltine's hands gripped the wheel. "The A-bomb is a big thing. Maybe even big enough to be of concern to people on other planets." Now that he had seen the danger, his sense of duty was finally aroused.

After that they were both silent for a long time, trying to absorb the import of his statement. Soon Hesseltine turned on the radio and picked up the ten A.M. news out of Albuquerque. Then there was a soap opera, *Young Doctor Malone.* Gray listened without interest to the complications of the doctor's life.

It was nearly one when they finally reached the outskirts of Roswell. "Let's stop at my house for lunch," Gray said. "I want my son to see this stuff."

"You sure about that?"

"I'm certain."

"It's gonna be classified."

"Well, it's not classified now, and I want my boy to see it and hold it in his hands. It'll be something to tell his grandchildren."

"He's twelve. Say he has grandchildren when he's fifty. That'll be, let's see, nineteen-eighty-five. By then everybody will know all about this. There'll probably be aliens living down the block. And the fact that he saw a few pieces of a wrecked disk in 1947 won't amount to a hill of beans."

"Well, Jennine still makes a better ham sandwich than you'll find in the officer's club."

"I could use a whole ham. A couple of hams. Those poor devils live on beans and bread."

"And I've got a six-pack of White Label beer."

"Trommers? Where the hell did you get that?"

"Three hundred ninetieth Air Service at your service. Some of the guys brought it back on a run from D.C."

"Does Jennine know how to make a hoagie?"

"Which is?"

"It's real food from Philly."

They dumped some of the stuff on the kitchen table. Gray called Don Jr., who was in his room struggling with a balsa model of a Zero.

Don Jr. is now a doctor living in Southern California. His office bustles with patients; he is a successful man and honored in his community.

I asked him to please tell me if this really happened. He looked me square in the eye and said, "Mr. Duke, it did." And he proceeded to relate the story of how his father had showed him the debris.

"Identify it," the major had told his son.

The boy looked at it, touched it. "Private plane?"

"See the balsa parts."

"Is that Egyptian writing?"

"Nope."

"What is it, then, Dad?"

Jennine took out a box of Cut-Rite and compared the wax paper to the parchment. "It certainly isn't normal wax paper," she said.

"Donnie, I'll give you a dime if you guess correctly. The debris comes from something that crashed up near Maricopa."

"Not a balloon, not a plane." He looked at his father, smiled. "Flying disk?"

"Smart," Hesseltine said.

"Don't be silly, Don," his mother told him. "Your dad wants you to learn these things."

"Jennine, the boy has just won a dime. He's exactly right. Our opinion is that this material came from a flying disk like the ones they've been reporting in the papers."

Donnie was awed, and the awe remains with him to this day. Gingerly, he touched some of the wooden beams. He looked at his dad. "What happened to the pilot?"

Don's mind went back to that wild, awful howling. "There wasn't a sign of a pilot."

He thought of the poor rancher with his wife and kids. Tonight and every night, they would be out there alone with whatever had done that howling.

He bit into the sandwich that Jennine had made for him, and ate with the gusto of the survivor.

Chapter Six

The Chronicle of Wilfred Stone

It is curious that distant memories become so vivid in old age. I first noticed this perhaps ten years ago; I remember my father commenting on it when he was in his seventies. When I was fifty my recollections of early childhood were little more than shadows. Now I can remember the lace collar I wore, and how Momma tied it behind my neck, and the smell of the lucifers they used to light the gas.

I remember other things too, oh, I certainly do. They are most appalling things, and I don't know how to cope with them.

Are they real, or is my mind beginning to mix memory and imagination?

That would be fatal to understanding, of course, and I cannot know if it has happened.

However, I do know that what I am about to describe has been done to many children of *this* generation. The Children's Circles that the others formed in the fifties and sixties were part of this phenomenon.

I should know all about that: I personally agreed to let them enter the lives of fifty of those children. They submitted a list.

I did not allow myself to suspect that they would use my agreement as an excuse to affect thousands more. But they did, of course. I told myself, only fifty. A small price.

Were they doing it as far back as 1916, and did they do it to me? The question makes me sorrow and makes me ache. It is so important to my understanding of what has happened to me—and to us all—and so impenetrable.

All I can do is focus myself on those days, and repeat the

recollections that age has returned to the forefront of my mind.

Once again it is early July, but this is the year 1916 and the location is Westchester County.

This is not the suburban glut of today, but another place entirely, a land of rolling hills and comfortable, elegant homes. There are farms in the valleys, and wagons are more common than trucks and cars. Where great malls will spread across the land there are now apple orchards, and the trees show promise of a rich harvest in the fall.

One of these houses in particular is of interest to us. In July of 1916 the house was owned by Herbert Stone, a man skilled in the application of law to the problems of the corporation. Among his clients are the National Biscuit Company and the Hill Coffee empire.

He was there with his wife, Janet, and their two children, Monica and Wilfred.

Monica was four, and I was three.

Before God, I wish I could go back with a warning.

The children are playing, the parents sipping scotch and water. The katydids are arguing, the butterflies fluttering. Westchester smiles.

Like his father, Herbert is a lawyer. He loves us with the kind of simplicity that I value so much and do not myself possess. My work has denied me peace in these aged years. Instead I live like an anguished ghost. They were the last family I had, mother and father and my dead sister. I have been cursed to outlive my generation, and to do so without the comfort of a family.

When this young journalist appeared, attracted like a little trout to the bait of my letter to his paper, he found me as I am now, and as I will no doubt be when I finally expire.

If I ever do. Two years ago my doctor told me that my disease would kill me in six months. My death is as hesitant as were my loves.

I am sitting in my garden here in Bethesda, smoking and watching the weeds grow, and scribbling in what young Duke calls "my dense and careful hand" on a yellow legal pad.

He has never met any of the young men from the agency, and so he does not know what they call me.

I am the T.O.M. The Terrible Old Man. They think that I am infected with alienness, that I am not really human anymore. Overexposed, they say.

Deep in the night I sometimes awaken and feel a sense of passing presence, and I must admit that I long to join the drift in the sky.

Some say that they eat souls. That is not true. What they do is more profound, more private, more final. "Don't let him catch your eye," the young men say. *"They'll* see you, and they'll get you, too."

I wore my lace collar and my Fauntleroys and was washed in Pear's soap. My voice was high and happy when I was three.

This is what I remember.

When they came I was rolling a red fire truck up and down across the board floor of the porch, causing a rattling that reminded me of an engine.

I have established the time as approximately five-thirty. My father had just driven up from New York, arriving perhaps half an hour before. He was still wearing his black broadcloth suit, tie and waistcoat. He had come from a meeting with Vincent Carney, a developer of office buildings. Mr. Carney had entered into an agreement to construct the new National Biscuit Building, and Herbert Stone, Esq., had made ten thousand dollars in an afternoon.

Father was sitting in a big wooden chair with his feet up on a stool.

He leaned his head back, imagining that he was lying in the castles of summer cloud that were passing by. Janet also closed her eyes.

As far as they were concerned they were innocently drowsing on a summer afternoon. Neither of them imagined that somebody very strange and very close was generating a sound that was causing their drowsiness.

Or that they were being watched by careful eyes.

Only we children remained active. Monica played with a doll she had named Ricardo, and I with my beloved red fire engine.

What my father had seen as a cloud in the sky was something very, very different. It was gray and tremendous and slow, this thing that had come over the house. Had he seen it as it really was, my father might have thought it an organic thing, something like a gigantic wasp's nest floating in the sky.

And what watched from within, with great, black eyes and spindly limbs—what would he have called them in their thousands? Giant hornets? He would have understood the fierceness, but never the intelligence.

Afternoon became evening, and cowbells began to sound lazily across the valley below. A woman's voice rose, calling the cows to their barn.

This voice was dampened by a sound that could almost be heard, a deep buzzing that seemed to pulsate in the gut and chest, to caress the heart and slow the blood.

The voice faded away. The cowbells stopped. Birds stopped, katydids and cicadas stopped. A snake paused in its patient stalking of a rabbit, and its nictitating membranes slipped over its eyes. The rabbit paused in its chewing and fell to its side.

Still we children played.

"Rum-m-m," I said, "clang, clang, clang!"

"Ricardo, are you ever going to get married? Only to you, my dear. I love you. You need a wipe. Okay . . ."

Nobody saw the line of dots that were coming from the gray thing, saw them twisting and turning in the sky, moving as gracefully as a column of geese, slipping quickly down from the land of the clouds to the land of the stones.

These appalling things stepped lightly into the yard, into the soft, hot grass, and they began to move forward in lockstep, closer and closer to the porch where our parents slept and we played.

They were small and fragile, as gray and spindly as insects. Their heads were huge and had the texture of something that had been inflated. Their prominent eyes glittered in the afternoon sun. As they moved their heads bobbed.

Every few moments there would be an angry buzz and they would sail a few feet through the air.

"Ricardo, I love you!"

"Rum-m-m—clang!"

They came closer. Someone watching might have thought that these creatures were engaged in some sort of ritual. In addition to their lockstep and their gliding jumps, they were

81

making a whole host of other gestures, moving their thin arms, chattering their mouths, turning their heads first left, then right, then toward the sun.

Again they stepped, jumped, jutted out their hips, twisted their arms together, then turned their black eyes toward the sun.

"Rum-m-m! Clangclangclang!"

"Ricardo is sleeping! He is a man like daddy and he is sleeping in my arms."

"Brum-m-m-m!"

"Please don't wake him up, Wilfred."

Three steps forward. Monica wrinkled her nose. There was an overpowering odor coming with the dancers, a stink of molten sulfur.

Abruptly the adults stood up. They began walking like robots. Down the porch they went and into the living room. They stood staring at the floor like tongue-lashed children.

"Mother and Father are marching," Monica said happily. But as her parents passed her she fell silent. She was not afraid, just confused. Why was everybody marching into the living room?

When she got up to follow, carefully cradling Ricardo, she found herself looking into a pair of huge, black eyes.

She experienced a burst of extreme dizziness and reeled back, twisting as if a bullet had hit her in the face. She lay still, her doll beside her. There was a movement too rapid even to perceive and the being had twined its arms and legs around her.

She knew it too. It must be understood that she was totally conscious during this ordeal. Her mind was not in any way altered. She felt, heard, saw everything that happened to her. And she suffered. It was the first of the secret, stifled memories that would in the end destroy Monica Stone.

With a loud, droning buzz she was taken off into the sky.

I had stopped running my toy firetruck and was staring at the creatures that now stood around me. I was completely calm. It had not occurred to my three-year-old mind to be afraid.

"Monkeys," I said brightly. I suppose that I smiled.

And then there was somebody else there, somebody very much more graceful than the men with the bobbing heads. One instant this person arrived on the porch, a fleeting shadow. The next she was standing before me. She was perhaps five feet tall, with a long, narrow face and slim arms and legs. Her skin was the texture of baby-leather, even more fine than that of children.

"My momma went inside," I said.

"Come with me."

She embraced me. I remember next a whirl of roof and clouds and sky.

Then I saw gray. There were buzzings and scrabbling noises and the frequent rush of wings. I did not know where I was and for the first time I felt fear.

I saw Monica staggering, being hit by flashes of light so bright that I thought they were knives. She screamed and jerked when the light hit her.

I tried to help her but the thin lady held me back. I fought the frail arms but they were as hard as steel, and I remember how she breathed with a hissing burr. Monica was being hurt! Her screams were terrible to hear, so loud they hurt my ears. In my young life I had never heard anything like it before.

The light would hit her and she would throw up her hands and bellow and try to run away. Then it would hit her again from another direction and she would turn and run. On and on it went.

Something was jammed down on my head, ground into my temples. It hurt terribly, I had to get it off but she was holding me and hissing and then I saw a vivid image of my mother when I was very young, reaching down as if from heaven and lifting me with hands that made my whole body tingle with delight, and all was gold.

Monica shrieked. I saw her in a blaze of light and smelled burning hair and burning cloth.

In 1977 my sister died in a bedroom fire. A sleeping pill worked faster than she had expected and her last cigarette of the day dropped from her fingers into the sheets. Or perhaps it was more than one sleeping pill.

We were returned to the porch amid a great clamor of buzzing wings. They sat me in my father's chair and poured out his glass of whiskey in the grass. Monica they returned to her doll.

A moment later they were gone, and the gray object had

become nothing but a glittering white dot, and then nothing at all.

The farmer's wife let fly with a boisterous "Ooooeeeeeee!" The cows mooed and went trotting up the path to their barn.

Monica said, "Now, Ricardo, what woke you up?"

Birds began to sing, katydids and cicadas to chatter, and the snake got its rabbit. Trout and sunnys fluttered again in the clear streams.

Nobody noticed that fifteen minutes had been stolen from their evening. Why should they? They had gone inside and discussed the news. What news? Well, wasn't that funny, they couldn't remember.

But that was quickly forgotten, because a problem presented itself as soon as they returned to the porch.

I had apparently swallowed my father's highball and gotten drunk.

"I seed de moon comin' up over de bally," I said. "Them monkeys come show Willy—"

"Oh, Herb, you left your highball!" Our mother was amused and annoyed at the same time.

"You could call Dr. Hovermanns, darling, but I think he'll just tell you to let him sleep it off."

That night we had a dinner of ham and sweet potatoes and green beans, and afterward Father read to us for a while. Nobody seemed to notice that I was not, in fact, drunk.

After we kids were in bed Mother and Father sat out under the stars and listened to the Victrola.

To the strains of Beethoven's Sixth Symphony, the "Pastorale," they counted shooting stars.

Monica was sick in the night, but it soon passed and by morning all was well.

Chapter Seven

As I read Will's narrative, I wondered if he was deluding himself, misleading me or telling the frank truth.

One glance at his face told me that this was, in his opinion, an authentic record.

He was terribly distressed. Being touched by them so early meant that he might all along have been nothing but a pawn. I asked him about it. "I wish it was true," he said. "It'd be a relief to find out that they were responsible for my actions." He looked at me with that sudden, sharp way of his that so effectively compelled frankness. "Do you think I'm a high-level robot of some kind?"

I shook my head. "I'm afraid I don't."

"No, you wouldn't. Otherwise you couldn't place blame, could you?. Yours is a punitive generation."

"That's a bit of a generalization. But I do think you're responsible for your own actions."

A bottle of Pinch stood on a table beside his summer chair. Sometimes there would be empty sardine cans there, too. I think whiskey and sardines were his whole diet. He went for the bottle, poured a substantial drink into his glass and knocked it back. He lit another Camel.

"Every man has to be responsible for his actions, Nick. Otherwise you're not a man. You wouldn't be human, except physically." He gave me a helpless, haunted look and returned to the bottle.

His childhood memory was full of disturbing implications. Had the others *implanted* him as they apparently have so many? If so, did it mean that his entire life was lived under their influence?

Perhaps it will never be possible to resolve that question. All I can do is redouble my efforts to be clear, to tell this story as perfectly as I can. To do that I must return to the central narrative, but this time with the knowledge that the visitors probably had Will to a degree under their influence. I do not wish to suggest that he wasn't making his own choices; I prefer to think that he was.

They were watching him, had been since he was a child. He was their man in Central Intelligence, picked from an early age to do their work.

But to do it as *he* saw fit.

This understood, it is appropriate to address once again the events that were taking place in Roswell in July of 1947. These enormous events.

The Gray file lies on my desk. I pick it up, turn to page twenty-three of his careful narrative.

"I returned to RAAF with my detail at approximately 1330 hours on the afternoon of July 8, 1947. We parked behind Hangar B-2 and commenced unloading the debris that had been collected on the Ungar ranch."

Major Gray was a sensitive man, and seeing the pitiful mess that was being laid out made him consider the courage of whoever had flown in it.

"They came a long way," he said.

Hesseltine nodded, lighting a cigarette. "Yep. And they're not going back." Everybody fell silent, looking at the debris. "I guess we'd better inform Colonel Blanchard," Walters said at last.

"Which is going to be very interesting."

"You think there'll be a problem?"

I doubt if Gray answered. He says only that "Walters suggested we inform the colonel." What he does not add is what must already have been going through his mind. He must have known that there were going to be a number of serious problems. He would have done his thinking on the way back from the ranch.

If he understood Air Force brass at all, and I think it is obvious that he did, he undoubtedly felt that they would try to classify the hell out of this.

Gray had most certainly established his own very private set of priorities, and he intended to fulfill them.

He had observed that most military officers were earnest and patriotic. They were not, however, deep thinkers. They did not see things in long perspectives.

What he intended to do was probably going to make a lot of people very mad, and he had to be careful or he could very certainly ruin his career. He was carrying out his duties as he saw fit.

"Mr. Hesseltine, why don't you three try to piece some of this stuff together while I get the colonel? Maybe there's enough here to get an idea what this thing looked like."

Hesseltine touched the debris with his foot. "It looks hopeless."

"Blanchard'll expect to see it in the best order we can manage."

Soon Walters and Hesseltine and PFC Winters were moving pieces around on the floor.

Gray went back to the administration building. On his way up the hall to the colonel's office he stopped by to see the base press officer, Lieutenant Jack Hope. He liked Jack, and he knew that he would do his job well. The key thing here was to be as casual and offhand as possible.

Hope remembers the moment vividly. I met him at his small, tidy home in Roswell. He was frank with me. I found that his story fit what was in both his file and Don Gray's.

There is only one element of it that I question. He and Gray both very specifically claim that he never saw the debris. I find that hard to believe. It would have been so natural to go over to the hangar, if only to satisfy his curiosity.

Nevertheless, I have recorded this as if he didn't go to the hangar, as if he cannot confirm the appearance of the debris.

"You need to interview me," Gray said to him. "I've got something that the papers'll be interested in."

Hearing the major's promise, Hope smiled. He had his frustrations, working for a unit that dealt with so many top secrets. Most of the really interesting things that happened at Roswell

Army Air Field were classified and couldn't even be mentioned. On the day that an atomic bomb got stuck in the bay of a B-29 and created a harrowing two-hour emergency, Jack Hope had spent his time trying to place a story about the fact that the Bill Cornell Band was going to play at the officer's club on Saturday night.

Gray told Hope his story, about how they had found the rubble, and what it meant. Hope scribbled frantically. He was delighted. This was a fine story. "I'll get some good play with this one."

He read his notes back to Gray. "If you work fast, you can get it on the radio tonight."

"Yeah. Y'know Don, I want to thank you. This is a real good piece. I appreciate it."

"Buy me a beer *mañana?*"

"Will do!"

As Gray left, he heard the music of Hope's typewriter. Now the story would be out before anybody made any decisions about classification. And that was right. None of the others understood that this was the largest event in human history. It was something that every single human creature had an absolute and inalienable right to know. As Don Gray must have seen it, his obligation to the American people and to mankind superseded every other consideration.

Well, he had informed the people. Now he would tell the brass.

He entered Blanchard's sanctum. The clerk let him through immediately.

The colonel was affable and smart. He had been an extremely successful officer, and he was next in line to take Eighth Air Force. Although he was a West Point man, the colonel seemed much more Air Force than Army. His command style was informal and consultative. Mostly, he was pleasant, although small problems could cause outbursts of temper. One morning he had chewed Hope out for tying up the base telephone lines. A few minutes later, though, he was laughing about it.

He was a heavily decorated officer. He had the Legion of Merit, the Silver Star, the Distinguished Flying Cross with an oak-leaf cluster, the Bronze Star, the Air Medal with a cluster, and the Presidential Unit Citation for his work as operations officer of the Twentieth Air Force that had been responsible for bombing Japan.

Gray had a simple relationship with him. He respected the colonel and made that clear. In return, Blanchard trusted his intelligence assessments. As he approached the inner sanctum, Gray wondered how the old man was going to take what he was about to say.

Blanchard looked up at him, his eyebrows raised, a question in his face.

There was only one way to handle the situation. Just come right out with it. "Colonel, we found the debris from a flying disk this morning."

Blanchard stared a moment, then his eyes crinkled into a smile. "I thought Hesseltine was the practical joker," he said. "If you guys are looking for suckers I suggest you try another colonel."

Gray looked straight into his eyes, trying to communicate the high seriousness that he felt. "Sir, I'm not kidding."

He watched a series of expressions cross Blanchard's face. The smile became a more wary expression, then a long stare.

"Was there any hostile action?"

"None."

"You have wreckage? An accident?"

"Apparently."

Blanchard pressed his intercom. "Get Payne in here," he said. He was always a man to involve his deputy. A moment later Lieutenant Colonel Payne Jennings appeared. He was a compact, intense man, a polished officer. Even though he wasn't a West Point graduate, he projected the formality and to a degree the rigidity of traditional army. Still, people liked him because he was fair and always willing to push for you with the colonel if he felt you had a good argument.

"Don found a crashed flying disk," he said to Payne. The deputy reared back, his eyes widening. Then he burst out laughing.

"Let's see if we can get General Ramey to buy into that when he comes down." He looked from the colonel to the major, saw they weren't laughing and pursed his lips. "This is for real?"

"Yes, sir," Gray said. "Ray Walters and Hesseltine have the wreckage over in B-2. They're trying to piece it together."

Without another word Blanchard and Jennings headed out to the hangar.

Very little headway had been made putting the pieces together. "The nearest we can tell, what we have here is a part of a larger device." Hesseltine sounded very professional, and Gray was pleased.

Blanchard picked up a piece of the parchment, ran his fingers down the columns of squiggles. "Gentlemen, I have to say that I'm a little awed."

"I thought it was a historic occasion," Gray said. "That's what I told Lieutenant Hope." Blanchard and Jennings nodded absently. That was a hurdle jumped. They'd just agreed that this story would be given to the public. Gray was proud of them.

Blanchard held some of the parchment up to the light. "It's like wallpaper. You wouldn't have wallpaper in a military vehicle."

"We can't know that," Walters said. "I don't think we can assume anything."

"This is just a pile of tinfoil and wallpaper. What I'd like to see is the rest of the thing."

"If this was a mortal wound." Gray had thought about it, and he had his doubts. If he'd been piloting the disk and it had sustained damage, the first thing he'd have done would have been to get it into outer space where there was no gravity. Then he could make repairs at his leisure, without fear of crashing.

"Well," Blanchard said, "if there's anything out in that desert, we can find it."

Jennings picked up one of the wooden I-beams. "What about the Russians?"

"A Russian blimp coming after the 509th," Gray said. "We considered that possibility."

"And?"

"It's a no-go, in my opinion. First, the material's just too strong. We don't have anything remotely like it, and I doubt that they do either. Second, none of the writing is in any known language. Third, that wood you're holding is too light and too hard to have come from earth. It isn't from an earth tree."

"You're certain about all this, Major? You've done your homework?"

Gray was quite certain. "Yes, sir."

"Where is the object it came from?" asked Jennings.

"We don't have knowledge of any other debris," Gray replied.

"You looked?"

"It's a big desert, Colonel."

"True enough," Blanchard said. He glanced at Jennings. "You think an air search is warranted, Payne?"

"Yes, sir."

"I agree."

Jennings started toward the door he had just entered. "I'll get it up right away. The 830th Search and Rescue Group. They're our highest-scoring search mission unit." Jennings left the hangar.

"Private," the colonel said to PFC Winters, "get this stuff into my office on the double."

"Yes, sir!" The PFC began gathering up the pieces.

Gray met the colonel's eyes. His expression of sardonic good humor was gone, replaced by a grave look.

Gray wondered if that was what Colonel Blanchard looked like when he was afraid.

Blanchard turned and headed back to the office block. As they passed Hope's office the publicist started toward the colonel with a piece of paper in his hand. Gray intercepted him. "Not now," he said. "We're sending up a search mission. The colonel thinks we might find the rest of the disk."

"Wow."

"Wait a while before you release anything. I'll call you." Hope nodded and took a step back.

"Don't leave me sitting on this, Don," Hope said. Gray thought he sounded rather desperate.

"Wait for my call." Now Hope looked forlorn. Gray smiled. "You aren't going to lose the story. It's just that, if we find the disk, it'll be really big."

"Big isn't the word. I'd get both papers and play on every radio station in town."

Gray clapped him on the shoulder and left the office. If

he realized just how big this really was he'd probably freeze up.

He followed Blanchard and the other officers into the 830th's briefing room. Captain Gilman was ready to brief. Three helicopters and a Stinson reconnaissance plane equipped with cameras were being prepared to go to the Maricopa area. As the navigation officer began to speak, Gray glanced at his watch. They'd had six minutes to prepare the mission, from the time they had been given the order. That was an impressive performance.

"The site is sixteen miles east-southeast of Maricopa," Gilman said. Hesseltine had already prebriefed. The officer pulled down a map of New Mexico—the same one that was in Gray's office, except the details of the White Sands Proving Ground and the high energy radar areas were simply marked "restricted airspace."

"Lieutenant Hesseltine, will you please pinpoint the location?" Captain Gilman stepped aside.

Hesseltine went up to the map. Together he and the navigation officer worked with the compass and protractor. "This is the approximate position of the Ungar house," Hesseltine said. "The wreckage is two miles west of that location. It fell in a fan pattern, indicating that the device was moving due west when the explosion took place."

"So we search west from the impact site," the navigation officer said.

"What's the appearance of the debris," one of the pilots asked.

"From the air what we saw will probably look like about a thousand square feet of torn-up tinfoil and paper. You'll see glints. The stuff is shiny. We didn't pick much up. Maybe less than one percent. It's a pretty big debris field."

The pilots and observers filed out, some of them still adjusting their parachute straps. One of them stopped. He turned around and addressed the squadron exec. "Sir," he said, "why weren't we told what we're looking for? What kind of device?"

Blanchard answered. "Anything out in that goddamn desert that looks like its made of metal."

"Yes, sir! Does that include windmills and tin roofs, sir?"

"Get going!"

The search party headed for the flight line. Gray followed

them. As intelligence officer, he felt that he had to participate in this part of the mission as well. If a disk was located, it would be his job to examine it. He got issued a chute and climbed into one of the helicopters. They were uncomfortable, noisy and slow, but they were truly amazing machines, the very latest in aircraft.

He knew about the incredible speed of the new jets that were under development, and was duly impressed, but these astonishing little craft would always seem like miracles to him.

The pilot introduced himself. "I'm Lieutenant Kephart," he said. He reached across and shook Gray's hand.

Gray nodded. "Let's go," he said.

The pilot flipped a switch and the helicopter's engine wheezed to life. A moment later they rose into the air, the nose pointing downward as the rotors grabbed for speed and lift. It was a strange way to take off, watching the apron spread out below you instead of fall away behind like in a normal plane.

It was now fifteen-thirty hours. It would take an hour to reach the crash site. The slowness and short range of the helicopters meant that there would be no more than another hour of search time before they would have to return to base. Gray watched the hot, empty New Mexico countryside pass by beneath them. Every so often they would see a house so dusty it looked like it was part of the land, a lump of mud and wood.

The three copters were at an altitude of fifteen hundred feet, and caused a good deal of notice below. People came out of their houses and waved, and observers waved back. Pilots concentrated on flying their cantankerous ships. To keep one of them in the air required continuous concentration. Gray didn't even want to think about their crash rate, which was horribly high.

They flew along Highway 370 to Picacho or Sunset, Gray wasn't sure which, then turned north, keeping the red dirt road to Maricopa and the looming peak of El Capitán to their left.

It was not long before they were in the crash area. One of the other observers, more trained in visual search techniques than Gray, was the first to spot the wreckage. From the air the fan shape of it was clear. The explosion had scattered debris widely, and bits and pieces had continued to fall from the craft as it moved west. "Take us in an absolutely straight line from where the debris field forms that point," Gray said. The pilot radioed this instruction to the others, and the three helicopters formed a line abreast with a thousand yards of separation.

The navigator aboard the Stinson reported the exact location of the debris field to Roswell.

The helicopters dropped to a few hundred feet and proceeded in formation. Above them, at a thousand, the Stinson took detailed pictures of the route of flight, even though nothing was being spotted. Wartime experience had taught the AAF that objects missed by airborne observers could often be found by experts examining photographs.

They flew for thirty minutes without seeing anything. The land was absolutely flat, but it was rising and there were hills ahead, and a mesa to the north. Searching hills was going to be a lot harder.

They'd come about sixty miles from the debris field. The farther they went the less likely they were to find something, in Gray's estimation. The absence of a crash site this far out meant that the craft must still have been under power. The pilot could have maneuvered, maybe even returned his ship to the safety of outer space.

Searching the empty land, Gray's mind turned toward that magical notion, outer space. What did it mean? And what worlds hid in its folds of darkness? Could the craft have come from Mars or Venus? Who was to know? Gray had a feeling, though, that it was from farther away, from another star. There were no trees on Mars, and wood and paper had been involved in the construction of this craft. Of course, Venus was covered by cloud. Was it a teeming jungle underneath? Nobody knew. But Gray doubted it. He had observed that the most vital civilizations arose in temperate areas. At best Venus was something like equatorial Africa, a gigantic hellhole seething with mosquitoes the size of rump steaks and snakes big enough to swallow a mule.

"This is one-two-one. I observe a glint of metal two o'clock approximately one thousand yards out," a voice said in the earphones.

"Change course zero-three-zero, drop to two hundred," came the reply from the Stinson.

A moment later the second copter spotted it. "We have

gleaming metal eight hundred yards out dead ahead," the observer stated.

Gray didn't see a thing. The earphones were alive now, as observers and pilots coordinated their observations. "We see an object," said the Stinson. "It is a metal disk. Repeat, a metal disk."

Gray peered ahead, feeling helpless.

Then he saw it, just ahead of the copter, seemingly so close that he could touch it. The disk was on the ground at the end of a swath of broken soil. It was the color of burnished aluminum. How these men had managed to spot gleams of sunlight off its dull surface he could not imagine.

They went down to approximately fifty feet, each helicopter in turn circling the craft so that the observer could get a close look. Then they cleared out and the Stinson made a series of low-level photographic passes.

Don Gray said nothing, but he literally ached to get out there and have a closer look at that thing. He'd deliberated asking the pilot to let him go down the rescue rope and remain with the device overnight, but he found that he was quite uneasy about being out here in the dark. More important, it seemed too radical a departure from procedure, and he'd already done enough rule-stretching for one day.

They flew back to base, arriving just after eighteen hundred. Blanchard and Jennings were waiting on the apron with Hesseltine and Walters. As Gray dismounted the copter, he saw the observer trotting off to the photo unit with his film for processing.

"What was it like," Blanchard asked Gray.

"A featureless disk. It had torn up a lot of dirt on impact."

Blanchard ordered everybody into Operations for debriefing. Each observer reported what he had seen. Gray was surprised to learn that they had observed pieces of wreckage in the broken soil behind the craft. He'd seen nothing.

Then the photo unit reported. Lieutenant Baker himself came in with the portfolio of pictures. He took his time setting up ten crucial shots on the map board, while everybody in the room squirmed. He had to be allowed his moment of drama; the photo unit had prepared the pictures in record time.

Since he'd gotten back Don Gray had smoked up the rest of

his Old Golds and was working on Hesseltine's Luckies. His mouth tasted dry and his head was still roaring with the noise of the chopper.

When Baker started to talk, however, all feelings of fatigue left the major.

"We have here a disk approximately thirty feet in diameter, of unknown thickness, content and construction. There are a hundred and sixty-five observed fragments in the impact area, most of them located in the soil that the object traversed as it slid into the hillside. There is also this." He pointed to a blurry enlargement.

Total silence.

"Is it a body?" Colonel Blanchard asked. His voice was gentle.

"An apparent cadaver approximately three feet long, in a distended posture, showing some signs of predator action. If you observe carefully, you will see that the cadaver appears to have a deformed head, unless the skull has somehow exploded."

"Are we looking at an alien, Lieutenant?" Jennings snapped.

"I wouldn't know. We are looking at a small cadaver that has a deformed head, and reveals signs of having been damaged by predators, like coyotes. That's all I can say."

Blanchard was so excited that he had gotten to his feet. "I want a full recovery party on that crash site as soon after dawn as practicable," he said.

"Yes, sir," said his exec.

"This is the goddamnedest thing I've ever encountered in my career, gentlemen. I want every man to realize how important this is. This is an alien spacecraft, for God's sake. We cannot even build such a craft at this time. This is going to be of the greatest interest to Washington."

"Sir, what do we do on site?"

"Obtain all visible debris and the craft itself if possible, and bring the material back to this base." He looked at Jennings. "Let's have a powwow, buddy. Gray, tag along." He turned and left the operations room.

Gray allowed his two superior officers to get a little ahead of him. He paused at Lieutenant Hope's office and got a rather desperate smile. "The piece is written, sir."

"Here's a change. You can say that the disk was recovered

intact and brought to this base for transfer to higher headquarters." He thought a moment. "No, say it was *loaned* to higher headquarters. Got that—loaned."

"I have just one question, Don. When can I circulate this baby?"

Blanchard was about to call Eighth Air Force. "Do it," Gray said.

"Yes, sir."

When Gray entered the colonel's office he was leaning far back in his chair. A cigar was clenched between his teeth. Jennings was standing at the window, staring out at the flight line. Walters was there, slumped against the wall. Hesseltine sat more or less stiffly, nervous to be with so much brass in the absence of his own boss.

"I thought you'd gone home," Blanchard said acidly to Gray. He hated to wait.

"I had to tilt a kidney." Was his quite intentional failure to mention his stop at Hope's office a breach of duty? No, he'd made it clear to Blanchard and Jennings both that there was a release being prepared. He didn't have to do more.

"We've got to tell Ramey," Blanchard said. "I want you to get on the horn with us, Don. He's gonna be pretty damn sure his leg's being pulled and I want you to make it clear to him that we're being straight with him."

Gray made a play for time. "Sir, I think we ought to wait until we have men on the scene and are in radio communication with them before we report this up the chain."

"Why so?"

"Well, I'm sure that we have an alien vessel, and so are you. But how is the Commander of the Eighth Air Force going to react from the far end of a telephone line? He could order the base sealed. Forbid us to touch the wreckage. Send a team of white coats to net us and ship us off to the funny farm. Any damn thing."

"I've got to tell the man. It's my duty. Not only that there are regulations involved. This clearly qualifies as an unknown event. The way I understand my mission, I'm required to report such an occurrence to higher headquarters. This is a sensitive installation, remember."

97

"We need to be able to tell him that we've examined the craft."

Payne Jennings unexpectedly spoke up. "I think Don has a good point, Bill. We've got to be able to say to Ramey clearly and in no uncertain terms that we are not dealing with some sort of Soviet device. Also, there's another thing—if it's ours."

There was a silence. Nobody had thought of that. Gray was a little disappointed in himself for not considering it. Then he thought of the hieroglyphics and the strange foil and the rows of numbers. No. No way it was ours.

He couldn't say that though. "We need to cover all our bases."

"Okay, guys. But if he starts hacking and slashing, I'm going to tell him it was a staff recommendation."

"Can't do that," Jennings said. "Makes you look weak."

Blanchard laughed, loud and hard. He looked around the room. "I think I can let you guys go home, if we're putting off the report till morning." He looked at Gray. "I want you out on that flight line at dawn, you and Walters both. I want both intelligence commands covered."

Walters spoke up. "Is this still considered a counterintelligence problem? It's pretty obvious there's no commie involvement—"

"Somebody flew that thing. And they did it for a reason. That *reason* is a counterintelligence problem, Mr. Walters."

"Yeah, I can see that, Bill." A sort of half smile crossed his face. "I can see that as kind of a big counterintelligence problem."

As the meeting broke up, Major Gray hurried back to Lieutenant Hope's office. "You released it yet?"

"Well, sir—"

"We're going to do some final confirmation in the morning. What say you release it at ten hundred?"

"You tell me, Major."

"Ten o'clock tomorrow morning, you tell the world."

Without a backward glance Major Gray left the office. He went out to the parking lot and got into his car and drove home, eager for a good supper and a clean bed.

Late that night he awoke very suddenly. For a moment he thought there was somebody in the house. So clear had this impression been that he got up and checked around. They didn't lock doors in Roswell in those days, but on this night Donald Gray dropped the latches.

He listened to the night wind rushing in from the desert. There were faint sounds, very faint, the cries of the things that lived in the dark land.

A car passed in the street. From behind some black window a woman sighed. He laid his hand on his wife's breast and also slept.

And the stars crossed the sky.

From the Roswell *Daily Record,* July 8, 1947:

ARMY AIR FORCE CAPTURES FLYING DISK
IN ROSWELL REGION
No Details of Flying Disk are Revealed

The intelligence office of the 509th Bombardment Group at Roswell Army Air Force Base announced at noon today that the field has come into possession of a flying saucer.

According to information released by the department, over authority of Maj. D. O. Gray, intelligence officer, the disk was recovered on a ranch in the Roswell vicinity, after an unidentified rancher had notified Sheriff Geo. Wilcox, here, that he had found the instrument on his premises.

Major Gray and a detail from his department went to the ranch and recovered the disk, it was stated.

After the intelligence office here had inspected the instrument it was loaned to "higher headquarters."

The intelligence office stated that no details of the saucer's construction or its appearance had been revealed.

Chapter Eight

The Chronicle of Wilfred Stone

Washington, D.C., July 8, 1947. Time: 7:40 A.M. My condition: standing naked before a mirror. I have a slight paunch, noticeable and a little upsetting to me. It is composed largely of beer, steak, Hershey bars, champagne, sweet rolls and whiskey. It is there because I have been trying to eat my way out of my war nightmares.

A boy called Jamshid was still dying in my mind, in those days, still dying at the hands of the Sûreté, his genitals tied off, his belly bloated with wine. I remember the Sûreté and the Gestapo men as extremely clean, eating huge Arab meals in nameless backrooms in the souk of Algiers, their voices melodic with confidence, softened by self-importance. They cherished the secret knowledge that great pain takes any man to his truth. If a human being reaches a sufficient depth of agony even his attempts at deceit will contain useful information.

Another of the truisms of tradecraft: torture always works. Human beings, it seems, cannot lie. If we do not say the truth then we indicate it another way. It's an endearing trait.

Jamshid worked for me because I paid him a dollar a week. In his family he was therefore more important than his own father. He was twelve and quick of eye. He was full of humor and bitter hatred for the French and the Germans.

He would slip from house to house with messages, helping me to forge a network of agents provocateurs that later served Franz Fanon so well. And then one night while I lay beneath my ceiling fan naked and slick with heat, my belly dotted by festering fly-bites, a woman came and murmured like a ghost that Jamshid was in the custody of the police.

First they scraped the skin of his buttocks raw with metal files, then sat him in a bath of acid. They raped him, they forced themselves on him, shattering his innocence and causing him in his torment to cleave to them. He became the slave of his tormenters. They used the Roman whip on him, an instrument of punishment known in that place from the time of the Third Augusta, the Roman occupation army. This whip has twelve cords of leather, and into the end of each is knotted a little hook.

I can remember him lying in the sun, and I thought grandly of the innocence of the child, and the weighty sophistication of my own twenty-eight years. I smoked, he was too young. I tied one on now and then. His Moslem eyes widened in horror and amazement at the sight of a liquor bottle. I relaxed in the carpeted fastness of Madame Jouet's while he squatted on the porch and heard the sharp voices of the French girls inside reciting exhausted *amours*.

There was an orange tree in the courtyard, and I cannot remember a time when it was not in bloom.

He screamed names, dates, everything he knew.

My agents were rounded up, tortured in their turn, and I became a hunted man, creeping through the back streets like some movie spy, being followed by men in tailored suits who soaked their bullets in garlic and habitually aimed at the stomach.

I was hiding in my room, half drunk, down to my last bottle when the Allies came marching into the city and it was over.

Those of my agents who were still alive were released.

In Washington I was growing fat on the fruits of victory, plotting the ruin of the French colonial empire and eating every night at places like Harvey's and the Occidental. Broiled sea trout at Harvey's one night, Hoover two tables away eating the same; a steak the next night at the Occidental, and then midnight and the whip cutting Jamshid's back like butter.

I would wake up shaking and pour myself a glass of Pinch, drink it and listen to records on my Victrola: "Deep Purple," from the days that I was dating Rose deMornay, "Sweet Leilani" from *Waikiki Wedding,* one of those fluffy prewar movies. They were enchanted days in America, the late thirties. The depression was pretty well over, and Hitler was kind of funny and the

Japs . . . well, they were awfully far away. "Whaddaya say to them Tokyo babes—I wanna nip on nese!"

Tokyo Rose . . . there is to terror a pure romance.

We fox-trotted our way from *Waikiki Wedding* to Pearl Harbor.

Now I would wake myself up by crying in my sleep.

Then came the Alien Estimate. I regarded it all as rather amusing, like a scary movie. I had not the faintest idea that it had electrified the Joint Chiefs, and scared General Vandenberg so badly that he'd spent a good bit of time literally staring at a wall. For me it was empty of reality. I was still ignorant of events in Rosewell. I wouldn't be for long.

I drove over to the office that morning, parking the Chevy as usual on E Street, relying on my license number to keep the officer of the watch from writing me a summons. When I got into my office there was a message from Vandenberg. Please call as soon as convenient.

As per standing orders, I informed our new boss, Admiral Hillenkoetter. He called me in and told me that I was free to see General Vandenberg as long as I didn't sell the agency to him. We were all afraid that CIG would be absorbed and dismembered by the Joint Chiefs, something that they had been trying to do since the war ended. Our new boss viewed any contact from his predecessor as a reconnaissance in strength.

I went over to the Pentagon in one of our staff cars, driven by the sort of clean, hard young man we liked to hire, most of whom we later expended in the Soviet Union. "Moscow rules" were written by such young men. I'll tell you another thing about "Moscow rules," which consist of planting messages in hollow trees, not using real names or telephones and doing a great deal more sneaking around than usual: they don't work. What works are the right implements, the leather cord, the naked electric lead, the soldering iron in the anus. Insert it, turn it on, then ask your questions. You will have the correct answers.

We had a tough outlook, those of us who were left over from the war. Want a woman to talk? Grab her lower lip and slap her until it starts to tear off. Women have a horror of disfigurement; she'll talk. Women believe in their faces.

"Goddamn it, Willy, what the hell is this?" Vandenberg

blurted as soon as I walked into his office. He snatched up the estimate and tossed it at me.

"I think it's accurate, sir."

"It's no joke?"

I saw the fear in his eyes, and grew instantly wary. It has been my unfailing experience that men of power are randomly dangerous when they are afraid.

"No, sir."

"We called the Mounties." He produced a thick folder. "They damn well investigated that situation up in the Northwest Territories. The bastards stole an entire village! Holy God, Willy, what if the S.O.B.'s steal Peoria? What in God's name does the Air Force do about it?"

I did not expect that my estimate would cause this much upset. "I think we ought to develop some cases around it, General."

"You're damn right we will! But tell me what these disks can do in the air. We've developed our own data, but we haven't got much. All we know is that they're fast, and some of them are big. Are they armed? Will my cannons work against them? What the hell do I do, Willy?"

"You've prepared your own background paper?"

"S-2 pulled something together. You can read it in this office. Eyes only. Two copies. The other one is at the White House."

I didn't like the drift of this conversation. Admiral Hillenkoetter wasn't going to be happy to hear that Van had already involved the President. "I think we need to present all of this stuff to the board—"

"No, sir! This is an Air Force matter, as of this moment! You are ordered to withdraw this estimate. No board meeting!"

"General, Hilly's gonna raise a stink."

"The hell he is. I called Truman at seven o'clock this morning and told him that he either gives this thing lock, stock and barrel to the Air Force or I'm out. I gave Harry an ultimatum!" Van was serving notice to me that this was of absolutely paramount importance to him. You did not threaten Harry Truman unless you were genuinely prepared to resign. Van cleared his throat, sucked his cigar hard. "He listened to me and then he says,

'Okay, Van, you take it. It's your baby.' " Vandenberg laughed bitterly. "I am not about to sit down in any NBE meeting and say to those men that my opinion is that the Air Force is completely helpless, *impotent* to prevent the mass kidnapping of Americans by monsters from outer space!" He glared at me, chewed the roaring cigar. "Goddamn it!"

"I realize the problem."

"You and your fancy suits and your shot cuffs and your goddamn Aqua-Velva! Why don't you ever get upset, Willy!"

"Would it help?"

Vandenberg glared at me. "Of course not. You're here because you don't get upset. We've built this magnificent Air Force and more-or-less survived the most stupidly conceived demobilization in the history of armed conflict—and now I find that it cannot fulfill its *basic mission* right here at home. You don't have to get upset, Willy. But I do. And I am."

"Okay, Van. I understand your position perfectly. If I was to put a reliability number on that estimate, I would give it about a seventy. Seven out of ten chances it is correct. What else could have happened to the Canadian villagers?"

"They even took the goddamn dead out of the graves! It implies that they were taken somewhere—some other place and planted there, like you say. Somewhere those villagers are living, with their dead in new graves. God. Willy, I looked up at the stars last night, and I have to tell you, I felt for those poor Eskimos."

"We can surmise a few things about the matter. First, the *dead* were taken. They were Inuit people, and their ancestors were vitally important to them. Meaning? They were not simply murdered or enslaved. Their beliefs were respected."

"They were taken somewhere. Intact."

"Exactly."

"What happened to the others? The boy that disappeared into the sky? And the poor man that went underground, Willy? I just—my blood ran cold!"

"Van, maybe—" He looked at me. I hesitated, unwilling to finish my sentence. I had been about to soften the stand I took in the estimate. But I thought better of it at once. *If* there was the remotest possibility that I was right, the position I had taken

105

was the correct one. "Maybe we'll find out it isn't as bad as it looks," I concluded rather lamely.

Vandenberg stared at the ash on his cigar. "Should I bother to ask what Hilly thinks?"

"Hilly's still getting into the job. He's going to be fine." Vandenberg raised his eyebrows. "He's concerned about this, naturally. He said that he felt we should wait for events to unfold a little further."

"I think that we should get aggressive. I think we should attempt to shoot down one of the disks."

"Hilly won't agree."

"It's a decision for the Air Force, the Defense Department and the President." He paused. "Truman is interested in this. He's read your estimate, as well as ours."

I concealed my amazement. This was not being handled according to established procedures. The National Board of Estimate should have read my paper, questioned and revised it, then transmitted it to the Defense and State departments. Then it would have come to the attention of the White House, and only if a presidential decision was needed. "Secretary Forrestal?"

"He'll be informed in due course."

Van looked at me. At last, I thought, he's coming to the point. Van could be very subtle. The blustery, tough exterior was there at once to confuse his enemies and make them imagine that he was vulnerable. He was a master bureaucratic infighter, and a brutal one. "I have a copy of a report from the 509th Bomber Wing in Roswell, New Mexico to Eighth Air Force headquarters." He handed me a piece of carbon paper.

I still remember the feeling of the blood rushing from my head as I stood there looking down at the laconic message from Colonel Blanchard to General Ramey, the commanding general of the Eighth Air Force.

"We have this day obtained debris from a flying disk of unknown origin and have located the remains of the object intact by photo recce. Please advise how we should proceed."

"The pictures are being flown here right now."

"Manna from heaven," I said quietly. I tried not to reveal my fear. Were we about to find people disappearing from New

Mexico? Empty towns? Graveyards full of holes? "You realize that this is at present the most sensitive secret that the United States possesses. Even more sensitive than the formula for the atomic bomb."

Vandenberg did not reply directly, and I realized that I had just condescended to a man who had bypassed his own chain of command and mine in order to restrict knowledge of this secret. He obviously understood the level of sensitivity involved.

"Hilly has to know," I added.

"I think we should convene a meeting with the President as soon as we get the photographs. You, me, Hilly and the secretary. We'll decide what to do from there."

"I'll brief Hilly."

"We can get the President one-fifteen to one forty-five."

"The pictures?"

"Barring weather delays, the plane will land at Andrews at twelve-forty."

"You need to think about containment. Ramey knows. The 509th's Colonel knows. Presumably his staff knows. Was the debris found by a member of the public?"

Vandenburg nodded.

"I'll tell you, Van, I think we should be damn sure that *none* of these people will say a damn word. And any of them we can't be sure of—well, this is a very sensitive matter. If we have to take extreme steps, I don't think we should hesitate."

How safe we felt, plotting our strategies deep in that Pentagon office. We were already doing the work of the others, playing into their hands, doing it *their* way.

If only we had understood, but we did not understand. Sometimes wars are fought without battles, won without weapons. The best strategist conceals his attack behind a shield of confusion. The best strategist can make even an invasion seem like an accident.

The others understood that fantastically powerful principle of warfare.

We did not.

Chapter Nine

That was not the only principle of strategy that our government didn't understand. It is fascinating and rather infuriating to me that Will literally cannot think about our relationship with the others except in terms of conflict. Strategies. Battles. Subterfuges. His war years have so warped his perception of the world around him that everyone is an adversary and every action a stratagem.

Understandably, the one thing he won't fight is death itself. It's obvious that he welcomes his cancer. The only reason he resists at all is to get this book finished. The closer we get to the end, the more he smokes and the harder he hits the bottle.

I have cried because of this man.

As much as I feel that he misperceived the others, he was in a sense right that they had a strategy. It would probably be more appropriate to call it a plan. A simple, staggeringly deceptive plan.

I like to think that I discovered its outlines on my own. Will missed it, precisely because of its simplicity.

While Washington stumbled the others were acting with decision. The government seems to have perceived the others as being rather ineffectual—which was no doubt exactly how they intended themselves to appear. They had advanced ships, yes, but they'd crashed one. Washington fell into the trap of viewing the event in Roswell as a failed attempt to scout unfamiliar terrain.

Meanwhile, the others were capturing the night.

Obviously they knew that an unbalanced government would

be easiest for them to control. They began to achieve this control by taking an action that was calculated to cause panic in high places. They did this out in far West Texas, on the vast and dreary reserve known paradoxically as Fort Bliss.

Second Squad, 4th Platoon, Company D, 53rd Infantry dropped their weapons to the hard West Texas ground and watched the sun go down. They were recruits just out of basic, attending infantry school while they awaited orders to occupation duty. They were involved in a war-game maneuver and wishing they were almost anywhere else.

I have reconstructed what happened over the next twelve hours from the reports contained in Will's files. These start in 1947 and end in 1956, when all the members of 2nd Squad were hypnotized to uncover hidden memories. That was the year Dr. Steven Reich discovered that the amnesia induced by the visitors could to a degree be broken by this process.

It is interesting to me that Will never allowed himself to be hypnotized, even though his agency routinely required that all other personnel exposed to direct alien contact undergo the process.

According to a report prepared by the Fort Bliss MP's who investigated the events that transpired that night, the squad was on a practice combat patrol. They had been assigned an area far from any expected "aggressor" activity, and I suspect that they anticipated a quiet night.

The squad leader, Corporal Jim Collins, would have put the men at ease when they reached their destination. He himself sat down heavily, and pulled off his pack. After a moment he signaled to his radioman, who came trotting over with his antenna bobbing. "You working, Lucas?"

"Yes, sir." Lucas bent his back and Collins pulled the handset out of its cradle and turned the radio on. He waited for the "ready" light, then made a brief transmission to Platoon.

"This is Baker Delta Mike at Checkpoint zero-two-two-Harvey-eight. Out."

The radio crackled. "Acknowledged," came the laconic reply. "Order: Rockabye."

Collins flipped off the radio. "We got an order to bed down for the night," he said. There were a few groans of relief.

No fires were allowed; they ate cold C rations. According to a typical C ration chow manifest from the period, supper could easily have been Vienna sausages, peas, processed cheese and rice pudding. There was no bread, and water was the only drink. No lights were allowed, which meant no cigarettes, and many of them wanted a smoke right now more than they wanted a woman.

There were ten of them, plus Collins. The oldest was twenty-two. That was Mastic, who had a tattoo of a long-stemmed red rose on his chest.

The youngest was a boy from Lufkin, Texas, called Sweet Charlie. Charlie Burleson.

Officially, this monster was eighteen years old. According to his birth certificate as recorded on November 7, 1931, in Austin, Texas, he was actually sixteen.

For some reason nobody had bothered to check his age when he enlisted. It could have been his looks: Sweet Charlie was also known as "Bullhog."

His great hope was to become a member of the Army boxing team and go professional after his tour was up. His hands were as big as most men's heads, and I believe that he had the disposition of somebody who'd swallowed a razor blade.

This kid was scraping grease out of the bottom of a vienna sausage can and staring off across the darkening landscape when he saw something strange. "What the fuck they throwin' at us," he muttered.

The whole squad looked where he was pointing.

"Goddamn."

"That's them Marfa Lights. I know what that is."

"We're way the fuck away from Marfa, boy. You ain't got no goddamn sense. That's some kinda aggressor flare."

Collins looked at the glow. It rose a little distance from the surface of the desert and hung in the air, a round, yellow ball about the size of the full moon.

"Lucas, get HQ on the horn."

After a moment the radiotelephone burped. HQ sounded a million miles away. "Permission to transmit in the clear."

"Granted."

"We are observing a stationary yellow flare south-southeast our position at approximately nine o'clock. Advise please."

There was a fairly long silence, during which Collins watched the flare. "This is Lieutenant Ford, repeat that location."

"South-southeast our position, approximately nine o'clock."

"That is off the game board, Corporal. Assume it's unconnected activity."

"Yes, sir. Over and out." He put the receiver back into the unit. "That flare is unconnected activity," he said aloud. "HQ says to disregard."

The men hardly heard him. They were watching the flare, which was now moving about in the sky, fluttering from side to side like a leaf. For a long time nobody said anything.

The disappearance of the thing was as sudden as a light being turned off.

The men remained still and silent. Finally Mastic farted, which brought a snort of derision from Sweet Charlie. "Season the fuckin' bivouac, right Mastic?"

"The more you eat, the more you toot."

"Vienna sausages ain't beans."

"All C rations are beans. See the numbers on these cans? This means they were made in June of 1944. That's three years ago."

"Hell, they're new. I hearda guys openin' these cans and findin' hardtack and molasses. The U.S. Army ain't issued rations like that since the Civil War."

"What the fuck war is that?"

"You don't know about the fuckin' Civil War, Sweetie? You must be some kind of moron."

"Who're you callin' a moron, Mastic, you corn-holin' homo."

"Fuck you, you big puff! Them cigar butts is just a act."

"Knock it off, you guys."

The men settled down.

The night returned to its rustlings.

The light reappeared directly above them, covering the central three-quarters of the sky. The squad was caught in its glow. At this point they came under the direct influence of the others—in fact, entered their control.

As elsewhere in this book, I have constructed the interactions between ourselves and the others on the basis of the secret psychological studies I have read, as well as my own interviews with witnesses and astute UFO investigators. Will has

111

contributed virtually all of what understanding I can claim. Always I have adhered to his admonitions, "This is about the soul, the body is secondary," and, "The others are so old that they have rediscovered innocence. That is what makes them terrible."

I have also watched about a thousand feet of eight-millimeter film that Will says was made by the others at the request of the United States government, of a group of people they had taken into their possession.

In this strange, pale environment the people look like great, fleshy bags. The others flit around, fragile and almost invisible on the film. People scream, they pound their fists on the walls, they try to dig through the floor. The fear and terror are impossible to describe. Every so often a pair of those black alien eyes will glare into the camera.

Is it rage or fear I see there, or desperation?

In addition, in the case of the 2nd Squad I had the advantage of reading transcripts of the hypnosis sessions of Corporal Collins, PFC Lucas and Private Mastic.

On that night back in 1947 the men looked up at the huge object that was now directly above them. They saw the faint lines and rivets of the underside of the great ship. There would have been sobs, muttered prayers. Some probably went to their knees.

Jim Collins called the radio operator, who sat frozen, staring. "Lucas!"

"Momma says no."

"What the fuck!"

"Momma said no turn on radio."

"What the hell is this?" Collins stood up. His men were lying on their sides or hunched or kneeling. "Hey you guys!"

As is typical of the others' methods, a human being they had contacted before remained in a more-or-less normal state. Only later would his memory be affected.

Under hypnosis Collins recalled seeing three children in white suits hanging back at the edge of the light, watching him. "We won't hurt you, Jimmy," a voice said. Collins stared hard at them. How had they done that? The voice sounded like it was inside his head.

"Hey," he said. "You kids." In reply there was a sneering giggle, also inside his head. "This is a military area. You kids aren't supposed to be playing around here."

"Come with us, Jimmy. We won't hurt you."

"Who are you?"

One of the "kids" pointed upward toward the object. Collins had never heard of foo-fighters, flying disks or aliens, and had only the sketchiest knowledge of outer space.

His first thought was: a blimp.

Immediately the voice answered, "No."

Then what is it, Collins thought.

He began to receive instructions subliminally. They sounded to him like somebody whispering in his ear. He cocked his head to listen, but couldn't quite understand.

He was aware that a group of about half a dozen of the children in white had just floated down out of the craft and were touching the foreheads of his men with little sticks.

A shaft of blue light hit him and in a moment he was completely changed. He was no longer the dumb creature he had been, a dull kid leading a bunch of other dull kids. Another, extremely secret life had returned to memory. He knew these people, knew them well.

Why it would be like this it is difficult to know. Apparently certain people are leading double lives, unknown even to themselves. They are the facilitators, the ones who help the others with the rest of us, who are much wilder and more difficult to handle.

"I remember," he said.

"It's been a long time, Jimmy. You were a baby. Now look at you!" The voice that spoke was old—ancient—and came from the night wind. And it was feminine.

"I grew up, ma'am."

"Yes. You are a strong boy."

She came close to him, and he looked into her dark, dark eyes.

"I am preparing these soldiers. They belong to me now, Jimmy. They are part of the Good Army."

These words filled Collins with a happiness he could not contain. He smiled from ear to ear and clapped his hands like an excited infant.

113

In response he was flooded with love. Meanwhile the ones in white went about their work. The ship came slowly down until it was no more than five feet above the group. One by one the 2nd Squad was lifted onto stretchers, which then floated up to the ship's softly glowing surface and disappeared.

She put a thin arm around Jim's shoulders.

"They will receive insertions like the one you got when you were a boy."

Together the two of them rose on a stream of light.

Jim went to the familiar cabinet at the end of the room and took out the tiny gray boxes he knew would be there. He knew exactly what to do—he'd seen it done it before and he remembered every detail.

He removed a long needle from the first box and inserted it into Sweet Charlie's brain. "Not him," she said softly. "Withdraw the implement." He pulled out the needle.

She did not interrupt him again, remaining silent until he had completed the operation on each squad member. "Now I will test them," she said. One by one the squad members opened their eyes and sat up. Then they slumped over, rendered once again unconscious.

"You have done your work well."

When she spoke in his mind it was like melody. "You will be married soon, Jimmy. The union will be with your childhood mate Kathy. Together you will conceive five new ones. The last two of them will be for you, the first three for me. Is this understood?"

He nodded.

"These soldiers are from the nation that has used the atomic bomb?"

"Yes."

"The earth grows heavy with her burden of men. She calls out to me to midwife her. She tells me that her *yuni* is opening to the stars."

"Yes."

"Do men want to go among the stars, Jimmy?"

"We don't think about that."

"You will raise the children I give you. That is your primary task. Now take these little ones back to their encampment, and be mindful that they have all suffered this night."

"Yes."

She sent them all back, all except the one she had not implanted. This one was suitable for another purpose, and she gave him over to the ones who wanted him.

"We love you, Sweet Charlie," they said. It sounded to him like a group of children speaking in rough chorus.

Their faces were pale and soft. They looked as pretty as babies.

—Smile, Charlie.

—I don't want to.

—Smile!

—I ain't got no reason!

Charlie decided that it was time to get out of here. He thought he'd gotten up, but his body didn't work. It just didn't do anything.

He struggled, pulled, tried to stand. He didn't move an inch. Now his breath came in gasps. His throat practically closed. He couldn't breathe. They were watching him, drawing close, leering at him.

Why did it seem so right? Was it somehow connected with the life he had lived? He wanted another chance.

Then he saw Clara. "I was carrying the baby for them," she told him.

How was this possible? Clara was dead! He knew because he'd killed her.

She'd let him knock her up, she'd goddamn well known she was doing it, she was trying to hang him on a fucking meathook! "They would have taken the baby before it was even born."

And then he was in the woods, deep in the pines and Sweet Charlie had that little shotgun and he was hunting Clara down, and he caught hisself that lyin' little vixen while she was gathering pinecones.

To decorate her Christmas tree.

—I was drunk.

—You can repay your debt to Clara by helping us.

Charlie saw something horrible, something he did not want to face, to think about, ever *ever* to see.

115

There are mirrors that reflect the soul. There are mirrors in which we see ourselves *as we are.*

—Momma, help me, Momma!

The other squad members were gone, only Jim was here. Jim also saw Sweet Charlie, saw the black, knotted ugliness that was the very essence of him.

"We can help you." The voice was as sweet as spring wind.

Charlie had understood that he was seeing his own soul. "Please, please . . ."

They took him then into the darker depths of their ship.

A moment later the screams started and they were wretched with a despair unlike anything Jim Collins had ever imagined. He was made to hear them for only a moment. Then somebody closed a door.

A girl came, walking toward him across the broad room.

She was wearing a thin summer nightgown with yellow flowers down the front and a lace collar. With her she brought a beautiful scent, the odor of gardenias, and there was a gardenia in her hair.

Tears of recognition sprang to Jim's eyes. "Kathy," he said, "Kathy O'Mally!"

Then darkness filtered down into him, and with it the forgetfulness of deep, deep sleep.

The next thing Jim knew he was hearing the birds. He opened his eyes, stared up into a pink and fragile dawn. He was cold, his face covered with dew. He coughed, then slipped out of his bedroll.

He felt incredible. The world around him, the sweep of land, the distant hills, the deep morning sky—never in his life had he seen such beauty.

What had they done last night? He remembered voices, laughter, excitement.

A party?

No, something else. Something incredibly beautiful. They'd seen a flare and then turned in and he'd dreamed.

Yes, a dream.

Some sort of justice had been done in his dream. He remembered a judge telling him about Sweet Charlie, that creep, and saying he was free, he had paid his debt.

Collins looked around him. Where was the big lug, anyway? Well, he'd turn up.

He moved off toward the latrine area.

There he thumped himself to get rid of an oddly persistent erection. He was so damn excited he could barely stand it. His knees were weak. He wanted a woman. In fact, it was a specific woman: Kathy O'Mally from back home. Kathy of the sandy blond hair. Kathy of the soft voice, of the laughter in the dark, of the welcoming arms.

He was feeling waves of longing for Kathy so great that he could barely endure them. And here he was out in the middle of West Texas thousands of miles from her. But, God, she was a wonderful girl. He had to write her more letters, to let her know how much he cared for her.

God forbid she wouldn't realize and she would get married before he came back. Once he had kissed her at Emmeneger's Drugstore. She'd presented her cheek and laughed.

Her laughter echoed. Had he dreamed about her last night? No. He'd had a nightmare about an owl, a huge owl carrying him off into the dark. He shuddered to remember it. A creepy sort of a dream. And then Charlie—what had Charlie had to do with it?

Nightmare or not, he knew one thing. Somehow in his sleep he had made a final and absolute decision. He was going to marry Kathy O'Mally.

When he got back from the latrine he called his men out of the sack.

Sweet Charlie had gone AWOL in the night. "We'll find him back at the goddamn mess gobbling steaks," Lucas said.

"I'll put him on report," Jim Collins replied. He didn't like that mean cracker any more than the others.

He was listed AWOL.

By the next afternoon an entire company was searching for him. But Sweet Charlie was never seen again.

Chapter Ten

The Chronicle of Wilfred Stone

The President was uneasy, I could hear it in his voice. Had I been interrogating him instead of participating in a meeting, I would have thought it time to make my move.

Before him on an easel sat six excellent aerial photographs of a debris field, a crashed disk some sixty miles from it, and two small bodies near the disk. One was clearly visible; the other hardly more than a shadow.

"I don't see any relationship between this crashed object and disappearing people," the President said. There was the snap of challenge in his voice, and beneath it the quavering disquiet. More accurately, he should have said that he didn't *want* to see any relationship between the object and the earlier disappearances.

General Vandenberg knew Truman well, far better than I did. He sat on a couch across from the President, his knees comically high, a cigar stuffed into the corner of his mouth. Even sunken into that ridiculous couch, Van was an imposing man. He also admired Harry Truman, for which reason I did not like the look he sent me as the President spoke. It was almost a plea, as if he was asking me to somehow soften the blow of my estimate, and not to be too hard on his hero.

Did he fear that Truman would crack? Surely not the man who had dropped the bomb.

Admiral Hillenkoetter was standing at the windows overlooking the rose garden. Some of Bess's roses were still blooming, and the windows were thrown open to the fragrant summer air. Now he committed himself and CIG.

"I'm a hundred percent behind the intelligence estimate."

"This is crashed hardware and bodies. It isn't disappearing people. I want evidence of a direct relationship. Otherwise where the hell do I stand with this thing, Hilly?"

If the President appeared uneasy, Secretary of Defense Forrestal was absolutely appalled. He sat staring at the pictures like a man looking into the face of death. From time to time he would sip noisily from a cup of cold coffee. "Of course there's a relationship," he said. "That's the whole point."

"Goddamn it, nothing's proven! It's speculation."

The secretary glared at the President. "There is no question in my mind but that we should shoot one of these devilish things down forthwith."

Van leaned forward. "I concur, Mr. President."

Hilly still stared out the window. "I think it's too soon for that," he said. The President looked toward him, his eyes flashing behind the famous glasses.

"Hilly's right. We don't need to shoot one down. We've got one, plus the little fellas that drove it."

"Mr. President, it would be a show of force. I think it's vital that we come on strong in this. These people must possess tremendous power. God knows what they might do."

"Exactly my point, Van," Hilly said softly.

Vandenberg chewed the cigar. Forrestal sighed. He knew when a point had been won or lost with Truman.

"Any order to take aggressive action comes from me," the President said. "Is that clearly understood, Van?"

"Yes, sir."

"For now I want all AAF orders of the day to include a statement that there will be no hostile action taken against any unidentified flying craft entering or being found within U.S.-controlled airspace anywhere in the world, until such time as said craft is specifically identified as enemy aircraft or acts in an overtly hostile manner, which means shooting first."

My own obsession with secrecy alerted me to the flaw in this order. "Say aircraft, Mr. President. We don't want to draw any attention to our level of concern over this."

"Yeah, okay. Just bleed it into the standard orders. Nothing unusual. Aircraft."

119

"It's dented," Forrestal said. He had taken up the magnifying glass and was peering at the object.

We waited, expecting him to make a point. At that moment Blanche Deisinger came in with a note for the President. He looked at it and then at Van.

"The AAF base at Roswell has issued a press release about the disk."

Secretary Forrestal's face drained of color. He dropped the magnifying glass on the President's desk and bowed his head. He reminded me of a mourner at a funeral.

Van just sat there, obviously too shocked to speak.

There was a small, ironic smile on the President's face. He took off his glasses and rubbed his eyes, leaning far back in his chair. He seemed swallowed by his office.

Hilly broke the silence. "We'll correct this problem forthwith." His voice sounded calm, almost indifferent. I knew what that meant, though: he was feeling off-balance. When he got a really bad shock was when he appeared most calm.

"I think it's obviously my baby," Van said.

"Yes," Forrestal agreed. "Your damn problem. There's never been enough discipline among those airmen of yours! My God, the things they get away with, cutting up the way they do. Van, this is outrageous!" He looked toward the President for approval.

Truman was simply listening. His eyebrows were raised. He was expectant, waiting for the suggestion that would solve the problem.

"I'll issue orders to silence them," Van said. It sounded weak, and it was. You can't silence the press with orders.

"They must be pleased as punch out there," the President said. "Think of it! They've put their goddamn base on the map." He laughed mirthlessly, in a way that told me heads were going to roll. God, Truman was a frightening man.

"To control the press, you're either going to have to use me or Hoover," Hilly said.

"Oh, brother, not him," Forrestal muttered.

Hilly smiled. "I'll agree that I'm the best of two evils, Jim."

"For God's sake, Harry, don't bring that old pansy in on this," Van said.

"Is he really a pansy?" Forrestal asked.

Truman's eyes twinkled. "I pity the President who doesn't know Hoover's weakness. Thank God FDR told me. Kindest thing he ever did." He laughed. "But if I ever get beaten by that goddamn Tom Dewey I'm taking the Hoover file home with me."

Forrestal snorted. "I don't like Hoover either, but the man runs a goddamn good department."

"As long as you have his balls in your hand," Truman said mildly. We all laughed. Truman's remark meant that Roscoe Hillenkoetter had just been given control of what would become the largest, most important and most secret activity in the history of the United States or any other human nation. Vandenburg didn't realize what Hilly had accomplished, but Hilly did. He flushed so red that he turned to the window. I wanted to clap the man on the back, but Truman suddenly eyed me and my blood went cold.

"He's heading this thing up, Hilly?"

"Yes, sir," I replied softly. A crucial moment was upon me. All Hilly had to do was cough, and I was dead. If he but remained silent this incredible command would be mine, and the Central Intelligence Group would be established over the Air Force's S-2 Intelligence unit in control of the whole alien project.

"I think that Will Stone has guts to spare," Hilly announced. He turned around. His face had returned to its usual pallor. "He's also a damn good thinker."

"He writes a good intelligence estimate," Van added.

"Scared the shit out of me," the President said. "If the goddamn thing is right."

"I believe it is, sir," I said.

"You better, kid! Unless you want me to kick your boss's head in. So tell us what we should do."

Typical of his style. Demand the goods.

I started to reply, but Van interrupted. "First I gotta pull that press release back," he said.

I parried for control. "We'll do more than that, of course."

"Of course," Van snapped. He had no choice but to agree even though it meant CIG management.

Silence followed. They settled back to listen to what I would propose. All I could hear on that distant summer day was the pottering of a lawn mower, that and the soft crinkling sound as Van sucked his cigar. I spoke my piece. "The press is going to go wild when they see the release. The 509th Bomber Wing is big news already. The only operational atomic bomber wing in the world. As far as the press is concerned, that release was generated by the hottest soldiers in the Air Force. They're going to believe it."

"And they've got it? The thing's been sent out?" The fear had returned to the President's voice.

Hilly gave me support. "Will Stone will get the dimensions of the thing sorted out immediately, Mr. President. General Vandenberg, I'd appreciate it if he had the cooperation of S-2 Intelligence and AAF Security."

Van went to the President's desk and picked up the phone. He spoke for a few minutes, talking to General Nathan Calkins, commander of the intelligence division. He handed me the telephone. I mustered all the authority I could, consciously lowering my voice. As I spoke, I could see the slightest of smiles in Truman's eyes. A young man asserting himself. It must have amused this master of authority.

"General, this is Wilfred Stone of CIG. I'm going to be in command of this for CIG. We'd like to know immediately how many news organizations have received the press release, who wrote it and who put their name on it."

I received a muttered reply that he would get back to me, then put the telephone down. "Gentlemen, I think that we must realize that this situation could be very far out of control at this point. We have a crashed disk, and the bodies of aliens. We have a press release. These two things add up to a spectacular press affair. They're going to be very excited. The story of the century, of the ages. Bigger than the bomb. We have to act instantly. I want a team to get out to Roswell with me. Small. People who are ultimately trustworthy. The minimum number needed." I went on, thinking fast. "I want to arrange to control all wire service activity in and out of Roswell. Remember that the news has to travel by wire. Also, all local radio broadcasts."

"You can use AAF Communications out of the proving grounds," Van said. "They'll have the capability you need. And there are Counterintelligence Corps officers out there who can make any personal visits needed, to set the radio stations straight."

"Gentlemen," Truman said, "keep me informed. I want you all to realize that I consider this the number one event of my administration. Beyond winning World War Two. Beyond dropping the bomb. I want to make one thing abundantly clear. There could be interservice rivalry between Air Force Intelligence and CIG, or with the FBI when they become involved. As far as I'm concerned, rivalries in a situation like this are treasonous. They will be dealt with as such. Is that understood?"

"How about Hoover?" Hilly asked.

The President sighed. "I'll deal with Hoover."

A moment later the meeting was concluded. Hilly, Van, Forrestal and I stood together waiting for our cars to be brought around. "I expect to be giving the President reports three or four times a day," Forrestal said. Now it was his turn to assert his command position. Neither Van nor the admiral, of course, wanted a single thing to do with him.

"That's a good idea," Hilly said. "I think we'd all be wise to do the same."

"We don't want to flood him with paper," Forrestal said. "I think we'd be best off sticking to the chain of command on this one."

"Except if it's an emergency," Vandenberg added. The general and the admiral were jockeying furiously with Forrestal. Officially Hilly probably had a better case in bypassing the secretary. But Van was stuck and he knew it.

Forrestal firmed his position. "If it's an emergency, Van, I'd expect to be informed immediately." The secretary's voice was acid. As his car pulled up he stepped away from us. "I'm going home to dinner with the French military chargé. We'll confer on logistics at eight." He looked at Van. "I'll expect your call. I want you to tell me how you're going to turn that press release into a joke."

With that bitter offhand comment Jim Forrestal unwittingly hit upon the ingenious essence of the cover-up that has remained intact for nearly fifty years. Ridicule. It still works, even today.

TOP SECRET
ARMY AIR FORCE
S-2 INTELLIGENCE ESTIMATE

Over the past half century there have been
a number of incidents of qualified observers
reporting unusual aerial objects. The March
1904 edition of the *Monthly Weather Review*
indicates that Lt. F. H. Schofield, Cdr., USS
Supply, reported observation of three large
luminous objects moving in formation across
the sky at 2300 hrs. This observation took
place in mid-Atlantic. The largest of the objects was estimated to have a diameter six
times that of the sun. Their size was not known
as distance/altitude could not be computed.

The March 1913 issue of the *Journal* of the
Royal Astronomical Society carried a report
by Canadian astronomer R. Chant indicating
that numerous objects consisting of "three or
four parts with a tail to each part" passed
across the sky. Thirty-two objects were observed over the course of an hour, moving in
formations of various kinds.

An analysis of reports indicates that
large luminous objects have been recorded in
the night skies by qualified professional observers at a rate of two to ten per annum since
immediately before the turn of the century.

The first official investigation of such
objects began on December 28, 1933, when the
4th Swedish Flying Corps commenced a study of
"ghost aeroplanes" which had been observed
flying in impossible weather conditions and
often shining powerful lights on the ground.
The investigation concluded on 30 April 1934
with a statement by Major General Lars Reuterswaerd, Commanding General, Upper Norr-
land Aerial Sector. General Reuterswaerd
stated, "There can be no doubt about illegal
air traffic over our secret military areas.
. . . The question is, who and what are they?"

Ghost aircraft continued to be sighted
over Finland, Sweden and Norway, and caused
extensive local forces recce, to no firm re-

sult. It is now known that no nation then had
aircraft capable of operating in the areas
and manner in which the ghost craft were observed to operate. Interestingly, 35% of
Scandinavian sightings took place during se-
vere weather conditions.

25 February 1942 saw unidentified aircraft appearing over Los Angeles. 1,430
rounds of antiaircraft were expended in an
attempt to bring down these apparent Japanese
planes. Shelling commenced at 0316 and continued until 0414 by 37th Coast Arty Bgde
using 12.8 lb HE shells. Three persons were
killed by the barrage. A large oval-shaped
object was targeted in lights and struck by at
least fifty rounds over a period of twelve
minutes. The object then proceeded southward
at a slow rate of speed. Chief of Staff Gen.
George C. Marshall informed the President of
the incident on 26 February 1942. GHQ officially denied that the incident had occurred.

In recent years so-called "foo-fighters"
were observed by both Allied and Axis airmen
during aerial maneuvers. These objects often
appeared to maneuver in context with aircraft
and were sometimes fired upon, but never with
any visible effect. The British set up the
Massy Project under Lt. Gen. Hugh R. S. Massy,
ret., which studied the phenomenon in 1943,
to no result. Similarly the Luftwaffe created
Sonderburo 13 under Prof. Georg Kamper. U.S.
8th Army investigated similarly, also with no
outcome.

During 1946 numerous apparent rockets
were observed over northern and central Sweden, Finland, Norway and Denmark. A total of
2,000 sightings were officially logged. Our
own intelligence indicates that these were
not Soviet-generated, and their source remains a mystery. 11 July 1946 U.S. embassy
Stockholm cabled "one landed on beach near
Stockholm without causing any damage and according to press fragments are now being
studied by military authorities." 12 October
1946 the Swedish government announced that
200 objects had been detected by radar and

could not be attributed to known celestial phenomena, hallucinations or airplanes. Subsequently the Greek government investigated many reports of such objects in their territory, but once again there were no conclusive results regarding nature and origin. The objects were not Soviet missiles, because they were observed to outrange any Soviet device.

The objects observed may be controlled by some intelligent agency, whether it is a human government, a clandestine private group in possession of powerful technology, or another as yet unknown source.
End.

Part Two
THE LOST SHIP

Take wings to climb the zenith,
Or sleep in Fields of Peace;
By day the Sun shall keep thee,
By night the rising Star.

—THE EGYPTIAN BOOK OF THE DEAD
Translated by Robert Hillyer

10JLY47
MOST SECRET
FROM: ROSCOE HILLENKOETTER, DIR. CIG
TO: STONE, WILFRED
EYES ONLY
COPY ONE OF (ONE) COPIES

1. You will proceed to Roswell New Mexico at 2200 this day aboard State Department Aircraft 003 and proceed to the site of an apparent crashed alien disk and commandeer this disk and all related material and objects connected with this disk.
2. You will convey this material to the Los Alamos National Laboratory Complex and expedite its study by a blue ribbon panel of scientists now being assembled. This group will complete analysis of all material obtained. You will operate in an observer/adviser capacity with this group, reporting daily to me on its proceedings.
3. You will contain any leaks of information and end the present free access that the press has to information about this material. You will use flat, blanket denial as your primary means of covering the truth, and will orchestrate a program of ridicule against any individual who makes public statements. You are officially authorized to use all necessary means to insure absolute and continuing silence from witnesses. The use of extreme or final means must be approved by this office.

Chapter Eleven

Ridicule certainly proved to be the right tool for the job Will Stone wanted done. Forrestal may have counseled its use, but it was Will who formed the idea into policy. I envy Will the brilliance of his youth. In 1947 he was hobnobbing with the President. In 1989 I'm fighting the Bethesda *Express* over the validity of my unemployment insurance claim.

Will wasn't alone. The Central Intelligence Group in the late forties was one of those unlikely bubbles of talent that on rare occasions rise to the surface of the federal bureaucracy.

Hilly chose two of the best of them to go with Will to New Mexico. Like him, they were former OSS types originally brought into intelligence work by "Wild" Bill Donovan.

Donovan had found some remarkable people to spy on the Nazis for Uncle Sam.

Joe Rose was in the Russian Division of CIG and was set for big things when it became the Central Intelligence Agency and acquired a believable budget.

Joe's background was pretty extraordinary, even as the backgrounds of such men go. He'd graduated Yale Law in '33—at the age of 15. He was a large, rather somber man whose hobby, of all things, was the study of medieval secret societies. His German was excellent.

When he died Joe left Will his library. I have looked through it, searching, of course, for the man. I found a first edition of Harold Bayley's classic, *The Lost Language of Symbolism*, a marvelous treatise on the hidden meaning of watermarks in medieval papers. The book does not identify any secret societies *per se* but by its incredibly detailed analysis of thousands of symbols suggests that the whole of the Middle Ages must have been run by them. And they seem to have conducted their affairs in a hidden language of watermarks.

Joe was not simply amused by secrecy; he obviously studied it as an implement of government: Martin Philippson, *Ein Ministerium unter Philipp II*, essentially a book about the network of spies created by this notorious Spanish monarch; books on the Cathars, the great heretics of southern France, on the Knights Templar, on the Order of Our Lady of Mysteries.

During the war Joe had functioned as a deep-cover assassin in Germany, murdering targeted Gestapo agents in order to interrupt investigations when they got too close to Allied spy networks.

According to Will, Joe's genius was that he had made the Gestapo itself his chief ally. How? He gave them assistance in their work against the Reds. Thus the Gestapo was in the position of trading the lives of its own operatives for information about Stalin's Red Choir.

How he managed all this and still maintained "deep cover" Will did not say. Maybe Will's love for his old friend has combined with time's notorious corrosion of memory to enhance his stature a bit.

Even if that is so, the man's books do suggest that he was remarkable.

After the war Joe had become known as one of the best interrogators we possessed. He cut his teeth on the very Gestapo officers who had helped him during the war, and after that shifted to work with home-front communists. (Will still calls them "commies.") He was a master of persuasion, moving with the greatest care from one level of tension to the next, until his subject finally broke. He worked only with words, having like Will acquired a dislike of violence during the war.

Then they had Sally Darby. Every once in a while I fall in love with Sally Darby, looking at the pictures of her Will keeps around. She had a complex, distracted expression and the darting pace of a sparrow.

Did Will love her? Of course he did.

She had graduated Smith with honors, and she could if she wished fulfill the image of the Smith girl.

This is how she came to CIG.

In 1938 she moved to Paris and met Janet Flanner and William Carruthers. Even after the fall of France she stayed on, so certain she was that the United States would remain neutral.

When occupation shortages became annoying she took a vacation in Geneva, where she met Bill Donovan. Or rather, as an American resident of occupied France, he sought her out.

She returned to Paris as a newly recruited OSS agent—and was trapped there when Germany declared war on us. Her friendship with Countess Eva Rollentz meant that her German social connections were excellent. She specialized in going to parties with generals and field marshals, then wrote richly insightful essays about them that ended up in Washington. My guess is that she must have slept with them, but it was never mentioned and I certainly never brought it up with Will. I don't think *he* ever slept with her.

It must have been idealism that kept this wealthy and well-connected woman with CIG, or it may have had something to do with the grudging love that certain people develop for their organizations.

Even bureaucracies have their patriots.

The three of them were a strike team. Will says, "We thought we were generals, but we were really front-line soldiers, dog-faces, poor bloody infantry."

They were sent to Roswell by the fastest possible means, which turned out to be the secretary of defense's personal airplane.

This must have added to their hubris. It is important to remember at all times that Washington felt as if it would be able to control the situation. The spaceship had *crashed,* for God's sake.

To hear Will talk about Forrestal's airplane, it was a sort of flying Yale Club with cigar humidors and fine brandy and Persian stretches on the floor.

I have done some research, and it's true that the plane was exceptional. It was more than nice enough to make three smart young strivers feel very, very important.

In addition to the pilots there was a communications officer with a radio shack up front. He was capable of reaching the telephone operator, and there were ordinary phones throughout the plane. You could call anywhere in the world from the craft, as you could on some of the more extravagant ocean liners.

As soon as they were airborne the threesome had a meeting. Joe Rose smoked one of the secretary's superb Havanas and Will indulged in old cognac. Sally sipped a Prior's.

Will reported their conversation to me as if he remembered it verbatim. Given his prodigious memory and his ability to call on pretty extensive notes and diaries, it might *be* verbatim. If so, it was so pompous that, given the circumstances, it was rather poignant.

"Is Van going to shoot one of them down?" Sally asked. To his face she would certainly have referred to him as General Vandenberg.

"Harry nixed it," Will replied. I imagine that he sniffed the bouquet of his cognac, perhaps even took a sip. "We discussed it this afternoon in the Oval Office."

Joe examined his cigar. "We'll have to get compliance from any civilians involved." He blew a reflective stream of smoke from his mouth. "I can manage that, I suppose."

"The civilians?" Sally lit a cigarette. "They'll object."

"They didn't object in Frankfurt, Sally."

"The law—"

"Moves slowly."

Joe was looking out a window, staring long at the passing blackness. "I can see a few stars. Quite a few, actually."

"Any of them moving?"

"What if there were, Willy boy?"

"We might be in danger."

Will insists that he said those words. I wonder. Had he been genuinely afraid, I think he might have actually been more open to the others. He would have bargained with them, then, or recommended that the President attempt to do so.

Will reports that the three of them spent some hours discussing how they would handle matters in New Mexico. It was decided that Sally would proceed to Los Alamos and start groundwork there, preparing a secure area to receive whatever Will managed to send her for analysis, as well as finding housing for the scientists they were expecting CIG in Washington to locate and make available.

Joe was to open an office in Roswell and comb the airfield and the countryside for people who knew something about what had happened. His mission was to spread silence.

They slept from about two-thirty in the morning. Will was awake for a short time at four, Washington time, and found that his stateroom was filled with blue light. His immediate impression was that an engine was burning.

Even now he doesn't know the meaning of the blue light. He is aware that it is associated with the near presence of the others. When I brought up that blue light is in folklore connected with the presence of ghosts, he gave me a sidelong look and said, "If they have developed a technology that enables them to control the soul, they might have some sort of contact with the dead."

He has worried that the world of the dead might be the primary human reality, and that the others have invaded more on that level than on this.

For my part, I wonder if the dead exist.

The changing pitch of the props woke Will for good about half an hour before they were due to land. He called for coffee and lit a cigarette. The right side of his head hurt, just behind the ear. One of the stewardesses said it looked like a spider bite.

One of the many signs of close contact with the others is a painful red mark on the temple, just like that. Did they revisit Will while he was on his way to Roswell, perhaps renewing whatever they had implanted into him when he was a boy?

I don't doubt that they did. He hated the idea of it, and refused even to speculate.

The radio operator appeared with a message from Hilly, which he and Sally decoded. In those days they used a code book and a sheet of paper. The codes were kept secure by frequent changes. Now of course codes change constantly and everything is done by computer. I suppose in 1947 it was still conceivable that a spy might carry his codes in the heel of his shoe.

The message explained that AAF Intelligence had contained

the press leaks by intercepting all wire-service copy leaving New Mexico and sending agents to every radio station that had picked up the story.

That must have been reassuring, but they still had an enormous problem. The news release was now appearing in places like the San Francisco *Chronicle* and the London *Times*.

They landed in Roswell and prepared to meet the Army Air Force officers who had found the disk and so irresponsibly announced this fact to the public.

They were waiting on the apron, and Will recalls them as an impressive-looking group of soldiers. Colonel William Blanchard was flanked by two men he recognized from their file photos. One was Lieutenant Peter Hesseltine and the other was Major Donald Gray. Even then Don Gray was considered one of the best Intelligence officers in the Army Air Force. Will admires him tremendously. In 1979 Don Gray admitted before television cameras that the debris of an alien craft had been located in Roswell. It is a testament to the effectiveness of Will Stone's work that the press *still* considers the whole thing a fraud, even after that.

Chapter Twelve

Gray, Blanchard and Hesseltine were obviously wary of the three CIG officers. Blanchard was motionless, his legs spread apart, his hands on his hips. Will recalls that Gray stood at attention, perhaps awed by the impressive Defense Department plane. Hesseltine fidgeted, his fingers drifting like nervous ghosts to the knot in his tie.

Like so many soldiers they had a boyish quality to them.

Men like Blanchard, who had flown in long-range bombers in the Pacific, were a singularly untroubled group. They had done more killing than anybody else in the war. But they did it from such a height and in such safety that it remained quite abstract to them. They read paperback thrillers on their long journeys to Japan, then spent a few minutes blowing women and children to pieces. On the way home they returned to their books.

Men like Blanchard looked as they felt: invulnerable.

By comparison, the CIG officers were tense and obviously uneasy. They were squinting, troubled by the blasting desert sun.

The first one out of the plane was Will Stone—a pale young man in what was probably the most expensive suit any of them had ever seen. The way Colonel Blanchard looked at him, Will thought that he was sizing him up as a pansy.

During the war years, Will had acquired the ability to read lips, meaning that he was able to tell what the three officers were saying to each other before he got into earshot. The conversation he reports is most revealing.

"The second one's the hired killer," Blanchard said softly.

"He looks like he could break you in half with his breath," Hesseltine added.

"Shut up, Hesseltine," the colonel muttered.

When Sally appeared the soldiers reacted again. "Wow," said Hesseltine, "I could stand to nibble that sandwich."

"Don't worry yourself, boy. Gals like that don't eat Army meat."

"Yes sir, Colonel."

"You'd be lucky to get her to bed the Duke of Windsor."

"Hell, Colonel, try the Pope."

"Saint goddamn Francis of Asskissi."

The irreverent Hesseltine laughed at Colonel Blanchard.

"You'd blister your lips on that hot little ass," the colonel said in reply to the sneer.

Major Gray, most proper, was disgusted with them. "You gentlemen are sick."

"I've got it figured," Lieutenant Hesseltine said in an insincere twang. "These palookas are the team that pulled down Al Capone."

"Those were T-men."

"Hell, Colonel, I'm not talking about the team that arrested him. I'm talking about the team that gave him syphilis."

"Not the Virgin Mary? Don't shatter my dreams."

"Hell no. The pansy dancing up the front. The way they did it, the guy danced up and breathed on old Al. Presto, one case of drippy dickie."

Now even the Colonel was disgusted. "I'm going to have you up on charges for language like that before breakfast."

"Yes, sir!"

As the CIG party approached, Blanchard locked eyes with Will. "Look at him," he said under his breath. "My opinion has changed. Fancy-pants is the gunman. The other guy's a toughie with a heart of lead. And that lady's probably some kind of whiz kid. Nobody's ever managed to get in her pants. That's as good as law."

There were introductions all round, and then they moved to a bacon-and-eggs breakfast at the officer's club, which was a barracks full of surplus furniture and steam tables. In lieu of air

137

conditioning there was tinfoil on the windows to reflect the heat.

Will recalls being surprised to find that the food was more than passable. No powdered eggs here, no Spam.

He made an immediate frontal assault. "I propose that we go to the site at once," he said around a mouthful of sausage.

Colonel Blanchard responded nervously. "We've got to have confirmation on that from Eighth Air Force."

It was as Will expected. Those words meant to him that Vandenberg was going to try to keep the whole affair under his own authority. Will would perhaps have preferred to play a more cunning game, but he had no time. He decided to use his strongest card at once. "We should have brought a doctor's note," he said to Blanchard. " 'Dear Colonel, Please let these children do what they have to do.' Signed, Dr. Harry Truman."

Blanchard was the hottest colonel in the AAF. He didn't want any waves that might disturb his shot at becoming commanding general of Eighth Air Force. Undoubtedly Will was right to threaten him with serious waves.

He capitulated, at least partially. "Okay, fair enough," he said. "Hesseltine here will take care of it."

"Very well." Will relaxed. He thought he'd won his point.

Major Gray got up from the table. "I'm afraid I've got to leave you folks in capable hands. I'm off to Wright Field with the debris we collected."

Will was furious. "We expected to see that material!"

Gray glanced at Colonel Blanchard. The colonel spoke quickly. "It's already loaded aboard a B-29. General Ramey's going to press conference the stuff at five this afternoon. My own second is flying it up to Forth Worth and Major Gray is going with him."

Joe was charged with the practical task of keeping things quiet. He exploded. "Press conference! That's just what we need."

"We're saying it's a mistake. A rawinsonde. That's a type of radar target." Will was uneasy about Major Gray. He told me that he would have "taken care" of the major in short order. In Will Stone hate and envy are essentially the same emotion. "In the end Don told the truth," he says. "It took him thirty-two years, but he did it." His tone is curt because of his envy for the man's moral clarity.

Not that the statement helped. Don Gray's words collided with the brick wall of Will Stone's cover-up and quite simply died.

Now Joe went to work on the colonel. "We want air transport," he said. "Mr. Stone wants to be on site within the hour. And we want full support. CIG intends to stay physically with the disk and the bodies until they are delivered to Los Alamos."

"I understood they were following the other debris to Wright Field."

Legally, the AAF had jurisdiction at Wright. Los Alamos had just shifted to Atomic Energy Commission control and was thus no longer within the reach of the Joint Chiefs, specifically Van. That was the main reason that Hillenkoetter had decided to park the disk there. Smoothly, Joe made his case. "The best scientists in the world are located at Los Alamos, and it's only a few hundred miles away."

"Washington already set it all up," Sally added.

Colonel Blanchard raised his eyebrows. "I don't know if we have the whirlybirds available to take you to the site."

"You have them," Joe said. "I counted six on the apron as we landed."

"I meant unassigned."

Once again Will played his high card. "Reassign them. Surely you can do that for the President."

Blanchard gave Hesseltine a curt nod, and the young officer went off to arrange matters. The CIG group finished breakfast and went over to the colonel's office to wait. On the way Will picked up a copy of the Roswell *Daily Record.* The headline made him furious.

RAAF CAPTURES FLYING SAUCER IN ROSWELL REGION

Will was so enraged that he was afraid to speak lest he jeopardize their tenuous rapport with the colonel.

Once in his office they looked at more photographs of the disk. These were copies of the aerials they had seen at the White House. "What is the status of these pictures," Sally asked.

"Restricted."

"I'm officially changing them to Top Secret. Take them off the walls and place them under covers, please, Colonel." She had no legal right to change the classification level of anything, but her action was typical of the way these people regarded themselves.

Blanchard and Hesseltine fell all over each other to get the pictures off the walls. They stacked them backside up on the colonel's steel desk, and covered them with pink sheets of paper stamped TOP SECRET in block letters.

Joe, as liaison with Air Force Intelligence, made a call to S-2 at White Sands to confirm that all wire-service output from the area was still being intercepted. Given the headline that had just appeared, it was probable that reporters by the hundreds would be on their way to this place within a matter of hours.

Will was leaving for the helicopter port when he received word that Hilly was on the line from Washington.

He took the call in an empty office he later found out belonged to the base press officer who had issued the offending press release. Hillenkoetter was abrupt. "What's it look like?"

"Well, Admiral, I'm not sure. We only arrived here an hour ago. They didn't have any transport prepared. Then they wanted to send me in convoy. Now I'm in a whirlybird. It's a struggle dealing with them. And they've hijacked the debris they've already collected. It's on its way up to Wright via Eighth Air Force in Fort Worth. Ramey's going to hold a press conference claiming the debris is a crashed radar target."

"Don't get your back up. The President approved that last night. By the way, Blanchard doesn't know it yet, but he's going on leave this afternoon. His second's gonna take the heat. Van wants to make sure nobody throws up on his favorite boy's pretty blue uniform."

"I want support from Van. So far it looks like I'm getting anything but."

"I'll have to go through Forrestal."

"Van will totally ignore you."

"Forrestal is too weak a weapon, Truman too strong."

"Meaning that I'm on my own."

"Get out there and get that disk. And the bodies. Especially the bodies."

Bodies. Disks. Debris. Huge newspaper headlines. Will experienced a moment of despair. How were they ever going to hide this thing? "I've got to tell you that I don't think the radar-target story will work. The press'll never buy it."

"They will, old son."

"But it's absolute, obvious crap. Admiral—"

"You add together all the reporters west of the Mississippi and you still haven't got enough smarts to tune a radio. They'll buy it. Anyway, I read reporters as frustrated egos. They don't *want* to hear anything about superior aliens when they're already suffering from the sneaking suspicion that they're nothing but pieces of shit themselves."

"You're being briefed by the headshrinkers again, Hilly. And you're believing it."

"No—"

"Remember what happened last time? When we tried to psychoanalyze Stalin and we predicted—"

"Never mind that. Truman forgave me."

"Good luck with your radar targets, Admiral. You and Van and Ramey are going to need it."

Will said nothing of this disturbing turn of events to Sally and Joe as he hurried through the beating sun to where the helicopters were firing up. His two associates would remain at the base to begin setting up a field office.

Will had never flown in a helicopter before. As a matter of fact, none of them had. In those days they were quite a new technology. Will was strapped into a miserable plastic seat and given a helmet that was not sized for him. It stank of the sweat of many heads.

The machine rose into its own cloud of dust. A moment later Roswell AAF was swinging away below. The pilot soon set a course to the north and west.

On the way the machines seemed to make dozens of banks, all of them very steep. Will held tightly to the edge of his seat and the lip of the windshield. He vividly remembers the feeling that he was going to fall out at any moment.

"Want to listen to the radio? We can pick up KGFL in Roswell."

Radio. What more could a man want? "Yeah, fine." Will tried to sound enthusiastic. Unfortunately the station did not offer dance music, at least not at nine-fifteen A.M. Instead, he was forced to listen to something called *Trading Post*. A rancher called in wanting to trade a "black shoat" for a set of golf clubs. A beauty salon owner would trade a Toni Professional Permanent for three nights of baby-sitting with her two sons.

And Will was on his way to view the bodies of beings who had been born in another world.

The sun was already high, pouring through the cockpit, burning against everything that it touched. Hot, exhaust-filled wind swirled in the sides. The stink of gasoline mixed with the stink of two sweaty men.

Roswell sank away behind them. They were alone now between the sky and the land. It was so big, so empty.

When Will saw the disk he almost choked with excitement. They swept around it in a long circle, and it gleamed in the sun. It gleamed and glimmered, and beside it he saw two khaki tarps.

They landed in an area that had been roughly marked with some cloth tape. Here the brush had been hacked away, but not enough to make much difference.

A hundred feet away lay the most extraordinary object on the surface of the earth. Will had appropriately large thoughts: the pyramids, the Acropolis, the Colosseum at Rome, the Eiffel Tower, the Empire State Building, all the works of man. Among them there was no such work as this.

Our history, too: clambering up from the muck, making the first fire and the first pot, building our cities and our empires, the dreams of sultans and kings, the hoarse chorus of the modern democracies—in all of those thousands of days, there was no such day as this.

And Wilfred Stone was here.

CARSWELL ARMY AIR FORCE BASE PRESS OFFICE
PRESS CONFERENCE REPORT

8 Jly 47

LOCATION: HQ 8AF Ft. Worth Tx.

PARTICIPANTS: Brig. Gen. Roger M. Ramey, CinC 8th AF; Major Donald Gray, S-2, RAAF; Warrant O. Vinton Yancey, Base Weather Officer, Carswell AAF.

Various newspaper reporters identified herein as "QUESTIONERS."

General Ramey and officer specialists met with members of the press on the evening of July 8 to discuss the misidentification of a rawinsonde (type ML-306) as a so-called "alien flying disk."

GENERAL RAMEY: Thank you, gentlemen, for coming to this conference. I trust that we can rectify some pretty exciting reports that have been circulating about the pile of debris I have here. [Points to debris on desk and floor of office.] With me I have Major Donald Gray who is the expert intelligence officer who originally recovered the material, and Warrant Officer Vinton Yancey of our weather office, who can make a positive identification of the material. Now I'd like to open it up to questions.

QUESTIONER: So this is all it is? A pile of tinfoil?

GENERAL RAMEY: That is correct. Perhaps Warrant Officer Yancey can explain.

W. O. YANCEY: This debris is from a so-called radiosonde. A rawinsonde-type device. It is very familiar to me. We release these sondes as target devices for airborne and land-based radar. It is one of the primary things we do here at Carswell.

GENERAL RAMEY: Radar practice is one of the fundamental training functions of the AAF. They also do it at Roswell, don't they, Major Gray?

MAJ. GRAY: Yes, sir.

QUESTIONER: Major Gray, aren't you an intelligence officer?

MAJ. GRAY: Yes, sir. That is correct.

QUESTIONER: And yet you thought this was a flying saucer? This is just tinfoil.

MAJ. GRAY: The misidentification was a result of a series of miscommunications.

QUESTIONER: Didn't you personally gather this debris in a field near Roswell? And personally identify it as a crashed disk?

GENERAL RAMEY: There are misidentifications of one object for another all the time. This was a case of mistaken identity. This is a complicated business, identification of one object or another.

QUESTIONER: This rawinsonde is a weather balloon? Can we say that?

W.O. YANCEY: No, sir, this is—

GENERAL RAMEY: Say that. That's fine. It's close. You can tell the way the wind is blowing looking at these things. A mistaken identification of a weather balloon. As far as I can see, there is nothing to get excited about. Would you concur, Major Gray?

MAJ. GRAY: Absolutely nothing here to get excited about. What we have here is a common device in use in the Air Force.

GENERAL RAMEY: Thank you very much, gentlemen.

Chapter Thirteen

Describing his first moments on site, Will leaned back and coughed a long, productive cough and closed his eyes. "It was like being in heaven," he said. "It was the highest of high adventure."

Will was a romantic, and as such a dangerous man. Romanticism rejects the ordinary, seeks the impossible and demands death for failure. The ultimate romantic was the Waffen-SS officer standing in the turret of his Tiger tank, battling the cold plains and blood of Russia.

I am not a romantic.

As the helicopters wheezed into silence Will strode up to the disk. So far nobody had entered it, nobody had even come this close.

A breeze brought an unusual smell, a sort of sulfurousness mixed with decay. It was coming from beneath the two tarps that covered the bodies of the pilots. Flies buzzed around them. Death was death, the flies knew.

To Will's absolute astonishment a civilian came strolling out from behind the disk. "Hiya," he said congenially, "I'm Barney Barnett."

"Who?"

"Barnett. I'm with the survey."

Will was thunderstruck. Surely nobody had been so remarkably stupid as to assign a civilian survey team to this site. "You're surveying this crash?"

He laughed. "Nah, not this. The mapping survey."

The man had blundered into the most secret place in the country. His unexpected appearance reminded Will that things were in a profound state of disorder. It went deeper than a simple lack of security, and it arose from a number of factors.

At this moment in history the government was undergoing intense change. The Air Force was being split off from the Army; the Department of Defense was being formed out of the Old War Department; the CIG was becoming the CIA; the American war machine was being dismantled and the Cold War was just starting.

The U.S. had no agency in place to meet the aliens, no properly positioned personnel, and no organization at all. Will felt as if he was being rolled in a wave.

"Mr. Barnett, go sit over there," he said, pointing to where the copters had landed.

"Is this a flying saucer?"

"We're just examining it."

"Because I had a look at those bodies before you guys got here, and they surely aren't human beings. No, sir."

"All right."

One of the enlisted men escorted the surveyor away. Will returned to the business at hand.

The device was about thirty feet in diameter, dented and collapsed in the front. You could see where it had skidded across the ground, making a track about sixty feet long. He walked around it, looking for an entrance.

Given the circumstances, his approach was admirably straightforward. One would have thought that considerably more caution was in order.

There was an opening on the bottom. When he bent down he could see a small chamber inside, but the hatchway was too tight for him. At that point he considered looking for a more lightly built volunteer, but the thought of not being the first to enter the craft was unacceptable to him.

Then he found the place where the blast had occurred. It was a tear about eight feet long toward the rear of the craft. Inside he could see shreds of what looked like wax paper and bits of tinfoil. This was a much more promising point of entry.

He called to Lieutenant Hesseltine, who—still green from the flight—came reeling up with a flashlight and—absurdly—a pair of pliers.

"I'm going in, Lieutenant."

"Is that wise?"

"There's nothing left alive around here."

"I mean—what you might encounter. Booby traps."

"I doubt if they had time to set traps."

"I gotta tell you, I'll back you up but I don't like this."

As they talked Will examined the wound in the disk. The debris found on the Ungar ranch had obviously come from this area. He looked inside, shining the flashlight around.

Then he leaned into the opening.

His head was in a small room that had been badly damaged by the explosion. The gray floor had collapsed into the base of the craft. The walls had been made of sheets of wax paper with yellow flowers pressed between them. He recalls the cheerful shambles as seeming very sad.

He wanted to get into the room. The trouble was finding a handhold. Everything was torn, bent or broken and it all looked extremely fragile. Experimentally he pulled at a shred of the paper. It proved to be as tough as the soldiers had claimed it was, and as it turned out he had no difficulty using it to pull himself up into the craft.

Beyond the damaged room the machine seemed to be largely intact. It was gloomy and he had to use the flashlight. He went deeper into the ship.

He told me about this in such matter-of-fact tones that I must surmise that it never occurred to him to be afraid. It would have occurred to me, I can tell you.

In 1947, of course, they barely considered issues like the danger of alien bacteria and viruses. Were such a craft to appear for the first time now we would immediately take steps to isolate it from the environment, and would approach it only with the most carefully prepared personnel and the greatest caution.

In those days, though, a vaguely briefed young man seemed completely adequate to the task at hand.

He must have been mad. That was the most dangerous place on earth, the interior of the disk, and it was being penetrated by an ignorant kid in shirtsleeves. His only equipment was a flashlight that kept going out.

He called back to Hesseltine, "Looks okay."

"See any controls? Equipment?" Children in the cookie jar.

"Not yet," he reported. He had expected to find a flight deck complete with rows and rows of dials, sticks for the pilots and perhaps a couple of jumpseats for deadheading buddies.

To move forward he almost had to crawl.

Then he arrived in a round central room, and there had his first taste of what he had come here to find, the deep unknown.

The floor below him was black and shiny and curved. It looked and felt as if he was standing on the top of an enormous bowling ball. To his left and right were two more of the wax-paper doors. They were really just wooden frames with the paper glued to them. It all looked delicate and oriental. Had it been a few years earlier, they would have been suspicious that this was a Japanese secret weapon.

The black curved surface he was standing on was extremely slippery, and he fell forward when he shifted his weight. He hit the wall, which was made of a gray substance as thin as the wax paper that formed the doors behind him. It wrinkled but snapped back into place as he regained his balance.

He thought he heard something on the other side of the wall.

He shone his light but it seemed dim, and the outside world was far away. Not only was the interior of the ship extremely dark, it was incredibly quiet.

Behind him he could see Hesseltine's head and shoulders as he squinted into the craft. There was a strange effect, as if the man was underwater.

Nobody then understood the significance of the black object Will had walked across. He has told me that they eventually decided it was a gravity motor, and still operating at very low power. It was distorting space and time. Without knowing or understanding, Will was feeling the effects.

He called Hesseltine, but the man simply stared. He hadn't heard a thing.

"Hesseltine?" The lieutenant was no more than eight feet away. "Hesseltine!"

He frowned. "Are you there, Mr. Stone?"

"I'm here."

"Where?"

"Right in front of you!" Will stepped across the black object into the destroyed room.

148

"I couldn't see you."

"I'm going to go through into the front. Time me. Fifteen minutes. If I don't call or come out, come in and get me."

I asked Will if at that point he was afraid. He stared at me for a moment, then continued his narrative.

Again he crossed the slippery black object. This time he shone his flashlight into the darkness beyond the door.

The room was empty. He proceeded.

Where was he now? Surely he should be up against the front of the craft. But there appeared to be more rooms beyond this one. This seemed completely impossible. He shone the light around, finally hitting on another hatch like the one he had just come through. He wriggled through it also, and finally found himself at the front. Here the ceiling was dented, corresponding to the damage that could be seen on the outside of the ship.

There were three tiny seats before a small, disappointingly simple control panel. It consisted only of a thick black rod with a round knob on top, protruding from the center of a console in front of one of the chairs.

That was all there was in the way of controls. Beyond the console were two half-moon-shaped windows in the lower part of the nose. They were embedded in the dirt, which he could see when he shone his light on them.

The shape of the windows, like two slitted, glowering eyes, made Will distinctly uneasy. They seemed familiar—or perhaps simply *right*—and that unsettled him. It was as if he was being affected by a powerful unknown beauty or horror, he could not tell which.

At this point things began to happen to him that the scientists he has worked with all these years still cannot explain. It was things like this that first made Will aware of the fact that the others had something to do with the life of the soul. As with so many people, merely being close to these high artifacts drew him toward his soul's denied truth.

Suddenly a scene swam up before his eyes, a terrible scene from early in the war. In 1940 he was working in France, before his transfer to Algeria, which had taken place after the United States entered the war.

He was in Marseilles developing contacts with the infant

French Resistance, building an investment against future hardship, as it were.

He had just met Sophie Tuttle.

Never in all the time I spent with Will did he so much as allude to having a sexual relationship with a woman. Sometimes he would mention Sophie, though, and stare long into space or take a hit from his bottle.

Now her face seemed to come looming up out of the dimness of the room. He describes himself as profoundly shocked. It seemed to him that time had been erased, that Sophie was back, real and alive.

He even smelled her perfume, L'Heure Bleu. She'd had a bottle of it. She'd worn it when they met for the last time, in Marseilles. He heard her sigh, heard the rustle of her dress. A snatch of song from the war, "Radio-Paris ment," to the tune of "La Cucaracha." Radio Paris lies. Children would sing it, "Radio Paris lies, Radio Paris lies, Radio Paris is German." Sophie would also sing it.

He lost her the same way he lost the others, because the Gestapo was an excellent organization and he was a confused, underfinanced, frightened man alone in an enemy land.

His feelings were extremely intense. He was crying, and amazed at his own tears. It was as if she was just as wonderful and alive as she had been when their sun shone.

Then he snapped back, aware that he was not sitting in a café listening to old Jacques Reynard relate the manner of her death. Werner Roetter's triumph.

He told me that he had been friendly with the Gestapo chief—in a distant way. They had strolled together along the waterfront while Will knew that Roetter's underlings were boring holes in his lover's teeth. The strategy was to break her by disfiguring her.

After the war Werner Roetter joined West German intelligence and had a fine career. A sudden heart attack took him in 1977, and Will had sent a note to his wife, Hildegard. From time to time over the years they'd exchanged Christmas cards. "Why not? You get tired of hate, and Sophie is dead."

My God, I'm glad I've never fought in a war.

The sun in wartime, the songs of the birds, the rattle of children's shoes on the cobblestones, sudden rain, it all came back to him.

I don't think that he ever truly forgot Sophie, and I feel sure that she was his only real love.

He remembered that first time in the ship as a confrontation with deep personal truths. "I recalled the way a forty-five feels in your hand, kind of ugly and kind of beautiful at the same time. Then you fire it and the top of a man's head flies off. Against the red blood the brains look white, and his skullcap and hair make a slap when they hit the wall. His arms fly akimbo and he drops. The face of a man suddenly dead captures all the sweetness life offers—if the bastard didn't suffer."

His friend Reynard told him that Sophie tucked in her chin before they hauled up the rope. Even at the end she was trying to live, hoping against hope that the noose would slip and give her a few more minutes.

It was like Will to have kept up with Sophie's murderer but to have lost track of the man who tried to save her. Will claimed that he'd lost track of Jacques, but I discovered that he had been a Resistance hero and had not died until 1983. He was well known in Marseilles.

To see Jacques again Will would of course have had to face the pain of his love.

He told me, "I had the feeling I was being examined, as if my soul was being evaluated."

The room was tiny and hot and it stank, something he had not noticed at first. He described the smell as being a mixture of sulfur and Sophie's perfume.

He began to touch things. It was almost compulsive, as if some part of him was trying to hold reality that way. He ran his fingers along the little seats, the console, the black control stick, the ugly, squinting windows.

And then he saw the boy.

He screamed—finally. I would have done it a long time before. In his surprise he dropped his light, which rolled across the floor, making wild shadows on the walls and ceiling.

But for its dismal glow, now coming from beneath one of the chairs, the room was dark. He tried to fumble for it but he had entered a state of fear so deep that he could not coordinate his actions. He jerked and twisted, then sank to his knees.

He was helpless, sinking down, crouching, his head touching the cool, soft floor. And the being was there before him, a figure no larger than a child, grown in his mind to the proportions of a giant.

From the San Francisco *Chronicle,* July 8, 1947:

DISK SOLUTION COLLAPSES
"Flying Saucer" Find Turns Out to Be a Weather Balloon

A platter-puzzled nation thought it was about to get the answer to the mystery of the "flying disks" yesterday.

A press relations officer at the Roswell Army Air Force Base in New Mexico announced without qualification that the 509th Bomber Group had picked up a flying disk on a nearby ranch last week.

There was immediately much telephoning from the Pentagon in Washington, and then Brigadier General Roger M. Ramey, commanding the Eighth Air Force at Fort Worth, said the object had been identified as the wreckage of a high-altitude weather observation device.

Originally, he said, it consisted of a box-kite and a balloon.

"The wreckage is in my office right now and as far as I can see there is nothing to get excited about," he said.

General Ramey later made a radio broadcast further to deflate the excitement caused by the first announcement.

The device, a star-shaped tinfoil target designed to reflect radar, is incapable of speeds higher than the wind.

The mysterious flying disks, which have been "seen" all over the nation (except Kansas, which is dry), have been described as traveling at speeds up to 1,200 miles an hour.

Chapter Fourteen

The Chronicle of Wilfred Stone

The small figure started to move forward. I could see its shadow coming quickly down toward me. I reared up and, shrieking like an animal, slapped at the thing.

It fell lightly against me and all of a sudden I was holding a dead child in my arms.

He felt almost like nothing. He was only a shadow in my arms, but he was so dead. It seemed to me that I was in the presence of an overwhelming tragedy or sacrifice. This was no "alien" disk, it was a thing of God's and I was holding a dead angel.

I cradled him in my arms. He was amazingly light; I doubt if he weighed more than ten pounds. I turned toward the entrance and started to carry him out. But it was too dark. I had to put him down on the floor and get the flashlight. Going down into the more intimate darkness of the floor I scrabbled around as if I was in my own kitchen hunting for a dropped matchbook in the night. I could feel dust there and the slight indentations made by many steps and sharp heels, and the base of one of the seats stuck down with glue.

There was such a feeling of something being alive in that room that I was almost unable to remain there when I finally grasped my flashlight. I shook it and got some dim light out of the stubborn battery.

I shone it into the dead face. There was an absolutely immediate and stunning sense of recognition.

He was—I remembered him.

I was confused. What did these reactions mean? I could not understand them and decided that they must stem from the sheer strangeness of the situation. Obviously this being could not be familiar to me—not him. At that time I never imagined I'd seen the aliens before. Never dreamed it.

In fact this *specific being* had carried me in his arms in 1916, and now had given up his life for me and for mankind. I did not understand this until quite recently.

Roswell was playacting of the most serious kind. The crash was intentional, the deaths were intentional—and it was all done to present our deepest souls with a clear choice.

I am sorry to say that we chose fear.

The being's skin was as white as chalk, his lips were thin and his nose was small. His eyes were sunken into his head, black pools. The most notable thing about him was that his head was large, almost grotesquely so. Had I seen him on a streetcorner I would have assumed that he was a child with water on the brain.

But he was beautiful. Incredibly beautiful. His skin shone in the light, as delicate, as pure as the wings of a moth. Beside him I was big and ugly and coarse. My hand came up and I felt the wonder that a dog must feel close to the thin and glowing skin of his master.

He smelled of sulfur I thought at first, but then I noticed something else familiar about the odor.

In the terror of his death he had soiled himself. If you have never been in war that might surprise you. But I have seen situations where every man present has done it.

What was he? I cradled him and felt again that he was as light as a cloud. Had he been alive I wouldn't have been surprised to see him turn into a gas, or just disappear. I carried him through the strange central area, slipping across the curved black floor as I hurried toward the light of the familiar sky.

I pushed my way out through the shredded paper room and stepped into the welcoming familiarity of the desert.

The light made me squint, but as my eyes got used to it I was shocked to my depths by what I saw. There were people here, about a dozen of them, sitting around smoking and chatting about the disk. Hesseltine darted around among them like a nervous fly.

Cradling the body I turned away from the bland, staring faces. It seemed to me that I was protecting something sacred.

"Get them out of here!"

"They won't move! They're from the University of Pennsylvania, and—"

"We're out here in the middle of nowhere and we might as well be in a bus station." I glared at the obstinate, curious people. They seemed ugly, vicious, as if they were heartlessly intruding on my private grief. "Get out of here or I'll have you arrested!"

They stirred a little. "We're archaeologists," one of them said, "we'd like to know the age of this artifact."

The arrogance did it. "Can't you see you're not wanted here!" I was actually screaming. "This is a restricted zone! It's against the law for you to be here."

"Maybe we need a new law," one of them said.

"The hell we do, we need new people, if you're any example!" They were the enemy.

"I think our Congressmen are going to hear about this."

"Draw your gun, Hesseltine."

"Look, I—"

"Draw the goddamn weapon!"

"I haven't got a gun. Sorry. We didn't have armory orders."

I stared at the civilians. "You're moving out. Or I'm filing charges of spying with treasonous intent." This seemed to make them uneasy.

Long sun was shining on my burden, a perfect child in a silver suit, the most beautiful person I had ever seen. If God's angels must meet death, then surely they looked like this.

The ground quaked and rolled. Then somebody was pulling at my shoulder. "Mr. Stone!"

I realized that I had fallen forward into Hesseltine's arms. The little being was between us. Hesseltine took him and laid him beneath the shadow of his craft.

Seeing this the civilians grew visibly uneasy. They began moving away in uncertain little clumps.

"My God, that thing is ugly."

I looked down at it, confused by Hesseltine's comment. My heart was full of tenderness, reproach rising in my voice. And then I saw it in the light of the setting sun.

How I could *ever* have viewed this thing as beautiful I did not know. It was worse than ugly, it was something from the depths of hell.

The skin was like wet, white paper. The eyes were black slits, the nose as sharp as a blade. Even in death the lips seemed to be twisted into a sneer.

I became aware that the thing had leaked fluid all over my bare arms. I wiped them, trying to get it off.

Quite abruptly, his face completely expressionless, Hesseltine leaned forward at the waist and vomited. When he straightened up he commented only that he hadn't eaten all day.

For the first time I realized that it was late, and I had entered the disk early in the morning. "What time is it?"

"Six-twenty."

"How can that be?"

"Well, you were in there all day."

I was astonished, and then angry. "Why didn't you come in and get me!"

His face hardened. He swallowed. There was a mirthless laugh. "I must have asked you to come out fifty times—"

"And I never answered and you—"

"You told me and told me to leave you alone! And frankly I didn't like your tone. I'm an officer and I expect the same minimal respect from civilians that I get from the enlisted men. And that stands even if you are some kind of goon from CIG."

"I didn't say a word to you. And I was only in there ten minutes at most."

He turned away. I watched him moving in the pale light, looked toward the civilians now bunched in nervous little knots, at the enlisted men leaning up against the truck that had arrived during the day.

"Hesseltine." I drew him a short distance into the desert, out of the others' hearing. "Let's try to talk coherently about this."

"Sure. Coherently. I'll make a note of that."

"Listen, we're out here alone with this thing, and I think we ought to at least try to be on the same side. You're Air Force and I'm not and that makes me suspect. I realize that and I accept it. But you've got to work with me because I'm who the President sent down here."

"I can't be faulted for my performance, if that's what you're driving at."

How was I going to reach him? "You've performed excellently. You're a top man in a crack outfit and it shows."

157

"Well, good."

"Look, I don't know what the hell happened here today. It *felt like* I was in there ten minutes scouting around and bringing out that body. End of story."

"You didn't talk to me?"

"Not to my knowledge."

He lit a cigarette, took a long puff and faced into the sunset. "You were in there for approximately nine hours and we spoke every fifteen or twenty minutes. You refused water and food and threatened me with arrest if I entered the disk."

The young man stood with his feet apart, wearing his lightweight summer uniform, his cigarette between his fingers and an expression of hatred on his face. During his day at the door of the disk, he had come to dislike me intensely.

"It's obvious that there's a lot more going on here than we can as yet even begin to understand. We need to proceed with ultimate caution."

"I just don't want to hear any more threats from you."

"Lieutenant, just scratch them from the record. I don't remember them. As far as I'm concerned they won't happen again."

He had stopped listening to me and was watching the desert. I followed his eyes. There was a light out there, winking on and off, moving slowly closer. It seemed to drift first to the left and then the right, then disappear for a few moments, only to pop up closer.

Hesseltine seemed transfixed.

"Hesseltine?"

"Yeah."

"Shouldn't we take some steps?"

"Oh, yeah." He trotted over to the site. "Okay, guys, get ready for chow. We'll be doing guard duty two by two all night so they'll have sent a couple of vats of java. Chow's from the officer's mess if you can handle food that good."

The light was boring down on us, glaring malevolently through the evening.

Fear literally rolled over me, transforming me in an instant from a competent if slightly uneasy CIG officer into a terrified little boy.

One moment I was standing there and the next I was racing through the underbrush. I had no clear thoughts. I just wanted to get away from that light. I was drowning in the ocean of desert.

The light was boring into my back, I could feel it. Terrible, as if it was cutting right through to my soul. It was huge behind me now, and I could hear it snarling and grinding and roaring as it came down upon us like a runaway train from the beyond.

And then it rumbled past me, an ordinary ten-ton army truck.

I tried to change my wild flight into more of a trot, but everybody had seen me capering in the headlights. The men looked at me as I strode into the light of their gasoline lanterns. I tried to manage a dignified appearance.

My obvious vulnerability must have been reassuring to Hesseltine, because he seemed less inclined to hostility. "We figured you'd seen a snake," he said.

"No. I thought—"

"That they were coming to get back their own? Not yet. It was only the supply wagon. Since we're obviously staying the night."

"Good thinking," I muttered.

The arrival of another truck meant that we could finally strip the area of unwanted civilians. Hesseltine's men had efficiently gotten identification from all of them. I put the sheet of names and addresses in my briefcase.

As soon as the food and field kitchen were unloaded the civilians, docile from an afternoon's barrage of threats, were put aboard the trucks for the trip back to their base camp near Lincoln.

I intend now to confess everything that happened on that hot July evening. A Wednesday night my yellow diary tells me. It says, "Stars. A late moon. Toward morning clouds racing from the south. Didn't drop below seventy-five."

That is all it says, just those few words to describe the night on which my soul was wrapped with chains.

Some were chains of love. And some were chains of death.

Chapter Fifteen

The Chronicle of Wilfred Stone

The trucks pulled out at seven-thirty, and I made a note to address the issue of FBI coverage on the civilian witnesses in my next contact with Hillenkoetter.

The civilians took all the color and chatter with them when they left. The atmosphere of the camp became charged with order.

Airmen talked quietly together, busying themselves with tent erection and food preparation. Soon the smell of spaghetti and meatballs filled the camp.

Once the sun set an impenetrable darkness seemed to rise up out of the land itself. But for the interior of a cave, I had never been in a place so dark. The moon was past its last quarter and not due up until after midnight, so there was nothing but starlight and the gas lanterns of the camp.

The evening star was Mercury, and I found that I could make it out quite easily on the western horizon until nearly nine o'clock. It's light was a pure, heartbreaking green. When it finally followed the sun it carried with it our last link to the day.

The disk reflected the yellow-white light of the lanterns, all except the tear in its side, which was absolutely black.

The meal was served off the back of the field kitchen by the cooks. It would have been nice to have some beer, but only ice tea and Cokes were offered. I set myself up in front of my tent and dug into my rations. Hesseltine followed me. He pulled his camp stool over and sat down.

"Look, I'm sorry about earlier. It was a rough day."

"Forget it. Instantly. You were out there for nine hours waiting for me, for God's sake. You had every right to be angry."

We ate in silence, two men in a wavering pool of light. "We're in radio contact every half hour," he said.

I watched an enormous moth lurch into view. It was so big I thought at first that it was a bat. It seemed like something from a time of giants.

The smell of the alien bodies drifted through the camp. I lit a cigarette, defending myself. "When'll they be bagged up?"

"They are, unfortunately. But they need cold storage. Even rubberized canvas can only hold in so much stink." Hesseltine gazed at the disk. "You sure you don't know what happened in there?"

"I haven't got the faintest idea."

"You're sure you weren't knocked out? But then how the hell did you keep answering me. I mean, we talked."

"I can account for ten minutes, maybe fifteen."

Something howled out on the desert. As it died away it was answered by the low, uneasy laughter of the men. "Coyote," Hesseltine shouted.

One of the noncoms wailed the animal a reply.

"The men'd be more comfortable out here if there was more of a moon," Hesseltine said.

"All we have to do is wait it out until morning, then we'll get transport instructions from Los Alamos."

"Probably gonna be a long time to morning."

The cooks had brought a portable radio, and they set it up in the middle of the camp. At nine-fifteen a program called *Musical Showcase* was broadcast from KGFL in Roswell.

The men sat around smoking and talking softly while Texas Joe Turner's voice echoed into the desert night:

> *Love, oh, careless love,*
> *You see what careless love has done to me. . . .*

As one grows older even the hardest parts of the past acquire beauty. Days I tried to forget now return to me transformed, Algiers balanced in evening light, the rains of winter sweeping old Marseilles, that black camp night with the disk and the bodies.

The last of evening slipped into the sky and Hesseltine went to his own tent. I hadn't brought my bags, not so much as a razor, so there was little I could do but lie back on my cot. When I'd set out this morning, I had no idea that I wasn't going to come back tonight.

I was still suffering from the lack of depth in our planning. What I had to do was to concentrate on my immediate objective, which was not to let the bodies and the disk out of my sight until they were safely inside a facility controlled by the Central Intelligence Group. I could only trust that Sally was preparing that facility and sending me the transport I needed to reach it with the disk.

I coughed, realizing that my mouth was dry and filthy with soot from the chain-smoking I'd been doing since I got out of the craft. In those days I don't think there were filter cigarettes. If there were, they certainly didn't work the same way they do now. I recall cigarettes that could really give you a hit. It was wonderful to smoke in complete innocence, unaware of the dangers and oblivious to the discomfort of the few nonsmokers. I don't think that we could have made it through World War Two without cigarettes. Smoking was practically the only relief.

I gave Sophie a Pall Mall when I first met her, and she threw herself back in her chair, making great clouds of smoke and laughing. "Do not smoke any more of these," she announced. "Cigarettes this good can be traded for lives."

The radio station went off the air at ten-thirty and the camp settled down. It was reassuring that there would be sentries on duty through the night. I could not have slept at all without that.

It seemed to me that I'd just closed my eyes when I suddenly found myself wide awake. It was extremely quiet. I sat up on the cot. The air in my tent was thick and stifling. I was thirsty. My head was pounding.

A child was standing in my doorway.

I practically leaped through the back of the tent.

Then he was gone. I took a couple of deep breaths. Hallucination? Walking corpse? I was prepared to believe anything.

I told myself that I must have been having a nightmare which had mixed with some real event, perhaps a sentry passing my tent.

I felt for my shoes, found them and carefully knocked them against the ground as Hesseltine had advised. Scorpions were a constant problem in the desert. I put them on and stepped into the night, guiding myself with my flashlight. By the radium dial on my watch it was three-fifteen A.M. I was at once exhausted and unable to sleep.

I went to the field kitchen to try to find some water. There was a big canvas bag sweating on the side of the truck. I drank from the aluminum cup attached. The water was on the warm side and tasted strongly of the rubberized canvas of the bag. I almost gagged, thinking of the rubberized stink of the body bags that held the aliens.

The moon was now a yellow sickle on the eastern horizon. Despite its presence the desert sky was so clear that I could see the firmament in detail. The Milky Way stretched from horizon to horizon. Color was clearly distinguishable among the stars.

As I watched I began to notice a curious phenomenon. One by one the stars were winking out. Now what did that mean? As I looked I discerned a line almost halfway across the sky. Ahead of that line there were stars. Behind it, none. And it was moving in our direction.

I assumed that it was a cloud. It had been a clear night. Where there had been a breeze earlier it was now still. I watched the cloud continuing to cover the stars. The night was also extraordinarily quiet, so quiet that I could hear the hiss of the match as a sentry lit a cigarette all the way on the other side of the compound.

In the brief glow of his match I saw a large owl standing right behind the man. I was quite surprised. I'd not been aware that owls got that big, nor that they walked on the ground. "Hey," I said softly in his direction. "Look behind you."

He pulled out his flashlight and turned around. The bird's eyes shone. It didn't move or blink. Fascinated, I began walking closer. I'd forgotten all about the disk.

We kept it in our beams as we walked forward. One moment it would look like an owl and then next there would be the flash of something else. The sentry was beginning to breathe hard.

"It's an owl," I said. My voice sounded thick, as if the two of us were shut together in a closet.

"No, sir."

The creature made an abrupt move, causing the sentry to jerk back. His light tumbled away into the brush.

I gasped in a breath and forced myself to a state of control. I told the sentry to be calm.

The next instant there was an echoing shriek above us. I looked up into absolute blackness. There was nothing, not a star, not a glimmer of reflected light, not a cloud.

Then from high, high up there came pitiful cries.

"What the hell is that?"

There was no reply. I shined my light around.

No sentry. No owl.

The dark was clutching at me. I turned around, thinking to go back to the camp and get the others.

I heard something moving in front of me, as if the creature we'd had in our lights was coming closer. When I turned back I saw nothing.

Events began unfolding with the mysterious grace of tragedy. I heard the sentry babbling and whining—but he was close now.

He kept saying something—"Oh, no, oh, no"—over and over.

As his voice died to whimpers I tried to call for help.

I felt a curious, soft, deep blow to my belly and wound up on my back on the ground. I was winded and my flashlight was gone.

When I tried to sit up I felt strong hands against my shoulders.

"Oh, God."

"Why do you call on your gods? We're the only ones here." The voice was swift and breathless and tough and far from human.

"We have the bodies," I said. "We can give you the bodies."

The reply was a snicker, then another sentence also delivered in that curiously breathless, mechanical tone: "We're gonna take you for a ride."

I remember next a wild jumble of dark images: cactuses, shrubs, running animals, then grass and sheep and suddenly rushing up a mountainside and flying off into midair. I was kicking and grabbing at things, totally disoriented.

And then I was high in the sky. As I passed over the summit of a mountain I saw the twinkling lights of a city arrayed before me. It was beauty so extreme that I wanted to somehow link myself to it, to melt into it.

When I was a boy I used to lie on the roof of our house watching the sunset, and sometimes when it was orange and red beyond the hills, I would wish that I could somehow let the beauty fill every molecule of my being.

I was free in the empty sky, slipping like a night bird through the air. Before me were those living diamond lights. There was something so wonderfully perfect about it, so very right that it seemed like a part of heaven. Beyond the vision but emerging from it there was a sense of what I can best describe as something a religious person might call purity.

I went down close to the silent streets, passing the Plains Theatre with its darkened marquee for *Cheyenne,* looking into the window of a shop called Mode O'Day. Even the mannequins in their frocks seemed incredibly beautiful.

And then the street ends and there are great hangars around me and lights buzzing with june bugs and moths and the huge planes of the 509th with their atomic babies in their bellies and I am rolling, floating, swimming in the air.

I saw a soldier walking along the tarmac with a rifle slung on his shoulder. Closer and closer I drifted, until I was just above him. I grabbed the hat off his head.

He looked up but I was pulled into the sky before he could see me. Then he searched the empty tarmac around him. "Well, shit," came his echoing shout.

I had that hat clasped in my hand and no intention of letting go. It was damned important and I knew it. If this fantastic thing was really happening the hat would be proof. I watched the world race and swoop past. There was a measure of control, and I found that I could to a degree influence my height and direction by twisting and turning.

I was feeling grand and alone in the sky when I turned onto my back and found myself face to face with a wall of dull gray metal. It looked like the same substance as the disk.

The thing must have been there all along. But how could it have been so silent, so stealthy? The base had obviously failed to detect its presence and it was huge, far larger than the little ship that had crashed.

A question flashed through my mind: Why hadn't they simply picked up their machine? They must have the means to do practically anything.

The metal was no more than two feet away from me. I stretched out my hand but it moved away, remaining an inch or so out of reach.

I heard a buzzing in my head. It got rapidly so loud that it hurt. Involuntarily I clapped my hands to my temples but the sound was inside. I couldn't protect myself from it. It began to shriek like a desperately straining motor.

I dropped about fifteen feet. Then the buzzing got low and I felt as if I was swimming in butter. There was a smell like burning rubber.

Was this magnificent device breaking down the moment I thought it invincible?

I fell another thirty feet, a truly sickening lurch. I tried to turn over, to see how close I was to the ground. No luck. Couldn't do it. The burning rubber smell was strong now. A dusting of what appeared to be warm ash was drifting down onto me from above. The buzzing changed to a noise like continuously shattering glass, a crashing that went on and on and on.

Again I fell, this time it seemed for miles. My muscles knotted against the feeling that the land was going to slam into my back any second. I kicked and screamed and grabbed air. So much for self-control.

Then I stopped falling. It was so abrupt it hurt. I drifted a little in one direction and then another. Throwing myself from side to side I tried to turn over, somehow to get my bearings. More of the ash sifted down.

I seemed to stabilize. Better. Now I was regaining a measure of stability, even moving forward. They must have fixed it, thank the good Lord.

It was like the bottom dropped out of the world. Again I raced downward, the wind screaming in my ears. Above me I saw all the stars of the sky.

The disk was gone! They'd left me here in midair and I was dying.

Crying, my throat aching with grief and dread, beyond panic, I fell to my final end.

Then I realized that I wasn't moving anymore. It took a long moment to understand that the absolute lack of motion meant that I had landed.

I felt around beside me. Dirt. Weeds. I was on the ground! I sat up. Incredible. Out in the middle of the desert. When I stood up I found that I was pretty weak at the knee, but otherwise I seemed well enough.

Very suddenly a wave of nausea overwhelmed me. I staggered, but it subsided without developing into anything.

I took stock of myself. Physically undamaged. Badly shaken, though. Alone in the middle of nowhere. The stars above me, the empty land around—I could be hundreds of miles from the camp.

There was little point in walking. In this darkness it might even be dangerous. I thought I might at least try to get my bearings, though, and began trying to locate Polaris. First I searched the sky before me. Then I turned carefully around, making certain that I was in exactly the opposite position.

I found myself staring at the camp, which was ten yards away.

For a moment I thought it might be a mirage. Then I walked forward. No, it was quite real.

One of our sentries challenged me.

"Wilfred Stone."

"Oh. Couldn't sleep?"

I walked into the gleam of his flashlight. I fought back my panic, my wild disorientation. "Actually, I was thirsty, but I got a little sidetracked." My voice shuddered toward a calm I did not feel.

"I wouldn't leave the perimeter again. We've got a guy lost already."

"Really?" It was as if cold fingers were compressing my heart.

"A PFC name of Flaherty. Sentry on the last watch. Nobody can find him."

I remembered him screaming in the sky. But I—hadn't that all been a nightmare? I'd been getting some water, then—

I realized I was carrying an overseas cap. I held it up, looking stupidly at it. The sentry looked at it too. "You find that in the desert?"

What could I say? "In the desert." The lie was essential, and not just to protect my reputation. It defended my sanity.

He took the cap, looked at the name in the band. "It's his all right," he said. He trotted off toward Hesseltine's tent, which was lit and active, no doubt because of the missing man.

I walked into the center of the group of tents and vehicles. The disk still glowed in the lantern light.

I at last understood that I wasn't looking at an accidental crash.

This disk hadn't crashed at all. It had been put here, and the bodies along with it.

It was bait. And we had taken it, and were wriggling on the line.

In some murky place our struggles must be ringing a bell. Somebody had heard the sound and grasped the line and set the hook.

And now they were going to reel us in.

TRANSCRIPT: INTERROGATION OF ROBERT UNGAR
LOCATION: ROSWELL ARMY AIR FORCE BASE, BRIG
INTERROGATOR: JOSEPH P. ROSE, SPECIAL OFFICER,
  CENTRAL INTELLIGENCE GROUP

1ST INTERROGATION SESSION

JPR: Let's get names clear. You are Robert Ungar?
RU: Bob.
JPR: I should call you Bob?
RU: I've been Bob so long I ain't gonna hear you, you say Robert.
JPR: Bob. Age forty-seven?
RU: Yes, that is my age. Sir, why have I been brought here?
JPR: Informally. A few questions.
RU: This is a room with barred windows. I would like to know if
   there are charges against me.
JPR: Well?
RU: Because I am going home if there ain't. I can go home. That's
   the law.
JPR: You are in a special federal compound.
RU: I am returning home.
JPR: Yes, that's right. And so please before you go answer me a
   couple of questions.
RU: No! Hell, no!
JPR: For your country, sir.
RU: Oh, Lord.
JPR: Did these alien beings say anything to you?
RU: I—I—they—who?
JPR: What did you see?
RU: There was a big blast in the sky the night of the second. There
   had been a hell of a thunderstorm out in the desert. Strange. We
   looked at it. The lightning was striking the same places over and
   over again. I was worried my sheep was gonna bunch against a
   fence. I went out there first thing in the mornin' and my daughter
   and son and I picked up a lot of junk. We thought it was a crashed
   plane so we told the sheriff—

JPR: Right away?

RU: Naw. A few days, maybe—when I got to town. Ain't got the telephone out there.

JPR: Did you see any of these alien beings?

RU: What the hell are you asking me? I saw some wreckage that a military officer told me was from a spaceship. I didn't see none of these beings you talk about.

JPR: But you stated to the papers that you had seen this crashed disk. But in fact you saw no such thing.

RU: I saw what I said! Now look, are you trying to twist my words, or something? I didn't see no alien beings, sir. I saw what I said I saw.

MR. ROSE CONCLUDED THE FIRST INTERROGATION SESSION. THE PRISONER WAS KEPT IN ISOLATION UNDER CLOSE GUARD FOR TWENTY-FOUR HOURS.

2ND INTERROGATION SESSION

JPR: Good morning, Bob.

RU: I have committed no crime but I can't even get to a telephone. I want a lawyer now.

JPR: Let's just finish these couple of questions and you can go.

RU: Go home?

JPR: Yes, sir.

RU: Well, what is it now? I still ain't done anything. They had me in a cell in a brig. They fed me pancakes and water and coffee.

JPR: Would you like a cigarette?

RU: I sure would. What are those?

JPR: Medallions. A fine cigarette.

RU: [Lights up.] It tastes like hot air.

JPR: Sir, you are going to have to change your story for the press. You are going to have to tell the truth.

RU: I did that! I ain't never done nothing else in my life, fella!

JPR: We know that it's fun to get in the papers with a big story. But you have to tell the truth.

RU: The whole story was from them officers! The base wrote it! I am hardly even mentioned.

JPR: You have to tell the truth. And the truth is you found a weather balloon and pretended it was a flying disk, and you did that for the fun of gaining publicity.

RU: Oh, Lord. You are twisting—changing—why don't you put them officers in jail?

JPR: We have to do this. They have to say this. For the country, Bob. For America.

RU: (Long silence.)

JPR: How many kids do you have?

RU: Two living at home and one married up in Albuquerque.

JPR: Kids are a beautiful thing. Do you hunt and fish with your boy?

RU: And with my girls. My oldest is an excellent shot.

JPR: Yes. Now, what you are going to do is to tell the papers that you found the weather balloon and called it a flying disk as a practical joke.

RU: I told the truth!

MR. ROSE CONCLUDED THE SECOND INTERROGATION SESSION. THE PRISONER WAS KEPT IN ISOLATION UNDER CLOSE GUARD FOR ANOTHER TWENTY-FOUR HOURS. THE PRISONER WAS STRIPPED AND THE FURNITURE WAS REMOVED FROM THE ISOLATION CELL. THE PRISONER WAS GIVEN ONLY WATER.

3RD INTERROGATION SESSION

JPR: Good morning, Bob.

RU: I am in a lot of trouble.

JPR: You certainly are. Your country needs your help and you aren't helping. America needs you and you are saying, "No, not me, America. I am sticking by my story so I will look good."

RU: How can I get myself out of this mess?

JPR: Say what we need you to say. You were telling a tall story. There was no flying disk. Only a weather balloon.

RU: The officers said it! I didn't! Make them say the truth!

JPR: They gave a press conference in Fort Worth with the commanding general of the Eighth Air Force, and the officer that said it, Major Gray, he has taken it back. He is doing this for America. Because he loves his country even more than his own reputation.

RU: I love my country, but what am I doing in a cell without even my clothes! This is not what I call America.

JPR: But you love your country.

RU: I sure do.

JPR: Well, that's progress.

MR. ROSE CONCLUDED THE THIRD INTERROGATION SESSION. THE PRISONER WAS RETURNED TO CLOSE SECURITY, BUT HE WAS ALLOWED A WALK IN ROSWELL IN THE COMPANY OF OFFICERS. HE WAS FED A LARGE MEAL AND ALLOWED TO SLEEP IN A BED IN A ROOM IN THE VISITING OFFICER'S BILLET.

4TH INTERROGATION SESSION

JPR: Good morning, Bob.

RU: Hiya. I want to go home. Are there any charges against me?

JPR: You can help your country. We cannot let it be known that this disk is real. We are just not ready.

RU: *Why not!*

JPR: Look, Bob. I hesitate even to tell you, but I will. I will tell you as long as you promise me on your honor—and I know how important that is to you—promise me that you will go to your grave with this secret.

RU: Yes, sir, I will do that.

JPR: Well, the truth is that we have reason to believe that these aliens have stolen a number of people. Men, women, children.

RU: Oh, my Lord.

JPR: We cannot allow the people to know this until we can defend ourselves. Bob, America is being invaded by an alien force. And they are doing strange, awful things that we do not understand. That is what is secret.

172

RU: May the Lord be with us.

JPR: I agree. America has a need for you to say it's a weather balloon, so the people won't panic. For the sake of the country. Uncle Sam needs you.

RU: Not to lie, he don't.

JPR: Oh, Bob. There must be something.

RU: I don't lie. I ain't never done it.

JPR: Then what will you say?

RU: I want to help my country. Damn right I do. But not with a lie. I found what I found and I know it. I will say that I am sorry the whole thing happened. I'll say that and you can make it look like what you want.

JPR: I have your word of honor? You will say in a press conference we call that you are sorry you ever reported you'd found this? And we will imply that you were wrong about what you found.

RU: I will not lie, but I cannot stop you from doing it if that is what you feel you gotta do.

JPR: We all have to make sacrifices. You say you are sorry in a press conference and we will handle the rest.

From the Roswell *Daily Record,* August 1, 1947:

HARASSED RANCHER WHO LOCATED "SAUCER" SORRY HE TOLD ABOUT IT

Robert Ungar, 47, Lincoln County rancher living 30 miles southeast of Maricopa today told his story of finding what the Army at first described as a flying disk, but the publicity which attended his find caused him to add that if he ever found anything else short of a bomb he sure wasn't going to say anything about it.

Ungar related that he and an 8-year-old son Bob Jr. were about 7 or 8 miles from the ranch house of J. H. Foster, which he operates, when they came upon a large area of bright wreckage made up of rubber strips, tinfoil, a rather tough paper and sticks.

On July 3 he, his son, Bob Jr., and daughter, Mary, age 12, went back to the spot and gathered up quite a bit of the debris. There was no sign of any metal in the area which might have been used for an engine and no sign of propellers of any kind, although at least one paper fin had been glued to some of the tinfoil.

There were no words to be found anywhere on the instrument, although there were letters on some of the parts. Considerable Scotch tape and some tape with flowers printed on it had been used in the construction. Ungar said that he had previously found two weather observation balloons on the ranch, but that what he found this time did not in any way resemble either of these. "I am sure what I found was not any weather observation balloon," he said. "but if I find anything else besides a bomb they are going to have a hard time getting me to say anything about it."

Chapter Sixteen

I had been eager to follow up on the story of Corporal Jim Collins. What had happened to him? Had he married Kathy? And what of their children?

Will agreed that we might find out a great deal if we contacted them. I wondered, for example, why the visitors had been so intent that he marry Kathy, and what had been meant when they said that the first three children out of the marriage would be theirs.

Like everything the visitors seem to do, what happened that night at Fort Bliss had significance on many different levels.

Fortunately it wasn't hard to locate Jim and Kathy. Because of his visitor contact, Jim has been quietly monitored by the government for most of his life.

The Collinses live in Everly, New Jersey, a small town near the Pennsylvania border. As I drove up from Maryland I expected to enter a devastation of refineries. I found farms and trees budding with spring, and a town of big old houses and wide porches.

Jim is now sixty-one, Kathy sixty.

They live in one of the big houses, and there is a swing on their wide porch. Kathy cultivates a wonderful garden and they make their own wine from the grapes grown on an arbor in the back. On the walls of their living room are large framed photographs of their children, and they have a friendly old dog named Horace. I found it all very annoying.

They were at first extremely suspicious of me. I gave them the cover story that Will had recommended, that I was a new caseworker with the Agency and I just wanted to reconfirm some details. Given what I already knew about them, having read Jim's hypnosis and all the secret memoranda about the incident at Fort Bliss, I was entirely convincing.

Once they were sure that I was genuine, they became warm, friendly and open.

The Jim Collins who had never heard of any aliens and thought that flying saucers were "crazy" was transformed into a knowledgeable individual with considerable information about the visitors. His wife claimed ongoing contact, and suggested that some of their children were involved.

What I wanted to know was whether or not Kathy had ever given a baby to the visitors. When I asked her, she grew furtive.

I didn't quite understand, then. But I do now.

Although shocked by my question, Jim and Kathy were fascinated that I wanted to know more about their personal relationship with the visitors. In all the years that they had been in contact with MAJIC, the secret group that controls human/alien affairs, they had never once been interviewed about this aspect. All of the other interviews had centered around the design and function of devices Jim had seen and touched. When he was lifted by the blue light, did he feel a tingling sensation? How hard had it been to insert the needles into the heads of his fellow soldiers? That sort of thing. MAJIC wanted to know how things worked, not what was being done with them.

Typical shortsightedness, in my opinion. The problem with keeping things like this secret is that they are removed from the free market of ideas, and understanding proceeds at a much slower pace.

I wanted to concentrate on Kathy's childbearing years. Why would the visitors *want* human children?

I went to Everly expecting answers to some very weighty questions.

I got Jim and Kathy. Even though their happy marriage and successful lives put me out a bit, I also found them a winning, charming couple. They were intelligent and full of humor.

And they told me this story.

Jim knew exactly what he wanted to do when his squad was granted compassionate leave just after the disappearance of Sweet Charlie.

Obedient to the subliminal instructions of the others he rushed straight into the arms of Katherine O'Mally.

He took the train to New Jersey with the explicit intention of asking Kathy to marry him. Since the night he'd fallen in love he'd been writing her a letter every couple of days.

By the time he arrived home he had just three days left before he had to report to his new unit in Pennsylvania.

He beat his most recent letters, so nobody knew he was coming. His own home was dark when the night train let him off. He went to Kathy's house and stood under the porch light nervously twirling his hat in his hands. Finally he gathered the nerve to ring the doorbell.

And there she was, her hair up, her robe fluttering about her, her face shiny with night cream. He gaped, he couldn't help it. She was more beautiful than anybody he had ever seen in his life. She was even more beautiful than she herself had been when he last saw her.

"Oh. My. God. Jim." Her voice was like a touch of air in the summer leaves.

"Hey."

"I'm a mess!"

"Nah."

"J-Jim—oh! Come in, come in!" She swept the door open. "Mom! Dad! Jim is here. Jim is here at home!"

He entered the house, feeling huge. Everything seemed too delicate, chairs that you could sit right through, pictures that would fall off the wall if you so much as brushed them. A vase of white flowers on the hall table might wilt if you breathed your beery breath upon them.

And it was so quiet! He was used to Army places now, green and gray and hard, full of loud guys who didn't know how to talk without dropping "fuckin' " or "cocksucker" at least three times into every sentence.

The flowers were gardenias. He looked hard at them, as if trying to consume them with his eyes. Though he couldn't say it or even think it very clearly, the obscure hurt that filled his heart when their scent reached him was a dirge for all the Army had taken from him.

Uncle Sam had stifled the little bit of poetry in him, but he

177

didn't know that. He only knew that the gardenias were real nice.

There were greetings then, Seamus O'Mally and his wife Angela meeting him halfway down the hall, and the embrace of his pipe-smelling and her Lanvin bodies. Then there was a lot of laughter and Kathy disappeared to put on a new face.

"What about your folks?"

"They—I'll—do you want me to come back later?"

"No, son, but your mom would be glad to see you."

He recalled his own dark front porch. "I think they're at the movies. That's what I think."

"They didn't know you were coming?"

"I just got leave—I guess I got here ahead of my letters."

"Kathy didn't get a letter, she would have been singing the house down."

He laughed nervously. He was no good at these conversations with the parents. All he wanted to do was talk about her. Kathy looks real nice. Kathy smiled when she saw me. Was she surprised!

But he couldn't do that. That would be so incredibly embarrassing. He slid his hands along the tops of his legs. Seamus O'Mally lit his big Kaywoodie.

"I think the Dutch are falling apart in the Far East," he said.

Jim thought vaguely about the little boy who put his finger in the dike. The Dutch were in the Far East? Where? "Yeah," he said, to cover his ignorance.

"The only empire that will survive the war is the British. The sun never sets on the British Empire. Except for India, sadly enough."

"India," Jim said. "Gandhi. He's—I like him." He thought of the little Indian man in the newsreels. Jim knew a good man. "He's got a lot of good things to say."

Seamus O'Mally stared at him, puffing slowly. Angie sipped her coffee, and he had the feeling that he'd just dropped his pants, somehow.

And then all of a sudden here came Kathy. Lord, she was pretty! Her skin was glowing. He'd never seen such a glow. And the smoothness of her skin. He prayed to God to let him touch his lips to her skin and he said God, if you will help me to kiss her lips—

He felt smiles in the air.

She laughed. "Emmeneger's is open till ten now."

"I thought they closed after supper."

"Not anymore. You've been away too long. Everly is a big town now."

"We got a Chevy dealership," Mr. O'Mally said. "Modern times have come to Everly."

"Cab Calloway came to Newark," Kathy said. "I didn't go, but Jane Krebs said he would put his handkerchief to his nose. They weren't supposed to know what he was doing, but they all knew."

"Hi-de-ho," Jim said.

"What was he doing?" asked Mrs. O'Mally.

"He was clearing his nose," her daughter replied.

Jim realized that he was desperate. Never had he had intimate dealings with a girl. Never had he asked a virginal, pure American girl—

His body was now thinking for him. "Let's go to the soda fountain, Kathy."

She smiled. "I'd like to very much, Jim."

"Don't forget your own folks," Mrs. O'Mally called after him.

"I won't, ma'am. We won't be long."

As they passed through the front hall Kathy took one of the gardenias from the vase and put it in her hair.

They went out together, running in order to avoid Seamus O'Mally's sprinkler.

They had been raised in the American middle class with its puritan traditions very much intact. You didn't make advances, let alone kiss a girl, except after a number of dates and a declaration of intent. You never "took advantage" by touching her in intimate places. And certainly you never, ever did that thing.

Kathy and Jim went down to the end of the block, walking in the intoxicating scent of the gardenia.

The odor calmed Jim and made Kathy seem familiar and accessible. They had a choice of walking around a small park or going through it. Jim didn't even ask; he led Kathy into the park. They passed up the first two benches, then found one in a more-or-less secluded corner. It was backed by a hedge, so that it could not be seen from the street. It overlooked the small pond at the center of the park.

"Remember ice-skating," Jim said, "last winter?"

"It seems so long ago."

"My tour of duty is up—"

"Don't say it. I don't want to think about all those months!"

She remembered the strange dream she'd had of him. "I dreamed about you," she said. She did not say how real it had seemed, how she'd waked up thinking she'd really seen him . . .

"I dreamed about you, too. I'm not good at puttin' stuff in letters, though."

"I got your letters."

"What did you think?"

She leaned her head against his shoulder. His hand stole into hers. She squeezed encouragingly and he gave her a kiss on the cheek.

The other fellows' talk about their sexual exploits had amazed him. He would never talk about Kathy, but he wanted her more than ever. He understood his longing more clearly than he would have before his exposure to Army talk.

He remembered the night he had fallen in love with her. It was the same night that Sweet Charlie had disappeared. He'd waken up that morning and realized that he loved the woman who now sat beside him.

"I love you, Kath."

There. It was said and so be it.

"Oh, Jimmy, I love you too."

He felt himself tremble all over and suddenly he had her in his arms and her lips were touching his. Then her lips opened and she let him into the secret contact of her mouth. Never before had he kissed a girl in this manner.

It crossed his mind that he might be going too fast. Dutifully, he broke away. "Sorry."

She sighed. "Last night I had another dream," she said. "I wasn't in my bed, I was somewhere else." She giggled a little. "I don't know if I should tell you this, but in my dream I was naked. Are you ever naked in your dreams?"

He was almost unable to speak his reply. As soon as she had said the word "naked" his body had gone on fire. He had a boner so huge she must see it in his pants, even in the dark. "Y-yeah. I have been."

"A beautiful child came to me in my dream. He was dressed all in white."

A deep and distant chord sounded in Jim's mind. He felt vaguely sick.

"This little boy had a wand. He waved it over me and dust came down on my body. Fairy dust. It was so beautiful and so clear, like it really happened. So I woke up thinking something good was going to happen today."

"Did anything?"

"Anything what?"

"Did anything good happen today?"

She laughed. "You came home."

"Will you do what I said in my letter, Kath?"

"Say it to me, Jimmy."

"Marry me?"

A flush entered her cheeks and her whole body became covered with dampness. This dampness melted certain particles that had been dusted on her in the night, and they released chemicals of subtle concoction, which reacted with her skin.

She began to smell of an ancient and pure essence. Jim could not perceive this odor consciously but it affected his deepest self. He became almost mad with desire.

He kissed her again, this time pushing against her, seeking to drive himself into her. "Oh, Jimmy," she gasped. "Jimmy, I will!"

Kathy was frantic. She'd never felt like this before. She knew he had an erection. It took an intense effort not to reach out, to grasp it as if she was grabbing a lifeline. The earth seemed to be heaving beneath the bench, the grass, the hedges, and the trees to be sighing with their passion.

Then she had an absolutely delicious, crazy idea. It would let her behold him, drink in the nakedness of him, at least that. "Let's go swimming in the pond," she whispered. And she thought: I'm crazy. I have gone crazy.

He shuddered and she could not help brushing her wrist against him. Even that slight touch made him recoil as if slapped. He was so hard in there! They really got *very* hard!

"We can't do that. It's—"

"I did it years ago."

"But we're not kids anymore." He crossed his legs.

She planted a kiss on his lips. For a moment he resisted, then he could not resist. She was mysterious wine and she made him drunk with her sweetness.

"We can undress in the hedge," he said.

He could hardly believe what was happening. She was as hot as he was. Hotter. He got up, stiff-legged, and moved into the hedge behind the bench.

Should he undress her? And what if they got caught. It wasn't even ten. People might come through the park. She turned away from him and dropped her head, presenting him the zipper of her blue frock.

He unzipped it and it fell away from her pale skin, and from the workings of her brassiere. "Unhook it," she whispered. In the dark he couldn't see. He'd never encountered a hook and eye before.

She reached back and unhooked it and it all fell away and suddenly she was naked above her waist. She turned around. He was awed, she could not be this beautiful. It was as if the very glow of life came out of her skin. She smelled like a rose, an angel, a baby. He drew near to her, hovering like a hawk above the leaping body of the mouse.

She laughed a little. "These are buttons!" She was touching his pants.

"GI issue. No zippers when buttons will do."

She did not fumble with them. Her hands were deft. He almost collapsed when she pressed her fingers against him to gain purchase on the buttons. Rockets of sheer delight shot from the places where her fingers were in contact with him. She was touching it! Touching it!

And then his pants were open. She unhooked his belt and they dropped to the ground. "Even the underpants are olive-drab." She giggled.

"They look clean longer."

"Look!" She knelt before him and kissed him, a little peck on the GI-issue boxers. But in just the right place. "Come on, be brave," she said, "gentlemen first."

A part of her told her quite calmly and rationally that she had gone mad. She was undressing a man in a public park! It could not be this way. She wasn't doing this. Not Katherine O'Mally, recently vice-president of the senior class at Our Lady of Sorrows. No, not Katherine O'Mally, the snow-pure daughter of Seamus and Angela O'Mally of Dexter Street in Everly, New Jersey. She had gotten her embossed Sunday missal for being the best religion student, and she was president of Sodality.

She imagined her next confession, "Bless me father for I have sinned, it has been one week since my last confession. I committed the mortal sin of lust and went on a naked swim with a boy in Town Pond." What would happen on the other side of the confessional? The sound of poor Father Dougherty having a heart attack?

With a wild laugh that was so strange it scared her a little she pulled Jimmy's drawers down. His penis caught in the elastic and got tangled. Never mind. She grasped the shaft and pulled it free. Then she slipped the pants down and there he was just like that.

She knew at last what they looked like, those bulges that appeared in their pants.

"Kath." He was weak at the knees. No girl in his life had ever seen him like this. No man had, not in this state. The night air touching him intensified the feeling of nakedness. She pulled off her dress and panties and stood before him, her hands hesitantly covering breast and pubis. Then she raised her chin and looked him straight in the eye. With a little flourish she dropped her hands to her sides and stood with the palms open in a familiar posture. "Our Lady of Sorrows," she said.

The sharpness of her laughter made him hesitate, but only for a moment. He took off his shirt and held out his arms. She came close and he felt himself tight against her naked flesh.

The night was warm and the world seemed full of a kindness that he had not known about. He kissed her lips and then her cheeks, and then her breasts, crouching and cupping them in his hands. Gently she pressed his shoulders, and he knelt and kissed the soft tangle between her legs. It smelled very strong there. She pressed against him for a moment and he got on his lips the sensation of a warm clam. He drew back, confused. He had no clear idea of what a woman's genitals were like. He didn't quite know what he had contacted hiding there in that thatch of hair. He looked up at her.

"Do you really want to swim?"

"Oh, I don't know. It's so crazy. We're in the *park!*"

He wanted to. He wanted to very badly. "It'll be warm. The water is warm in July."

Hand in hand they stepped through the hedge. The asphalt walk was almost hot against their feet. Jim could feel the stones pressing, tickling. He was aware of his penis bobbing before him. Kathy was too, because she took it in her hand and led him toward the water.

He stumbled. "God, Kath." He was looking around for other people. But the park appeared empty.

Warm or not the water shocked them. The mud of the bottom squirmed up between their toes. They didn't care; their bodies were free. Their secret intoxication took them far beyond their capacity for caution. All the careful repressions of their lives fell away and they were animals in the water.

Jim gave a shout that echoed across the pond, returning flatly from the houses that stood guard on all four sides of the tiny park. The delight in his voice startled people, and one or two porch lights went on.

Kath spread her arms wide and twirled round and round laughing.

More lights went on, and figures came out onto a couple of porches. The O'Mallys, living as they did at the far end of the block, heard nothing.

Jim splashed down into the water and rolled around. It was at its deepest about three feet, so he couldn't exactly hide. Kath fell on top of him and they rolled over and over, each acutely aware of the sexual presence of the other. Jim became knowledgeable about the extraordinary beauty of a woman's skin in the wet and dark. He slipped his hands again and again down her breasts, rubbing the nut-hard nipples with his palms.

They sat in the shallows like two babies playing with each other. They splashed and giggled and squirmed at one another's tickles and most intimate invasions. He came to know by feel the clam within her pudendal thatch, and she stroked the rod of him and hefted his scrotum again and again, playing with his balls, rolling them between her babyfat fingers.

Red light reflected on the pond. First it brought Kath to her senses. She was horrified: There was a radio car at the curb with its lights flashing. A policeman with a flashlight was hurrying along the bank toward them. He was followed by a small crowd of citizens.

They had cavorted their way almost to the middle of the pond. The crowd was going to come between them and their clothes. "It's naked kids," shouted a voice as tight as wire.

That was what collapsed the fairy-fort of their dreams.

They stood up.

"Run, Kath!"

They could not go toward their clothes. There was no choice but to get out of the pond on the far side. Leaping like dolphins they surged from their water, their young limbs carrying them across the pond much faster than the bulging cop and his tow of inquisitors could make it around.

The hedges and shrubs afforded some protection. But they dared not go back in the direction of their clothes lest the garments be discovered before they could put them on.

Kathy was scared but she was also still excited. She was beyond concepts like fear. A creature of the night had emerged from the depths of her soul, an ancient maenad, the mystical being at her core.

Jim was just plain scared. As he ran along, hopping in the thistles and briars, he kept thumping his penis and making little whistles of pain.

"Why are you doing that?"

"Gotta get it down, man! I don't want to go to jail like this!"

They ran then like the wind. They fairly sailed out of the hedges and onto the wide meadow that surrounded the band-stand. Wind swept past their bodies and rushed in their hair; they flew as the witches must once have flown and suddenly they were in the street.

A car caught them in its lights but the driver was so star-tled that he killed his engine. As they sailed down Dexter Street they could hear behind them the rattle of his starter turning over.

"The oak! Follow me!"

Kathy clambered up an oak, managing to get to the bottom-most branch. Jim saw her plan: they could cross its branches and get onto her roof that way. The window to her room was right there.

The car had started. It turned on two wheels and came roaring down Dexter. "Hurry, Kath!"

"Help me!"

They were whispering as best they could. The O'Mallys were right in the front room listening to *The Hour of Charm.*

He put his palms against her buttocks and shoved. She was so light, dear Kath! Then he came up behind her. One of his legs was caught square in the lights of the car. It screeched to a stop at the end of the walk. A man in suit and hat got out and came marching into the yard. Behind him in the car a woman could be heard bawling hysterically.

"Get down out of that tree! What do you mean running around like that, you kids! How dare you!"

The Hour of Charm turned off. Kath slipped into the open window of her room. Jim froze against the trunk of the tree. He prayed, "Dear blessed Virgin Mary I will offer up ten rosaries if you let me get away with this."

Seamus O'Mally came onto his front porch. "What gives?" he said in his mellow brogue.

The driver's attention was diverted for just a moment. It was all Jim needed. He crossed to the roof and was in the window in an instant.

Kath was there. She pulled him into her closet and closed the door behind them.

"Thank you," Jim breathed. Ten rosaries it would be. After a hell of a confession, of course.

"Don't even breathe. Oh, Jimmy, what about our clothes? They'll find our stuff."

"We'll say something, some lie. We were robbed and we got scared."

"And took off all our clothes?"

"People do crazy things when they get scared."

"I've got it. They made us take off all our clothes! The robbers!"

"Don't whisper so loud, somebody's coming!"

Angie O'Mally's voice drifted up from below. "Be sure and check the attic. Don't forget the attic."

Jim found his hand touching her breast again. It was just so beautiful!

"It was a naked man! Possibly two naked men!"

Her fingers squeezed the tip of his penis. She barely breathed, "I don't think I like that man."

Seamus O'Mally's voice drifted up. "An odd thing. You're sure you saw this? And they climbed my tree?"

Jim put his finger into her thatch, driving it deep. She groaned.

Light burst in under the door. Jim gritted his teeth. Kath held her breath. He probed deeper and she tickled and they both almost fainted with the pleasure of it all. "Nobody in here," Seamus said.

The light went out. Kath kissed Jim. She smashed into him and forced his lips open and jammed her tongue into his mouth. He felt as if he had become an electric fire of nerve endings.

And then they were coupled together. "Oh it hurts," she breathed.

"Sorry!"

"No, it hurts and feels good at the same time!"

Distantly they heard voices in the street and then the grinding of a starter. That was the signal they needed. They leaped to one another and their bodies pounded like two pile drivers, thundering against the floor.

Downstairs there was absolute consternation. *The Hour of Charm* went off again and both elder O'Mallys looked in horror at their living-room ceiling.

The chandelier was swaying, the plaster was thundering as if somebody was literally leaping up and down on it.

"Burglars," Angie shouted.

"The devil! It's squirrels, woman!"

"The naked burglars, and they're in our baby's room!"

"There ain't any naked burglars. Couldn't you see that man was daft? It's squirrels or it's rats!" Seamus went clumping back up the stairs, his pipe between his teeth.

He got a tiny .410 shotgun out of his closet and went into his daughter's room to dispatch the varmints that had gained entry.

The closet door was shaking like the boiler in the machine

shop where he was foreman. "Must be a 'coon," he muttered as he snapped a shell into the gun.

He threw the door open.

At first he did not understand what he was seeing. Wallowing like savages in a heap of dresses were two completely naked human beings. They were obviously doing what he always referred to as "their business" together.

"The hell, that loony was right!"

Such was the extremity of their passion that they moved in a blur. It never even occurred to him that his beloved daughter lay abnegated before him, not until they expended themselves and became suddenly as quiet as thieves.

"Katherine O'Mally, oh Lord! And *you*, you Army tramp!"

Jim couldn't think. So mad had been his pleasure, he had almost forgotten his own name. It took him a long time to notice that there were lights on. He burrowed up to the surface of clothes, pushing a girdle and a couple of slips away from his face.

"Mr. O'Mally," he said in what sounded to him like the voice of a twelve-year-old, "I can explain."

"Explain! Get out of my house, you home wrecker! How dare you sully my only daughter! Oh, Katie Kate, are you hurt, my dearest?"

Mrs. O'Mally came in behind her husband. Jim had leaped to his feet. Now he grabbed the brassiere that had been tangled around his head and held it to conceal his still rigid penis. Why wouldn't the thing go down, anyway? Wasn't it supposed to, now?

Mr. O'Mally had knelt down, seeking toward his daughter, who was barely visible in the pile of clothes. "My baby, has he hurt you, precious? Shall I kill him for you, beloved?"

"Oh, Daddy," she gasped. "Daddy." He reached his huge hands into the clothes and lifted her out. She swooned in his lap. Her eyes opened, and she looked up at Jim. "Oh Daddy, I like to *fuck!*"

That was enough for Seamus O'Mally. He fell back in a dead faint, dropping his daughter as he toppled.

"We're getting married tomorrow," Jim shouted.

"Yes! Oh, yes! And we're going to make love forever!"

Angie O'Mally began keening. She knelt to her husband. "Oh, why did you die?" she moaned.

One eye opened. He lifted his head. Very methodically, as if he hadn't fainted at all, he picked up his shotgun. "Young man, get out of this house. Katherine O'Mally, go and bring me my razor strap!"

Jim heard the smack of the strap as he climbed down to the lawn. Twenty or not, she was getting it. He was furious but he was also helpless. He stole back to the park and found their clothes. By the time he had dressed he'd come more or less to his senses. Rather than appear again at the O'Mallys' door, he stuffed Katherine's things in their mailbox.

He then went home to his own family.

The next morning a very perplexed postman found the clothes.

James Thomas Collins and Katherine Mary O'Mally were driven by their parents to Maryland where there was no waiting period, and married before a justice of the peace on July 14, 1947.

The issue of their first night together miscarried exactly three months later, and I got another piece of this most extraordinary puzzle.

I do not believe that the baby died. My strong suspicion is that it was taken from the mother, most probably by three fragile creatures in the dark-blue coveralls they tend to wear on night missions to populated areas. Undoubtedly they did their work with precision, following a tradition many hundreds of years old. I have found records of this sort of activity in the folklore of many human cultures. The women of Northern Mexico call them *campeches* and welcome their coming.

Why would they be doing this, and why would it take so long? To more than one witness they have described themselves as "God's workers."

It takes many generations to create the gold of a new species out of the clay of the old.

The tiny spark of a child was delivered up a shaft of golden light to the one who would be its mother.

She was a superb surgeon, and she operated immediately on the eyes and the skull. The rest of the child she did not touch, but bathed it rather in a pink fluid made from the blood of its natural mother.

It prospered and lived and grew in a few months to its strange maturity.

Katherine O'Mally Collins called it in her secret heart Seamus, and in tears she told me that she knew that it lived, and whispers love to it still when the night wind might carry her words to heaven.

From the very heart of the mystery I believe—I hope—that her child listens.

Chapter Seventeen

His encounter with the others had put Will Stone in a very awkward situation. The problem was that his experience was spectacularly strange, even irrational. It was no doubt intended by them to challenge his comfortable model of reality, to communicate the notion that they were not what he assumed.

But all it really did was serve the psychosis of suspicion that underlay his personality.

He said to me, "How could I possibly tell what I remembered—flying through the air and such? It was so totally absurd. I'd have lost the most extraordinary job in the world." For a romantic and an adventurer, Will Stone was surprisingly cautious.

The others' actions must have seemed spectacularly irrational, but I think rather that they were the result of very large-format thinking of a kind we have not yet developed.

That possibility never occurred to Will. How could it have? He simply did not have sufficient intellectual scope.

As far as he was concerned, the possibility that the "aliens" were working according to an irrational plan left him feeling very vulnerable indeed.

Did it mean that reason was so flawed that they didn't use it? If so, then reason was actually irrational, and people who used it could never hope to outwit those who had surpassed it.

If only Will had possessed the courage to sit the others down and say the truth: We do not understand.

They were wedded to the straightforward assumption that the so-called aliens had a scout ship and that the larger body of aliens would be along soon. And yet Will's original intelligence estimate indicated that they had been here for at least sixty years prior to 1947. A search of folklore and legend would have turned up suggestions that their presence was much older.

So the Roswell crash might not have been a scout ship from another planet on an initial reconnaissance mission. For the same reason that Will wouldn't admit the strangeness of his own experience, none of them would address that possibility.

They preferred to pretend that they knew what they were dealing with, and invasion was something they could understand.

In his own defense Will told me that he was too frightened to think clearly, that the screams of the poor sentry who disappeared into the sky were echoing day and night in his head. And that sneering voice: "We're gonna take you for a ride."

Had they ever! There is something so wonderful about the idea of that dignified, serious man gliding over the streets of Roswell with an overseas cap in his hand—and then finding, to his horror, that the cap he'd taken to prove to himself that the incident had really happened had somehow come from the head of the very sentry who was missing!

He has never thought that the others have a sense of humor. Of course not: victims never think that practical jokes are funny.

There was also the sad side of it, the terrible side.

They had searched what remained of the night for their lost comrade. The base sent up six helicopters with powerful searchlights and they crisscrossed the desert for miles around. Will watched them like stars gliding in the dark, and then saw the silver light of first sun on their Plexiglas cockpits.

"No joy," the radio would crackle, "no joy, no joy."

They organized themselves and set out on foot. Men linked arms and scuffled through the brush trying to find a button, a bit of cloth, anything more than his cap to tell them that PFC Flaherty had existed.

No joy.

By nine it had become obvious that they weren't going to find him.

Even so the entire MP company turned out to search, and began bouncing off in all directions in their jeeps.

Right on schedule at nine hundred hours the flatbed truck Sally Darby had sent down from Los Alamos arrived. It was huge and extremely well built, used for transporting experimental atomic weapons.

Will noticed a profound change in the men of the detachment. They were sullen and silent. He was glad that the disk and bodies would be removed today. It was not clear to him that the AAF would let its men remain another night out here.

They set about getting the disk onto the flatbed.

The thing was so light that thirty men standing around the edges could with effort lift it off the ground. Their problem was that they couldn't move it more than a few feet, much less haul it onto the flatbed.

Will was worried that they were going to have to bring in a crane and waste at least another forty-eight hours. He was considering bringing a CIG crew down from Washington to guard the disk if the Air Force withdrew its personnel.

Then a very odd accident took place.

The men had the disk and were moving slowly toward the truck. Lieutenant Hesseltine was calling out like a rowing master. "Step! Step! Step!" Each time the men would all make their prescribed movement, some stepping backward, others sideways, others forward, depending on their position around the circle.

It was almost as if the disk had a gyroscope running somewhere inside. Every time they moved the thing it would resist and heave.

Again Hesseltine shouted, "Step." Two of the men who were supposed to go forward went backward instead. They lost their grip on the underside of the smooth surface. One of them toppled back and fell.

In an instant ten men were down and the disk was sliding out of the hands of the others. The fallen ones scrambled to get out from under.

The disk did not drop like a rock. To their amazement it settled softly to the ground—a result of the semifunctional gravity motor.

They soon learned to take advantage of the thing's subtle resistance to gravity. They would lift it and push it a distance.

It would slide to the ground a few feet from where they had started.

In this way they got it to the huge flatbed.

As the men worked to lash it down, Will and the lieutenant turned their attention to the three alien bodies. They'd had chests of ice brought, but in those days they didn't possess decent insulation and nothing but slush had survived the desert heat.

They opened the bag containing the freshest body, intending to check it before icing it down as best they could.

The smell was dreadful. But more disturbing by far to Will was the degree of deterioration that had set in overnight. The flesh was sunken, the eyes shriveled and collapsed. There was a considerable amount of thick, maroon liquid in the bottom of the bag.

"We've got to get this embalmed," Hesseltine said.

Will looked at it in horror and amazement. Unless he did something fast there wasn't going to be anything left for the scientists. And this one—this body was the strangest of the three. The other two were obviously alien.

But this one: Unless he missed his bet this was something very close to a human child.

He acted with his characteristic decision and commandeered a helicopter, his objective being to get the body to Los Alamos as soon as he could.

He gave Hesseltine instructions to wait with the disk, and then radioed Joe Rose to come up from Roswell and take command of the loading and transport process.

They resealed the body in its rubberized bag and got it strapped onto the runner platform of the chopper. He got in beside the pilot and in a moment was on his way back to the base. Leaving the disk made him nervous, but he saw no alternative. He was by then deeply mired in the absurd and wasteful interservice rivalry that characterized the MAJIC project all through the forties and fifties. The Air Force had already created its Blue Team to organize recoveries of crashed disks, bodies and debris. Air Force and CIA would work in competition along parallel tracks for years. Unfettered by any congressional oversight, they lavished their energies on wasteful competition while the others—as always—proceeded with clear direction and careful method.

At that moment, though, the only thing on Will's mind was his now desperate effort to get this body where it belonged before it was reduced to gristle and liquid.

He realized that Van had strengthened his position on the base by sending Colonel Blanchard on enforced leave and placing the much more rule-conscious Jennings in command.

He did have one hope, and that involved Jennings. The man was so bound by the chain of command that he was likely to report first and await orders rather than do anything overt when Will arrived on base with the body.

Will's fear was that the Air Force would commandeer it. Admiral Hillenkoetter was obviously in no position to prevent this. In return for his support in other matters, the President was likely to continue to side with General Vandenberg.

As they bounced along toward Roswell Will tried to find the view he had seen last night. Sure enough they swept across a small range and there it was, the town now washed by morning sun. He had been here, flying on wings of dream.

He shuddered, remembering the freedom and the fear. Two feet away from him the strange body rode in its canvas shroud. Given the incredible pressures of the situation, I find it remarkable that Wilfred Stone was functioning at all. But he was functioning, and well. As a matter of fact he was acting with considerable intelligence and decision.

The others had very intentionally shattered his model of reality. He no longer knew what to think about them or what they were doing.

Still, he acted. He tried.

They landed on a round helicopter target, and two medics trotted over to take charge of the corpse.

"What are your orders?" Will asked, as if only mildly curious.

"Place the object in the meat locker pending transport."

That sounded extremely suspicious. "Transport to where?"

"Unknown, sir. You'll have to ask the exec."

Jennings was moving with unexpected swiftness.

Will accompanied the bundle to the kitchen of the officer's mess, where it was placed in a walk-in freezer. He then went

195

to the HQ building and called on the lieutenant colonel. He was annoyed to find that he had communicated with Ramey and already had orders to transport the bodies and everything else immediately and under guard to Eighth Air Force HQ in Fort Worth.

He was a tight, intense man and he obviously intended to exert the authority he had been given. "I have a direct, written order," he told Will. "I don't even know your credentials."

"You know I'm CIG, and I obviously report to Admiral Hillenkoetter."

"Then the *admiral* will appreciate the way we do things in the Air Force."

What Will did at this point was completely outrageous.

Without another word he went directly down the hall to the intelligence offices. Joe Rose had his setup there, a cubicle with phone and a typewriter.

There was a set of keys to Rose's rented Chevy hanging on the wall, left there according to standard station procedure. Will picked up the keys and went over to the officer's club.

There was no guard on the meat locker in the kitchen. They weren't expecting him to turn into a body snatcher.

But that is just what this audacious man did. It's too bad that he had to use his best qualities, his quick intelligence and decisiveness, to outsmart the Air Force instead of understand the others.

When the odor from inside the locker hit him he almost passed out.

He drove into the town with the bundle on the back seat. It was already a hot day and the inside of the car was sweltering.

He went up Main Street to the Gawter Funeral Home, chosen because it was the first one he found.

"I'd like to see Mr. Gawter," he said to the young woman at the reception desk.

"Who?"

"The owner."

"Mr. Steinman. Mr. Gawter died three years ago." She made a call, glanced up. "Is this in reference to a bereavement?"

"Yes." In a sense, it was.

"I'm so sorry for you. Mr. Steinman will meet you in the

Contemplation Room. He'll show you our memorials and explain the different plans that we offer here at Gawter. Is your dear one still at the hospital?"

"No," Will replied evenly, "he's in a bag in the backseat of the car." Macabre though it is, Will Stone has a very definite sense of humor.

She blinked very rapidly for a moment. Then without a further word she conducted him to the "Contemplation Room," which turned out to be a showroom where coffins were lined up like late-model Buicks. A man of about fifty in a dark-blue suit approached. He was wearing a sad smile.

Will introduced himself and showed him his CIG credentials.

"This is a national emergency," he said. "I'm commandeering your place of business and your services forthwith. You are to close your doors at once for the duration of the time I am here. And if you ever speak to anybody concerning what you are about to witness you will be committing high treason and will be punished accordingly. Do you understand me?"

Steinman's lips opened with a dry rasp. In those days nobody would dream of impeding a government official in pursuit of his duties.

"I want you to send all your workers home until one o'clock this afternoon. Tell them that I am a federal mortuary inspector."

"Yes. Please come with me to my office."

They were soon watching the last of his six employees hurry out of the back of the building. Will got the bundle from the car.

He'd never been backstage in a funeral home before. There were three porcelain embalming tables in the preparation area, which was air-conditioned with an evaporative cooler. The result was that the air was warm and damp instead of hot and dry.

Each table had a drain in one corner, and was so angled that any fluids would flow right into it.

"Where do the drains go?"

"City sewer."

"I want every bit of fluid from this body saved."

"I'll get a bucket."

Will put the bundle on the table. It was so carefully tied that he had to cut the knots with his penknife. When Steinman came back he was confronted with the little man.

The odor was overpowering. Steinman handed Will a tube of Baume Ben-Gay. "Put a dab under your nose," he said. Will informs me that it didn't help.

Steinman opened a glass-fronted cabinet which contained trochars and rubber gloves and packages of Rock-Hard Cavity Fluid.

He put on some rubber gloves and lifted one of the arms. It was then that he noticed something very wrong. No doubt it was the extreme lightness of the limb. He gasped and looked at Will in consternation. "What happened here?"

Will did not answer directly. How could he? "What can you do to slow down decomposition?"

"Embalm him or freeze him."

"I have to take him somewhere. Is there a freezer truck?"

"No truck can maintain temperature low enough to stop decay in a cadaver this far gone. It has to be frozen solid."

Will had no choice but to go for embalming. He saw that he would have to drive the thing up to Los Alamos himself.

"Sir, is this—may I ask—a child?"

"This is the body of a soldier."

Steinman peered at the face, then looked at Will. His eyes were stricken. "What happened to this man?"

Will tried for a believable answer. "An atomic accident. The rest is classified."

"Lord, Lord. What hath God wrought?"

Will had to get out of that room. The odor was just too much. He stood for a moment in the hall, gasping for breath. But he didn't dare leave Steinman alone with the body so he soon went back in.

"It's a mistake to leave the room when you have a stinker on the table," Steinman said casually. "Got to get used to it twice."

Will describes the humid, sultry atmosphere of the preparation room as feeling like rotted grease. He slopped too much Baume Ben-Gay under his nose, inhaled some of it and went into a sneezing attack so violent he was afraid it was going to turn into a virtual epileptic fit. The powdered eggs he'd swallowed earlier for breakfast threatened to come up while he was still trying to control the sneezing.

Then he saw the mortician start trying to open the little man's coverall. It was silver with dozens of pockets and flaps and buttons on it.

While he fumbled around in complete confusion Will finally brought himself under control.

"Where's the zipper on this thing, anyhow?"

They couldn't find a zipper. There were no buttons, except on the pockets and the flaps. The little man was like a cheap doll that had been sewn into its dress.

"We'll cut it," Will announced. Steinman brought scissors, which were hopeless. Then he got a surgical scalpel. It didn't work either.

He looked hard at Will. "Mister, I want to know what's going on here. What is this?" He gestured at the corpse.

"I told you. A soldier—"

"Who got himself shrunken in some kind of atomic accident? And his coverall is made of cloth that won't cut and he looks like a cross between an angel and a troll? Mister, I want to know what all of this is about or I think that I am leaving this area. Why aren't you in some government facility? The Roswell Base is a mile from here. And there is the national laboratory in Los Alamos."

"The deterioration is happening far faster than we anticipated. You have the best facility in southern New Mexico."

"Is it some sort of spaceman? Is that what you are bringing in here?"

"I don't know what in the world you're talking about," Will tried to butter his voice with scorn. "That nonsense belongs in the back pages of the newspapers. I have a dead man here, and he has a family that loves him."

"Which reminds me of the matter of payment."

"You'll be paid five hundred dollars."

"Well, that is good."

"So let's figure out how to get this damn coverall open and get on with it before we both suffocate."

Inch by inch they examined the garment. There were no

seams anywhere. When Will touched it he could feel the slight, bony skin beneath and his flesh crawled.

"I found it! Damn, this is a cunning thing." Steinman had made a small opening in the cloth. As he pulled it got wider. It made a curious ripping sound, but he wasn't tearing anything. The two sides of the open seam were covered with strips of what looked to Will like stiff fur. It was composed of tiny hooked hairs that tangled when they were pressed together. The seam they made was almost invisible.

I don't know whether mankind invented Velcro independently, or if MAJIC secretly leaked the technology to the rest of us.

They opened the garment and lifted it off the body.

And it was a perfect body. Heartbreakingly perfect. The size of a boy of about ten. The skin was gray-white and completely hairless. The genitals were about as formed as those of a three-year-old. But they were there, uncircumcised. There was no belly button.

"My God, this is a little boy!"

"I told you—"

"You told me there was an accident. A soldier—shrunk I thought. Somehow."

"A boy soldier. Doing a very brave work for the good of his country."

"You people have gotten to killing children with your damn atomic shenanigans? For shame!"

"For America!"

"Let me tell you something, Mr. Government. You people forgot what America was a long time ago. This boy in this here uniform—there isn't anything in the world important enough to bring his young life to an end like this. And what did you do to his face? Operate on his eyes? Why, he's no more'n a human guinea pig."

Will made a note that Joe Rose was to work on this man, make certain he kept his lip buttoned.

"Embalm this cadaver, Mr. Steinman."

"I'll do it, but I need a death certificate. I want to know where the parents are and where to ship this child. There's no way this little fella is leaving here in the back of a Chevrolet!"

After Steinman had made his incision a brownish-red fluid drained out into the bucket Will had put under the table. He collected the fluid in a jar.

Steinman brought out a syringe and a large bottle of embalming fluid. As a test Will had him swab some on the skin. When there was no reaction he let him fill the body with the fluid.

"I'm going to get a pine box," Steinman said. "It's all I have available for a child. I'd have to order a nicer coffin from San Antonio or somewhere." He gave me a sad, lost look. "We don't get many dead children in here."

The moment he left Will wrapped the body in the rubber sheet that covered the table. Bundling the uniform, carrying the specimen jar and the body, Will took everything out to the Chevy and drove off.

As he left he saw Steinman standing on the front steps of the Gawter Funeral Home, looking angry.

Steinman never revealed what he knew, and Will has no record of what may have happened to him.

My supposition is that Joe Rose did his work well, and the funeral director took the story of the government man and the strange little child with him to his grave when at length he became one of his own corpses.

July 12, 1947
CLASSIFICATION TOP SECRET ULTRA

Central Intelligence Group
EMERGENCY REPORT ON MISSING MILITARY PERSONNEL

Prepared by Field Headquarters Unit, Los Alamos
Central Intelligence Group
Copy 1 of 1
FOR IMMEDIATE TRANSMISSION

Circulation: The President; the Secretary of Defense; Joint Chiefs of Staff; Director, Federal Bureau of Investigation; Director, Central Intelligence Group

To be passed by hand and destroyed on return to CIG

Purpose

The purpose of this report is to assess the significance of the disappearance of two military personnel in connection with extraterrestrial alien activity within the borders of the Continental United States.

Background

1. Burleson, Charles, PFC 0998721943, USA, 53rd Inf. Sta. Ft. Bliss. Disappeared during nighttime maneuvers on Fort Bliss 7/8/47.
2. Flaherty, Michael, PFC 549112174, 1395th MP Company, RAAFB. Disappeared while on sentry duty at the site of a crashed alien disk in southern New Mexico at approximately 0335 on the night of 7/10/47.

Detailed Analysis

1. PFC Burleson
PFC Burleson disappeared during or after a night of unusual flare or light activity reported during field training maneuvers by a detached squad of 4 Platoon, D Company. There was no indication of any morale problem. Private Burleson was absent at squad muster at 0600 hours 7/9/47. A search was made of the squad bivouac area without results. The search was extended by the squad to nearby ravines and gullies, also without results.
As there were no roads out of the area it was assumed that the soldier had met with a mishap. No trace of this soldier has been found.

2. PFC Flaherty
PFC Flaherty was detached for sentry and guard duty at the site of an alien object crash near Maricopa, New Mexico. He was part of a six-man unit under the command of S/Sgt. Peter Dickson. PFC Flaherty had four years experience as an MP and had a series of highly successful evaluations. He had a K-Type Security Clearance and was cleared to serve posted guard duty at nuclear weapons depots and in secured armed nuclear weapons storage locations. PFC Flaherty had no charges or negative comments in file, had never been AWOL or on charges of any kind. He was a bachelor age 23. He did not drink or smoke. He had received a high school diploma and had plans to study civil engineering after his period of service. He was on his second tour of duty. On the night of 7/10/47 PFC Flaherty disappeared, apparently into the night sky. Despite a wide air and ground search over

203

a 72-hour period no trace at all has been found
of PFC Flaherty.

Conclusion

We conclude that both of these disappearances
were the probable result of unknown alien activity. This conclusion is based on their known
habit of causing bizarre disappearances, as per
"Intelligence Estimate on Flying Disk Motives"
prepared for limited Top Secret distribution
7/8/47. In both cases, there was apparent alien
activity in the area.

Recommendation

It is urgently recommended that the following actions be taken:
1. No nighttime military maneuvers to be conducted in areas where flying disk activity is
   being observed by the military or reported by
   the public.
2. All nighttime guard duties throughout all
   military commands to be placed on War Alert
   status until further notice, all sentries to
   be briefed and armed and to move in squad formation only.

Chapter Eighteen

The Chronicle of Wilfred Stone

I drove north into a fierce afternoon. As long as the car was in motion I had the wind, so the fact that the car stank of formaldehyde and rot wasn't unendurable. The merest whiff of it bothered me, however. My impulse was to light a cigarette but I was already half sick from too much tobacco and coffee.

It was just me and this road and the thing in the backseat. The previous night obsessed my thoughts. What had happened out on that desert? I remembered the enormous, glaring eyes of that owl, the impossible flight—

I was hit by a bout of shaking worse than a malarial ague.

It was all I could do to get my foot onto the brake and get the car pulled over to the edge of the road. Mike Flaherty's screams were thrashing me.

All of a sudden I was just so afraid.

And I couldn't talk to a soul about it. By doing such odd things to me the aliens had isolated me from my peers.

They were breaking me, and I knew it. The devils were out to destroy my mind.

The minute the car stopped the stink became overwhelming.

I jumped out and went a little into the desert. The heat almost took my breath away. It was as if the sun was actually squeezing me. I crouched down, instinctively covering my head. The smell was in my clothes, clinging to my skin, making my insides crawl with disgust.

To the east Haystack Mountain rode in sunlight. On another day I would have enjoyed a view like this, but today its empty silence was oppressive.

There was no movement at all, no sound except the lazy rasping of grasshoppers. Away from the car the air smelled of hot, dry grass. I imagined cowboys riding this range, silent in the heat, restless for booze and poker. Fifty years ago that had been the norm. Fifty years, barely a generation. And here I was in a car and carrying an alien corpse in the backseat. What would they have thought? Would they even have begun to comprehend?

A sound startled me—echoing in the silence, carrying from far away. It rose, desperate, a woman's scream.

Sophie.

No. A rabbit being attacked by a hawk.

Then there came a buzzing, low at first and insistent, the kind of thing you felt in your chest rather than heard with your ears. I searched the skies, expecting to spot a small plane swimming from horizon to horizon.

When I saw that the sky was empty I had my first twinge of fear.

The sound got louder. I tried to identify it as something familiar. If not a plane, then what? Oh, God. I didn't want this to be happening. I wasn't going to be able to handle this.

Instinctively I clapped my hands to my head and ran for the car. What if they were coming after their fallen soldier? God help me. I was alone out here in the middle of nowhere. Who the hell knew how they regarded their dead.

How stupid I'd been to just take the thing and come out here like this. I was miles from Roswell and there wasn't another soul around.

The buzzing got louder, began to pulse in my ears. I grabbed at the car door, fought my way in. When I fumbled for the keys they seemed to hop out of the ignition on their own.

They jangled down under the seat. I bent, trying to force myself to be calm. The buzzing got louder and louder as I scrabbled. I sobbed and shook, fighting to control myself, to somehow grab—and then I had them. I had the keys.

All right, calmly now, put them in the ignition.

The buzzing became an angry whine.

Turn on the engine.

Now it was a roar, shattering, massive. Something huge was landing right on top of me.

The engine turned over once and then just plain died.

I screamed into the hell of noise as a huge shadow obscured the sun.

And a trailer truck loaded with sheep rumbled past, leaving the Chevy rocking in its wake.

A man can slip so easily over the edge.

I wished to God for talk. Just casual conversation. "How about Dewey? Think he's gonna announce?"

An SS officer had once said under interrogation, "You learned not to get near them when they were dying. A human being will do anything if he is dying. Once a girl was being hanged in the women's section. The bindings came loose. A female officer reached up to tighten them. Before anybody could stop her, the girl had torn the woman's arm off."

Where had that man been stationed? Was it Sobibor? Belsen? I can't remember if we hanged him or promoted him. I can't ever remember. What is justice?

The man's fate came to seem very, very important. I thought of his boots, of his black uniform, of the excessive politeness that marked him in my eyes as a killer.

I was hanging over the steering wheel with tears tickling my face. The car was a prison cell in an infinity of light.

Finally I sat up, took a deep breath, re-started the car. I could hear the engine nattering to itself, could hear the grasshoppers again, could hear my own breathing.

I lit a cigarette and returned to the road.

I flipped on the radio.

The first thing I heard was the Vaughn Monroe song "Ghost Riders in the Sky." I turned the damn thing off.

I started singing to myself like I had in Algiers and Marseilles when the Gestapo was breaking my networks. I would walk in the back streets and sing under my breath in English a song from childhood, "Oh, slow up, dogies, quit roaming around, you have wandered and trampled all over the ground. Oh, move slow, dogies, move slow."

My father seemed to be in the car with me, singing again on an early summer night. I was small and lying upon his lap and the whippoorwills were calling.

I had been safe then and, oh, how I longed for it now. I

knew that somebody was talking to me as I drove. I had known it for some time. I just hadn't been ready to look at the fact that I was alone in a car with a dead body and someone was talking to me.

I remembered hide-and-seek in our enormous yard, laughter in the night, cool and mysterious, and where I hid somebody else hid, too. . . .

They touched me with cool hands, cool and little and white.

I drove on and on, the tires pounding on the pavement. I was in a white world. My body was tingling. Some part of me told me that I was nowhere, not in the desert, not in the car. And yet I heard the engine throbbing, throbbing. . . .

Suddenly the shadows were long.

I'd driven all day and hardly noticed it. Where had the time gone?

I stepped on the gas. Fifty, sixty, beating toward Santa Fe and Los Alamos beyond. Los Alamos. It was Spanish for "the Cottonwoods," known to locals simply as "the Hill." A bastion of science and power hidden atop a mesa. It was my City of God, the place where the truth would be discovered.

Why was this road so long?

I did not want to be out here in the dark, not with the thing in the backseat and the memory of what had happened last night still fresh.

I felt such an overwhelming poignance, as if in some secret part of myself I had touched my ancient childhood.

Evening became night and the road seemed to stretch ever longer. Soon my world was a glowing dashboard and a smear of light on the highway.

Outside the desert seemed to sigh, restless in the dark. It appears peaceful, the desert, but it is actually a place of endless terror. There is fierce competition in the desert, all the time. The snake stalks the mouse and the mouse captures the roach. And everything is always a little thirsty.

It is man alone who brings light to this world. Nature is dark, brooding and cruel. What compassion there is in the earth flows from the sterling heart of man.

Slit a man's throat and his dog will lap up the blood. Slit the dog's throat and the man will save him if he can.

What *did* we do with that SS officer?

I was hungry and thirsty. In fact I was so hungry and thirsty that I was shaking like a leaf.

There had been somebody in the car with me, somebody sitting right there on the seat beside me. A woman. She was little and pale and I think in that moment I loved her enough to sweat blood. She'd been so sad!

A horrible thought crossed my mind, but when I pulled over and checked the bundle I found that everything was perfectly in order. My precious cargo hadn't been taken from me by some cunning deceit.

Still, I felt that the aliens had been with me. I knew they had. But when? Didn't my thoughts stretch back unbroken to morning. A long, hot day of driving . . .

There were lights down the road. Distances are deceiving, though, on a desert night, and it was another half hour before I reached the town of White Lakes.

There was a gas station and thank God a little place warmly lit that had a sign in the window, CAFE.

I pulled the Chevy up beside a couple of Fords and went inside. There were a few tables covered with checkered oilcloth and a counter. The place smelled of hamburgers and cigarettes and coffee.

"Burger basket, and gimme a Coke. Cherry pie and coffee after."

I was surprised at how crowded the place was, considering that it was nearly nine P.M. I had to take an end stool at the counter and I was lucky to get that. I'd already ordered my burger when I noticed the intense buzz of conversation around me.

"It was silver. Shiny."

"You seen it closer than me, then. I just saw a big disk."

"It was a blimp. One of them German airships like they had before the war."

Had I heard that right? "What's the stir?" I asked the man beside me.

"We seen one of them flying disks, that's what's the stir!"

"Really?"

A woman at one of the tables chimed in. "It was unearthly!"

"Godless," her husband muttered.

"Big! It came up the highway not ten minutes ago. You musta seen it."

I knew my blood was draining from my face.

"You seen it, traveler?" a man called out. He had a Stetson on the back of his head. The homey country voices were getting mean.

I clung to my damp glass of Coca-Cola. It was a handle on the familiar world. Dark waters were engulfing me. The café, the people, all began to slip away.

Had there been someone in the car with me? I thought—a woman. Yes . . . but I couldn't remember clearly. My head was whirling, my ears ringing.

"Hey, traveler, you seen it? You were right out there on the road."

"I had—had—car trouble. I'm running late and flat-out tired. I don't think I could see fifty feet."

"Well, everybody in this town saw it. Yes, sir! It was as big as one of them blimps."

A blimp. My mind raced. Weren't they all in mothballs? I grasped at a straw. "Maybe that's what it was."

"Hell, this thing went up so fast you wouldn'ta believed it." The man who spoke wore a sloppy uniform. A local sheriff's deputy, I thought.

A woman spoke up. "I was lookin' at it outa my pickup, mister. I saw that car of yours. I saw you drivin' right under it."

The whole room became silent. Even the cook at the grill turned to look at me.

"Like I say, maybe it was there. I just didn't notice! I mean, who expects a thing like that!"

The woman from the pickup was regarding me with eyes like pins. "That Chevy of yours looked like it came down outa the thing."

Oh dear God, surely that couldn't be! If my car—no. It would mean that I was nothing more than a little trout being played on a line, played until I was tired.

"Maybe we oughtta have a look at that Chevy of yours, mister."

I had to get out of there.

I drank down my Coke and cranked up what was probably a pretty bad smile. "I didn't realize the time. I've really gotta be going!"

The cook glanced at one of his checks. "You got a hamburger comin'. I'm just gonna put it together."

"Oh, I'll pay."

The woman was like a snake. "He came outa that thing," she murmured to the deputy, who nodded. His hand was on his gun.

I put a dollar down on the counter. "Will this cover it? Keep the change!"

"You spend two bits and you leave a simoleon. That's real generous, mister. You take your burger basket with you." He laughed. "And you can keep the basket!"

I edged toward the door. In a moment I was outside. I started to open my car. The deputy had the movements of a jackal. He grabbed my wrist with a hard, thin hand. My fingers let go of the car door.

"Yes, Officer?"

"We all saw it. We saw your car come out of it. It came right out of the bottom and the thing flew away. I want to know what the hell you are, mister. What the hell was that thing? You like to scared us half to death!"

"I'm a federal officer," I said. I flashed my wallet at him, hoping that he'd be satisfied with a glimpse of a Washington, D.C., driver's license. "You saw secret military activity. You keep your mouth shut, and tell the rest of those folks to do the same."

He leaned back on his heels. "The hell."

"That was it!" I tried to get in the car.

"You're—"

"Let me go! You can't hold me like this!"

"Mister, I want to search this car."

"No! You have no cause."

"What's that smell, then? What stinks like that—you got something in there—what is it?" He peered into the backseat. "What's rolled up in that bag?"

I took the moment to jump into the car. Frantically I inserted the key and hit the starter.

He grabbed into the window, clutched my shoulder. "You're under arrest!"

"I'm a federal officer!"

"Get out that thing."

I slammed it into reverse and jammed the gas pedal down so hard his strong grip was instantly broken.

I slurried into the highway and stepped on it.

For a long time I saw a flashing red light behind me, but he couldn't overtake me. Mobile radios hadn't penetrated to small New Mexico sheriffs' departments in those days, so he wasn't able to call for help.

But he was tenacious as hell and he drove well. No matter how fast I went he kept getting gradually closer. And he knew every slight bend in the road.

I couldn't arrive at the Hill with an infuriated hick sheriff on my tail.

In desperation I cut my lights. We were entering the mountains south of Santa Fe and the road was beginning to twist and turn a good bit. I jammed the gas pedal to the floor and started taking bends on two wheels.

Finally I found what I was looking for—a dirt road leading off the main highway. I turned hard, sliding into it amid a cloud of dust.

Then I backed right out into the highway and tore off around the next bend.

It was a trick I'd learned during the war. He saw the dust I'd left and took off down the side road.

I almost wept as I pulled up an hour later to the main gate at Los Alamos. I had never in my life been so glad to see armed men and lights and to hear my credentials questioned.

I was reassured to see that the guards were wearing snappy new Atomic Energy Commission uniforms, blue like cops rather than khaki soldiers' things.

I had challenged the night and won, or so it seemed to me. Actually, I was more like an ant who finds the poison the housewife has laid. Delighted with its sweetness he carries a piece of it deep into his nest. Because it is so good he hides it away at the back of the the food tunnels.

That way only the best and brightest ants may feast on the treasure.

Part Three
CONGRESS OF LIES

They know not, neither will they understand;
they walk on in darkness: all the foundations
of the earth are out of course.

—PSALM 82

Chapter Nineteen

The same night that Will arrived at Los Alamos, Roscoe Hillenkoetter seems to have become personally involved with the others. Nobody, least of all Hilly, realized that anything like this had happened until 1960, when the old man, retired now, suddenly threw caution aside and called for a congressional investigation into unidentified flying objects.

It was a direct attack on Will and his agency—an agency that Hillenkoetter had literally created during a midnight session with Truman.

By 1960 Hilly was long retired. After making his statement he very publicly joined a group called the National Investigations Committee on Aerial Phenomena. Will says that he was forced to infiltrate it, take it over and ultimately destroy it.

In order to get Hillenkoetter to back down Will finally briefed him. He saw at once their predicament and left NICAP, commenting quite correctly that the government had revealed all it could and it was up to the "aliens" to tell the rest of the story.

During that time MAJIC interviewed the former CIA director. When he was placed under hypnosis the first thing he remembered was the remarkable night that he conceived of the new agency.

Hilly's encounter was not simply a matter of a flying disk landing in his backyard. Like all the most profound encounters with the others, it was also an encounter with a powerful aspect of self.

Roscoe Hillenkoetter was not sleeping well on that

night. His dreams were troubled by familiar storms. He was having a ship nightmare of a kind that had dogged him since he'd gone through Pearl. This time he was on the bridge of a tired old cruiser somewhere in the South China Sea. She burned coal and every seam sweated. The wind was screaming and there were Jap subs about. He didn't like the flying whitecaps or the evil green sky. He listened to the distant laboring of the engines and gave an order to come about into the wind.

Then he noticed that the steersman was a twelve-year-old. He was shocked beyond words. How the hell had a kid like that gotten into the Navy!

He shouted for his first officer. A high, piping voice replied. This one was ten! Then he saw babies crawling on the deck, hundreds of them, and women in the rigging, little girls on watch without lifejackets!

They were singing sea shanties while the typhoon came down on them. Nurses, babies, children. An elderly couple covered with coal dust helped each other up from the engine room, looking for a breath of air.

His ship was crewed by the innocent and the old. And then he saw three white torpedo tracks dissolving in the crest of a wave. "Hard a-starboard," he screamed, "flank speed!" As the ship heeled a box of pickup sticks fell to the floor of the bridge and went scattering reds and greens and yellows down the ladder.

Then the ship took the first torpedo. A geyser of water burst up, and in the rocking, plunging aftermath all the hatches flew open and screaming crowds of children poured up from below like a desperate horde of ants.

She took the second fish and he felt the shuddering snap of the keel and knew she was going down.

He was half out of bed and running for the pumps when he finally came awake.

"Lord God almighty!"

He dropped back onto the bed. What a hell of a nightmare. Damn the war that it left a man with dreams.

He turned over and plumped his pillow, then closed his eyes and tried to fall back to sleep. He was shaking. He deliberated about waking his wife. But he was too old to admit even to her that he'd been frightened by a dream.

He was methodically calming himself down when he began to get the feeling that there was somebody in the room.

He opened his eyes but didn't move. A prowler? Surely not. But then who? He wasn't a man given to flights of fancy. There was damn well somebody here. He could hear them breathing right over by the closet door. In and out, in and out. Breathing as regularly as a damn machine.

He kept a .38 Special in his bedside table. If he was quick he could probably get his hand on it before they moved, but he'd be bound to take at least a couple of shots before he could bring his own weapon to bear. Hell.

Moving his head very slowly he tried to look across the room.

A woman was standing there, big as life. As on a stage she was lit from above.

He sat up. She was young, and so beautiful he all but cried out from the pain of seeing her. There was recognition, shocked, confusing. He loved this woman as if he had always known her—as indeed he had. She was mother, daughter, lover, the betrayed woman within us all. She was the one in whose lap we lie when we are babies and when we die.

When a boy on the battlefield calls for his mother, it is she who comes. She is why we make love so often. No matter how deeply we penetrate the bodies of our lovers we never reach her.

Our eternal striving for her has brought the whole human race out of our loins.

With the softest of smiles on her lips she rose into the air and went right through the ceiling, disappearing in a swirl of flimsy blue skirts.

The synopsis of his hypnosis states dryly that he cried when he described her departure. And now in Will's garden, with the traffic hissing beyond the wall and a child singing next door, now I am also betrayed by the old man's traitorous tears.

His unease, on that distant night, finally got the better of the admiral. He woke his wife. "I'm having trouble sleeping," was all he cared to tell her.

"Would you like me to make some hot toddy?"

"That would be a sainted act."

She stretched and kissed his cheek and slipped from the bed.

The admiral got out of bed and went to the divan under the window. From here he could see the moon's low sickle riding the oak tree that stood in the side yard.

She brought the toddy and he sat sipping it. His mind went back to the dream, and he reflected that an old man running an organization like CIG really was playing with the futures of hundreds of young people.

He knocked back the drink and returned to bed with his wife. He entered what was for him an unusual state between waking and sleep. The transcript of his hypnosis revealed a very strange encounter.

A beam of blue light came down from the ceiling and began to move slowly back and forth in the room. Hilly was paralyzed. Finally it found the bed. It moved up the sheets, then up Hillenkoetter's cheeks, until it rested just between his eyes.

The center of his forehead glowed white.

And the beautiful lady walked into his dream. She was young, no more than twenty, and wearing a light-blue summer dress. He thought that she was the prettiest girl he'd ever laid eyes on. She had a piece of chalk in her hand.

She turned to the blackboard (he seemed to be in a schoolroom) and wrote a single word in block letters.

"MAJESTIC."

Then she lectured. Even under hypnosis he was so taken by her beauty that he could not remember her words. That was the cunning part of it, of course. They were probably standing right around his bed with their big bobbing heads, pulling that girl out of his unconscious and making her their tool, their way into his deep mind. Their weapon.

She laughed and tossed a curl from her eyes. And there his hypnotized narrative ended, as he recalled waking up. His ordinary file contained the rest of the story.

He remembered being filled with a sense of malignant, creeping evil. Something awful was about to happen, some slouching horror to come through the dark window.

Damned if he was going back to sleep now. Anyway, he'd

had an idea. Really a hell of an idea. He put on his robe and slippers and went down to his study.

There he wrote out the organizational plan that remains to this day the basis of MAJIC. He created an agency that would oversee every detail of our relationship with the aliens, and designed it in such a way that it has kept itself almost perfectly secret.

When he was finished he looked over the sheets of legal paper. He was excited.

As he worked he had become more and more aware of just how urgent this really was. He saw that he also had a chance to make a lightning strike against Vandenberg and close this thing up now and forever as a CIG/CIA project.

His sense of urgency was so great that he began to think that he ought to bypass everybody, Van, even Forrestal, and go to the President right this second.

He'd also figured out something else. Once the initial leaks were fixed, this business of the aliens was going to stay secret forever.

He knew exactly how to accomplish that goal. The secret would be permanent and it would be total.

He had not only this night created the Majestic Agency for Joint Intelligence (MAJIC), but also conceived of this foolproof method of entombing it behind an impenetrable wall.

It was twelve-thirty. A hell of a nervy time to call the President.

He looked at the phone.

Roscoe Hillenkoetter was not close to Harry Truman and right now that was a problem.

He had not often before availed himself of the private number in the apartment at the White House. But he didn't want to go through the staff. He wanted to reach out to Truman man to man. There wasn't any other way to do something as sensitive as this.

He dialed the number. A woman's voice answered on the second ring.

"Mrs. Truman?"

"No. This is the night maid."

"This is Roscoe Hillenkoetter. May I speak to the President?"

"I will give you Mrs. Truman. She's up reading. The President is asleep."

Bess Truman came on the line immediately.

"Oh, hello, Hilly. Just a minute." He heard her waking him up, then a brief exchange as she identified his caller. Then the President's distinct "What does that old shoe want?"

"What's the matter, Hilly. Can't sleep?"

"No, sir."

"Urgent?"

"Yes, sir."

"I'm up for it, if you don't mind pajamas and a robe."

"I'll be there shortly."

Hillenkoetter replaced the instrument. He went upstairs and dressed as quietly as he could. Then he kissed his wife's cheek and slipped out of the room.

He took with him in his briefcase the report on the two missing soldiers, which he had received that afternoon, his handwritten outline of the Majestic agency and another couple of documents that would be relevant to the meeting.

It was a muggy Washington night; he went to the garage and pulled out his car.

He drove almost automatically, staring out the windshield, trying to frame his proposition in such a way that the President would accept it. Above all, he did not want to frighten Harry Truman. That was the trouble with this whole business: it was so full of scary implications that it made sound judgment almost impossible.

Despite the late hour there were, of course, plenty of lights at the White House. The west entrance was actively guarded. He pulled up and got out of his car. He was taken through the dim public rooms to the private elevator. He was taken up to the apartment.

Now things changed. Suddenly he was in the Truman home, a family's private sanctum.

The President was in the sitting room. He wore the promised pajamas and robe. There was a smell of freshly brewed coffee. Harry Truman stood up and took the admiral's hand. "Hello, Hilly. We'll have coffee in a minute."

"Thanks for seeing me, Mr. President."

"Glad to. Since you've never before called me out of bed, I'm expecting something special." His eyes narrowed. "What happened? Stalin shave his mustache?"

"My news isn't that big."

"Then maybe it's something we can handle."

"You've read this?" He handed the President the staff report on the two disappeared soldiers.

"God, yes. It makes my blood boil. These bastards are kidnapping our boys."

"Yes. And look at this." He brought out one of the other documents, this one from the FBI. It was a synopsis of the annual report on crime statistics for the period 1944–1946. "A substantial jump in missing persons."

"A man comes home from the war. Finds out he doesn't really like his old life, decides to start all over. One more missing person. A lot of men have been coming home from the war just recently."

"What if that's not what it means?"

"Hilly, it's a horrible thing to contemplate."

"It seems possible."

The President looked steadily at him. "I wish I had something more than provocative speculations. These aliens or whatever they are could be entirely innocent."

"Not entirely. The boy who disappeared at the crash site. That is certain. They took him."

"Look, Hilly, what are we supposed to do?"

"Well," Hillenkoetter replied, "first I want to point out to you that we're taking the disk and the bodies to Los Alamos for analysis."

"Van made a case for taking the disk to Wright Field."

"I know that!"

"You and Van are fighting like a couple of tomcats in heat over this thing."

"More like a couple of crazed weasels, Mr. President."

Truman laughed. "You're an honest old bastard for a spy, Hilly. And I'm not unaware of the fact that the Hill is now under control of the AEC. And that the new administrator is a Navy man. Admiral."

"Aye-aye, sir."

221

They both laughed, this time. "You've got your disk unless Van stages some kind of a raid or Hoover commandeers it as state's evidence."

Hillenkoetter went white. "I hadn't thought of that!"

"Don't worry, Hoover hasn't either. So far all he's done is phone me and whine about the Joint Chiefs. He thinks it's Van's show. The question is, Hilly, how do we prevent this squabbling from messing up our project?"

Hilly jumped at the opening. "That's why I came here so urgently, Mr. President. I would like to propose the immediate creation of a secret agency to handle this. It would be a sort of clandestine Defense Department."

"A big agency?"

"As big as necessary."

"Big is hard to hide. Especially if it has to stay hidden for years."

"I've thought of that." He took a deep breath. The woman of his dream swam into vision. He pushed the memory aside. "We tell each man we involve that the aliens themselves are the architects of the secrecy, and that they will destroy the nation if we reveal the secret."

Truman threw back his head. He made a short sound like a bark in his throat. "Goddamn. That'll sure as hell do it. That'll bury this thing deeper than King Tut's tomb." Suddenly the public face was there, bright and cheerful and reassuringly tough. "That's a hell of an idea, Hilly. A real motivator!"

The public face collapsed, and Truman was Truman again. The fighter, and quick. He took a cigarette out of a silver box on the coffee table.

As he was lighting it the night maid brought the coffee in. She placed the silver service on the table and poured. Hilly took his black, and found that even White House coffee could be overboiled.

"Okay," Truman snapped as the maid withdrew, "you've had your pregnant pause. Get on with it."

"I see the agency as having sealed compartments, sharing secrets on 'need-to-know' basis only. All reporting to a single administrator."

"Tried and true structure for a secret operation."

"It kept the bomb secret."

"What're you going to call your baby?"

"Majestic."

"What a horrible name."

"Why do you say that?"

"It sounds like the King of England had a hand in it."

"Well, something to identify it as awesome."

"Majesty. Magic. The Magic Group."

"There was a Majestic Group at one point. It would be a bit of a diversion if there's ever any digging."

"Fine, then. Do what you want."

"Yes, sir. We'll call it Majestic."

Hilly saw Truman's eyes literally glaze over. It was as if he'd been turned off by some hidden switch. "I'll read your proposal and get back to you in the morning with any comments."

"I'm sorry to do this in the middle of the night, sir."

"You and me both, Hilly. Now do you think you can sleep?"

"I wonder what happened to those boys."

"We have about four thousand unknown soldiers. Now four thousand and two. Missing in action and presumed killed. It happens to soldiers. That's why they get their dogface pay."

Hillenkoetter was surprised by the depth of emotion in the President's voice, the tenderness and deep anger behind the hard words. He could see why this man had dropped the bomb.

He took his leave of Truman.

What happened next isn't quite conjecture on my part, but Will does not possess a written record. He knows that Vandenberg visited the President shortly after Hilly left. What exactly was said we don't know, but I think we have the gist of it.

The moment Hilly walked out the door the President called Van.

Before he arrived Truman read Hilly's rough proposal a number of times, thinking matters over. He was forced to agree that secrecy should be maintained until we knew more. But it wasn't right and he knew it. The public should be told at the first possible moment.

If he waited too long he would never be able to tell, because he would never be able to explain the reason for the delay.

The first essential step was guaranteeing U.S. airspace against the intruders.

He had worked himself into a state of considerable agitation by the time Van arrived in full uniform.

"Why the hell'd you waste time putting on all those duds, Van? I've been waiting."

"Sir, I'm ten minutes from a dead sleep."

"Well, that's not too bad considering the brace of medals you've got to hoist. I've got a brilliant proposal from Hilly and I'm going to go ahead with it tomorrow morning. I'm setting up a new agency within the purview of Central Intelligence to handle this alien business."

"Sir, the Air Force—"

"I'll tell you what the Air Force is going to do!"

Vandenberg looked shocked.

"Sorry, Van. I'm on edge. Disappearing soldiers. Kids. That bothers me like the dickens."

"What can I do to help, sir?"

"You have full and complete authority to take immediate hostile action the next time one of these disks shows up within shooting distance of any gun in the possession of the Air Force! And you take that as an order!"

"Mr. President—"

"Look at this damn FBI report. Disappearances doubled between 1944 and 1946. Is that related? These two soldiers— you've seen Hilly's report?"

"Yeah."

"Van, we are under attack and I want action! I want *response!*"

"Mr. President, you will get armed response from the Air Force."

"You tell your pilots to *shoot down* anything that looks like those gun-camera photos you have."

The visitors had very cleverly left him without choices. Tell the public they might be kidnapped by aliens and the government was helpless? Hilly was dead right. You had to bury this in a tomb.

"Mr. President, it's possible that I will be unable to shoot the craft down."

"Then get the capability! If you can't shoot one down then I'll declare a project bigger than the Manhattan Project on this. We've got to regain control of our airspace, General!"

Vandenberg's eyes hardened. "We will, sir."

Truman dismissed him. For a few minutes he sat smoking and thinking, shuffling Hilly's papers. But he was not a reflective man. Shaking off his upset he returned to the bedroom. He tossed his robe on a chair.

Bess half woke. "Is it all right?" she asked.

"Hell no," he said as he got into bed, "it's not all right. Not by a long shot."

Being Harry Truman, he then turned over and slept like a baby until morning.

TOP SECRET/MAJIC
EXECUTIVE ORDER
SUBJECT: ESTABLISHMENT OF MAJESTIC AGENCY FOR
JOINT INTELLIGENCE (MAJIC)

Copy 2 of 12

The purpose of this agency will be to coordinate all United States activities connected in any way with nonhuman alien presence, including the management of the MAJESTIC scientific group, military BLUE TEAM activities and FBI/CIA(G) surveillance activities designed to establish and maintain all MAJIC-related operations at the highest level of security obtainable. The TOP SECRET/MAJIC classification is now the highest level of classification.

MAJIC Initial Organizational Structure—MJ-1
MAJIC is a coordinating and management group, reflecting the same centralization concept contained in recent legislation establishing the Central Intelligence Agency.
MAJIC will be overseen by the Director of Central Intelligence, who will report on all MAJIC activities to the President as appropriate and advisable.
DCIA will receive the MAJIC Designation MJ-1. Admiral Hillenkoetter is appointed MJ-1(1) by order of the President.
Positions MJ-2–4 are MAJIC administrative positions. Should project SIGMA (referenced below) succeed, MJ-1 will institute project PLATO, seeking to establish ongoing communications of a diplomatic or negotiational nature with the aliens. The first objective of this project will be to attempt to control alien incursions into US airspace and alien contact with US citizens.

MJ-2 Position
MJ-2 is the designation for director, MAJIC Operations. Mr. Wilfred Stone is appointed Director, MAJIC Operations,

MJ-2, by order of the President. Further appointments within the Operational Group to follow. The primary responsibilities of the MJ-2 position will be two. The first will be administrative and collational, gathering and synthesizing all output from all other MAJIC positions and transmitting them in an orderly manner to MJ-1. The second will be diplomatic. MJ-2 will create an office (Designation: SIGMA) that will seek means of communicating with the aliens.

MJ-3 Position
The MJ-3 position is the Civilian Operations Coordinator responsible for propaganda and maintenance of public ignorance in the face of extensive and obvious alien activities, which include substantial and publicly visible flyovers of Unidentified Flying Objects (UFOs) and Identified Alien Craft (IACs). They also apparently include the abduction of civilians as well as military personnel for unknown reasons. The primary MJ-3 mission is to guard the fact that government cannot prevent these activities and does not know their purpose. MJ-3 will operate a program of denial and ridicule. The natural skepticism of journalists will be enlisted by total, absolute and blanket denial of any and all sightings, disappearances, observations of landed craft, etc. This program will be carried out no matter how obvious the truth of a given report. It is *essential* that NO sighting no matter how obvious be explained as an "unknown." Such explanation may lead to difficult questions and journalistic demands and *will threaten this program.* Further, MJ-3 will orchestrate the ridicule of civilians who come forward with witness accounts. If they are persistent, such civilians will be methodically discredited. Persons associated with scientific institutions and universities who are too interested in this subject will be warned away. Should they persist strong measures will be taken as appropriate. The atmosphere of denial and ridicule is intended to curtail public understanding, and frighten non-MAJIC-associated scientists into ignoring the whole area.

MJ-3 will also be responsible for the infiltration of "flying saucer" study groups now springing up as a by-product of recent radio and newspaper attention. All cover operations will be coordinated by MJ-3.

MJ-4 Position
The MJ-4 Position is Coordinator of Military Activities. The Army Air Force BLUE TEAM set up to retrieve alien objects and remains will advise MJ-4 of all its activities. All MAJIC-related military operations will be coordinated by this office, including those carried out after the impending transfer of BLUE TEAM to Air Materiel Command from its present S-2 Intelligence status. MJ-4 will manage Project REDLIGHT in cooperation with AFMC and AFOC with the mission of flying any intact alien craft that may be recovered. A civilian-based National Reconnaissance Organization will be established to provide site security for all activities relating to alien craft, their movements and attempts to fly them.

MJ-5 Position
The MJ-5 Position is Coordinator of Security. All incoming personnel must receive MAJIC clearance. This clearance can only be granted to persons able to pass the most stringent tests of background and loyalty. MAJIC clearance will be given only after stringent FBI clearance investigation. Should a situation develop where MAJIC clearance cannot be extended to a given elected individual above the MJ-1 level, that individual will be isolated from all knowledge of MAJIC for the duration of his term of office. MAJIC clearance procedures apply to *all* persons exposed to any MAJIC information, no matter how trivial, and will be applied to elected as well as appointed officials.

MJ-6 Position
The MJ-6 position is an internal executive position. MJ-6 is responsible for all record-keeping and isolation of MAJIC-related files within the Library of Congress and related col-

lection centers such as military document centers. This position will maintain not only a record-keeping division but also a research division that will be devoted to the discovery and classification of related isolates from other branches, such as FBI or Air Force documents that incidentally refer to MAJIC, MAJESTIC or related activities. It will coordinate all activities with MJ-9.

MJ-7 Position
MJ-7 is Coordinator of Allied Relations. MJ-7 will develop liaison with presently forming Allied alien activities organizations. MJ-7(A) will provide civilian liaison to these organizations, and MJ-7(B) will provide military liaison.

MJ-8 Position
MJ-8 is Coordinator of Soviet Bloc Relations. MJ-8 will attempt to create an atmosphere of complete and open sharing of information, in view of the apparently hostile nature of the alien incursion and the obvious need to cooperate at the highest levels in order to achieve a meaningful and effective human response to the possible arrival of massive alien force.

MJ-9 Position
MJ-9 is Project Historian. The historical mission is twofold. First, historians shall be enlisted to attempt to determine the extent of alien activity prior to the present time. Second, a MAJIC Historical Bureau shall receive *all* documents from all units and prepare and maintain a large-scale historical resource for use in briefing and as a source of reference.

MJ-10 to MJ-12 Positions
These are scientific positions.

MJ-10 Position
MJ-10 is Coordinator for the Physical Sciences. Subgroups will include Astrophysics, Propulsion, Electromagnetics, Particle and Atomic Physics and other areas to be added as

needed. The primary mission of the MJ-10 position is to collect data and provide meaningful answers regarding the science behind the amazing alien craft and their apparent mastery of such forces as gravity, and the nature, capabilities, and limitations of their weapons.

MJ-11 Position

MJ-11 is Coordinator for Biological and Behavioral Sciences. The mission of the MJ-11 position is to collect information as to the nature of alien biology, brain function and behavior. It is especially important it be determined if any viruses, bacteria, gases, chemicals or radioactive elements might be effective as weapons.

MJ-12 Position

MJ-12 is overall Coordinator of Scientific Activities. Under MJ-12 will be two subsidiary positions, MJ-12(A) and MJ-12(B). MJ-12(A) will be coordinator of defense-related scientific activities, with priority on the development of weapons/strategies which will provide the US with an effective deterrent where none whatsoever now exists. MJ-12(B) will be coordinator of other scientific activities, with priority on the understanding of the physical nature of the aliens and their motives/objectives.

Chapter Twenty

While Hillenkoetter was meeting with the President, Will Stone was having a deeply shocking personal experience, one which I believe was intended either to lead him to deep inner understanding, or to shatter him.

When he had arrived at Los Alamos he had found that things had been magnificently organized by the talented Sally Darby. Her timetable, however, did not allow for what he really wanted to do, which was sleep for about twenty hours.

Sally now had a team of six CIG personnel working with her, and they were getting the full cooperation of ZIA, the private company that arranged all the Hill's logistics, supplies and construction.

Will could detect the hand of the White House in all this; he allowed himself to hope that Hilly had gained ground with Truman.

While Sally got the cadaver into cold storage he called Washington to report to Hilly. It was one o'clock in the morning Mountain time. That made it three A.M. in Washington.

The director had just returned from the White House. Will was informed that the President would probably approve Hilly's plan for a new agency. If he did, Will was going to be its head.

It was a tremendous vote of confidence for a young man still reeking of formaldehyde and covered with road dust.

He hung up the telephone and tried to take a little time for himself in the room that had been provided for him at Fuller Lodge, the Hill's hostel for visiting dignitaries.

After a fitful ten minutes trying to nap he had a shower and a shave. He was surprised to find GI soap in the bathroom. It reminded him that, until literally a few days ago, Los Alamos had been a military city.

When he finished his shower there was a message from Sally under the door. As he dressed again he looked wistfully at the bed.

He went to her office in the Big House a short distance from Fuller. Both buildings had been part of the boys' school that had been here before the government moved in, and as a result they were fairly well constructed. The rest of the Hill's residential area was a mass of Quonset huts, prefabs and trailers.

There were people everywhere; the place was a hive of activity even at one o'clock in the morning. Lights blazed along the perimeter fence and all through the Tech area.

His obsession with secrecy made Will dislike the small-town feeling, the frank and curious looks that he got as he walked down the street. Even though everyone here was cleared—and many of them at a very high level—few really accepted the "need-to-know" concept that was beginning to redefine American secrecy. Nobody, no matter how exalted their clearance, had a right to know everything, not even the President. Knowledge was only to be shared as required by very specifically defined need. Will could see these people gossiping among themselves, confident that their clearances made it legal.

He did not like Los Alamos for another and more curious reason. That was its exposure to the sky. He would rather have gone underground with the disk than take it up onto the top of a mesa like this.

The sky was like an open door.

If a car could be taken off a road and the driver not even know it, they were going to lose this thing flat. That was too much power, too much capability.

Will simply refused to believe that the people of White Lakes had actually seen his *car* coming out of a huge disk. Because he remembers nothing more about what happened, it is impossible to be certain. Maybe all he encountered in White Lakes was a little hysteria.

He himself was close to that point. Every innocent stranger

seemed full of hostile intentions. If he'd been armed he thinks now that he might have shot somebody. It took everything he had not to dive for the shadows and make his way to the Big House as though he were back in Algiers.

The building wasn't designed for offices. There was no receptionist, no phone and it was the middle of the night. He didn't know where to find Sally. He was so exhausted that this simple problem actually choked him up.

He surveyed the large, silent room. There were books everywhere. Despite the lateness of the hour people crowded the library, browsing, reading, all reflecting the tremendous intellectual energy of this place.

Finally Will spotted a staircase at the far end of the room and mounted it, passing through the haze of pipe and cigarette smoke.

When he had opened the door every head in the room had turned toward him. And every eye followed him as he went to the staircase.

Of course it wasn't hard to find Sally. Her office was the only lighted room on the second floor.

"Will," she said, "congratulations!" She looked absolutely glorious. She was glowing. He had seen her as a pale, effective woman haunted by her own vulnerabilities. Now he understood why Hilly had chosen her. Pressure was obviously her milieu. Confidence, competence, effectiveness poured from her.

He tells me now that Sally Darby should have been MJ-2, the leader of MAJIC. I can't pass judgment.

"How in the world did you know? Hilly only told me a few minutes ago."

"I talk to Hilly, too. He called here half an hour ago looking for you. And he asked me if I thought you could do the job."

"Thank you for your support."

"Hell, I told him I could do it better."

"Will you second me?"

"Maybe, MJ-2. Assuming your appropriation is big enough."

"I want the disk guarded. Heavily."

"We have tanks and antiaircraft guns at our disposal."

"This place has tanks?"

233

"A company."

"Get them deployed. I want the whole place on full alert status against attack from the air."

She picked up her telephone. A moment later Drew Shelburne came into the office. He had been a bright counterintelligence expert in the British Division.

"Hello, Drew."

"My Lord, Will, when did you die?"

"I've been on the road for eleven hours. Why do you look like a flower at one A.M.? Both of you."

"I guess we're just too enthusiastic to get tired," Drew replied.

Sally gave him instructions to relay to the guard units.

When Drew left Will dropped into a hard chair, the only spare one in the office. "I'm an exhausted man in a place where nobody ever sleeps. Have you got any headache powders, dear?"

"Bromo-Seltzer."

He poured the stuff directly into his mouth and swallowed it before it foamed up too much. Sally brought him water from somewhere and he washed the residue down. "I feel like hell and I'm scared to sleep alone."

She raised her eyebrows.

"It's not a proposition. But they come in the night. Last night, that sentry—my God."

"Look," she said, "I hate to tell you this but you have a meeting with the scientific group at seven in the morning. The pathologist wants to get to work as quickly as possible. He's the only one from off the Hill. The other three are locals. A physicist, an electromagnetic expert and an aerodynamicist to examine the disk."

"Tell me about this pathologist."

"Gene Edwards. University of California at Berkeley. Working on a top secret radiation pathology project. Married, two children. Prominent New Dealer during the thirties. Flirted with the Party in '33–34."

"A Communist? You got me a Communist?"

"His security clearance is his bread and butter. We promised to erase his record in return for absolute secrecy."

234

"Don't actually do it."

"Of course not. The point is, he can be blackmailed if necessary."

"Good. And the others?"

"Straight-arrows, nothing to hold over them. One of them once had a mistress."

"Big deal."

"Exactly. We just have to rely on them being good, loyal Americans."

Will recalls that he took her hand. She seemed beautiful and desirable to him at that moment. Had she reacted differently it probably would have been the beginning of the only love in his life.

"You're tired and scared and you need a friend."

"Hello, friend."

"I'm a colleague, Will."

"And I'm just a scared hick kid from upper Westchester. I think I need a lap to put my head in."

Her response was to call the security service and ask them to post a guard outside his room.

She accompanied him back to Fuller and helped him get settled. "Everything you own stinks," she commented offhandedly.

"Call the laundry."

"They have a laundromat."

"I thought I was in a hotel."

"With GI soap? I'll hire a day laborer to get you clean. Maybe if we soaked your clothes in Oxydol for a couple of hours."

"Find me fresh clothes. My suitcase is still in Roswell, anyway."

"We can manage a suit by morning, I expect."

"I'm a forty-two long. Remember that. I don't want to be forced to wear a bag."

That was the last thing he remembered until he woke up abruptly at three-thirty A.M.

The room was dark except for a line of light coming in under the door. Will felt reassured; a faint smell of cigarette smoke told him that his guard was at hand, no more than twenty feet away.

In the next instant he discovered how very far twenty feet can be.

There was somebody crouched on the foot of his bed.

At first he thought it was a shadow, but as his eyes adjusted to the light he could see that the form was solid and very much alive.

He called to the guard—and all that came out was a puff of air. His next thought was to turn on the reading light that was clipped to the head of the bed.

A small man sat there as solid and real as any living person. Will called out again but there was only more hissing.

Will cannot describe the man in detail but his impression is distinct that this was a human being. He had the disquieting impression that it was a child, a boy with a huge, bobbing head.

Will threw back the bedsheets and started for the door. A hand pressed against his chest, delivering what felt like an electric jolt. The man's arm was clad in silver cloth.

Will remembers vividly how startled he was by the effect the touch had on him. Blackness came around his eyes.

"It's all right, Willy, it's all right," the creature said. His voice was ugly and low and rattling as if his lungs had given out. "We're going to capture you, Willy."

It took him an hour to mutter the rest of this story. Will is terrifically reticent about sex, and even after all these years the embarrassment of talking about what next took place was painful to witness.

First he felt a terrific blast of pleasure in his groin. Then fingers were touching him intimately and their strange electricity was pouring waves of pleasure into him. In the shadows he could see the head come forward, closer and closer. He thought that he saw the face of a demented child. The lips smacked wetly.

Will toppled back into the pillows, swooning with terror and pleasure. An instant later his body gave a spasm and he experienced a terrific blast of sexual release. "It's all right," the thing repeated, "it's all right, Willy."

My heart went out to Will as he described enduring an intimate and protracted exploration that he was helpless to prevent. All the while it continued the voice kept repeating that it was all right.

As far as Will was concerned, it was very far from all right.

At last the strange creature withdrew his hand. The bed springs creaked as he jumped down to the floor.

He took a few steps toward the window and the next thing Will remembers the creature was gone and he was screaming.

This sound the guard heard. He responded instantly. The door swung open.

Will managed to quiet himself down. He could not tell the man what had happened. Finally he croaked that he'd had a nightmare. He apologized to the guard.

He could not tell anybody that he had just been, in effect, raped. It was a secret he kept for forty-two years, until yesterday.

In his day homosexuality was the darkest of secrets, a deep personal shame for any man. Had he been able to gain access to his own sexuality, I suspect that he might have discovered that he was somewhat attracted to men.

As the guard left he called out, "Get me a pot of black coffee. And if I fall asleep wake me up."

"Yes, sir."

He lay down to wait for the coffee. It was a long moment before he was aware that somebody was stroking his cheek. "Sleep, little one," said the voice of the strange man. Will's eyes flew open.

He was alone.

He buried his head in the pillow. "Stop," he shouted, "for the love of Mike stop!"

A sweet voice sang in response. "Sleep and rest, sleep and rest, mother will come to thee soon."

"God help me! Stop them! Stop them, God, stop them!"

Then the world faded to black and he slept. The guard said in the morning that he tried to rouse him but couldn't.

He had slept *their* sleep, perfect sleep, the sleep of babies and old men. They had given him a gift, I think, the chance to see himself as he was. I cannot blame him for passing it up. It takes great courage to love one's true self.

The next morning Will ached with disgust. He loathed what had happened to him. And yet . . . there was also something else.

He didn't only feel attacked and raped and captured. He felt loved as he had not since he was a boy. Cherished, even.

This did not reassure him, and for a rather odd reason.

As son of a master fisher of trout, he knew the secret of the stream, that the man who takes the best fish is the one who loves them truly, and feels a genuine compassion as he drags them exhausted from the water and drops them to suffocate in his creel.

He was just like that, Wilfred Stone, a fish being loved to exhaustion.

And he was just about out of fight.

Chapter Twenty-one

His forty-eight hours of grappling with the others had reduced him to a furtive, huddling creature aching with secrets he dared not tell. He was closer to a complete breakdown, I think, than he realizes even now.

It was in this state that he held his first meeting with the scientific team that became the nucleus of the group that formed under MJ-12.

Three of the four scientists were bursting with confidence and good fellowship. Two weeks ago he would have craved the company of such men and counted them as critical assets to the team he was assembling. Now he had no more faith in them than a tired commissar might in the latest rabble of slaves from Moscow's dungeons.

There was Walt Roediger with his churchwarden pipe and academic demeanor. And paunchy, fluffy Dick Toole, the electromagnetics whiz who had been working until two days ago on the linear accelerator project.

The two of them stood up and advanced on Will as silently as ghosts when he arrived in the cramped conference room of Tech 21, the building Sally had commandeered to house the project.

It had once been a massive generator room. Now it was mostly damp cavernous space, smelling faintly of machine oil.

The communist pathologist Gene Edwards was what Will described in his old-fashioned manner as "a real Arrow Shirt man." Tall, youthful, strong, he reacted to Will's arrival only by putting down his *Los Alamos Times* with a considerable amount of paper rattling. His body language spoke resentment. This was understandable, in view of the fact that he had been coerced into coming here.

They did not feel that they could risk telling anyone anything until the individual was on site and under their control. One word to the newspapers that the government was looking for scientists to study alien artifacts and the desperate and fragile cover-up would fall apart.

So he'd been forced to cooperate by a threat to his clearance. Without it he could not work on the program to which he was assigned at the University of California, which sought to understand and mediate the effects of radiation poisoning.

Edwards was the most serious security risk and his area of expertise was the most vulnerable to disclosure.

The group's last member was costumed rather than dressed, in what Will assumed was his own carefully considered notion of intellectual disarray.

According to Sally he was more than just brilliant like the others, he was something of a genius. He was an astronomer by profession. He had been chosen for Majestic because of his combination of backgrounds. Not only did he have a degree in astrophysics and an outstanding record of discoveries and achievements, he'd also worked during the war as a propagandist. He had been damned good at that, too.

Privately they would work Gerald Benning the astrophysicist to the bone. His public role would be a propaganda function. As an astronomer of significant academic standing he would explain every sighting that came to Air Force attention, taking the position that they were all bunk.

To make the group's chief astrophysicist also its chief propagandist was a stroke of cunning. It minimized "need to know" while it also meant that the propaganda would be fine-tuned to hide the real situation.

I have read some of Benning's books, *Flying Disks* and *The Saucer Enigma,* and they are indeed masterpieces of the propagandist's art, making utterly insupportable and absurd claims that the disks can be explained by things like nonexistent atmospheric "lensing" effects.

Benning truly was a genius and he must have been a man of courage as well, a moral man. While keeping the public calm with his debunking books he secretly fought to understand the others. And he knew that he would be publicly discredited when and if his secret labors bore fruit.

Was CIG lucky, or was their real insight at work when these scientists were picked? I have a feeling that Roscoe Hillenkoetter was a far more extraordinary man than history yet realizes.

Will made an opening speech which was designed to disarm his small audience as much as possible. "Good morning, gentlemen," he said, "I'm your resident bureaucrat here to interfere with your work in annoying ways."

"Thank you," Edwards replied in a surprisingly pleasant voice. Will had expected a file like his to whine.

"I realize that none of you know exactly why you're here."

"But we're damn interested," Benning said. "I just gave up a week's telescope time at Palomar, so this had better be good."

"Gentlemen, this is probably the single most important thing that has ever happened."

"Tom Dewey's decided to get off his duff and whip Harry Truman," said Walt Roediger around his pipe.

Edwards looked disgusted. "This is supposed to be important. That excludes both Dewey and Truman."

"Gentlemen," Will said, "we've captured a flying disk and three of its occupants and we would like you to participate in a program of greater potential impact than the Manhattan Project—"

"Hold it," shouted the hitherto silent Toole, "did you say a flying disk?"

"I did."

He burst out: "Poppycock!"

He would not be the first to submerge fear beneath a shout of derision. Will quickly learned to use that tendency of the intellectually arrogant as a tool in maintaining secrecy. A man proud of his own intellectual attainments does not want to believe in superior aliens, not when their mere existence threatens the validity of his knowledge and therefore his self-integrity. I believe that this is the reason that scientists such as Carl Sagan continue to delude themselves about the reality of the disks.

Will decided that the best way of responding to Toole's outburst was to ignore it for the moment. "You must understand

241

that we have a need for absolute secrecy. There is substantial evidence that our alien visitors are extremely hostile."

Edwards shook his head sadly. "Of course. The only motive strong enough to bring intelligent life across the universe turns out to be conquest."

Out of exhaustion and nervousness Will downed an entire cup of coffee, almost gagging with the heat of it. There were sweet rolls and he began gobbling one.

Roediger stared at him. "Mr. Bureaucrat, this is about the most unnerving pause for refreshment I have ever endured. Will you get on with it, if you can stand to stop feeding."

"These sweet rolls would be good if they had more than the single raisin among them."

"Hostile aliens! Talk!"

"Yes."

Toole's eyes twinkled. "I'd want proof. Absolute proof in the form of a corpus delicti to autopsy."

"Dr. Edwards will be starting his autopsy in fifteen minutes."

"I'm beginning to suspect that you aren't kidding."

Sally pointed to the large double doors at the far end of the room. "The disk is through there. The bodies are in cold storage next door in T-22."

"I'm going to autopsy these things?" Edwards had gone pale.

Roediger gave Will a frank look. "There's physical material? This disk is what—I remember the papers saying something about debris being recovered."

"A rawinsonde. It was a rawinsonde that was recovered. I think that was the official verdict." Dr. Toole folded his arms.

"Gentlemen, we ought to begin. First, this project is going to be tightly compartmentalized. That means that every research team reports only to its own supervisor."

"No cross-fertilization?" Will wondered if Toole rather than Edwards was going to prove the more difficult.

"Initially there will be. But when we begin to gain some perspective we will divide according to subject area. At that point cross-fertilization will stop and need-to-know will replace it."

"Stupid, but predictable," Toole said.

"I would like to begin with a walk-around of the disk. Then we will observe Dr. Edwards's first approach to our most intact body." I went to the doors and pulled them open.

There was absolute silence. Then Toole spoke. "It looks a bit like something from a movie. Is it a prop?"

"No, Doctor, it is not."

Roediger walked up to the disk. "I'd like to go inside. Is it safe?"

"It may be partially operational. Personnel entering it have experienced extreme time disorientation. We don't know why."

"Time," Dr. Toole said. "In what sense?"

"A man subjectively perceived himself as being inside for a few minutes. He was actually gone for nine hours."

Benning was examining the damaged area. He reached his arm in and waved it up and down. "I wonder if we have a time machine here."

"Could such a thing exist—I mean, as a frankly physical object?" Roediger touched the edge of the disk as he spoke.

"Has it been tested for radioactive output? Are there disease factors possibly involved?"

"The AAF men who found it put a Geiger counter on it," Sally said. "There is no radiation."

"What about X-rays? Neutrons?"

"Doctor Benning, the main reason we're here is to develop a program. To make a beginning."

"Mr. Stone."

"Yes, Dr. Toole?"

"This temporal effect interests me. Is there a written report? Were any measurements taken, data gathered?"

"The man went on a brief reconnaissance into the vehicle, carrying only a flashlight. Nobody can account for the fact that nine hours passed, least of all the man himself."

Edwards regarded me. "Were you the individual who entered the craft?"

"Why do you ask that?"

"Just answer the question."

"Yes is the short answer."

"Then I have another question."

Will managed a smile. A weak one, I suspect. Edwards had a quick and challenging mind.

"My second question is, why do you look like that?"

"Like what?"

"Like you haven't slept in days, like you've just lost a great deal of weight. Did being inside the vehicle affect your health?"

"I went in, located and retrieved the best-preserved of the three bodies, then exited the craft. I apparently kept telling the people waiting for me outside that I was fine, and not to come in after me. They questioned me every fifteen minutes for the full nine hours. I don't remember saying a thing to them."

Dr. Roediger got a flashlight from the box of equipment Sally had arranged. He peered into the craft. "This is obviously living quarters. Wrecked by an explosion."

"The thing came down during a thunderstorm," Sally said.

"How odd," Edwards commented.

"Why odd?"

"That somebody this advanced would still have trouble with thunderstorms."

Roediger spoke. "Obviously they wouldn't. I think that we can safely assume that this thing was intentionally crashed. It's a plant."

"Complete with dead crew?" Benning said. "I hardly think so."

"Maybe the crew was supposed to eject. Maybe they don't care about things like dead crew." Roediger pulled himself up into the device.

"Doctor, don't do that." Will's voice revealed his fear.

"I won't go any farther in. I just want to get the feel of it."

"Gentlemen," Sally reminded them, "the first order of business today is the autopsy."

Edwards flared. "This is ridiculous. You want me to autopsy the bodies of apparent alien beings with no preparation, no prior knowledge of the anatomy—nothing at all to go on."

"It's deteriorating too rapidly. We can't wait," Will said.

"It was X-rayed last night," Sally added. "The whole body. The films will be there to use as a guide."

Will was relieved when Roediger emerged from the disk.

"There's decorative work in the paper screens," he said. "Flowers. Yellow primroses, I believe."

"Yes, we noticed that."

"And purple writing on the walls."

"Calculations, I thought."

"I wonder if it isn't poetry? Things written by men far from home." Roediger worked with his pipe.

"You probably shouldn't smoke in here," Sally said.

"Of course."

They were like bees in a flower garden, the way they circled and danced about the disk. They examined its skin, measured it with tape measures, took notes on the clipboards she had provided.

The scene from the night before kept replaying itself in Will's mind. He could still feel those clammy fingers on him. As a matter of fact, he feels them to this day. He said to me, "I'd been taken to one hell of an ugly place in myself."

Rape is more than an act of violence against the body, it is an assault on the soul. Worse for Will, though, must have been the fact that he had felt such a strong response.

"It's all right, Willy." Had he accepted those words, he would have been a free man. Even if he had still died alone, he would have been able to look back on a life with some love in it. I feel sorry for the man, never having been loved, never except when he was a tiny boy.

"Gentlemen," Sally said, "we have to get to the autopsy right now."

"We have three cadavers," Will added.

"And one middle-level pathologist," Edwards said. Will was worried by the bitterness in his voice. Was he going to let them down?

"You have adequate credentials," Sally said.

"Adequate! You need the best man in the world for this. What about Rowland or Dowling? Why me, plucked out of a pretty average sort of a career? Arguably, this is the most important autopsy that has ever been done. Why me?"

"And what about the rest of us? We're all good, I'll agree to that. But where's Fermi or Oppenheimer or John Von Neumann? Frankly, Miss Darby, why any of us? Where are the great men?" Benning's eyes flashed.

"I'll tell you why people like that aren't here," Toole said. "People like that can't be coerced. They also can't be fooled."

"You're all good men," Sally replied. Her voice was smooth, as if she hadn't heard Toole's implications. "We don't want people who might attract press attention simply by their movements. We had to find excellent men who weren't publicly visible."

Edwards was looking more and more unhappy. "Which brings us to the issue of secrecy. You are obviously desperate to hide this whole business, even from a security-cleared community like Los Alamos. I think it's fair to ask your reasons."

"We're still just feeling our way. There have been incidents that suggested hostility. But we aren't sure of anything. Until we *are* sure, I think you'll agree that things should be kept under wraps."

"I can accept that," Roediger said quickly.

"The people have a right to know." Edwards.

"I think its all damn good fun," said Toole. "It's probably some kind of psychological test—"

Will was fascinated by the man's stubbornness. "You still don't believe the disk is real."

"It's made of paper and tinfoil, and the ribbing is dark-brown wood. *Wood!* I'll say I don't think it's real. I think it was made in Hollywood."

"The tinfoil, as you call it, cannot be damaged in any way by any means we have yet applied. It's incredibly tough."

"What kind of testing has been done? Are there reports we can read?"

"Dr. Toole, the testing was *ad hoc,* in the field. We fired bullets into a piece of the foil. Tried to burn the paper, break and saw the wood. We couldn't."

"They came in a ship of tinfoil and paper." Absently, Roediger tapped his pipe against his leg. "Extraordinary."

"What's extraordinary is that the rest of you apparently believe this."

"Of course I do, Dr. Toole," replied Roediger. "If it was less than extremely strange, I would have my doubts."

Toole gave Will such a long, searching look that he felt he should add something. "You can reserve judgment until you see the bodies."

"Actually, I believe you now," Toole said. "Not because of this ridiculous disk. My reason is simple, Mr. Stone. I believe you because you are so incredibly scared."

Will could hear something dripping in the depths of the room. "I think that you should all witness the autopsy," he said. "If Dr. Edwards will agree."

They all followed Edwards into the autopsy room.

SUBJECT: AUTOPSY REPORT # 1
DATE: 7/14/47
COPY <u>ONE</u> OF THREE

INITIAL FINDINGS UPON EXAMINATION
AND AUTOPSY OF THE BODY OF AN
APPARENT ALIEN CREATURE

1. External Appearance

This body was observed to be in a state of significant deterioration. It had been preserved with formaldehyde solution but not otherwise dissected.

The cadaver was 44 inches long with a weight of 27 pounds when the preservative solution had been drained.

The external appearance of this cadaver was of a human embryo with an enlarged cranium. Hands and feet were normal. Finger- and toe-nails had been pared. Fingerprints of a swirl-left pattern were observed and taken. All ten fingers and toes were apparent. There was some vestigial webbing between first and second fingers and toes.

Sexual organs appeared to be those of a male. They were in an embryonic state and revealed no evidence of pubescence.

Ears were partially formed, and showed some evidence of surgical intervention. Folds of skin had been drawn out from the surface of the scalp in an apparent attempt to create the impression of a more fully developed ear than was actually present.

Lips were vestigial and the mouth contained no erupted teeth. The nose was also in an incomplete state of growth and had also received surgical intervention, resulting in what appeared to be a very thin and delicate organ.

Eyes were distinguished by extensive surgical intervention. They were almond-shaped and by far the most prominent facial feature. The eyeballs were not matured and appeared to have been sutured with artificial lenses of

an unknown type. Because of their extremely
unusual condition, dissection of these eyes
was not attempted.

2. Dissection

An incision was made from the thorax to the
scrotum. The skin was first extended from the
fascia and the fascia was observed to be consistent with the appearance of an immature
human male. The fascia were then dissected
and the internal organs were observed. The
position of the heart was observed to be ver-
tical, as would be consistent with a very
early fetus, prior to the fourth month. The
organ was prominent and was weighed to be
1/70th of the mass of the body. When the organ
was dissected it was found that there was direct communication between the two auricles
through the foramen ovale. The Eustachian
valve was observed to be large. A *ductus ar-
teriosus* was observed to communicate between
the pulmonary artery and the descending
aorta. This *ductus* opened into the descending
aorta just below the origin of the left sub-
clavian artery.
Alterations in the structure of the circulatory system suggested that this body had been
surgically corrected to detach it from placental dependence in an artificial manner.
The stomach was opened and found to be free of
any food substances. The cardiac orifice was
apparently atrophied, although the deterioration of the *corpus* made this difficult to
determine. It is possible that this individual did not eat.
The liver was prominent and it was clear that
the blood of the umbilical vein would tra-
verse it before entering the inferior cava.
The umbilical vein itself had been severed of
its placental crown and returned to the circulatory system by a means that was beyond the
scope of this dissection to establish.
The lungs were not developed. There were lat-
eral pouches on either side of the central di-
verticulum, open through into the pharynx.

The larynx was somewhat cartilaginous and the trachea was developed.

It is probable that this individual did not breathe any more than he ate. The means of sustaining life is unknown, if he was ever alive in any practical sense.

The cranium was dissected and it was found that the skull was formed of exceptionally thin and pliant cartilaginous material, appearing to be bone precursor that had been affected in some manner, making it more than usually thin and delicate. The brain itself was extensively and surprisingly formed. There was an unknown cortex superimposed on the forebrain and extending as far back as the fissure of Rolando.

Because of this extraordinary formation it was decided not to pursue dissection of the brain at this time. The organ was extracted and placed in fluid preservation pending further study.

Overall, this *corpus* presented the appearance of a human embryo of three or four months duration that had been the subject of considerable alteration and modification, some of it obviously surgical. Other modifications, such as that of the brain, were harder to understand. In addition to the alterations, there was the matter of the size of the body and the relatively mature condition of the epidermis and nails. It would appear that this fetus was separated from its mother and brought to a semifunctional state by artificial means.

3. Conclusion

This is a human male fetus that has been subjected to forced maturation without normal gestation. Its degree of functionality while living—if it ever was alive—is unknown.

SUBJECT: AUTOPSY REPORT # 2
DATE: 7/14/47
COPY <u>ONE</u> OF THREE

INITIAL FINDINGS UPON EXAMINATION
AND AUTOPSY OF THE BODY OF AN
APPARENT ALIEN CREATURE

1. External Appearance

This body was observed to be in a state of profound deterioration. It had not been preserved but was delivered in a container of rubberized canvas, to which some of the tissue had adhered. The cadaver was 36 inches long with a weight of 8 pounds. The external appearance of this cadaver was not of a human type.
The skin appeared smooth and a dark bluish-gray in color. There was no clothing on the body. There were no genitals and no way of determining sex, if any. The nose consisted of two slits, the mouth was a small opening that did not appear to be supported by an articulated jaw, and there were holes in the position of ears. The cranium was round and large in proportion to the body and the eyes were almond-shaped. The eyes were closed and could not be opened without damaging structures, due to condition of decaying tissue.
Arms and wrists were very thin. The hands displayed a three-digit arrangement without thumb. The arms extended to approximately three inches above the knee. The three fingers extended directly from the wrist, with no palm.

2. Dissection

The body was opened from crotch to chin. A green liquid emerged from the incision. The skin was not backed by fascia, and the bone structure appeared to be a cartilaginous substance of light green-blue color.
Internal organs were observed but their func-

tion was unclear. The thoracic and peritoneal cavities communicated and there appeared to be no respiratory system and no stomach. The esophagus was vestigial and dissipated before reaching another organ.

There appeared to be two multichambered hearts and it was surmised that body fluid could be pumped rapidly. There was an extensive circulatory system that involved three different types of vein. Some material was extracted from one of these systems and suggested possible waste, leading to the notion that waste may have been exuded through the skin.

The fluid removed from the body was analyzed under the microscope and found to be a vegetable substance, chlorophyll-based. It is possible that photosynthesis was the means of obtaining energy.

The cranium was dissected and it was observed that a ridge of cartilage separated the brain into two completely isolated components. The brain was severely deteriorated, but appeared to be extensively fissured and divided into numerous lobes. Because of the deterioration the degree of bilateralism of the two halves could not be determined with any accuracy.

This cadaver exuded an unusually foul odor.

3. Conclusion

This is not a cadaver of a kind previously observed by or known to this pathologist. It appears to be a form of creature utilizing elements of both the animal and the vegetable.

Chapter Twenty-two

An hour after Hillenkoetter got the autopsy reports Will received an urgent telex: return to Washington soonest. He flew by light plane to Denver and connected with the United Mainliner, scheduled to land at Washington National Airport at eleven P.M.

He'd had only fitful sleep for three consecutive nights, and had been operating under numerous incredible pressures, ranging from the efforts of the Air Force to take over the project to the repeated personal assaults from the visitors.

The least thing could unsettle him, and he found himself wanting to weep over the simplest problem, like whether or not it would be impolite to remove his shoes on the plane.

He kept trying to tell himself that the episodes he'd had might have been dreams, and yet he knew that they weren't. They were physical experiences—horrible and impossible, but entirely real.

Every time he dozed off the image of the little man with the bobbing head would reappear and he would wake up pouring sweat. It would take him fifteen minutes just to control the nausea, and sometimes he could not.

He was running entirely on coffee and cigarettes. He sat smoking and staring out the window, trying to think of someone in whom he could confide.

A psychiatrist was obviously out. He had all the symptoms of what was then called dementia praecox and would be so diagnosed.

When they landed at Washington National it was past eleven, closer to twelve.

A fog was rising from the Potomac. But for the lights and bustle associated with Will's flight the airport was empty. He was met by a young CIG man with a sign, "W. Stone."

This cheerful kid took his bag and conducted him to a black Chrysler. He assumed that he was on his way home to a bath, clean pajamas and blessed sleep.

They were turning onto Pennsylvania Avenue when he realized that their destination was the White House. For a moment he was furious, but on reflection he realized that this was inevitable.

The fact that he was being driven this hard is a testament to the level of concern felt by the President. Nobody had ever even questioned the basic assumption that this was an invasion by aliens with military ambitions.

Will was led into the Cabinet Room by a White House guard in full uniform and looking at midnight like he'd just been boiled clean and pressed to a razor crease.

The room was jammed with people, hazy with smoke and blazing with lights. Huge color pictures of the disk and the aliens were on every wall. The President was sitting at the far end of the table with a pot of coffee in front of him. Hilly and Forrestal were beside him. Van sat along one side of the table with the other Joint Chiefs. Eisenhower was there, looking extremely grim. There were a number of civilians present whom Will did not know.

When he appeared all conversation ceased, every head turned to face him. The silence was absolute.

He barely managed to keep on his feet, such was his fatigue.

"Mr. Stone," the President said, "I'm glad your plane was nearly on time."

Was he expected to make a presentation?

"May I see the agenda," he asked.

"There is no agenda, young man," one of the strangers said in a thick Middle European accent. "There is only you." Will fantasized stepping through a window and racing across the lawn, escaping into the night streets.

Vandenberg tossed a photo of the most startling of the visitors down the table. "We are given to understand that this is a deformed human child," Van said quietly. "Could you explain that a little further?"

"Well, that's what the pathologist found."

"But look at it," Eisenhower said. "Does it look human to you?"

"I don't think I'm ready to say. All I can do is point to the fact that it has perfectly ordinary fingers and hands, and that the pathologist is a good one. His finding was that it was a surgically altered baby that had stopped maturing at about five months gestation. The fingers were even manicured."

"Young man," said one of the older gentlemen there, "I am Dr. Kenneth Rhodes of the Ringer Clinic."

Hilly spoke up. "Dr. Rhodes is one of the leading embryologists in the country."

"To take an embryo of that maturity and somehow cause it to grow larger without maturing further—that's a complete impossibility. As the cells grow they also mature. This is—well, this is in the nature of things."

"I don't think that creature is in the nature of anything, Doctor. We saw all sorts of signs of surgical intervention. God only knows what else was done—drugs, electricity. Could be anything. If that creature lived it was human. We found it in the company of two obvious aliens. According to Dr. Edwards none of these creatures could have lived long, if they ever lived at all. But nevertheless, they are what we found."

The President suddenly slapped his hand down on the cabinet table. "I want to know what the hell's going on here and what I'm supposed to do about it. If that thing is human, where did it come from? Whose baby was it?"

"Mr. President—"

"Not you, young man. I've got five of the leading scientists in the world here. Gentlemen, tell us where that baby came from."

"And what about the 'hivelike' living quarters," Forrestal asked. "Does that mean communist?"

Despite the President's admonition, Will spoke up. "I don't know what it means. Who said the living quarters were a hive?"

"We got a telex from Darby while you were en route," Hilly

said. "They've begun making a blueprint of the interior of the disk."

"Hivelike," Will repeated.

"Are they communists?"

"I don't have any idea, General Eisenhower!"

Forrestal's eyes were almost popping out of his head. "Aliens in advance of us and they're communists. We must hide this at all costs."

"I can see *Pravda* now," the President said. "We have seen the future and it is communist."

A deep silence followed. Finally Van filled it. "We need to decide on a response. I think that we must prove to these people that we are sovereign in our own territory, land, sea and air."

"I agree," Truman said.

Eisenhower gave Will a challenging look. "How? Do you have any thoughts?"

"We have to face the fact that they're far ahead of us."

"How far?"

"Terribly far."

"Examples?"

"The condition of the fetus is an example. To us it is a human fetus—or was one. But somehow it was almost certainly functioning. The thing lived, breathed, thought. We do not know how that could be."

"I'll tell you what I think," the President said. "I think this damn infant was stolen from some family and monkeyed with by those—what are they, anyway? What was that stuff about vegetable material in the autopsy report?"

"The truly alien ones were more vegetable than animal. That was the key finding."

"Little green men," Eisenhower said. "Literally."

"More bluish-gray, actually."

"I think this is a kidnapped child," said the President. "That's my concern. And that's the reason for the order I have issued to the Army Air Force. Van?"

"The Air Force has orders to seek, engage and destroy the enemy. We will fire on these disks, gentlemen, and we will bring them down."

"Citizens are having their babies kidnapped," the President added.

Absolute silence filled the room. The President alone remained animated, looking from face to face with a strange half smile on his face. He must have looked like that at the moment he told his cabinet he was going to drop the bomb.

The decision was absolutely characteristic of Western civilization, the American government and Harry Truman himself. It was in its essence highly conservative. But ours is at core a very conservative civilization. This is why it has survived so long, and why it has absorbed so many changes without altering its essential form.

Will also held his tongue. Unquestionably, it was a moment when he should have spoken out. I want to blame him for not doing so, but I cannot. He was at his very lowest ebb, he had just endured too much. Above all, I blame the visitors for his silence. Had they not put him under almost impossible pressure he might have had the psychic energy to intervene.

But that was probably their purpose: to test him, Truman, all of them, to the absolute limit and see then what they brought forth of themselves, peace or war.

Eisenhower was the first to speak. "I'd think a lot of questions would be answerable before you did that," he said. "A thing like that could have unpredictable importance."

In later years Eisenhower would become almost completely impossible to understand, but his locutions in the late forties required no more than a moment's extra thought.

"Unpredictable *consequences,*" Truman snapped. "Do we have any ideas on that?"

"It's too early for us to make a cultural evaluation," Dr. Rhodes said.

"I want ideas!"

Van responded. "Mr. President, we have a five-hundred-mile-an-hour airplane on the drawing boards."

Hearing this, the President seemed to become suddenly exhausted. "Look, this thing first appeared over Roswell. In other words, over Roswell Army Air Field where our atomic bombers are located."

Van offered more disturbing information. "From May twenty-seventh to June thirteenth the 509th demonstrated its capability to deliver nuclear warheads to targets at intercontinental distance during maneuvers out of Wendover Field. This weapons system works, and that is the first time we demonstrated it. Two weeks later the aliens started nosing around and getting in our hair."

The President continued. "Then we had soldiers go missing. And that estimate you wrote, Mr. Stone, and the missing persons reports for '44 to '46 suggest that people in the civilian population may be affected. And now this—this—I don't know what to call it—"

"An artificially deformed baby," one of the scientists offered.

"—living in a communistic hive," Forrestal said.

"Look, I've got a feeling we're going to have a war with these people and I don't know a goddamn thing! Not a goddamn thing!" Truman was actually ranting. Will saw his weakness and he was horrified.

"There are certain things that we do know." The scientist with the Middle European accent looked around the table. "First, they do not wish to annihilate us or they would already have done so—"

"Unless they're bringing up the big guns right now!"

"Well—"

"Well, nothing, Dr. Rosensweig! I'm telling you there could be an invasion coming. And as far as this communist business is concerned, maybe that's why we were singled out and they weren't—they don't need to be invaded because they're already communist."

Dr. Rosensweig spoke gently, trying to calm Truman down. "What 'they,' sir?"

"The Russians, man! *They* aren't getting treated to this or they'd be screaming in my face right this damn minute, you can bet your britches! Maybe they're being ignored because they're already communists."

"We know so little."

"Hell, they live in a hive! A *hive*! My blood runs cold."

"Yes, Mr. President, but the fact remains that they *have not* yet harmed us. Another thing we know is that their craft are vulnerable to thunderstorms. Meaning high-intensity electrical discharges applied in a random manner. Lightning."

"So what? How does that help me regain control of my airspace?"

"There is the beginning of a weapon in that idea, if we must have a weapon."

The President slammed his open hand on the table. "I need weapons now! Give me aircraft cannons with atomic bullets! Give me something that will damn well *work* right this minute!"

Eisenhower spoke again. "Within the joint mission capabilities, Mr. President, there are capacities that we have that we can apply in this case workably."

"And get this man a translator!"

"He means that we have joint mission capabilities that can be useful now," one of the other brass hats said quickly. Eisenhower flushed purple, obviously furious at Truman's jibe.

"We have substantial forces worldwide," Eisenhower said. "These forces can be raised to a higher level of alertness, with an increase in ground security and air patrols. It is a matter of casting your net, and you will get your fish."

Truman set his jaw. "I don't want to fail. I don't want to see a situation where we shoot and miss."

Van responded. "Mr. President, we will shoot and miss. But we will also shoot and hit."

"The metal is strong," Dr. Rosensweig cautioned.

"The things are made out of tinfoil, sticks and paper," Van said. "This is what they have. The foil is formed out of millions of tiny, absolutely uniform welds, according to Darby's telex. Amazing. They have good tinfoil, good sticks, good paper. But we have bullets that travel a thousand miles an hour and are made of hot lead. We will have some success."

"I want to know generally if you are opposed to armed action or for it," Truman asked.

Forrestal replied, "I'm very uneasy, frankly. If it wasn't for this communist thing—"

"Yes or no!"

"Well, yes, given the situation. But proceed with caution."

"Hilly?"

"We must show that we are in control."

Will's heart sank. He knew that he should be speaking out. He knew that the President was making a terrible mistake. But he still remained silent.

"Dr. Rosensweig, what does your committee think?"

"Gentlemen," Rosensweig said as he looked around him, "does any scientist here want to shoot?"

The other scientists were silent. The President shuffled his notes.

"As you requested, sir, we discussed this at length before we came here," Rosensweig continued. "We feel that you should wait for developments. An effort should be made to make contact before shooting. There are those among us who believe that certain factors of human history would repeat themselves elsewhere. Throughout history we have been getting more ethical. We think that this will also prove to be the case with our visitors."

Truman leaned far back in his chair. "More ethical? Now you've really scared me. I fear men who don't know history. Auschwitz is more ethical than something we did before? I would say that we are getting less ethical. If they are more advanced than us, I can make a case that they will be monsters."

He looked from man to man in the room. The depth of his cynicism amazed Will. How did he go on, thinking as he did? And yet his eyes twinkled. No matter how serious the situation, Truman was always bursting with good humor. A complex man.

"Gentlemen, I am ordering armed confrontation. And I want a service co-ordinated response along the lines that General Eisenhower appears to have suggested. Worldwide, every U.S. base is to be alerted that they will rise to meet any and all unusual aircraft, and they will shoot first. Now, it's late and young Mr. Stone is obviously dead on his feet. Thank you."

He abruptly left the room. Will stood there blinking, surprised, confused. It was over. We were going to shoot.

And fail. Of course we would fail.

There was a low buzz of conversation as papers were gathered and briefcases snapped shut. One of Van's men began pulling the photographs off the easels and putting them in a large portfolio.

Van came over to Hilly, motioning Will to join them. "The President wanted me to tell you that the disk is being moved to Muroc in California for military analysis. We've got to find the weak points."

"What about MJ-12, the scientific group," Hilly asked.

"That'll have to wait. Everything is military right now. Until we regain control of our airspace."

Will thought then that we were never going to regain control of the skies—or of the dark night, or even of our own minds.

He had the feeling that we had just made a catastrophic mistake, and were lost.

TOP SECRET EYES ONLY!

7/13/47
ARMY AIR FORCE
ORDER NO. 677833
SUBJECT: UNCONVENTIONAL AIRCRAFT

TO: All Operational Commands, Continental US, Generals Commanding.

1. Sightings or reports of unconventional aircraft such as glowing objects, flying disks or airships will receive immediate scramble emergency response.
2. Such aircraft will be attacked and shot down without warning.
3. Gun cameras are to be turned on during encounters.
4. Combat flight rules are the order of the day.
5. There will be a report to higher command the moment any sighting takes place.
6. No public announcements are to be made without authorization from higher command.

Chapter Twenty-three

It was not long before the Air Force had its first engagement with a flying disk. Subsequently there were a number of such engagements, the most famous of which took place near Godman Air Force Base on January 7, 1948. In this incident Captain Thomas Mantell was killed after flying toward what he described as "a metallic object . . . tremendous in size." There are substantial public indications that Captain Mantell's body was never found.

In February 1948 Brigadier General Cabell, chief of the Air Intelligence Requirements Division, asked that each air base in the U.S. be provided with one interceptor on a continuous alert basis, to be equipped with "such armament as deemed advisable."

Will told me that no disk was ever shot down, and the program was abandoned in the early fifties because of the high casualty rate and the zero success level.

The first engagement took place in July of 1947, barely a week after the "shoot to kill" order had been issued.

This incident occurred over central Kansas.

Tech Sergeant Eddie McConnell was almost but not quite napping over his radar screen at approximately three-thirty A.M. when his half-closed eyes detected a blip and he heard a beep as the antenna of his radar swept through 160 degrees. He hit his mike and announced, "Traffic incoming one-sixty."

"Incoming one-sixty," the traffic controller replied.

Neither man was particularly excited. The American Airlines Skysleeper sometimes passed overhead at this hour. Or it could be a private aircraft.

The radar operator watched his screen. "Traffic at flight level five approximate. Speed seven-sixty."

Now the controller sat up in his chair. "Verify that speed, please, sir."

"Seven-six-zero."

The controller was aware of order to engage unusual craft, they all were.

He thought that he might have a scramble situation here, and so informed the officer in charge. "We have a bogey three o'clock at level five incoming seven-six-zero."

The officer jumped up from behind his desk in operations and vaulted up the steps to the tower. "Lookout, what do you see at three o'clock," he yelled as he ran.

"A star, sir."

"Give me those binocs," he said. "Get radar."

The voice of the radar operator came through the loudspeaker. "Radar here, sir."

"Is it exactly one hundred and sixty-two degrees at this moment?"

"Yes, sir, speed now seven-eighty."

One of the men in the tower whistled. Everybody was watching the star now. "I'm calling a scramble," the operations officer said. "Hit the button."

The claxon sounded. Seven pilots were in the ready room drinking coffee and telling stories about girls they'd bedded or failed to bed. "I hate unannounced drills," one of them shouted over the blaring of the airhorn. "Your coffee gets cold."

The flight line lit up as the pilots ran toward their planes. Mechanics were hauling quick starters for the powerful Merlin engines that drove the P-51's. The pilots hit their seats, buckled in and started their checklists.

"Flaps extended. Turbochargers on. Coils on. Heat. Prepare to turn over." One after another the engines sputtered and coughed and charged to full power. The ground crews pulled the starters away and signaled with their flashlights that the planes could proceed to the active runway.

"Wing abreast formation," said Major Jack Mahoney, the squad leader.

Headsets crackled. "You will attack incoming bogey," said

the ground controller. "This is not a drill. Repeat, this is not a drill."

"Oh, boy," one of the pilots said.

"We gonna get ourselves some action right out here in apple pie country."

"No chatter, men."

Control ordered them to seven thousand feet so that they would come in above their quarry.

"Arm cannons." No test firing was allowed off the range area, so they didn't carry out that procedure.

Lieutenant John "Lucky" Luckman fingered his firing button, wishing that he could have a test volley. He watched the altimeter. "Passing three," the flight leader said, just as his instrument indicated the same. Right on the money.

"Heading eight-two," ground control announced.

"Wide turn. Mark. Execute," Major Mahoney said.

Luckman began a wide turn to the right. Combat rules meant no lights, so he couldn't see the position of his flight mates without looking hard for the blue flames of engine exhaust.

"Two-two-one. I have a faulty compass." Without his compass at night Joe Lait was flying half-blind. He could easily lose his bearings.

"Turn back, two-two-one."

"Roger. Two-two-one leaving formation. Returning to base."

Now there were six of them.

"Two-two-three. Instrument failure. My board is dead."

"Drop back emergency two-two-three."

"Lights on at base," the controller said. His voice was now high with nervousness.

A dead board was an odd malfunction. Lucky Luckman had never heard of such a thing. He'd never seen it on the simulator. He surveyed his own instrument cluster. Everything was perfectly normal.

"Level seven."

"Continue heading eight-two until you have visual contact."

"Two-two-four. I have a hot manifold. Returning to base."

"Affirmative," the flight leader said.

That was a more normal problem, Luckman thought. He didn't like the idea of being without a board at night, but a hot manifold was something you could deal with.

"Two-two-three. Cannot see base. Repeat, cannot see base."

"Two-two-three, your heading is zero-five-six. Make a slow right turn."

Herbie Nelson in 223 would be lucky to get back. If he hit any cloud he was going to drop a wing and spin for sure.

"Two-two-two. I have lost my compass. Lost my board. Turn—"

"Repeat, Two-two-two. Two-two-two?"

There was no answer from Ev Wiley. "Call him, Lucky."

"Two-two-two. Do you hear me? Two-two-two?"

Silence.

Lucky thought to himself that there was total electrical failure on that airplane—or worse. He was scared now. Only three aircraft remained.

Then he saw it, suddenly huge and dead ahead, and not where it was supposed to be at five thousand feet.

"I have visual. Twelve o'clock."

"I do not see, repeat do not see." That was his wingman, handsome Bobby Virgo. Why the hell didn't he see it, was he blind?

"What is our position?"

Ground answered. "Approximately fifteen miles from target. Flying abreast in ragged formation. Separation four thousand feet."

"That thing looks closer than fifteen miles."

"I just lost my engine," Bobby announced.

Lucky broke into a sweat. Not Bobby. He loved his friend, loved him too much. "Jesus, Bobby."

"Leaving seven. Spin!"

"Bail out, Bob!"

There was no reply.

"Bobby! Jesus, Bobby!"

"Hey, Luckman! Snap out of it!"

Lucky twisted his head around, looking for some sign of another plane. He didn't know who had spoken. "Two-two-five," he announced. "What is my position, control?"

"Calling two-two-five. Two-two-five come in."

"This is two-two-five! What is my position, ground?"

"Two-two-five is off the board with two-two-one. Calling two-two-one, calling two-two-five."

"Bobby's in a spin, you jerks!"

"Calling two-two-seven. Two-two-seven?"

That was the major. Where was he? Luckman was closing on the disk fast.

"Two-two-seven. State your position."

The major didn't answer ground. He was gone, too.

"This is two-two-five! I'm still closing! Can you hear me? Can anybody hear me?"

No reply. So his radio was out. He was on his own.

The disk was now huge, filling his gunsight. He had no more time to scream uselessly at ground control.

Luckman dropped his nose to keep the disk in his gunsight. He cut in his supercharger and increased revs to the maximum. The airframe screamed. Exhaust flickered past the cockpit. Airspeed passed through four hundred. Four-fifty. The disk grew larger and larger and larger.

He got as close as he was planning to get. His hands were shaking. At the least sign of trouble he was getting the hell out of this thing. He suspected that he had dead friends out there. Somehow the thing had shot them down.

He pressed his firing button and watched his tracer disappear into the disk. "On target and still closing," he said automatically. "Firing. I observe tracer hits."

It has been universally true that the others have remained passive unless attacked. Even when they are attacked it takes a powerful weapon and an aggressive man to get a reaction. According to Will absolutely nothing we have thrown at them has ever had the least effect.

Will coached me very carefully before I began to write about what might have happened to Lucky Luckman after he pulled his trigger. He believes that he met both Luckman and the missing soldier, Charles Burleson, under very extraordinary circumstances, so his speculations about their fates may not be without foundation.

Of course we cannot be certain that it went as we have surmised. But it most likely did, or very close. Lucky's story also gave me a chance to illustrate the visitors' most astonishing capability, which is certainly their mastery of the soul. A soul is part of the physical universe, and can be affected by appropriate technologies. It can get sick and be nursed and even medicated. Often the visitors say that they are doctors. They are, but it is the soul they wish to heal.

Souls can die, in the sense that they reject all identity and become simply an empty mote of potential.

Sometimes Will seems to think that the visitors are like farmers, and they are here harvesting souls.

One moment Luckman was flying an airplane. The next he was tumbling totally disoriented through a hell of wind. For an instant his mind was blank. He did not register what had happened and went on trying to push a firing button that wasn't there. Then the wind spread his arms and he saw light flash past his goggles.

He realized what had happened: he was outside of his plane.

A rush of adrenaline made his heart start hammering. His vision cleared for a moment, then curtains of black started coming in. Lights were shooting past like meteors. Tracer? Stars? Ground lights? He couldn't tell. He tried to get his right arm in to pull on the ripcord, but he was spinning so fast his arms were like iron bars extending away from his body.

He couldn't see at all. Was he blacking out? Couldn't tell. He was sick. He hurt, shoulders, legs. He was pissing, goddammit.

Falling! You are *falling!*

Tomorrow he was going to wash his car. How would he ever wash his car? Goddamn, it was so sad.

His throat hurt. He couldn't close his mouth. The wind was tearing his cheeks open, ripping at his lips. It was so cold it felt like his skin was burning. He tried to get his arms in. He had to. God, this was death. This was what it meant to die!

Why the fuck did I ever join the Army Air Force? Oh, God help me. Momma. Momma!

I didn't mail your letter, Momma! I'm going to miss you, Bobby.

There was blue light here. With a slamming thud his arms wrapped around his chest. He was in a blue tunnel. He tried to pull the ripcord but it was no good. His hands looked like wet masses of blood-soaked cotton. There was blood all over him, too, sloshing inside his flight suit.

He tried to talk, couldn't. His throat hurt awful bad and he wasn't breathing. Straining, his chest bursting, he fought for air.

Then there was something dark blue and covered with tubes and things, and it was coming toward him. Dark blue. He saw it vaguely, out of agonized eyes. He was smothering. He felt his bowels give way.

Then he was naked. He was a baby. His mother was carrying him on her shoulder. "Rockabye baby in the treetop, wind will blow and cradle will rock. . . ."

Momma always sang it like that, in her bell-perfect voice, "Wind will blowwwwww. . . ."

What's going on here, I'm not a baby! He squirmed, trying to see around him.

That woke him up.

He was lying on a table in a featureless gray room. Aside from stiffness he didn't feel bad. He could breathe. The air stank of sewage. He sat up. "I've gotta wash my car," he shouted, "My friend and I—Bobby—" A hollow feeling filled him.

What the hell had happened? Bobby had been in a spin!

He swung his feet off the table. This was the goddamn infirmary. He could smell the iodoform. Out the window you could see the base parking lot and the maintenance hangars beyond.

He got up. "What the fuck'd you do, fill me fulla morphine? Hey! Nurse! Somebody!"

The door was funny. At eye level it had a round, shiny black thing embossed on it. No knob. "Open up! You got one pissed-off pilot in here! Hey!" Again he thought of his friend. "What the hell happened to Bobby Virgo? I've gotta know!"

He ran to the window. What the fuck, he'd go out that way. He could see his own damn car not a hundred feet away, his dusty-green DeSoto.

He raised the window. Now what? The outside looked double-exposed. There was a ghost DeSoto hanging over the real one. He blinked, shook his head.

Somebody behind him said his name. The voice was an eager, hissing whisper, nasty. It sounded like a vicious fag, like

those bastards he'd gotten tangled up with in St. Louis . . . and
he saw their greasy pale bodies . . . lying where the DeSoto had
been.

He whirled around. "Nurse!"

There were three men standing there in pale uniforms with
crossed Sam Browne belts. They were about four feet tall and
they looked as though they were made of puffed-up marshmal-
low. They had big, black eyes. A smell of sulfur had been added
to the medicinal stench of the room.

He reacted instinctively, rushing the three men. He
grabbed the first one he saw and hurled him full force against
the wall. There was a *splat*. His head bobbing, the thing crawled
away. Blue-green goo dribbled down the wall behind him.

The other two held their hands out to him with the wrists
limp, like they expected him to kiss their long, pale fingers. The
hell, he was gonna beat the shit out of these guys.

He took a swing at the nearest one. It was a good punch,
on the money—but he found himself whirling around, swinging
through the air.

"Man," he yelled, staggering, "you got too much morphine
in this soldier!"

What in hell was he doing, taking swings at nightmares. He
dropped onto the bed. Had he gone crazy? Was this a goddamn
padded cell?

Then he noticed the smear on the wall. He went over, felt
it. Real. Sniffed it. Smelled strongly of sulfur and some kind of
plant. Garlic? Celery? No way to be sure.

Either he had knocked hell out of a real mushroom man or
this was about the shittiest salad dressing ever mixed on this
airfield.

He was staring at the mess, thinking about tasting it to see
if it *was* salad dressing when something bumped gently against
the top of his head. When he looked up he found himself staring
directly into the ceiling. He looked down. He was standing on
nothing. He'd floated up to the top of the room.

"Oh, fuck."

On its own his body rotated to a lying position. Then the
door opened with a faint pop and he went shooting down another blue tunnel. He yelled but couldn't move a muscle.

He was aware when he stopped moving. He knew that he wasn't in any infirmary on earth; he wasn't a stupid man. He'd figured out where he was. A hell of a thing.

Realizing all this, he stopped being belligerent and became careful. He wasn't about to make these people even more angry. His mind raced with excuses for why he had already practically killed one of them with his bare hands, and maybe more when he'd fired into their ship.

They looked awful. He just hadn't expected to see them. He was really a very gentle guy, all he'd done—

"Is shoot at us and then injure one of my soldiers."

She was standing across the room, a perfectly normal-looking woman of about thirty. She had soft features, auburn hair and a small mole on her right cheek. Her dress was blue plaid. She reminded him very much of that strict Miss Bonny who was his fifth grade teacher. Miss Bonny had a big willow switch she kept behind her desk.

She came slowly closer, sort of drifting across the room. It looked weird and he got scared. He backed away. As far as he knew Miss Bonny was still teaching school. So what in God's name was she doing here?

"Why do you call on your god? I'm the only one here."

He hadn't talked. Did that mean she could listen to his thoughts?

The closer she got the more he backed up. All of a sudden something grabbed him hard from behind. Miss Bonny hissed, her eyes glaring with evil triumph.

He twisted, screamed, tried to run. But his legs wouldn't work. When he attempted to hit her his arms remained at his sides.

"Can you not see me as I am?" she asked. He frowned. That wasn't Miss Bonny's voice.

His whole life seemed to fall away from him. It was nothing, an annoying weight.

But he wasn't finished. He still had to wash his car and spend the evening with Bobby and send his momma that letter—

"We will find work for you, child."

Then he saw her truly, flood and fire and war and flower,

271

a baby struggling from the womb and a crone heaving in death, a woman at morning, splashing water on her face and she so young that his heart hurt, and a gate forever opening to secret light.

"You poor child. Your life is interrupted before the time of its completion."

He saw lovers he would never touch, moonlit nights he would never wander, lessons unlearned, a man who would never know real love, all because he had died.

Then he saw his father standing before a grave with his hat in his hand and he was so little and simple, was Dad, and all his hard work was buried there.

"Why would they bury his work?"

"You are remembered there."

"I'm here. I'm okay!"

"You are not in good fortune. You have died."

"Lady, I'm just as alive as I ever was! Look, my hands, my skin!"

He looked down and saw his own torn flesh.

"You cannot live like that. I must move your soul, little one."

When the woman put her hands on him the illusion that she was human faded away. "It's an alien," he thought, "she's one of them."

Her laughter tinkled. "There are no aliens, child." There was gentle derision in her tone.

He was dead! Hot tears poured from his eyes.

She began to look more deeply into him. In the middle reaches there was a yearning, unacknowledged element of the female. He felt her mind probing into his own and he recoiled. She was stronger than he was, though, and she drew him inexorably into his earliest memories, seeking the core of his fears.

And she did not forget that his innermost self was female.

Suddenly he was back home in Billings. He was on the potty. He didn't like this, there were things in the water and she was making him sit on them! They were going to come up and get him. "Momma, them is spidos in here! Spidos, they gettin' me!"

She came at him, her voice buzzing, her fingers darting.

"Nonono! Stay right there." He felt the overwhelming power of her hands holding him against the spider hole.

His howls of terror echoed in the quiet house.

Then he was on the floor. An elderly nurse was bending over him. To see her broke his heart, there was in her face such love, such caring, such total decency.

She picked him up. He lay in her arms. How could a fragile woman like this pick up a full-grown male? Then she turned him over and said in the softest, kindest voice he had ever heard, "Behold the flesh that was thine."

A savagely injured young man lay on the floor. From the way he was dressed he appeared to be aircrew. Lucky wanted to touch his young face, so innocent!

"That was thee."

"That?"

"Yes, child."

In an instant he understood. She had rescued him—his soul, his essence—from his own dying body! He was overwhelmed with such gratitude that he could barely contain himself.

"Never fear, child, for you are with us now. No more harm shall come your way."

She took him through the great ship.

The first room he came to contained rows and rows of what looked like little incubators, and each one contained a tiny baby. There was a hush here, as if in a church.

"They are the children of man," the old nurse said.

They all turned as he entered, watching from their strange incubators with huge, black eyes. He'd never seen babies that looked like that, or babies that were so aware of you.

"We are growing a new humankind, dear child."

She drew him through a door and into a place where there were tall, strong bodies hanging in tubes of pale pink liquid.

"This one will fit thee very nicely."

He felt himself drawn as if magnetically toward one of the tubes. The body seemed almost alive. He looked into its eyes.

There was a roaring sound and then the fluid was draining from around him. He ached as if he'd been asleep for a thousand years.

When the fluid had gone down he took a choked, rattling

breath. The air smelled strongly of human blood, an odor he knew from when his carrier had gotten hit by a kamikaze in August of 1944. There had been beautiful young sailors torn to pieces all over the deck.

There were forms outside. Then the tube was opened and three children stood before him. They were wearing silver coveralls. They smiled in unison. He could see that they were grown versions of the babies in the incubators.

Behind them stood a tall, blond man. He was more than six feet. "Hi there," he said.

"What's going on?" When Lucky heard how high his own voice sounded he cleared his throat.

"My name is Charles Burleson."

"I'm John Luckman, lieutenant, USAAF." What made his voice sound like that?

"I was in the Fifty-third Infantry. Grunt infantry."

"I was flying a fuckin' night fighter when—" As Lucky was speaking he glanced down at himself.

His voice died.

He was looking at rich breasts and long, smooth legs. When he breathed the breasts heaved; when he shook his leg, the woman's leg shook.

"Hey!"

"Calm down, you're okay."

"What the hell is going on here!"

Three voices came into his head, speaking in breathless unison. "It's the one that fitted you best."

"I'm a goddamn frail!"

"You and Charles Burleson can be mates."

"No!"

"They're artificial bodies," Burleson said. "They take your soul and move it."

"Get me the hell out of here! This is crazy! Nuts!"

Her voice came into his head. It wasn't a vague whisper as it had been before. In this new body she spoke as loudly as if she had been at his side. "In time you will find much happiness this way, child."

"I'm not a woman!"

"I think they're kind of new at this," Burleson said.

"I've got a major problem here!"

"Maybe we can convince them to move you later."

"Jesus, I can't feature this! I just can't feature it!"

"You have to begin orientation. We've only got a short time before our mission."

"Could you tell me what is going on?"

Burleson laughed. "Be patient, John. First things first."

"Well, who are all these kids around here, and what the hell's the matter with their eyes?"

"They're human kids, sort of altered. She's raising them. They're really incredible people. You'll like them."

Burleson suddenly stiffened. A sad expression crossed his face and his voice changed subtly, as if he was being *used* to speak the words, rather than speaking them himself. "I'm going to ask you to close your eyes. When you open them you'll be standing in front of a mirror."

Lucky closed his eyes.

"Now open them, child."

Before him in the oval mirror that had stood above his dresser at home was a face unlike any face he had ever seen. He blinked and it did, too.

It was as if a shadowy woman from deep within him had somehow floated to the surface. He felt charity toward her, and a curious sort of love. "I think my jaw is kind of heavy for a woman."

"Is it?"

"But I have nice eyes. Really nice eyes."

"It is well that you like them."

The mirror disappeared. Burleson sighed, relaxed. "She comes into your mind and takes you over sometimes. I don't think they actually have bodies of their own, not the ones in control."

Lucky wondered if he would get lipstick and stuff, but didn't dare to ask. A guy wasn't supposed to like that stuff.

"Sure!" came three eager voices in his head. "We can get all that!"

The three children came tumbling into the room in a state of great excitement. They were dragging clothes, shoes, they had a makeup case, all sorts of things.

A few minutes later he was wearing a flowered dress and comfortable if somewhat clunky shoes. He was extremely embarrassed by the clothes, but he was also a resourceful person and he was fighting to get used to it, to make this craziness work.

"Good," said the voices, "that's very good!"

"Dance?" asked Burleson.

"Yes," she replied. "I will dance with you." Slowly, without music, the two creatures moved about the room, their shoulders occasionally brushing the huge tubes where other bodies like theirs waited.

"I didn't know I had a soul."

"We all have them, and these people can do all sorts of stuff with them. Incredible stuff. You'll see wonderful things, man."

"I *was* a man."

"You were a male body. *She* says that inside you really wanted to be a woman. You've become your own truth."

"Were you a woman they made into a man?"

"I told you, fella, I was grunt infantry. A bad ass. And they gave me a lot harder time when I came with them."

"In what way?"

"Let's just say I had to pay a debt. But that's over now and this sure as hell has the U.S. Army beat."

Lucky laid her head against the grunt's shoulder. Somebody turned on a radio, and they danced to "Something to Remember You By."

"Let me lead, asshole."

"Okay, give me a break."

It was going to be possible to dance with Charles Burleson.

Chapter Twenty-four

Will stared at a laconic report from Eighth Air Force Command. Seven pilots had set out. Five had returned. One had lost his engine and spun his plane into the ground. Another had attacked the disk and disappeared, plane and all.

He dropped the report on his desk. At this point he felt that he could not go on.

They had broken him.

In those days they understood nothing of the motives of the others. According to Will it is now theorized that they will try to take certain souls to their absolute limits, to literally shatter them so that they can become free of all the ingrained ideas that had imprisoned them.

It is a testament to Will's strength that he did not go mad or, as happened in a number of other cases, commit suicide.

Instead he took action on his own behalf.

Maybe he didn't choose the perfect response. But it was the best he could manage: he ran.

Will and his father had shared many peaceful hours on the trout streams of upstate New York.

Herbert Stone had passed his membership in the Trout Valley Club on to his son.

Will realized that he could get on a train and be at the club by midmorning.

It was nearly ten. The late express would leave for New York in half an hour.

He put his papers in his safe and locked it.

On his desk he left a terse note that he'd gone fishing. No phone number, no address.

He intended to tell Hilly his plans personally. He picked up the phone and dialed the admiral's home number. Two rings and Hilly answered.

Will put down the telephone.

He told himself he'd call when he arrived at the club.

He packed a bag full of cotton shirts and canvas fishing duds. Most of his gear was at the club, so he didn't need to worry about carrying an eight-foot fly rod on the train.

I looked at pictures of Will in those days. There are only three, all taken of other people. His appearance is always incidental.

He was an excellent dresser. His suits were tailor-made and he had a Panama hat. He must have looked the image of a well-heeled businessman as he left his apartment building for Union Station.

The Pennsylvania Railroad's "Night Flyer" had a drawing room available through to Poughkeepsie. He engaged it and made a long-distance call to the garage in Poughkeepsie where he and his dad used to rent cars.

Since his father's death in 1945 Will had not been able to visit the club. So this journey was not simply an escape from intolerable pressure, it was also an attempt to come to terms with deep grief, and perhaps even to reconnect with the only love Wilfred Stone had ever known.

Sitting back in the cab, he remembers feeling as if life itself had suddenly returned to him. He enjoyed the geniality of the cab driver, of that old, self-confident America.

Our America is a ship in a dark ocean.

"Have a good day?" the cabby asked.

"Good enough."

"Y'know, I just don't remember it got this hot during the war. I think all the gunfire overseas broke up the air and made it cool."

"It's sweltering."

"You're sure?" He gave an easy laugh. "Here we are," he said.

When Will casually described his train trip to me my heart practically broke. What we have lost!

He was welcomed onto the shiny black train by the sleeping-car porter. He took his bag and showed him to his drawing room. "You'll want that suit ironed," he said looking at Will's wrinkled seersucker. "Just put it in the door when you're ready."

He inspected the room and the lavatory, then pulled down the bed and smoothed the blanket. "Would you like an immediate makeup, sir?"

"I think I'll read in the club car for a while after we get started."

"Well, sir, there's a midnight snack in the dining car starting at eleven. Or I can bring you something in here if you prefer."

The train pulled out at 10:29 on the dot. Will let fifteen minutes pass and then made his way to the club car at the back. He didn't expect to find anybody there but lonely commercial travelers, but there was always that pebble of hope.

He ordered a sidecar and a pack of Luckies. LSMFT— "Lucky Strike Means Fine Tobacco." Also stood for "Lord Save Me From Truman."

He sat with the commercial travelers watching the lights of Maryland flash past and dreaming idly of Her, the woman he hoped would soon walk in and take the chair beside him. She would be dressed in navy, with dark hose and high, high heels. On her head would be a pillbox hat and around her neck a discreet but expensive string of pearls. She would be perfectly made up right down to her spectacularly red lips and fingernails. She would order a Manhattan and lean back sipping it and smoking.

And Will would say hello. She'd laugh, raise her eyebrows and say something like "again," and they'd be off to the conversational races.

An impressively tall blond man came in instead, and took her chair. When the waiter came up he asked for a glass of plain water without ice. He sat erect, staring straight ahead. Like Will, he wore a seersucker suit. Oddly, there was a conventioneer's tag on the lapel, but no name. Will knew nothing of artificial bodies. He never imagined that a group of them were on a mission that involved him.

"Warm evening," Will said.

The man slowly turned his head. Will recalls a twinkle of laughter in his eyes, that and a seriousness. His eyes were violet, quite startling. Will was fascinated, and he introduced himself. "I'm Wilfred Stone," he said. "Going up to the City?"

"Where are you going?"

"Actually, I'm off to do a little fishing."

"Where?"

"On the Beaverkill. I'm a member of the Trout Valley Club—"

The man got up and left without a word. Of course, he had obtained the information he had come for.

Mildly perplexed at his odd behavior, Will watched him stride out of the car. He finished his drink while the Baltimore passengers were boarding, then went to the library at the end of the car and picked up a best-seller. He believes it was *The Story of Mrs. Murphy.* It proved to be a study of a woman's life rendered in the most meticulous detail. Normally he would have turned away from such a book, but he found himself desperately eager to participate in another, more normal life. Her loves, pregnancies, hopes, her happiness and sadness—he drank of it all like a thirsty man at a mirage.

The Story of Mrs. Murphy took him through the late supper of eggs and bacon. He followed it with a brandy Alexander and a cigar.

He sipped his Alexander and nursed his cigar through the midnight hour. Finally he returned to his room. The porter had opened the bed and laid out his pajamas, slippers and robe. He called for a final cognac and retired with the book.

In the distance the whistle wailed and the bells of guarded crossings sounded through the rolling, muted night.

He awoke in a vague way while they were stopped in New York and his sleeping car was being attached to the "Broadway."

As they pulled out of Penn Station the porter woke him. He shaved and went to the dining car, where he had breakfast as morning light glimmered on the Hudson.

He left the train in Poughkeepsie, a troubled man in a freshly pressed linen suit. He knew it would only be a matter of a day or so before Hilly found him and called him back. But he needed this time, had to have it.

Even at nine-thirty the day was already steel-blue and hot. As he walked up the hill to Van Alter's Garage to get his rented Ford, he felt himself sweating into the suit.

He guided the car down to the Hudson ferry and crossed to the country side of the water. There was a yacht flying up the river, and a couple of excursion steamers were dashing along with flags snapping and ladies holding down their summer dresses.

West of the river the hills rose wild. "Dad," he said into the throbbing privacy of the car.

"Never attack your enemies, Wilfred. Confuse them." So his father would say. "If a man accuses you of a crime of which you are innocent, you may be sure it is what he would do in the same circumstances." He was wise. "Never sign a contract with any man with whom a handshake would not suffice."

Silent tears appeared in the corners of Will's eyes when he talked about his father. I could never find out quite why his grief had stayed with him for all these years. Their relationship must not have been complete. I suppose that Herbert Stone lived on in his son.

After he died Will had discovered that his father had done undercover work for the Treasury Department for years. He was flabbergasted. It was his father's contacts in the secret intelligence community that had led to Will's OSS appointment.

To Will's knowledge his father had never kissed him.

Will arrived in Roscoe at eleven-thirty, passing the Roscoe Inn, the scene of many a fisherman's evening, then turning off onto the narrow road that led up the kill to the home of the Trout Valley Club.

The club was housed in a rambling Catskills mansion with enormous porches. In those days Ann and Jack Slater ran the place for the membership, keeping it open from March through October.

Before writing this chapter I took Will's journey. I will pass over without comment my experience on Amtrak—not because it was bad, but because it made me long for the wonderful rail journey Will had so casually described.

I rented a Taurus in Poughkeepsie and drove to Roscoe.

I found the former location of the Trout Valley Club, and

even the place where Will had fished—and had himself been so deftly caught.

The club has been torn down, but its view of the Beaverkill was unparalleled. From that hill one can see at least three miles of water, and each of those miles can tell a thousand stories.

This place, this stream, was the birthplace of American fly-fishing. I am no fisherman, but when I went to Roscoe and saw that dancing water, I was captured a little by the romance of it.

Will lived that romance. "Mr. Stone," said Ann Slater as he climbed the steps. "Mr. Stone, I can hardly believe my eyes. I thought you'd moved away."

"You can't move away from the Beaverkill."

"I know that and you know that. But people do try."

He found that his gear had been kept in perfect condition. His fine Orvis rod was supple and his reel oiled. His lines and flies were ready for him. His heart ached when he looked into his tackle box. All of his father's best flies had been moved in, and some of his older or less successful ones discarded. The rest of his father's gear had been discreetly removed from their cabinet.

"Mr. Dette came in and rearranged your flies," Ann said. This man was one of the most famous flytiers in the Catskills, and a longtime personal friend of Herb Stone. His daughter still runs Dette's Flies.

Will walked back to the kitchen where Jack was preparing lunch for the four club members who were there. Upon entering this place he really felt as if he had left the outside world and all of its difficulties behind. "I hope there's a good hatch," he said as he entered the kitchen.

"My Lord, Wilfred Stone. I thought this place was getting toney at last. Guess I was mistaken."

"What's for lunch, Jack—rat stew?"

"Well, the other fellas are having a little beef stew. But I can fry you up a couple of rats if you want to catch them. I think there are some living in the bottom of your cabinet."

"I'll take beef stew."

"As far as hatches are concerned, we had quite a big hatch last night, and they took some fish this morning with caddis."

"How's the evening action been?"

"Well, if there's a hatch going its pretty good just after sunset. Nine would be about right tonight."

"That suits me. I'm going to spend the day loafing and then I'll fish."

After lunch Ann put the radio on the porch and brought Will a pitcher of lemonade and the *Herald Tribune.* The club had a good aerial, so he was able to pick up many of the New York City stations. He remembered only that he used to listen to WQXR. I looked up an old radio log in the library and found that he would have heard a program called *Tom Scott Songs* at that hour.

The *Trib* was full of Truman and the Russians and the Marshall Plan. Will found it strangely thrilling to read the public doings of the President, knowing so much of his most secret affairs.

It was also extremely painful. He finally turned to the "Thronton Burgess Nature Story." I also looked that up. Will had read about the summer habits of the martin.

Nobody disturbed him, which was as well; he could not have spoken without sobbing aloud. He was a man without emotional resources.

Exactly in the state the visitors wanted him, in other words.

Once a large, black sedan drove slowly past the house. The other fishermen appeared. They were nobody Will knew and he has forgotten all but the idiotic nicknames by which they introduced themselves: Whisker, Pootie and Boy. They had no fish, and the luncheon talk was of throwbacks, big ones hanging under logs and better days.

As far as Will was concerned, he had left the others in Los Alamos.

He could not have been more wrong.

283

Part Four
THE FLOWER

*Except a corn of wheat fall into
the ground and die, it abideth alone;
but if it die, it bringeth forth much fruit.*

—JOHN, 12:24

Chapter Twenty-five

The Chronicle of Wilfred Stone

The Beaverkill at the turn of evening: mist rising, the rocky bed muttering with the water's many voices.

I had gotten well into an isolated stretch and was just making my first cast when I saw a figure standing on the bank.

I was astonished because of who it was: a largish blond in a white dress printed all over with yellow primroses. She could have been the twin of the oddball I'd seen on the train.

She hung back in the bushes, her hands flittering nervously along her sides. Was she embarrassed by her dowdy outfit?

She had distracted me enough to ruin my first cast. The fly dropped into swift water.

"Hello," I said. Her heavy jaw made her unattractive, but she had nice skin.

She did not reply.

I pulled back my line and started preparing another cast. All the while I was aware that she was watching me. It really wasn't very polite; nobody local would stand on the riverbank and stare at a fisherman.

Finally I waded out of the stream. "May I help you?" I asked as I clambered onto the bank. I had absolutely no premonition of danger.

When I straightened up from my climb I found myself face to face with her.

Why had she come so close? She was taller than me and her eyes were pools of shadow. Her lips were set in a mean line. I was suddenly aware that I was alone on the stream and far from help.

Her muscles rippled; she was obviously strong. I got the idea that she might be an inbreed from back in the hills. There were said to be a few pockets of such people in the Catskills.

Then I smelled something awful. I was thunderstruck. A familiar and terrifying odor of sulfur clung to her.

I threw my rod aside and leaped down the bank into the water. Fighting my hip boots I plunged across, keeping to the rocky shallows. I grabbed brush and tugged myself up the other side. There were fallen logs and brush tangled in the rocks, and beyond them huge cypresses. I ran into the darkness, limbs slapping my face, roots tripping me.

That smell, that smell! It was a woman, though, an ordinary woman!

A vision of that face came into my mind as I struggled toward the bluff beyond the woods. If I could get up there I could circle back and cross the Beaverkill on the covered bridge, and from there make my way back to the clubhouse.

The boots were never meant for this kind of activity. I could barely keep my balance, let alone move quickly.

I soon noticed that she wasn't behind me. Finally I stopped. I was well into the stand of cypress, which was so dark that I risked colliding with a tree trunk if I didn't feel my way.

Obviously I'd lost her. But I didn't relax. That smell—I could never mistake that smell again if I lived to be a hundred. She had to be connected with them. I started up the bluff.

Then I saw behind me a brief flicker of light.

I didn't waste an instant. That flicker told me everything I needed to know. She was herding me away from the stream. I had to move fast or I'd never turn her flank.

She was one of their *things,* like the gnomic man I'd en-countered at Los Alamos. I was literally dizzy with fear.

I dragged myself up the cliffs, tearing my fishing vest on the granite, lacerating my hands.

Behind me she seemed to glide through the trees like a ghost, her blue light flickering from time to time. I thought I heard her making a sound, a faint whistling.

Farther and farther up I went.

Soon she was behind me. She was climbing easily and she was very close.

288

I pressed myself against the rocks. Now I could hear her breathing, could hear the sound of her dry skin scraping on the rocks.

The beam of blue light flashed above me.

Then I smelled damp air, cave air. There was a hole to my left. I pressed myself back into it.

An instant later I saw a hand, then the top of her head. She was right here. As soon as her eyes appeared she was going to see me.

I forced myself back into the cave. I intended to go as deep as I could, to press myself against the stone until I blended with it.

The tunnel was low. I had to go on my stomach. Moss and damp earth got into my mouth. Creeping insects fouled my hair and went down my neck.

Finally the walls spread and I was able to rise to my hands and knees. I was breathing hard now. My eyes were tightly closed; there was no reason to open them, not in this dark.

I began to be able to stoop, finally to run with my head tucked into my chest and my arms out to feel for jutting stones.

Then I heard it again, that strange cooing sound.

Only it was in front of me, down deep in the cavern.

Three short, soft cries. They resonated with a tenderness of some sort, but to my ears it was the love of the leopard for the deer, of the snake for the frightened mouse.

I pulled out my lighter, flicked it but couldn't get fire. In the glimmer of the flint I saw huge shapes, old Indian paintings on the walls perhaps, and seething, glittering movement in the tunnel ahead of me.

They were here, deep in the cliffs, in the *ground*. God, what were they? Where had they come from?

The three cries were repeated, closer now. They were urgent, sweet sounds.

Behind me I heard her pushing herself along the tunnel. I was trapped, caught. All around me I could hear whistlings and rustles.

I couldn't run, could hardly move.

A hand closed around my ankle.

I yanked myself away and shrieked.

And suddenly I was falling. Wind rushed around me. I flailed and screamed. I didn't hit, I just kept falling and falling and falling.

There was light. My eyes flew open and I was staring with total incomprehension at a magnificent view. I didn't understand. Where was the cave? Where was I?

I had risen above the sunset and was in the light that ascending larks strive to reach.

The horror of dislocation so overwhelmed me that I was reduced to a primitive state. My humanity collapsed. I felt the man falling away like a flimsy costume, bits and tinsel fluttering in the sun.

My cries disappeared into the sky.

Below me the world was a purple shadow bisected by a glowing line of sunlight. Westward evening spread across the fields, and farther west the land rested in spreading day.

Nothing was holding me up or restraining me in any way. I gritted my teeth and moaned. The impression was strong that I was about to fall. Why did they keep doing this to a man afraid of heights?

The lights of Roscoe disappeared into the general shadow of the globe. When I tried to breathe it simply didn't work. I was freezing cold. There was no wind around me. My skin began to feel tight, my eyeballs as if they were working their way out of my head.

It must feel like this for the trout to be dragged from his lair. He gasps and gulps, his eyes bulge from his head. And the fisherman, chuckling to himself over the cleverness of the capture, tosses him into his creel.

They were treating me exactly as I treated the trout, and in that there was a lesson I have never forgotten.

Now the world was glorious below me, half of it in sunlight and half blue with night. I had been pulled from out of the shadow line. It was an appropriate moment to grab me: my life was lived in that deceptive edge.

There was a heave within me. My stomach knotted, my knees came up to my chest, I retched. White foam flew from my mouth, and in that instant I felt myself lying on a floor. I gagged; I couldn't help it. The combination of shock, cold and oxygen starvation had caused the reaction. I was having a fit, flopping and spitting and choking—exactly like a fish flapping in a creel.

By slow degrees my body recovered from the punishment it had received. I pulled myself to my feet. I was in an absolutely dark room, inky black. Experimentally I put my hand in front of my face. I couldn't see it, not even with my palm touching my nose.

I went for my lighter, flipped it open and struck the flint.

For a moment I didn't understand what I was seeing in its shaky flame. Then the rows of glistening objects resolved themselves. There were dozens of pairs of huge, black eyes around me.

With a bellow of horror I threw the lighter at them. I jumped back but their long arms encircled me in an instant. I felt their black claws pressing into my skin.

I knew what these creatures were. I had seen one autopsied. "More vegetable than animal."

I fought like what I was, a trapped beast.

The sentry's screams returned to my ears. He'd yelled "No, no, no" his voice rising to an absolute pitch of hysteria.

I would lash out and they would withdraw into the dark. Then there would be silence for a while.

I would hear stealthy movement. When they touched me it felt like the skin of a frog.

I fought with the strength of the mad. They twined themselves around me, grasped me with their wiry fingers, scratched me with their claws. I kicked, I hit, I bit, around and around I turned, lashing out with my fists whenever I felt their wet, soft touch.

Again and again they came and I fought them off. I didn't think, I didn't hope, I just fought.

Finally, though, I started to tire.

My breath burned my lungs, my legs wobbled. All around me they were cooing and whispering, and I heard in my head a woman singing a gentle song.

One of them came up to me and put its skeletal hands on my shoulders. Although I could not see I remembered from the autopsy how those hands looked: three long fingers and black, sharp claws.

291

I could feel the hands sliding around my back. The thing was drawing me closer. I was so exhausted that I could no longer raise my arms.

Another one was behind me now, grasping me, holding me, twining itself around me.

I screamed and screamed and screamed and they cooed and finally a voice spoke. It was like a machine talking. "What can we do to help you stop screaming?"

There wasn't a darned thing they could do! I screamed until my voice cracked and my shrieks became ragged blasts of air.

Then I could scream no more.

They were all around me, caressing me with their soft hands, their smell thick in my nostrils.

I sank to my knees.

"Can you take off your clothes or do you want us to help you?" The voice was breathless and strangely youthful, like a child of about fourteen.

Suddenly I was on the porch at home, playing with a toy when—hadn't they carried me, then?

I was a little boy then, and they had carried me, had *carried me!*

"You—you—"

They were touching buttons, scrabbling at zippers. There was rapid breathing and little snapping sounds. My fishing vest and shirt went off, my trousers opened.

And then there was a great deal of prodding and poking at my hip boots. Finally it stopped.

"What do you wear?"

"Rubber boots."

"Take them off."

"Why don't you do it?"

"We can't."

"What will you do to me when I'm naked?"

"We're naked."

I toppled to the floor. I just couldn't stand up anymore. I went down in a cage of supporting arms.

There was more fumbling and scrabbling with the hip boots. Finally they withdrew. I sat up, feebly waved around me. Nothing—the air was empty.

"Pull thy boots, child."

This voice was very different from the ones I had been hearing. It was clearly *ancient* and full of authority.

"What will you do to me?"

"I can do with thee what I wish."

"I don't want to take off my boots! I want to go home! I'm a federal officer. My government will rescue me. We have planes—"

"You have no weapons, child."

"We have the bomb!"

"No, child, the bomb has you. Take off thy boots."

I would not.

There appeared to be an impasse. But then the boots started to get warm. In seconds they were hot. I smelled burning rubber.

I got right out of them.

A sort of chuckling followed, slow and low and terribly sinister. "Don't you remember us at all?"

I saw my red fire engine. It stood bathed in golden light, the lost treasure of my boyhood.

I reached out, put my hand on it. Yes, it was real, my own beloved fire engine, the one I'd lost when I was three.

All through my childhood I'd dreamed about it. How lovely it was, my heart ached to see it.

They'd—I remembered when I was very young . . . flying . . .

The lights came on.

I was alone in a surprisingly small gray room. Although I was physically the only person here, I had no sense of being mentally isolated. Just beneath the surface, my mind was seething with voices, images, thoughts. It was as if I was skating the short-wave band with its static and half-heard messages from far away.

Then two blond people came into the room. I recognized both of them. One I had seen briefly on the train. The other was the woman in the flowered dress.

"We are here to assist you," said the man. He sounded as if he was reading a script.

Soon I would know the secret of the disappearances. What would Hilly find of me?

Late tonight they'd miss me at the Trout Valley Club and

decide that the stream had taken me. They'd search its length tomorrow morning, looking in all the places where a fisherman's body is apt to lodge. Would they find even my rod and reel? I thought not. My guess was that the woman had policed the area after I was captured.

Hilly would guess what had happened.

The government would lose balance completely. If Stone went, then they were all vulnerable.

The woman came up to me, grasped me firmly by the shoulders and kissed me on the lips. Her kiss was dry and firm and gave the impression of something a loving father might do to calm a distraught ten-year-old kid.

She embraced me in a wooden hug. She said, "It's gonna be all right, buddy."

The man in the seersucker elbowed her. "You don't sound a hell of a lot like a frail," he muttered.

The woman sent him a hard look.

He had some white stuff in his hands, which he unfolded into a robe. It was simply cut and made of soft paper. The two of them raised it over my head and drew it down.

For a moment it clung to me, then it seemed to take on a static charge and stood out from my body. I tingled.

"Come on," the man said.

Why were they like this? Were they robots?

"We aren't," the woman snapped. Her voice sounded petulant and very human. But when I asked them their names they gravely shook their heads. "Your name dies with you," the woman said. "We don't remember."

We went down a hall that was more a tunnel it was so low. I could see that it was made of paper of the same type that formed the inner walls of the ship we had found. Light came through it from the outside. The yellow flowers pressed into the paper seemed almost alive, so vividly did they glow.

We entered a round chamber that contained a circle of what appeared to my eye to be plush first-class airplane seats. As a matter of fact they were airplane seats, familiar to me in every detail. I recognized the United Airlines logo on some of the headrests, TAT on others.

When the man shoved at my shoulders I sat down. Considering his strength there was really nothing else to do.

"Are you in pain? Are you prisoners?"

The woman dropped a big hand onto my own. Her utter lack of grace was extremely peculiar. One expects a certain ease of motion from a woman.

How incredibly alien they were. Had I understood then *who* they were, I wonder if I would have acted differently. All of my life I have wished I knew what they thought of me. It must have been an incredibly funny, poignant experience—if they had the full range of human feeling available to them in those strange bodies.

"Open your mouth," the man said.

"I will not."

"Goddammit, I knew it. Look, I gotta—" He threw himself at me. He was huge and as hard as stone. I was too spent to resist him, even for a second. With one arm around my chest he held me from behind. With his free hand he forced open my jaws.

I tried to clench them but his fingers were powerful. The woman had a graceful little bottle from which she withdrew a curved dropper.

My jaws were open, I was helpless. She put three drops of ice-cold liquid on the tip of my tongue. When they let me go I smacked and coughed. I spat.

"You can spit," the man said. "It doesn't matter."

"What have you done to me?"

"You needed that. You're going on a trip."

"I want to go home."

They pushed me into one of the seats. I quelled a wave of nausea, but it was followed by another, stronger one. The man reached around behind my seat and came out with an airsickness bag from the pocket. TRANSCONTINENTAL AIR TRANSPORT was printed on it in red letters. I used it.

The air had changed. Far from being cold, it was now thick and hot. It was getting hard to breathe. Whatever was happening to me, my body was being taken to the extremes of endurance. In those days we knew nothing of hallucinogenic drugs.

Without a sound the walls of the room became clear.

At first I did not understand what I was seeing. A huge shining strip of light curved off into the sky. Beneath it there shone the amazingly complex surface of a gigantic sphere colored in a thousand shades of tan and green and blue.

Then I saw that it was all surrounded by reefs and oceans of stars, stars in endless numbers, stars beyond belief in a billion colors winking, as if God's own treasury had been spilled.

We appeared to be in the rings of Saturn. How far from earth would that be? I couldn't even begin to remember. However, I was completely convinced that we had come an awfully long distance in a very short time.

In the middle of the clear wall was a round doorway. It did not appear to open into the view around us at all, but revealed broad plains beneath the light of a strange, brown sky. It looked like a patch pasted on the wall of stars.

I had no intention of going through that door.

Chapter Twenty-six

The Chronicle of Wilfred Stone

The next second I was standing in a desert. It was strewn with sharp black boulders that shone dully in the weak light. A forlorn breeze fluttered my paper garment.

I was aware of the fact that Saturn was a ball of gas, so I did not imagine myself to be there. I didn't know where I was. They had removed me from reality. A few minutes before I had been struggling in the depths of a cave, now I was on a desert worse than the Sahara.

I have wondered at those events, trying to determine if they were physically real or if they happened in some other way.

I was here, and the grit underfoot was real and the air was crackling dry and the sky was brown.

I staggered a few steps, hitting my naked foot against one of the stones. I sat down, rubbing my ankle. I looked around.

In a way that is almost impossible to describe, this place was unfamiliar. Even the details were wrong. Perhaps especially the details. The shape and color of the stones, the quality of the sand, all of it was wrong. Even the air against my skin felt different.

I wasn't really thinking anymore. I was just here, my eyes looking out into the open.

Which was, of course, the whole point. My humanity had dropped away. I was still conscious, but I was an animal again.

And I was so lonely. I raised my head to the brown sky and keened. My sound was the only noise in the place. It seemed to be coming at once from far away and from deep within me, deeper than I had ever been. I took a breath, did it again. My spirit rose with the sound, for a moment to fill the empty air with the magic of being.

Then it died away and I was little again and it was getting dark.

I suspect that we made such sounds when we lived in the forest.

Grabbing a rock I stood up. I threw it a tremendous long distance.

It landed with an empty thud.

I raced across the plain, dodging and skipping with a grace I had never before possessed.

When I came to a high point I stopped. Seeking for the scent of water, I smelled the air.

A growl of frustration came from my throat. The sound startled me. At first I thought there was some kind of animal behind me. Then I thought, "No, that is how you're *supposed* to sound."

I was me, me alone. No name, no education, no expectations. Just me.

The sky was pale and unmarked by clouds. Not far above the horizon there was a powdery brilliance, which I presumed was the sun in deep haze.

Next I scanned the horizon, looking carefully for some sign of life, a swatch of green, perhaps, or the glitter of water. Then I looked for smoke or just the outline of a building.

The place was completely empty and entirely silent.

Again I smelled the parched air. I was already quite thirsty; I couldn't live like this for long. The air was so dry that it was leaching moisture from my body. My hands looked like paper, the skin puckered and shriveled. I touched my face, feeling fissures that had never been there before. And my nose was cracked inside.

Where would I go, naked except for a flimsy piece of paper? Graceful or not, my feet were thoroughly banged up from the mad run. I don't think there was a single rock that wasn't sharp.

For the most part the desert seemed absolutely flat, but off to my right the land rose. I could not judge distances. The views, though, seemed much longer than they had any right to be.

I walked in the direction of the rising land. At least this

would keep the sun behind me. What had appeared to be the gentlest of rises soon became quite steep. I wasn't going to be able to keep this up forever. My chest and head ached, my legs felt like lead, my feet were on fire.

Very suddenly I started to have trouble seeing. At first I didn't understand why, because I did not realize how fast night came. By the time I realized what was wrong the sun was already on the horizon.

It seemed as if the air literally absorbed light. The instant the disk of the sun disappeared it was absolutely dark. There were only one or two bright stars visible through the dusty haze.

God, this place was ugly.

I sat down. There was no point in walking farther without light. The dark was like ink, like something you could feel.

I wished they'd at least left me my lighter.

Then I was crying bitterly. The tears came without warning. I had been left here to die. It was so damn unfair and I was so far from home.

Later I heard something, or thought I did. Now that it was dark I didn't want this. I didn't want to hear anything that I couldn't see.

The sound was low and slow and high in the air. It was as if some tremendous thing was floating through the sky above me, breathing.

The breathing got louder and louder. I felt like it was right above me, huge. I cringed, waiting for it to land on me.

Instead it went away. I let out my breath.

No sooner had I begun to relax than there was a tremendous rattling noise in the distance.

It got closer and closer and lower and lower and I could hear the breathing again, fast and excited. There was urgency in it, like a starving prisoner inhaling the aroma of the jailer's soup.

A new sound started up, sharp scraping. It was very regular, as if somebody was slashing knives together.

Something whizzed through the air just above me, so close that my hair was touched with a breeze.

Involuntarily I shrank away—and saw a red glow out of the corner of my eye. I looked. Redness spread along the horizon on my left.

A moment later a huge red star popped up and the place was bathed in dim, bloody light.

There seemed to be a forest of thin trees all around me. It took me time to understand that I was looking at tall, black legs, many of them.

It took every ounce of my composure not to scream. I was under what appeared to be a gigantic insect of some kind, perhaps a spider. The rattling noise started again. I could see sharp mouth parts working.

Jumping, twisting, turning to avoid the legs I made a dash to get away from the thing.

It rose up into the air, making a gigantic leap. I had to scramble to avoid it landing right on top of me. Again I ran. This time I threw stones at it.

It leaped.

I evaded, but barely. I scrambled up the rise on the theory that those jumps would be harder uphill. They weren't. It sailed high into the red air and came down on top of me.

Legs clutched, mandibles scraped—and I was caught. I grabbed a rock and hammered against one of the limbs. For all the good it did I might as well have been trying to break steel pipe.

I fought against its quick, clever legs. Finally I went wild. I hit, kicked, bit. The jaws were slashing and I could see a bright green tongue darting in and out of its mouth. I was brought closer and closer to being sliced to pieces.

I could not possibly taste good to the thing. It was sure to tear me to pieces and spit me out. I was furious at dying so pointlessly.

Then the legs pressed me against the wide open mouth and I began to die.

As I sank away I saw around me a starry night of home. I was back at our old house. We were playing on the porch, my sister and I. I saw her beside me, attending to her beloved doll Ricardo. That word—I hadn't thought of it since I was tiny. The moment was bathed in a light that seemed to contain some essential emotion of loss and urgency.

There was between me and the thing that was devouring me a kinship of tremendous power. It pushed my fear aside and I lay like a raptured lover in the forest of legs.

If this was death, from where did love emerge?

I was dropped on the ground from a distance of a few feet—put down gently. For an instant I saw the complex face of the thing that had held me. It looked like nothing so much as a tremendous mantis. But those eyes—huge, reflecting the red air—were not blank. I was shocked. Somebody was *looking* at me. Joy rang out. There was peace, wisdom and then a cock of the head: the irony of our situation. Soundless in the charged air, laughter.

I was left collapsed on the ground, drained now not only of my culture and my name but also of my physical strength.

Bit by bit I was being demolished, reduced to the simplest nub of self.

I lay staring at the sky. Did I sleep? I don't know, but when I finally felt like getting to my feet I was stiff and ached in every joint.

Keeping the red sun on my right I forced myself up the rise. As I walked I understood that I had been brought a long distance. Before me there stood the most tremendous cliff I'd ever seen. It seemed to go up for thousands and thousands of feet.

On its highest ridge there was a very distinct blue glow. The glow was pulsating.

Life.

So the attack had not been an attack at all. Somebody had simply been helping me.

The cliff was not sheer. There were plenty of footholds, and I had already reached a dizzying height when the red sun sank below the horizon.

Again darkness came abruptly. I was left hugging the wall in front of me, afraid to go another inch.

I don't think it was dark for more than ten minutes. When the pale sun rose again I resumed my climb.

There were moments of dizziness when I would have to stop. I wasn't in shape for a climb like this. My throat felt as if it had been packed with powdered glass. My head pounded.

Not only was I thirsty, I was also becoming hungry. I kept remembering that beef stew I'd had for lunch. Once I even sucked a bit of it from between two teeth.

When that happened I hugged the rock and cried like a

baby. The loneliness came again, and stopped me for a long time.

The higher I went the more difficult the climb became. Worse, the soil up here was friable and there wasn't a single stable handhold. I had to dig down then haul myself up as the dirt collapsed around me.

Above me the blue glow was massive. I tried to call out but it was no good. I hadn't a trace of a voice.

At this height the cliff was more like a sand dune. To make headway I had to lie against it and squirm. I was so frustrated that I would have been in tears, but I had no tears.

It took me some time to realize that I'd made it.

Before me was a sparse but huge park. I dragged myself onto the surface, which I found to consist of tightly matted grass, bright green. I inhaled it, chewed at it trying to get some moisture. It was very dry.

I pulled myself to my feet. Off to my left there was a stand of tall, narrow trees. They were really huge, a hundred and more feet high by my estimation.

Directly ahead I saw a truly welcome vision, a cluster of buildings. They were obviously adobe. It looked very much like a Hopi town. I started stumbling forward.

A smell came to me on the air—or rather, a sensation. This was dampness. It loosened my drum-tight skin. It filled my nose with life, made my lungs open.

As best I could I ran.

Then I saw it. A fountain. It was made of black, shiny stone, round, with water playing out of a nozzle in the center.

I plunged my head in and opened my mouth. The water was glorious, cold and pure and perfect. I could feel my skin drinking, my mouth, sucking and drinking. Never had I experienced such raw pleasure. It was ecstatic, delicious, almost sexual in its intensity.

Finally I raised my head. Beyond the fountain there was a small garden.

In the garden stood a child. Her looks did not matter to me; what I saw was the radiance within. I ran to her as would a youth to his perfect love.

Chapter Twenty-seven

I finally felt what I should have felt from the beginning for Wilfred Stone. My youth and arrogance had prevented me, though.

I looked at that old man in a completely new way. I reached toward him. He looked down at my hand, and then at me. In his eyes was an emotion I cannot name. It sent a jagged edge of fear through me, as if I had scented death.

"Turn it off," he said. I put down the tape recorder. He flipped the switch. He didn't actually tell me to leave out the material that follows, but that was the implication.

I do not feel that he was right, but out of respect for him— yes, respect—I took notes on this part of his narrative of the other world, rather than record it.

The wise child walked quickly away, a chalky ghost in the gloom. She was the size of a three-year-old but her movements were mature.

Will called out.

She stopped when she heard him. When she smiled he sensed what he described as something almost vampiric about her. There was a sense of tremendous, overwhelming power, the night in the child.

He felt himself in the presence of tremendous wisdom. This was what it was like to be with somebody who had gone beyond the human.

His next words just popped out, as if formed from purest instinct. "Help us," he said.

The response was immediate. The next second he was back in his boyhood home in Westchester County.

The whole place was flooded with pure, sweet light. He could hardly believe it. And this was no illusion. Will says that he was *there*.

What's more, he remembers the event now from two different perspectives—that of himself as a little boy encountering a strange, shadowy man in his room . . . and also that of himself as the man.

The old red fire engine was there, standing against the wall opposite his crib.

He moved slowly around in his room. The wonder of it made everything seem jewellike and perfect.

Then he noticed movement in the crib. His own curly head, his blue eyes—the Willy Stone of thirty and more years ago rose up and climbed deftly out to the floor. Will could smell his baby freshness, could hear him, see him.

"Oh God, God," he told me, "Nick, my heart just broke in two. I was so little! And in that huge, shadowy, mysterious world, the courage in the eyes—"

The wise children, the others, had brought him home to the best and purest thing that he was.

He remembered a warm, huge hand that had come out of the dark . . . and suddenly the curtains blew and the moonlight came in and he saw a huge, terrible man, a nightmare man bending over him.

He screamed, a high bullet of a sound.

Feet pounded from downstairs. Will the man saw his father's balding head shining in the moonlight as he came up the stairs. Behind him his mother floated in her lace and silk.

He stepped into the shadows.

Will as child was terrified. "Daddy! Man! Man here!"

He saw his own father engulf him in himself and carry him like a limp offering back to the crib.

Then the room fell away, growing smaller and smaller until it was a dot of light in the air, and then was gone.

The vampire child was dancing slow turns around him. She stopped and smiled a dangerous smile. And he felt nothing but love.

At the far end of the oasis there was a tall arch, and beyond it a round, tumbledown building.

He wanted to go there, but she restrained him, pushing against his belly as a clown child might against her clown father.

Leaving him for a moment she ran to a small table. She pointed. On it there was a plain gray plate and three gray pancakes. Will realized that he was ravenous. He remembers still the taste of that food, the pure flavor of the buckwheat from which the cakes were made, the sense of a freshness he had never tasted before.

There was also a wide bowl of water. The girl came and scooped it up for him and he drank from her cupped hands.

Afterward she sang to him in a whispering voice, in a language he did not know. He began to feel sleepy and lay down on his side.

Much later he was awakened by a soft hand stroking his head.

He jumped to his feet. All the weight of his years seemed to have fallen away.

He walked, then, as his excitement rose; finally he ran to the ancient building. Where the blue-gray stones were intact their perfect fit reminded him of Inca work, but for the most part the place was cracked and crumbling.

He went up the steps and into a wide, cool hall. It was made of dark-blue stone worked with great intricacy. When he tried to follow the labyrinth of these carvings his head began to pound. Finally he had to stop looking at the walls, the ceiling, and keep his eyes on the floor.

There was a circle of children sitting before him. It was all so very *familiar.* Words came to him: beyond fear there is another life.

Was this the place the dead went?

Had he been killed? Was that what this meant?

He went to the center of the circle and waited, standing quite still. He soon heard a drum beating out in the corridor. The sound stirred him, infected him, made him start to move.

The children began to chant in repetitive notes, wonderful notes.

He spread his arms and started to turn. The room whirled and the drum pulsed and chanting hypnotized him.

He remembered his own beginning.

He was moving swiftly and secretly across the sky of home. There were little flecks of cloud. He went past them and down into the spreading summer trees. He moved around a great, gnarled limb, his heart full of love and delicious with the secrecy of his coming. His movement was so stealthy that not even a grasshopper stirred from her rasping as he passed by.

Then he saw a window. The shades were drawn but he passed through them as if there was nothing there.

The room was dim and very quiet. A young woman lay on a bed, her head turned to one side. She was as fresh and lovely as new light, covered only by a thin gown. Brown curls spread over her brow. Her belly was huge.

He loved her terribly, and could not resist going closer to her. Then he began to drift downward. He could no longer float.

In an instant he was inside her womb, a glowing cavern. Her body was roaring, the heart fluttering like a tent in the wind, her whole self a bubbling, oozing bladder barely managing to contain its liquids.

He swam into the fluid of her and drank her and smelled her essential flower, and was filled with the taste and sense of her.

There began a dialogue between them, long speaking together of the days they would spend as mother and son.

He would love her as a boy, but when she grew old he would abandon her. His love for deception would replace his love for her and so she would die alone, her breast weakly shuddering, on a cot in the hallway of a public cancer ward.

He sat before me, his head bowed, tears streaming from his eyes. So this was what he didn't want recorded and why he never, ever mentioned his mother. I wanted to help him, to offer him some word of comfort but I could not. We are all betrayers, all of us.

To find true joy one must first accept true pain.

Once again he was back in his old bedroom, only not as a man. This time he was a little boy again. He was dancing and dancing. It was a moonlit night and there was danger in the air. Terrible things were happening.

He saw waves of ships crossing the highest air. They were gray disks and the streets below rang with screams.

But more people were singing than were screaming and chains lay abandoned that had weighted their shoulders.

"The lamb will lie down with the lion." The secret meaning is that the son will love the errant father, the lamb will welcome the hungry nuzzling of the wolf-mother, the rat will perish of love as the owl's talons pierce his heart.

Beyond fear there is another world.

Chapter Twenty-eight

The Final Testament of Wilfred Stone

I was still dancing hard when I realized that the magic had slipped away. The room was silent, absolutely dark.

I heard a click, saw a flash of sparks, a flame.

The blond woman in the flowered dress was holding my lighter. Around us there were dim, dancing shapes on the walls, crude old carvings. I did not recognize their origin—perhaps they were Native American, or maybe even older. They were powerful, they spoke of dance, these flying red figures.

This was no ancient building, and the children's circle was gone. I was no longer a little boy.

We were back in the cave.

I felt as if I had been to death and back. I saw the brilliant thing they had done. They had stripped me of all except what was most essential, pure and true about myself.

"Will you take the flower?" she asked. In her hand I could see a little yellow blossom. "There's a field where the sins of the world are buried. The soil is forgiveness. These flowers grow there."

I wanted to take it, but when I held out my hand a terrible thing happened: I saw Sophie hanging in the Gestapo's basement, spinning slowly and urine spraying like rain from between her furiously kicking legs. A blast of hate exploded out of me and for an instant I thought that flower was the ugliest thing I had ever seen.

She laughed and dropped it to the floor.

At once I had a change of heart. I wanted it. *I* needed forgiveness too, after all.

The way she was looking at me, her eyes so full of love and humor, I saw that the aliens, as I called them in those days, were not evil. It was us, we were afraid. "We shot at you!"

An almost quizzical look came into her face. "I know all about that." She opened her mouth to say more, but was suddenly stopped. It was as if a switch had been flipped in her brain. Her mouth moved but no words came out. "Hell," she finally muttered, "I can't tell you about it."

Then she shuddered, her eyes grew penetrating and terrible and I backed away from her. It was exactly as if somebody else, somebody much, much greater had entered her and taken over.

Knowledge seemed to pour out of her and the whole impact of my experience struck me like a great slap.

This was what mankind was seeking, this incredible state that I had entered. I was beyond the boundaries of reason and the prison of history.

It was as if I had been in the forest of Eden, but with a tremendous difference. No longer did I wish to eat of the tree of knowledge of good and evil, for I had consumed the last of its fruit, and digested it all.

I was truly free, and this was what mankind was about.

"My God, what I've learned—"

"Have you?"

"I want the others to know. I've got to tell them. The President's gone to war with you! I've got to explain!"

"You have made your decision."

"No! This would be—it's terrible—we can't shoot them—you—are you—what are you, anyway? Are you part of them?"

"There is no 'them.' Only us. We are part of us, and so are you."

She was holding out what looked like a plain, ordinary glass of milk. "You're thirsty, you need a drink."

She was absolutely right. I took it and swallowed two huge gulps before I realized that it was incredibly bitter, so bitter my head was splitting. I spat milky spray but she grabbed the glass before I threw it down.

Then she was on me, taking me in a headlock and forcing the rest of the substance down my throat.

I choked and struggled but she was like a creature of steel, not a living body. "You will forget," she said, "until the latter days of your life."

What did she mean?

Then I realized that I was getting dizzy. The wise child, the children's circle, the ancient school—it was all becoming distant and indistinct and unreal.

My memories—but I couldn't forget! I *must not!* Finally she let me go. "You've given me a drug!"

"Yes, so that you can forget."

"For God's sake, I've got to tell them!"

"They aren't ready."

"Give us another chance, for God's sake!"

"When the time is right, you will take your chance. Nothing will be given. You are charged with the task of keeping our secrets until man is prepared to hear the truth."

The milk of forgetfulness made the room turn slowly round and round. The last thing I saw clearly as I collapsed was that dress. In the flickering light it became a field of yellow primroses.

Then I was standing in the stream. I had just dropped a cast. When I drew my line back I found that the fly was gone. How strange, I tie good knots. Then I remembered, hadn't I cast into some swift water?

It seemed only a moment ago, but also ten thousand years. A woman had come up . . . or a deer . . . yes, a deer had ruined my concentration.

I glanced at my watch. It said five-thirty. But how could it when I'd gone out at eight-thirty?

The light was very curious. Although the sky was cloudless there was no sun. In the western horizon I could see the pure stars of morning. The east glowed green and white.

I am not a fool in the woods: obviously it was dawn.

Just then I heard a bell down in Roscoe.

A trout slapped the surface of the pool I'd been fishing and I lost interest in the confusion of time. Knowing nothing of the style of the hatch that had drawn him to feed I simply chose a lucky fly and made a cast that turned out to be as soft as a drift of spiderweb.

My lure had hardly rippled the surface when I had a

smart strike. He took me and ran for cover. My line shook with his life.

I had always secretly loathed the wolf in me and loved the lamb. That was all changed. Now the wolf was my pride as the lamb was my joy, and I played that fish with skill beyond anything I had known before. My heart burst with love for him. I played my line and wept with the sheer beauty of it, the amazing *goodness* of the situation.

My reward was a phenomenal catch, a four-pound brookie struggling in my creel. To take such a large brook trout anywhere would have been marvelous. But from this stream in 1947 it was a miracle.

I stopped fishing then and returned to the club.

I was met with amazement.

One man reached his hand out, ran his fingers down my chest. I saw that my fishing vest was all torn. When in the world had that happened?

"You get lost up a branch?" somebody asked.

"No."

Then I realized the truth. I must have been out all night. How could that be? Had I fished in some water of dreams?

"Thank the Lord you're all right," said Ann. Her eyes were hollow.

"Yeah. I took a damned good brookie."

They did not exactly shun me, but they looked at me out of the sides of their eyes. It developed that I had been gone for three days. I had reappeared fishing happily in water they had dragged ten times for my body.

I called Hilly.

"I'm fine," I said. "I was fishing some pretty isolated water."

"For three days, Will? What did you eat?"

"Pancakes," I blurted. "I had some buckwheats."

Why had I said that?

"Get back here," Hilly said. "We've got a hell of a lot of work to do."

"I'll be there as soon as I can."

I stopped in Roscoe at the taxidermist and left my fish. Then I drove back to Poughkeepsie and chartered a plane, which bounced me down to La Guardia Field, where I took an American Airlines DC-3 to Washington National Airport.

When I landed in Washington an agency car was waiting for me. I sat back in the plush of it and watched the sights pass, the memorials and the White House, the Washington Monument gleaming like bone in the middle morning.

Hilly sat reading a report and gnawing on a roast beef sandwich. "We're having our problems in China," he said, "and the President wants to know if Gromyko can be made a friend of the Marshall Plan, and the Dutch are screaming that the East Indies are going to go communist and there will be an election in Italy that we could buy for about twenty million. If we don't, communism crosses the Danube and France will go next. I can give you and your little men five minutes, Will."

"Yes, sir."

"I want the detailed organizational plans for Majestic on this desk by the end of the week. No more sudden vacations, fish or no fish."

"It was a hell of a catch."

"I expect to see it mounted in your office."

It remained there for forty years.

Now it hangs in the shadows of my living room, its varnish browned with time. But the shape of the fish is beautiful to see. It hangs there frozen in the moment of its perfect death.

Now that the shadows of the dead come close around me I have at last remembered.

Flights of angels came and we called them hordes of demons. The light of the soul shone upon us and we hid our faces. A chance was offered to every man to extend himself beyond the boundaries of Earth. In the interest of maintaining the integrity of the nation, we denied you this chance.

If they should return with their wonderful offering, do not turn away. There will be tests and dangers. But be of courage, for at some point they will hold out to you a little yellow flower.

Take the flower.

Afterword

This novel is based on a factual reality that has been hidden and denied.

I have used what little is known for certain of the crash of a so-called alien spacecraft near Roswell, New Mexico, in July of 1947 as the springboard for my story.

My vision of the others, their world, their motives and their objectives is based on my own understanding. Where what I have seen with my own eyes departs from conventional wisdom, I have always trusted my personal observations.

Insofar as military and governmental involvement is concerned, I have adhered to the available facts as I understand them.

Thanks to the kind assistance of UFO researcher William Moore, I was able to interview many of the witnesses still living in the Roswell area.

When Moore took me there, I found that he and researcher Stanton Friedman, who along with Jaime Shandera have investigated the whole story with meticulous expertise, were well known to the local people, and well respected for their honesty and thoroughness.

By contrast, none of the "debunkers" like aviation writer Philip J. Klass, who have made so many facile pronouncements about this case, had ever so much as interviewed these witnesses.

After spending considerable time in and around Roswell, and reviewing the extraordinary admissions concerning this matter, it seems virtually certain to me that a disk crashed and this fact became top secret. This was done as part of what has become an elaborate process of "official secrecy and ridicule," as described by former CIA Director Roscoe Hillenkoetter in the *New York Times* of February 28, 1960, quoted in the frontispiece of this book.

The Roswell Army Air Field issued an initial press release that announced that the debris of an alien spacecraft had been found. I have personally met and spoken with Walter Haut, the press officer who wrote this report. Colonel (then Major) Jesse Marcel was the intelligence officer who originally picked up the strange debris on the ranch of William "Mac" Brazel. In 1979, shortly before his death, Colonel Marcel had the courage to admit in a number of videotaped interviews that the debris he found was really from an apparent alien spacecraft, and that the Air Force had covered this up.

I have met and spoken with his son, Dr. Jesse Marcel, Jr. Dr. Marcel assured me that his father was of sound mind when he gave his 1979 interviews.

As in my book, General Ramey, the commanding general of the Eighth Air Force, held a press conference shortly after the recovery of the debris. He claimed, in effect, that a group of the nation's best intelligence officers had mistaken a commonplace radar target of a kind they saw every day for the remains of an unknown craft. Marcel was ordered to participate in this press conference, an act which his family and friends claim made him extremely unhappy.

The press accepted the general's statements.

In their writings, "debunkers" avoid mentioning Colonel Marcel's interviews, no doubt because they are the key to the case, and cannot be refuted except by making the patently ridiculous charge that this honorable military officer was a liar.

The colonel was asked if he thought what he had observed was the remains of a weather balloon.

He answered, "It was not. I was pretty well acquainted with most everything that was in the air at that time, both ours and foreign. I was also acquainted with virtually every type of weather-observation or tracking device being used by either the civilians or the military. It was definitely not a weather or tracking device, nor was it any sort of plane or missile. What it was we didn't know."

Marcel went on to describe what he had found. "There was all kinds of stuff—small beams about three-eighths or a half-inch square with some sort of hieroglyphics on them that nobody could decipher. These looked something like balsa wood, and were of about the same weight, except that they were not wood at all. They were very hard, although flexible, and would not burn. There was a great deal of an unusual parchment-like substance which was brown in color and extremely strong, and a great number of small pieces of a metal like tinfoil, except that it wasn't tinfoil." Later "Mac" Brazel's daughter Bessie described the paper as having apparent flowers pressed in it.

Marcel took this material back to the base. He was so far from thinking that it might become a security issue that he stopped at home to show some of it to his son, who was then eleven. Dr. Marcel remembers the incident well and has described the material he saw to me.

If the major had actually mistaken the remains of a commonplace device for those of an alien spacecraft, and caused this information to become public, surely his career would have suffered. But it did not suffer. Far from it. Later he was transferred from Roswell to Washington, D.C., where he worked on the Air Force program that eventually detected the fact that the Soviets had exploded an atomic bomb.

In other words, after he found the debris and reported on it publicly, he was transferred from the 509th into the most important intelligence project that the Air Force was then pursuing. Far from being discredited, he continued to be held in the highest regard by the Air Force.

He reached the rank of colonel before retiring from a successful career.

That the cover-up has remained intact is astonishing, considering the existence of the Marcel interviews, and the statements CIA Director Hillenkoetter has made.

Interestingly, Admiral Hillenkoetter joined a prominent UFO organization after his 1960 admission of the cover-up. Later, on resigning from the group, he made an extraordinary declaration: "I know the UFOs are not U.S. or Soviet devices. All we can do now is wait for some action by the UFOs. The Air Force cannot do any more under the circumstances. It has been a difficult assignment for them, and I believe we should not continue to criticize their investigations."

Despite all this the "debunkers" are still taken seriously by the press and among scientists.

In their refutations of the Roswell incident, they concentrate on rancher Brazel's testimony.

After a week of being held in isolation by Air Force officials, in total contravention of his Constitutional rights, Mr. Brazel very understandably said that he was sorry that he'd ever shown the debris to authorities. Family members feel that he was coerced. It seems clear that he was forced to provide the government with support for its cover-up, and that his coerced testimony has been used by "debunkers" with close governmental ties.

In any case, Mr. Brazel was not a qualified observer. He knew nothing about radar targets and such. Major Marcel, the one professional who has spoken out, stated that the debris was of unknown origin.

The truth must be faced: this careful, professional man did not misidentify anything. When General Ramey told his press conference that the remains were of a weather balloon or radar target, he was, quite simply, lying on behalf of national security. This was the beginning of the cover-up that has remained in place to this day.

What happened in Roswell remains a deep, dark national secret over forty years later. Fantastically, despite all the obvious proof to the contrary, the fiction that the others don't exist is rigorously maintained as official policy and generally accepted by the scientific establishment.

It is time for our serious investigative reporters to wake up and do some digging into this matter. If they did so, they would soon discover the hollowness and the propagandistic nature of the "debunker's" assertions.

The apparent appearance of *someone else* in our midst—a marvelous event by any ordinary estimate—has ended up as an ugly secret and a source of nasty journalistic humor, irrational denial and sleazy sensationalism.

I do not wish, by this book, to create the impression that I am asserting that the others are aliens from another planet.

What I am saying, very specifically, is that they are an apparently intelligent *unknown.* That is all I am saying, and all that presently can be said.

The truth, if known, is held secret. I would be very surprised indeed if the government had the least understanding of the others. If what I am beginning to discover about them is correct, real understanding will change our most basic ideas about the nature of reality.

What secrets the government does possess must be opened to the light of common life. Only then will we be on our way at last to understanding the mystery that has appeared among us.

Despite all policy and no matter with whom it originated, our government must now take a calculated risk—perhaps even defy the others themselves—and officially admit that they are real.

When this is done we will finally begin to gain insight into what is happening to us.

It is time for the truth to be told.

—WHITLEY STRIEBER

A Note to Readers

Readers wishing to add a record of their own experience to the files of the Communion Foundation, to contribute to the work of that foundation or to inquire about receiving the Communion Newsletter are invited to write to the author:

Whitley Strieber
496 La Guardia Place, #188
New York, New York 10012